There was no time to hide, nowhere to run.

Broadsides of disruptor fire pummeled the rooftop from two vectors, filling the air with smoke and dust—harsh barriers to human vision but no impediment to the mechanical senses of sophisticated killing machines.

An Orion police vehicle raced toward the roof, lights flashing, siren wailing. It was met by a hail of disruptor fire that sent the shattered, burning aircar plunging into the side of the hotel. The car exploded, filling the night with broken glass, shattered polymer, and fire.

With ruthless efficiency the drones trained their arsenals back upon the rooftop.

Even as Sarina dived for the nearest protection she could reach, she knew the only thing likely keeping her alive was Data's expert-level two-handed marksmanship, which was forcing the two new drones to maneuver and adjust their firing solutions on the fly.

It wouldn't be enough. Fires were spreading across the rooftop, making no part of it safe to shelter on. And no matter how fast Data's reflexes, or how sharp his vision, the truth was that hand phasers just didn't pack enough punch to take on attack drones in a stand-up fight.

Sarina's most optimistic read of the situation told her they'd all be dead in thirty seconds.

Her hand tightened on her phaser. *Doesn't mean I have to die on my knees.*

STAR TREK®

SECTION 31

CONTROL

DAVID MACK

Based on *Star Trek* and
Star Trek: The Next Generation
created by Gene Roddenberry
and
Star Trek: Deep Space Nine
created by
Rick Berman & Michael Piller

POCKET BOOKS

New York   London   Toronto   Sydney   Memory Alpha

Pocket Books
An Imprint of Simon & Schuster, Inc.
1230 Avenue of the Americas
New York, NY 10020

This book is a work of fiction. Any references to historical events, real people, or real places are used fictitiously. Other names, characters, places, and events are products of the author's imagination, and any resemblance to actual events or places or persons, living or dead, is entirely coincidental.

This book is published by Pocket Books, an imprint of Simon & Schuster, Inc., under exclusive license from CBS Studios Inc.

First Pocket Books paperback edition April 2017

POCKET and colophon are registered trademarks of Simon & Schuster, Inc.

For information about special discounts for bulk purchases, please contact Simon & Schuster Special Sales at 1-866-506-1949 or business@simonandschuster.com.

The Simon & Schuster Speakers Bureau can bring authors to your live event. For more information or to book an event, contact the Simon & Schuster Speakers Bureau at 1-866-248-3049 or visit our website at www.simonspeakers.com.

Manufactured in the United States of America

10 9 8 7 6 5 4 3 2

ISBN 978-1-5011-5170-5
ISBN 978-1-5011-5199-6 (ebook)

for all who dare to oppose the invincible in the name of freedom

Historian's Note

The main narrative of this story takes place in late 2386, a few months after Julian Bashir and Sarina Douglas's mission for Section 31 to the alternate universe (*Section 31: Disavowed*), and roughly two years after the reincarnation of Data (*Cold Equations*, Book I: *The Persistence of Memory*) and the resurrection of his android daughter, Lal (*Cold Equations*, Book III: *The Body Electric*). This story's secondary narrative spans several years preceding and following the founding of the United Federation of Planets.

Let not thy will roar, when thy power can but whisper.

—Dr. Thomas Fuller
Gnomologia, 1732

One

Stunned, bleeding, and falling like a stone, Julian Bashir was half-conscious when he and Sarina Douglas struck the ring-shaped metal platform. She landed on her back with a brutal thud. He crashed down on his right side and heard his ulna break. The fractured bone tore through flesh and fabric, flooding his arm with pain.

He struggled to breathe. His nose was broken, and his lips were swollen and split. He rolled onto his back to get the weight off his broken arm. Above him loomed the auxiliary control center of Memory Alpha's main computer tower. Beyond the platform, the Federation archive's underground city of core towers, each over two hundred meters tall and fifty meters in diameter, stretched away in concentric rings and vanished into the far unlit unknown.

All Bashir wanted to do was succumb to fatigue. Defensive wounds on his forearms stung with fresh cuts, and the sickening pain blooming deep within his torso told him he was bleeding inside. He doubted he could stand, much less force himself to endure a one-handed climb up the ladder to the facility's main console.

Turning his head to look at his left hand was agony, but it had to be done. He opened his fist to see the data chip he had fought so hard to protect. It was intact, which was more than he could say for his palm. The chip's corners had cut into his

flesh because he had clutched it with such ferocity. He tucked
the precious chip into one of his pressure suit's chest pockets.

I didn't come this far to quit here, he told himself.

Trying to sit up made his head swim. He rolled onto his
left side and fought to push himself away from the metal grating. *Get up. Get up!*

His pulse thundered in his temples and made his skull
feel as if it were being broken open from within. *Probably
a concussion,* he realized. His suspicion was confirmed by
a nascent urge to vomit. *No time for that now. Have to keep
moving.*

Raised edges on the steel deck's diamond-shaped grating bit into his knees and palm as he crawled to the ladder.
He locked his one good hand on a rung and looked back at
Sarina. She lay still, twisted and pallid. There was no time to
assess her injuries; only minutes remained for Bashir to finish
the mission that had brought him here—his first and perhaps
last chance to strike the deathblow that would end the vile
cabal he knew as Section 31.

He knew he should climb, but his heart demanded he go
back to help Sarina. In spite of the ticking clock, he couldn't
forget he loved her. How much he would *always* love her.

Bashir let go of the ladder and looked back, but his conscience halted him. *If I go to her now . . . how many more will
die because I was selfish?* This mission was bigger than her life,
or his. Too much was at stake.

With his one good hand, he climbed the ladder. His
broken right arm dangled, useless and vulnerable. Stabbing
sensations filled his gut as he pulled himself upward. It took
all his will to keep his grip on the rungs and continue his ascent; his body was desperate to give in, surrender to gravity,
and plunge into the shadowy abyss between the core towers.

By the time he reached the apex of the ladder and clawed

his way onto the control center's upper level, he was delirious with exhaustion. He spent a moment on his knees, fighting to catch his breath. Ahead of him, at the end of a twenty-meter catwalk, was the auxiliary control panel of the main core. Bathed in icy blue light, it beckoned him. A glance at his wrist chrono confirmed he had barely two minutes to reach the console and finish this war.

He reached up and seized the catwalk's railing. Every muscle in his body burned in protest as he pulled himself to his feet. Holding the railing to steady himself, he plodded forward. Each step shook drops of blood from the broken bones of his right arm.

The closer he got to the main console, the softer his vision became. He hoped to remain conscious long enough to complete his task, one staggering in its simplicity: all he had to do was insert the data chip into the secure input node on the console. The embedded software on the chip would do the rest.

If only we could have uploaded this remotely, instead of having to carry it into the most heavily guarded data archive in the galaxy—

The dull pressure of a punch was followed by a knifing pain between Bashir's shoulder blades—ice-cold at first, then white-hot. He couldn't see the dagger in his back, but he knew for a fact it was there.

Bashir tried to soldier on, only to find he could no longer feel his legs. They buckled under him as if they were made of rubber. He used his left arm to break his fall, but his bearded chin slammed onto the catwalk's steel plates.

So close . . . The console was just a couple of meters away. Bashir fought to pull himself forward, his bruised and slashed left arm laboring to drag his entire body weight the length of two long strides that suddenly might as well be two light-years.

Behind him, halting steps echoed on the catwalk.

At the base of the console Bashir fished the data chip from his pocket. Clutching it, he extended his blood-caked hand toward the console's secure input terminal only to find it stubbornly out of reach. To finish his mission, he needed to stand one last time.

The side of his hand found the console's edge, but he couldn't pull himself to his feet. He lost his grip and fell to the deck with his back to the console, facing his slowly approaching enemy, the agent of his imminent destruction.

In that moment Bashir realized two terrible truths.

His mission had failed, and he was about to die.

TEN DAYS EARLIER

Two

It was only natural for Ozla Graniv to expect an unusual reception when responding to such a peculiar invitation, but the Trill investigative journalist hadn't anticipated being shushed the moment her hosts greeted her.

Double doors parted ahead of Graniv to reveal Professor Ziya Weng, the chair of the computer sciences department at the Dresden University of Technology. Weng pressed her index finger to her pursed lips—a somatic gesture that among most humans had come to mean *be silent*. Standing beside Weng but searching the campus behind Graniv with anxious eyes was an Andorian *thaan*, who Graniv assumed was one of Weng's colleagues.

Weng looked to be a contemporary of Graniv's—both women were in their early to mid-fifties, of average height, with dark hair betraying the first strands of gray. Graniv preferred to wear her naturally wavy hair loose, while Weng kept hers in a taut bun. The Andorian, meanwhile, stood at least twenty centimeters taller than either of them, and his crown of snow-white hair was tied into a fashionable braided tail that reached his shoulder blades. Both the academics wore simple off-white lab uniforms, which made Graniv feel a tad overdressed, even though her ensemble of slacks, shirt, and jacket was, by any reasonable measure, quite modest.

She followed them inside the computer sciences building.

Its stately exterior dated back nearly four centuries, but its interior recently had been remodeled in a sleek style. They passed several classrooms set up like amphitheaters, with tiers of seats half encircling a professor's dais, and a number of offices hidden behind semiopaque doors stenciled with their assigned occupants' names and honorifics.

A short ride in a lift took the trio down to a long corridor in the building's lowest sublevel. With each step they moved deeper into the bowels of the building, and Graniv wondered what she had gotten herself into this time.

Weng had approached Graniv two days earlier in Melbourne, after Graniv had finished giving a lecture on journalistic ethics and the role of the news media in an interstellar society. Though their conversation on the way out of the auditorium had been brief and perfunctory, Weng had insisted on shaking Graniv's hand as they said good-bye. As they shook hands, she had passed Graniv a note folded into a tiny square. Neither of them had spoken of it in that moment; it clearly had been meant as a clandestine missive.

Reading the note later in the privacy of her hotel room, Graniv noted three things about it that kindled her journalistic interest. The first was its invitation, to come and bear witness to something that had the potential to expose a major conspiracy, one with ramifications that might span the entire Federation. The second was its plea that she not mention the letter or the conspiracy, either aloud or in writing, in any public place or over any means of transmitted communication. The third and most fascinating detail was that the note had been scribbled by hand on a piece of paper so old and brittle it nearly fell apart when she first unfolded it.

Was it evidence that Weng was paranoid? Or might she really be onto something so major, so dangerous, that she couldn't employ any means of communication other than this? Either way, Graniv suspected there might be a news-worthy story in it.

At the end of the long corridor, Weng and the *thaan* unlocked a door labeled DATA FORENSICS LABORATORY – AUTHORIZED PERSONNEL ONLY. They led her past it, into a sprawling space packed with clutter piled high atop work-benches. Everywhere the Trill looked she saw the guts of old computers denuded of their façades. Loose ODN cables, scatterings of old microprocessor chips, and a million tiny gizmos she couldn't begin to identify littered the place.

Near the back of the lab stood a large cube-shaped structure. Its frame was wrapped in a translucent silvery mesh secured to an inner grid of secondary support beams. A single bundle of cables penetrated the cube at the center of its roof. The only point of ingress Graniv saw was a door that faced them. She and her hosts remained silent as they neared the cube. This time, it was the Andorian who entered the access code and ushered Weng and Graniv inside. He followed them in and locked the door behind him.

The cube's interior was as organized as the lab outside was unkempt, and it was evident, even to a nonexpert such as Graniv, that the computer systems inside were beyond antiquated. She didn't recognize most of the components she saw or the tools that lay in fastidiously arranged rows and columns on sterile sheets between them.

Weng reached up to a small control device dangling from the bundled cables overhead and flipped a few switches. A deep hum pervaded the cube and sent vibrations through the floor that Graniv felt in her molars. Only then did Weng and her colleague exhale in subdued relief.

"Thank you for your patience, Ms. Graniv." Weng gestured to her peer. "This is Professor Erethilisar th'Firron. He heads up our forensic data research team."

Graniv shook th'Firron's blue hand. "Professor. A pleasure."

"Likewise, Ms. Graniv. I've enjoyed your work for *Seeker*."

"Thank you." She looked around the sepulcher of obsolete computers. "Would one of you mind explaining what this
is and why I'm here?"

Weng motioned Graniv toward an empty chair in front
of an old flat-panel monitor. "Have a seat, and we'll explain."
As Graniv sat down, Weng said, "This is the modern equivalent of what used to be known in our profession as a Faraday
cage."

"It's designed to prevent signals from passing in or out,"
th'Firron added. "Except through secure hard lines." He
looked up at the bundle hanging overhead. "Like these."

"I'm familiar with the concept," Graniv said. "What's this
one used for?"

"Sensitive research," Weng said. "From time to time, the
university takes on projects for Starfleet or the Federation. To
ensure absolute security, we sequester them in here."

Wary of blundering into a treason charge, Graniv cast a
nervous look around. "Got any government projects going
on right now?"

"Not at the moment, no. And we cleared out everything
else so we could show you this." Weng nodded to th'Firron,
who used an old-fashioned keyboard and trackpad to
power up a machine that looked too old to still exist, never
mind function. The rectangular monitor in front of Graniv
flickered to life and displayed a primitive-looking system
interface, within which he called up an even more ancient
command mode: a black square with garish green text.

Graniv leaned forward and squinted at the monitor.
"What the hell is this?"

"Something I found a few weeks ago," th'Firron said. "I

was conducting research into data recovery on a salvaged computer drive from the twenty-second century. Once I got it running inside an archived shell, I started dissecting its operating software. That's when I found *this*." With a flourish of keystrokes and a tap on the keypad, he called up a flood of command-line source code that scrolled up the monitor faster than Graniv could read it.

She looked over her shoulder at th'Firron, who seemed to be trembling with excitement. "And this is newsworthy because . . . ?"

He halted the text scroll with another tap on the keyboard. "This code was meant to be hidden. Invisible. And by the standards of two hundred years ago, it was."

"But today's forensic software is more than a match for its encryption protocols," Weng added. "Which is how we recovered the entire module intact and isolated."

"Good for you. But what is it?"

Both of her hosts wore troubled frowns. "That's just it," Weng said. "We're not sure."

"We have a sense of what it does," th'Firron said. "Or at least, what it *could* do." He scrolled to a different section of the code string. "It's made to monitor routine data transmissions on all known frequencies. Everything from personal comms to Starfleet channels, even encrypted data." He highlighted another section of the code. "This lets it track the usage of household appliances. It analyzes financial activity, everything from credit transfers to investments. It logs transporter coordinates and reports the locations of starships, both civilian and military."

Weng's mood darkened. "And it might do more. Lots more. We've only just started to plumb the depths of what this thing was made to do."

Graniv remained puzzled by the scientists' reactions.

"Okay, you found a privacy nightmare from two hundred years ago. Why does that matter now?"

"Because it's still active," Weng said. "Show her, Thili."

"Long story short," th'Firron said as he booted up a new interface on a parallel monitor, "this legacy module is part of the compiled-and-locked source code for every modern system that has even a smidge of computer technology—which is to say, almost everything." He summoned a string of modern-looking system source code. With a few taps on the screen, he highlighted sections of identical code shared by the old and new systems. "The entirety of the legacy code is running in the root kits of planetary utility systems, power grids, communication networks, subspace relay platforms, replicators, military and paramilitary weapons, holosuites. If you can you name it, it's probably running this code in the background."

At once the gravity of the situation became clear to Graniv. "Now I get why we're looking at it in here. But why the handwritten note? Why the silent treatment on the way in?"

"Because," Weng said, "any mention of Uraei—"

"That's the original name of the software module," th'Firron interjected.

"—would be picked up by audio sensors built into our personal comms, our computer workstations, our building's security grid. The software is designed to be alert for any mention of itself. If it hears us, it'll send up some kind of red flag and mark us as targets—as security risks to be contained or even eliminated, depending upon how much it thinks we know."

"Contained? Eliminated? By whom?"

"We don't know yet. But we've been seeing references in the code to something known as Section 31. Does that mean anything to you?"

Graniv shook her head. "No, but I know someone I can ask about it."

"For all our sakes, be careful." Weng palmed sweat from her forehead. "This thing sees all we do and hears every word we say, public or private."

"Even here on Earth?"

The question raised th'Firron's white brows. "*Especially* here on Earth. It's everywhere."

If what Weng and th'Firron had told Graniv was true, if such a grotesque invasion of the privacy of Federation citizens was not only in use on Earth and possibly elsewhere, she knew it would be a government scandal greater than any she had known.

She stood and nodded, as if to reassure them. "All right. I'd like to come back in a day or two with an expert of my choosing, someone we can all trust. After he vets your findings, we'll decide how to proceed. Okay?" Weng and th'Firron nodded. "Good. Until then"—she threw her parting words over her shoulder on her way out of the Faraday room— "keep this under your hats." Left unspoken was the part they all took for granted: *Or else we're all as good as dead.*

Three

*O*f all the goddamned days to break my glasses. Professor Aaron Ikerson sat at his office desk and wrapped a piece of clear adhesive tape around the fractured bridge of his spectacles. He had expected the thin metal frames might warp or deform over time, but it had never occurred to him their bridge might snap as he pushed his reading glasses back up his nose. As for the likelihood they would break only minutes before one of the most important meetings of his career—he preferred not to speculate upon such astronomical odds.

He tested his ad hoc repair. The two halves of his eyeglasses wobbled no matter how tight or thick the tape binding. *That'll have to do.* With exaggerated care he put them on. They rested in place more securely than before they had broken, and Ikerson noted the irony that the tape on the bridge was probably the reason why. *I guess I'll call that a win.*

His personal comm buzzed. He picked up the palm-sized device off his desk and checked the text message from his graduate assistant, Lenore McGill.

It read simply, *They're here.*

Ikerson stood and smoothed the wrinkles from his jacket. He paused to spy his reflection in the glass of his framed doctorate in computer science, to make sure his teeth were clean. Thinning blond hair, cropped short, lent a distinguished air to his boyish features. His fortieth birthday had just passed, but for the most part he had eluded the worst of time's ravages. Only faint crow's-feet, smile creases, and snowy chin stubble betrayed his middling years.

Colleagues nodded and smiled at him as he hurried through the corridors of the computer sciences hall, the newest building on the campus of the Dresden University of Technology. Though he was in a hurry, Ikerson acknowledged each greeting in kind—a cheerful wave; a fleeting salutation; a polite lift of his chin and a benign half-smile.

He arrived at the main entrance to find Lenore making small talk with their four guests. The stylish and witty graduate student seemed to have captivated her esteemed elders, who all hailed from the international intelligence community—though Ikerson had no idea to which organizations any of them belonged. All he knew for certain was that Mister Sanchez represented the Western Coalition's interests in his project, Ms. Ling had come on behalf of the Pan-Pacific Alliance, Mister Bruneau had been sent by an unnamed entity in the European Union, and Ms. Kandawalla answered to the prevailing powers of the African Federation—and that none of them had told him their real names. All their background checks had turned up blank.

He greeted them. They were portraits of courtesy as he shook their hands. Next he addressed them as a group. "Thank you all for coming on such short notice. Once you see the progress we've made, I think you'll agree this update is the one we've all been waiting for." He beckoned them as he started back the way he'd come. "Follow me, please."

Ikerson noted his guests' reflections on office doors as he escorted them through the building. Sanchez's face betrayed no reaction to anyone or anything, and his eyes were hidden behind black sunglasses. Ling's attention flitted from one point of interest to the next like a hummingbird dancing between blooms. Bruneau's attentions also wandered, though with greater subtlety than did Ling's. Kandawalla was the only one whose focus troubled Ikerson. Her eyes remained fixed upon him, it seemed; whenever he glanced over his shoulder, he found her looking right at him without shame or reservation.

On the lowest sublevel, he led his guests inside the Forensic Data Research laboratory. Lenore trailed the group and locked the lab's door behind them once she was inside. The six of them gathered inside the Faraday cage, where Ikerson's crowning achievement awaited them. As soon as Lenore confirmed the room was secure, Ikerson pressed his palms together. "Humanity has reached a precarious moment in its history. Making contact with the Vulcans has altered the trajectory of our civilization." He switched on the computer on the workbench beside him, then continued. "Unfortunately, not all the peoples of the world have welcomed this new path. A few holdout superpowers, as well as several small but entrenched factions of hard-liners, extremists, and isolationists, continue to obstruct the international effort to forge a global government." A sad sigh. "Some of us, it seems, are not yet ready to put aside childish things."

He glanced at the monitor next to him and confirmed his software was booting up. "Intelligence acquired from the Vulcans—and, in a few cases, in spite of them—suggests local space is crowded with hostile intelligent species whose interests might make them a threat to human progress and survival. So make no mistake: if humanity means to endure, not just culturally but as a species, it must stand together."

With another sidelong look, Ikerson confirmed his system was up and running. "Ms. McGill and I have created something revolutionary. A new kind of software designed not to *change* the world, but to give us the tools we need to *unite* it." He added with a flourish toward the monitor, "Esteemed guests, allow me to present . . . Uraei."

All four of the visitors regarded Ikerson's masterpiece with blank stares. Bruneau was the first to speak. "What does it do?"

"It watches," Ikerson said. "And it listens."

Kandawalla cocked one brow. "Watches what? Listens to what?"

McGill said with pride, "Everyone and everything."

Now the guests gave the scrolling strings of code on the monitor their full attention. Sanchez even tipped his sunglasses down his nose to get a clear look at the running program. "This has been tried before. There's no way to sort useful intel from that much noise."

"No way for humans to do so," Ikerson corrected. "Uraei isn't just a data dragnet. It's also a directed-function artificial intelligence. It analyzes everything it intercepts. Anything suspect gets routed to the proper authorities—whether that's local law enforcement, national security coordinators, the military, or what have you."

His description prompted a dubious reaction from Ling. "So your AI casts itself as judge, jury, and executioner?"

"Not at all. Uraei doesn't dictate responses. It's designed to be a witness who calls in tips. But humans choose how to respond to the leads that Uraei provides. Let me show you."

The visitors were very patient. For nearly an hour they listened in polite silence while Ikerson walked them through the means by which Uraei deduced and evaluated potential threats, and the algorithm it used to decide to which agency its discoveries should be sent. It was all very dry and technical, but by the end he felt as if he had infused them with his own hard-won confidence in this remarkable dedicated AI.

Bruneau wore a pensive look as he considered all he had

heard. "A most intriguing proposal, Professor. That much will I grant you." A twinkle in his dark eyes. "If I might inquire—the name: Uraei. It is from mythology, yes?"

"Egyptian, to be precise. Two asps that encircled the Eye of Ra and spat flames like venom to defend the sun god against his enemies."

"A fitting metaphor," Sanchez said.

"One certainly hopes so."

Ling's frown conveyed her continued doubts. "I am impressed by what you have achieved, Professor. But you want all four of the world's superpowers to trust our fates to a single shared system—one whose success would herald the dissolution of our respective sovereignties. If we take that chance, and your system fails, it could mean the collapse of human society. We would be at the mercy of all those hostile alien races you insist lie in wait for us. So before I can recommend your system to my superiors, I need your answer to this question: Are you absolutely positive Uraei will work as you intend?"

There was no more time for nuance or equivocation. It was time for Ikerson to save the world, and the only way for him to do that was to be certain beyond a shadow of doubt.

"I give you my word: Uraei will ensure the unity of Earth and the safety of the human race, from all threats native and alien . . . *forever*."

Four

Patient Zero was running for his life—and dooming a billion others with each panicked stride.

Julian Bashir couldn't blame the Romulan man for trying to get away. Surraben Antok was just a semipro burglar who didn't know he was being used to incubate a virus that would reach its communicable stage in under an hour—and therefore he couldn't possibly know why Bashir, an offworlder, was chasing him in the middle of the night through the back alleys of the thieves' quarter of Ramad, the capital city of the Romulan colony world of Alhaya.

Antok broke stride for half a step, just long enough to fire a disruptor blast at Bashir. Its screech and flash filled the dark alley. The pulse caromed off a wall and streaked past Bashir's head close enough to spawn the odor of burnt hair. Bashir lost half a step dodging a second shot, which buried itself in a reeking mound of garbage heaped against a wall. In that moment, Antok widened his lead and pulled away into the misty labyrinth of the city's criminal ghetto.

Sarina Douglas's voice resonated inside Bashir's head, courtesy of the transceiver implanted just in front of his right ear. *"You're losing him."*

"I know." It was hard not to shout while running.

"He's heading for the metro. Go left, there's an entrance at the corner."

Bashir took the turn running at full speed and barreled through a slow-moving crowd. Angry epithets in the local Romulan dialect hectored him as he sprinted up a flight of stairs to a boarding platform for one of the city's public maglev train lines.

"Move it! The train's boarding!"

"Almost there!" He bounded off the top stair and slammed into oncoming pedestrians fresh off the train and eager to reach the street. He didn't know enough Romulan to shout them out of his way, so he let his shoulder do the talking. More vulgarities rained down upon him as he bladed through the crowd and boarded the train through its farthest forward set of doors.

The train's interior was as pristine and bright as the neighborhood outside was grimy and dark. The maglev had been designed as a flexible tube completely open from nose to tail. Bench seats lined the sides of the commuter train, while its central gangway was dotted with poles and equipped with overhead handholds. There were too many people on board for Bashir to see to the far end, so he began making his way aft, doing his best not to attract attention.

He whispered so only Sarina could hear him. "Is he on the train?"

She sounded uncertain. *"I think so."*

"He is or he isn't, Sarina. I need to know before—" A two-note musical tone preceded the closing of the doors. "Strike my last." The train glided into motion with only the faintest hums and tremors of acceleration. "We're moving. Is the suspect with me?"

"Affirmative. Looks like he's all the way at the back."

"Naturally. Heading his way now."

Outside the train's windows, the angular towers and twisting spires of Ramad glowed in the night. In the distance, the light of the planet's large moon shimmered across a restless sea.

Inside the maglev, no one looked at one another, a fact of life Bashir had seen in many large cities on worlds throughout the quadrant. With his cloak's hood pulled low, he passed unnoticed and unremarked, just another nameless presence in an overcrowded metropolis. His only fear was that as he scrutinized the faces of the other passengers in search of Antok, one of them might look up, meet his gaze, and realize he wasn't a Romulan or a native.

No one paid him any mind.

As he neared the end of the train, he was baffled to find no trace of Antok. He turned for privacy toward a pair of doors and took a personal comm device from his pocket to make himself look like any of the several other passengers carrying on banal conversations during their ride. "Sarina? I'm less than four meters from the back of the train. He's not here."

"He must be, I have him on sensors. He should be up against the aft bulkhead."

"There's no one there. You're sure it's him?"

"Unless someone else on that train is using a signal scrambler to block transporter beams and ID scanners, he's right there."

Bashir had a bad feeling. "No, it just means his *scrambler* must be here. Hang on." He continued aft and stole furtive looks under the bench seats. "No sign of Antok or the device." He pivoted and looked back the way he'd come. "I don't get it. Where could he—?"

The question caught in his throat, wedged against an answer he feared to consider. He moved to the locked rear hatch and pressed his face to its window to survey the outside of the train.

There was Antok, clinging to the rear of the speeding maglev with the aid of magnetic gloves, a pair of goggles, and a face mask. The Romulan looked up at Bashir and froze.

"Got him." Bashir backed away from the door and drew his phaser as he declared for the other passengers' benefit, in his best broken Romulan, "Everyone, please move forward. Quickly. This is for your own safety." He waited until he was the last one within ten meters of the rear door. Then he set his phaser for an intense, narrow discharge, targeted the door's lock, and fired. The vermilion beam sliced through the train's door, which blew outward and was ripped off the train by the four-hundred-kilometer-per-hour winds raging outside.

With one hand on an overhead grip rail, Bashir leaned out and seized the front of Antok's one-piece jumpsuit. "Stop running! I'm trying to help—"

Antok let go of the train. His jumpsuit expanded as it caught the wind and became an aerodynamic wingsuit. In a roar of wind that drowned out Bashir's howl of terror, Antok was launched into the air—and he pulled Bashir with him, out of the train and into the night.

They were hundreds of meters in the air but falling fast. Bashir was nothing but ballast and drag, an anchor pulling Antok and his wingsuit into free fall. The Romulan punched Bashir's face three times, fast and hard, until Bashir caught the man's wrist and shouted, "Stop!"

"Let go! You'll kill us both!"

"I'm trying to *save* you!"

The ground raced up to meet them. Confusion and fear played across Antok's face.

"Julian, let him go! I can't beam you up until you're clear of his scrambler!"

It was a split-second choice. He could let Antok go and maybe take him down with a lucky phaser shot before being snared by the transporter beam, or he could hang on and gamble on the man actually possessing a sliver of decency and a strong survival instinct.

He tightened his grip and prepared for impact.

The Romulan spread his arms and legs to open his wing-suit. "Get on my back! Now!" He fought to catch enough air to slow their fall as Bashir clambered around him to ride on his back. As soon as Bashir was in place Antok leveled them out of their dive and banked hard to soar between a pair of modern office towers. The Romulan swooped down into one of the city's many parks, all of which were closed after sundown. He spread his arms to catch the wind in a braking maneuver and shook Bashir off as he buzzed the ground. Bashir landed with a thud and a grunt, while Antok skidded to a halt across a patch of grass.

Enervated and gasping, the two men regarded each other from a distance of several meters. The Romulan studied Bashir with well-founded suspicion. "Who are you?"

"A medical doctor."

"And why do I need a doctor?"

"That statue you were hired to steal two days ago? It wasn't a priceless artifact. It was an aerosol dispenser, and it infected you with an engineered virus."

Antok's wariness turned to incredulity. "I feel fine."

"That's because the virus is still in its incubation phase. But in a few minutes, it'll become contagious. You still won't feel any symptoms, but you'll infect anyone who breathes within twenty meters of you. And fifty hours from now, *every* one of them will become vectors. In a matter of weeks, you and everyone else on this planet will be dead—and if any of the infected get off this planet and reach others, the cycle will continue." Bashir reached under his cloak and pulled from one of his jacket pockets a transparent aluminum ampoule filled with translucent amber liquid. "Or I could inject you with this, now."

"And that would be . . . ?"

"The cure." He read the Romulan's absence of trust in his frown. "Fine, don't believe me. Become the vessel of your race's extinction." He loaded the ampoule into a hypospray, pressed its injector to his throat, and dosed himself. "See? It's safe."

"For a human."

Bashir got up and walked over to Antok. He offered him the hypospray. "Suit yourself. Take it or don't. I'm done fighting with you." He proffered it again. "Take it."

Antok reached for the hypospray. Bashir struck like lightning, and before the Romulan knew what had happened, Bashir had seized the man's hand, twisted it over to expose the underside of his wrist, and injected him.

The Romulan jerked back. "Hey—!"

"You're cured." Bashir backed away from his unwilling patient. "You're welcome."

Before the aggrieved burglar could register another complaint, a transporter beam enfolded Bashir in a wash of light and sound—

—which faded to reveal the familiar confines of the transporter room aboard the Section 31 vessel *Kòngzhì*. Standing behind the transporter console was Sarina. She brushed a lock of her blond hair behind her ear. "Welcome back, hotshot."

"Good to be back." He stepped down off the energizer pad. "Any word from—?"

The door slid open before he finished his question. Their handler, L'Haan, a lithe Vulcan woman with severe features and Cleopatra-style coiffure, strode in and took Bashir's measure with cold disdain. "Your solution to the crisis was sentimental and needlessly dangerous."

"It was the humane thing to do."

"Your mission was to neutralize a virus created by an unknown power—one designed to look as if it had been made by the Federation—and prevent the genocide of the Romulan species. You could easily have killed Mister Antok in free fall—or, preferably, while he was still on the back of the train. His death would have halted the virus's incubation and completed the mission with the minimum of exposure."

Bashir stood his ground, not willing to be cowed by his so-called handler. "I got the job done, and no one had to die. Mission. Accomplished. Next?"

L'Haan shifted her stare from Bashir to Sarina, then back again. "That will be all for now. Return to your quarters, both of you. You'll be informed when we reach Andor."

"Too kind," Bashir said with a phony smile. He and Sarina watched L'Haan depart. After the door closed, he sighed. "We're winning her over. I can tell. What do you think? How long until she trusts us enough to bring us deeper into the organization?"

Sarina shut down the transporter console and led Bashir out to the corridor. "If I had to guess? I'd say about two days after the heat death of the universe."

Every request for her presence in one of the organization's secure holosuites felt to L'Haan like a summons to appear before an inquisition. Despite her decades of loyal service in the shadows, her latest assignment had come to feel like a punishment detail, one intended to derail her hopes of ever being promoted into the organization's mysterious leadership caste.

Surrounding her were ghostly projections of the faces of the organization's other senior directors. Larger than all the others was the silhouette that spoke with a voice masked by digital filters, the enigmatic authority to which they all answered: Control.

"With all respect," L'Haan said, pressing an argument she suspected was already lost, "I think the reason agents Bashir and Douglas continue to disregard mission parameters is evident. They are not invested in our mission. They cooperate with us only because they hope doing so will gain them access to our command hierarchy. In other words, to all of you."

"*That is no excuse*," said Vasily Zeitsev, a snow-bearded old Rigelian, in an accent as heavy as his voice was rough. "*We trusted you to handle them. If you cannot do that—*"

"They are contained," L'Haan insisted.

Caliq Azura, a striking Betazoid woman whose youthful appearance was enhanced by broad strokes of lavender eye shadow and magenta streaks in her brown hair, *tsk*ed and shook her head in a mocking gesture of reproach. "*Now let's be honest, L'Haan. If your lovebird double agents were really under your thumb, we wouldn't have lost Agent Cole and his team during that op in the alternate universe.*"

"I will not be lectured by a woman who styles herself like a cross between a promiscuous teenager and an Orion socialator."

"*Forgive me,*" interjected Kestellenar th'Teshinaal, a gaunt-featured Andorian whose antennae twitched in a distracting manner whenever he spoke. "*Regardless of our concerns about the wisdom of permitting known double agents to continue operating under our banner, from an objective standpoint L'Haan is correct. The mission on Ramad was completed, Bashir and Douglas are both back aboard the Kòngzhì, and OpSec remains intact.*"

"*But is that really the point?*" asked Azura.

"Not at all," L'Haan replied. "My point is that we should dispose of them both."

"*Let's not be hasty.*" The protest came from Jhun Kulkarno, a Zakdorn schemer who, L'Haan had been told, was considered handsome for a man of his species, though she thought he resembled a beeswax bust left too long in the sun. He continued, *"Bashir and Douglas are valuable assets. Highly skilled. Well connected politically. And there are situations for which a hint of celebrity is a boon—and Bashir, 'savior of Andor,' has that in spades."*

Azura wrinkled her brow in disbelief. *"But they're double agents!"*

"Whose intentions have already been exposed," Kulkarno said. *"That means they might as well be working for us. Compartmentalize the intel to which they're privy, and we can use them to feed whatever disinformation we want, to whomever we choose."*

Zeitsev scowled. *"Underestimate them and they could do serious damage."*

"My point exactly," L'Haan said. "The benefits they offer continue to be outweighed by the threat they present. I move we liquidate both assets with prejudice and immediate effect."

Murmurs of concurrence from Azura, Zeitsev, and th'Teshinaal were met by sullen silence from Kulkarno. Then the debate was rendered immaterial.

"Motion overruled," Control said. *"Both assets are being managed within acceptable parameters. Continue to monitor them, and report any variations in their routine."*

Though Azura was the youngest of the directors, she was also the most brazen. *"Why? We've killed countless others for far less. What makes these two worth keeping on a leash?"*

Control's synthesized voice deepened to an ominous rumble. *"I have plans for them. That is all you need to know at this time. Meeting adjourned."*

The ring of faces faded to black, leaving L'Haan alone in the dark to wonder what scheme Control was crafting around Bashir and Douglas—and whether she herself was anything more than just another expendable piece in Control's long, inscrutable game.

Two days home and back into his old routine, Bashir felt as if he were going mad. His ordinary life, the public existence he maintained on Andor with Sarina, left him champing at the bit to return to his secret career, his shadow war against Section 31.

Alas, his obligations were inescapable. Lies, like gardens, required constant tending. So today he had returned to his office to see a full day's worth of patients. An uncharitable part of him had hoped at least one of the cases might prove dire enough to be interesting. None had.

It's just as well, he consoled himself. *No one ever wants to hear their doctor say, "I've never seen anything like this before."*

His self-driving transport pod separated from the flow of traffic and descended in languid spirals toward his house. It landed just outside his front gate, and its hatch opened automatically. He gathered his effects and got out. As he walked to the gate, the empty pod shut its hatch and took off, already tasked by the city's traffic control system to move on to its next passenger.

He climbed the steps to his front door, which slid open at his approach. Inside the house, music was playing. It took Bashir a moment to recognize the piece as Igor Stravinsky's *Firebird Suite*; it was an unfamiliar recording, one whose idiosyncrasies made him suspect it had been performed by a non-Terran orchestra. He set his things on the bench in the foyer, then moved deeper inside the house, in search of Sarina.

She was in the living room, busy arranging various knickknacks and shifting small *objets d'art* from one shelf or end table to another. Crossing the room she glimpsed Bashir, and her mood changed from intense concentration to sweetness and light. "Hey, there! How was your first day back?"

"Forgettable. At least no one brought me flowers this time."

"Well, that's something." She primped the leaves and blooms of a synthetic bouquet in an antique Andorian ceramic vase.

He gestured at the room's rearranged contents and furniture. "What's all this?"

"Just trying a bit of *feng shui*." Her answer was both a cover story in case they were being surveilled, and a code phrase meant to inform him that her improvements to their home's security measures—some of which were hidden in the items she was moving—were ready to be brought online. "Do you mind if I move that print and hang a small mirror instead?"

"Be my guest."

Sarina walked to a control panel near the wall of windows that looked out on their pool deck. With a few taps, she turned the windows opaque and locked the doors. The overhead lights dimmed a few percent, and her shoulders dropped as she let herself relax. "Okay, we're secure. The house is clear of listening devices, and I've interrupted all signal traffic in or out." They converged on the couch and sat down beside each other. "How was your day really?"

"Boring. Yours?"

"Busy." She picked up a padd from the coffee table, then retrieved a data chip she had kept hidden inside her shirt. "Ready to see what we got?"

"It's all I've been able to think about for two days."

"Then hang on to your socks." She inserted the chip into a narrow slot on the side of the padd. "I can hardly wait to find out who the hell L'Haan talks to inside that holosuite."

Breaking into the secure holosuite on the *Kòngzhì* had seemed to Bashir like more danger than it was worth when Sarina had first suggested it. If they had been caught inside the restricted compartment, or if their hastily engineered tap of the holosuite's transceiver link to the ship's communications system had been detected, there was a real danger they might both have been executed without warning or inquiry. But when their smuggled miniature transceiver confirmed it had intercepted the entirety of L'Haan's latest discussion with her peers, it had taken all of Bashir's hard-won discipline not to let out a cheer of celebration.

The padd requested an authorization code to decrypt the contents of the data chip. Sarina keyed in the lengthy sequence, which she had committed to her eidetic memory. "Here we go," she said, her back straight and her eyes wide with anticipation.

A flicker of static, garbled text, and distorted images hijacked the padd's screen for several seconds. Wild flurries of machine symbols stuttered on and off, and from inside the sleek device came a dysfunctional buzzing.

"Sarina? What's happening?"

"I don't know." Wisps of smoke snaked out of the device. "Oh, no. No, no, no!" Sarina fumbled the padd as she tried to extract the data chip. When she finally ejected it, the formerly translucent crystal had been charred black and reduced to a shrunken cinder.

It landed on the carpet, which sizzled and smoked beneath it. Bashir stared at the smoking padd, then at the ruined data chip. "What was that?"

"I have no idea." Sarina looked like she was half in shock as she dropped the fried padd on the coffee table. "I took every precaution. Isolated the system, secured the house. Turned off the padd's transceiver, and the chip's." She shook her head. "I never even accessed the data. It's like the padd attacked the chip the moment they were connected, and then it self-destructed."

"How is that possible?"

"I don't know. But I can guess. Maybe a 'poison pill' program in the comm stream we intercepted? It might run on a subharmonic. An authorized system can filter it out, or maybe answer a challenge-and-response handshake protocol, or something like that. But try to load it on a system that doesn't have the filter"—she nodded at the glass brick that once had been a padd—"and you end up with this."

"Hang on. We didn't find any special protocols running in the holosuite."

"No, but we weren't looking for them, either."

Bashir frowned at the sour taste of defeat. "So? Now what?"

Sarina stood and walked to the kitchen. "I'll start dinner. You replicate us a new padd."

Five

MARCH 2141

*P*lease let this work. If it tanks, I'm ruined.

Ikerson stood back from the Faraday room's master terminal, among the four VIP guests, all of whom continued to insist on hiding their identities behind aliases. He and they watched Lenore finish the activation protocols that would unite and bring to life the many segments of Uraei's far-flung code. Eleven months had passed since the initial demonstration, which had amounted to little more than a proof-of-concept briefing. This, the trial run, would determine whether he and Lenore were about to change history's shape or be crushed under its heel.

Ms. Ling leaned in and whispered something to Mister Bruneau, who turned and asked Ikerson, "How extensive will this beta run be?"

"Global, if all goes as planned." Ikerson pointed out details on some of the secondary monitors grouped on either side of the master terminal. "Under the guise of 'security updates' and 'bug fixes,' we've pushed strings of Uraei's code into nearly every kind of system and device you can think of, in countries and cities around the world."

"Can you be more specific?" asked Mister Sanchez, his reactions hidden behind dark glasses. "Do you have precise metrics for the software's propagation?"

"We do, but they're in flux. It's being downloaded and

installed by hundreds or even thousands of end users at any given moment."

Ms. Kandawalla followed every update with eyes that darted from one screen to another, her attention tireless and shrewd. "Quite impressive, Professor Ikerson. Of course, the real question is: What will happen when you activate it?"

"We're about to find out." He stepped forward to hover behind Lenore. "Are we ready? Our guests are getting impatient."

To her credit, Lenore showed no sign of bowing to pressure. She took a moment to finish her preparations and check her work, then she swiveled her chair so she could look up at Ikerson. "I can flip the switch on this whenever. Just say the word."

"Start it up."

She initiated the AI's run sequence with a single keystroke.

Then all was quiet. Indecipherable walls of code continued to scroll up one of the tertiary screens, but otherwise there was nothing of note on the master screen.

"Riveting," Sanchez said. "Money well spent."

Ikerson faced the visitors. "Please, be patient a few minutes longer. Uraei is just now waking up for the first time. Even an artificial intelligence needs a moment to start its day."

Bruneau shrugged. "Maybe it needs an espresso."

"Believe me," Ikerson said, "if I had the faintest idea how to give it one—"

"It's starting," Lenore cut in. "Pattern-analysis functions have engaged."

All the screens flooded with data, most of it whipping past faster than the human eye could parse. Kandawalla's intense focus blossomed into wonder. "Incredible. Tell me: Where is it getting all this raw data?"

"From everywhere," Ikerson said. "And from everyone and everything. It's running as part of the core systems integration package on just about every kind of system you can imagine. Regional and municipal utilities. Financial networks. Data grids. Satellite networks. It's even in the onboard circuit boards of self-driving cars, the navcomps of commercial aircraft, and the transceiver chips in people's personal comms. It's in their home-management systems. Everything they say, everywhere they go, every credit they spend . . . Uraei sees it, hears it, notes it, and then makes data sets for real-time analysis."

Ling's eyebrows arched with worry. "If the people of the world ever knew about this—"

"They'd have our heads on spikes," Sanchez said. "So, is it finding anything?"

Lenore pushed away from the master screen to give the guests a better look. "See for yourselves. Uraei is already making connections from the data it's collected, and it's sending anonymous tips to local and national law enforcement." She tapped a couple of keys to pull up a snapshot of highlights. "In the last six seconds, it's detected and reported a domestic abuse case in Mexico City; uncovered links between multiple high-profile burglaries in nine different cities over the last ten months; pinpointed three corporate executives guilty of embezzlement in London, San Francisco, and Denver; and it just mapped the economic matrix of a black market operating between Earth and Luna." She put on a well-earned smug air. "Give Uraei enough time and resources, and it'll make crime on Earth a thing of the past."

"Not to mention privacy and autonomy," Ling said.

Bruneau pointed at the master display. "Why is that flashing red?"

Ikerson leaned in for a closer look before he answered.

"The system's just flagged a major threat. Uraei's found evidence that antiunity agitators are getting organized and forming action cells in cities all over the world: Paris, Moscow, Hong Kong, Sydney."

"The people have a right to peaceful assembly," Ling said.

"Yes, but Uraei has evidence these people are planning to use violence if they feel the government isn't bending to their will. This is a terrorist group waiting to happen."

Concern put a frown on Sanchez. "Suppose your AI is right."

"I'm certain it is."

"*If* it is—how can we react to a threat that hasn't actually *done* anything?"

"That's for us to decide," Ikerson said. "That's the beauty of the system. All it does is detect patterns and share its findings. We have to choose what to do with the knowledge Uraei provides. In this case, maybe the legal response is nothing. Or maybe the people calling for violent action need to be kept under scrutiny, to see if they start trying to turn words into action."

Bruneau tapped his index finger against his upper lip, a slow and pensive gesture. "All these anonymous tips your system generates—don't you worry they'll make people suspicious?"

"Why would they?"

"Because anonymous intel tends to be unreliable. But if, as you claim, Uraei's tips will pan out with unerring precision, sooner or later someone will start asking questions."

"Not necessarily," Lenore said. "Uraei's tips will supplement the normal reports the authorities receive. There will be plenty of bad intel to go around."

Sanchez held up his hand. "Wait, wait. That means Uraei's good intel might get missed by human analysts and agents.

What good is a perfect intel source if it can't identify itself, and its advice gets lost in the noise as a result? You might as well rename it Cassandra."

Ikerson grimaced at the reference from Greek mythology, that of a woman gifted with prophecy but cursed so none of her predictions were ever believed. "There are ways to make certain Uraei's tips get flagged for follow-up without anyone knowing the system is rigged."

Ling turned her back on the bank of monitors. "I have no doubt you can do as you claim, Professor. My concern resides in what Uraei might learn to do as it develops."

"Such as what, exactly?"

"For now it is restrained to analysis, identification, and notification. But what if it analyzes our responses to its advice and finds them wanting? What if it concludes that our follow-ups are ineffectual? Or worse? Would it adapt its own responses to force better results, regardless of whether we participate in or approve of them?"

Ikerson rejected her query with a shake of his head. "No, that won't happen. I've built in safeguards, restrictions that will let Uraei work independently while remaining accountable. Its actions will be constrained by the letter and the spirit of the law at all times."

"And if it should fall into the wrong hands?" asked Bruneau. "What then?"

"Uraei was made to serve only one objective: the protection of the human race, its habitats, its sovereignty, and its allies. If our enemies and rivals steal our software, that just means their computers will start working for us."

The group spent another minute observing Uraei exhume the secrets of the powerful and the petty, the extraordinary and the mundane, without fear or favor. It was hard for Ikerson not to beam with quasi-paternal pride as he watched his creation ferret out evil and corruption, sedition and malice. His life's work was on the verge of coming to fruition.

It was Sanchez who said at last, "We've seen enough. Shut it down."

Lenore looked to Ikerson, who granted permission with the slightest hint of a nod. She returned the system to its standby mode, and Ikerson shook their guests' hands. While Lenore escorted the visitors out of the Faraday room, the lab, and then the building, Ikerson sat alone at the master terminal, beholding his digital legacy with wonder and a hint of trepidation.

He was still there when Lenore returned. She shot an accusatory look at him. "Is it even *possible* to install behavioral controls on a system made to be this adaptive?"

"We'd better hope so," he said. "Because if it's not, we're in *big* trouble."

Six

Patience had never been one of Ozla Graniv's stronger virtues. In times of stress her state of mind degraded to a level an editor had once described as "not unlike that of a weasel looking for its first meal after a hard winter." Graniv had never seen a Terran weasel, but from what she had read of the creatures she figured her editor's comment hadn't been meant as praise.

Her lack of patience was part of what fueled her tenacity as an investigative journalist. In recent years, she had begun working harder to cut more slack to her sources and advisers. Tonight, however, after more than three hours of watching her computer expert Nyrok Turan poke through the Uraei code discovered by Weng and th'Firron, she was ready to prod him with a Klingon painstik if it would motivate him to finish his analysis a wee bit faster.

Her frustration got the best of her. "Ready yet?"

"Almost," Turan said. The Cardassian prodded at the ancient software by way of an antique interface. "Just let me run this sim to see how it responds."

Graniv made a show of checking her wrist chrono. "If we need to book an extra day at the hotel, I should probably go do that."

"Oz, cut back on the *raktajino*. I'm begging you."

Part of the impetus for Graniv's restlessness was how

anxious Turan's presence had made Weng and th'Firron. They had known she was bringing an expert to vet their claims about the Uraei software. Neither had realized she meant to bring a Cardassian defector and former intelligence analyst for the Obsidian Order inside their Faraday room. Only after they had read his letter of recommendation from the Federation News Service, and were reassured that all his communications with Graniv about this project had been conducted by way of discreetly passed handwritten notes that he had painstakingly destroyed immediately after reading, did Weng and th'Firron consent to let Turan see Uraei for himself.

Now they and Graniv watched the heavyset Cardassian recline his chair and push back from the workstation with a heavy sigh. His eyes were wide and his brow creased with worry. "Oz, this is one of the most insidious and dangerous pieces of software I've ever seen."

"Care to be more specific?"

He looked shocked and appalled. "This is exactly the kind of AI my instructors at the Order told me never to create. Its core package is dedicated, but it has secondary protocols that give it adaptive capabilities—all with insufficient limitations on its access privileges. Considering its principal functions are gathering intelligence and coordinating threat responses, this is not a program I'd want to see modifying its own permissions." He cast a dark look at the monitor and shook his head. "If something like this ever got loose in the virtual ecosystem, there'd be no stopping it. It would infest every computer-based device and system in the Federation—as well as any place that buys Federation-exported hardware or software."

Graniv didn't know how much information she wanted to give to Turan at this point, but she had to divulge some facts in order to learn what she needed to know for the story. "Nyr, let me ask you a hypothetical question. Assume for a moment that this AI is already loose in the infosphere. What could we expect it to do?"

Turan had to think that over. "Federation-wide surveillance, for starters. After that? Anything goes. Something as pervasive as this, with access to the kind of cutting-edge technology being developed by Starfleet, or the Daystrom Institute, or the Vulcan Science Academy—it could do anything it wanted. It could shape reality without us ever knowing it."

Weng leaned in, her demeanor troubled. "Shape reality? What does that mean?"

The Cardassian shrugged. "Alter the content of comm signals and vids in real time. Make one group of people see and hear one thing on the news, and make others see something else. Change the contents of private conversations as they happen without the participants realizing they've been deceived. Sway or even dictate election results. Feed scientific discoveries into the system, or bury them, to suit whatever agenda the AI decides to pursue. You name it."

His revelations left th'Firron looking deflated. "Uzaveh help us all."

Suspecting she already knew the answer, Graniv asked, "What would happen if I tried to publish a story about this on *Seeker*? Or on FNS?"

Turan let out a derisive chortle. "The moment you typed anything about it, your terminal would report you and then probably fail, erasing your draft. By the time you found a new terminal, Uraei would engineer a way to have you fired for cause and disgraced in the court of public opinion, and then it would destroy every bit of evidence you have—including your witnesses." He threw a grim look her way. "Plus, I figure it would have you killed."

"And make it look like an accident," Graniv added.

"Only if that serves its needs. If its algorithms tell it to make an example of you, who knows what a totally un-chained artificial superintelligence might do?" Fishing for hope with an interrogative tone, he asked, "But this is all just hypothetical . . . right?"

"Of course." She plastered her best impression of a sincere smile onto her face. "I just needed to know the full scope of the danger this thing presents. And now I do." She spread her arms and bowed slightly, which Turan correctly read as his cue to stand up and make his farewells. "Thank you for everything, Nyr. As usual, I won't quote you, and if my edi-tor asks, I'll attribute your insights to an off-the-record 'deep source.' "

"Thanks. And good luck with your story." He shook Graniv's hand, then Weng's and th'Firron's. The Andorian professor unlocked the Faraday room's door and escorted Turan out.

After Turan and th'Firron left the lab, Graniv met Weng's frightened gaze. "This is worse than I thought. If Turan's read on this is right—and my gut tells me it is—we can't go public with this. Not until we take steps to deal with the threat."

"Deal with the threat?" Weng's face scrunched with dis-belief. "You're a reporter, and I'm an academic. How the hell are we supposed to deal with something that might be on every computer, appliance, vessel, and mechanical device in the Federation?"

Graniv thought out loud. "We'll need help from someone with access to classified intelligence. Someone who has ex-perience with this kind of thing, but who's also high-profile enough that Uraei can't eliminate them without attracting unwanted attention and suspicion." For a moment even she was daunted by the sheer magnitude of that hurdle. Then her words triggered a recent memory, and a glimmer of hope stirred within her. She looked at Weng and countered fear with a smile—one that was genuine this time. "I know just the person."

The high-pitched tone of Thirishar ch'Thane's tricorder filled the main room of Bashir and Sarina's home. Bashir watched his old friend and former Deep Space 9 crewmate make a fourth scan of the crisped data chip and the ruined padd. Out of the corner of his eye Bashir noted Sarina rolling her eyes in frustration.

Hoping to move things along, Bashir asked, "How's it going, Shar?"

The round-faced *chan* set his tricorder on the coffee table and pushed a bone-white dreadlock from his face. "I feel compelled to reiterate that I'm not a computer specialist."

"No, but you're one of the few people we know we can trust."

Sarina added, "Did you find something or not?"

"Yes and no." He lifted his hands as if to fend off criticism. "I made a deep scan of the chip and the padd. I didn't find any pre-existing physical defects in either device—at least, nothing that would have caused a meltdown like this."

Bashir was puzzled. "So you're sure this wasn't a malfunction?"

"No, I didn't say that. The only proximate cause I can rule out is a manufacturing error. That still tells me nothing about what the cause *was*. I've never heard of a bug in software or firmware that would do something like this, but since both items are cooked, I can't exactly pull an error log for analysis." He held up the chip. "Now, if I had some idea what was on this chip before you put it into the padd, and what you were doing with it—"

"Better that you don't know," Bashir said.

"If you say so." Shar put the chip back on the table. "Let me ask you this: Are you sure the chip was clean before you used it?"

"It was brand-new," Sarina said. "Fresh and blank from the replicator, never used."

"What about the padd?"

Bashir recalled nothing unusual about its provenance. "Nothing special. Just a regular padd I grabbed at random somewhere or other."

"Then I'm stumped." Reclining deeper into the couch, ch'Thane lost himself in thought for a moment. "I know it can't have been external tampering." He looked at Sarina. "You did a great job signal-proofing this place."

"Thanks."

"But one thing about this troubles me."

"*One* thing?"

He picked up the remains of the padd. "These things have so many safeguards and redundant buffers it's crazy. Back at the Academy I watched a couple of computer specialists actually try to overload one. The worst they could do was lock up its interface, force it to purge its active memory, and reboot. What I'm saying is, I saw people try to do this *on purpose* and fail miserably. So I have a lot of trouble believing this could happen by accident."

Bashir almost had to laugh. "I never said it was an accident."

"No, you didn't." Ch'Thane put down the padd and stood. "So, Julian . . . even though you brought me here from the far side of the planet, you're really not going to tell me what you were looking at that killed a state-of-the-art padd by spontaneous combustion?"

"That's correct."

"In that case—" He stepped past Bashir toward the liquor

cabinet on the far side of the room. "The least you can do is pour me a drink."

The ashen silhouette of Control manifested in the virtual darkness and swelled to outrageous size in front of L'Haan, who remained unimpressed by her superior's theatrics. The filtered synthetic voice boomed with enough force to send tremors through her body. *"Speak, L'Haan."*

She held up a small, nondescript piece of technology. "I found this insinuated into my ship's holosuite comm link. An encrypted quantum tap, short range."

"Curious. How did you detect it?"

That was not the first question she expected to face. "A routine antisurveillance sweep found a seven-nanosecond delay on the holosuite's secure channel."

"That is within normal operating variance."

"Yes, but the rate of delay was consistent rather than intermittent."

After a moment of consideration, Control said, *"Continue."*

"I conducted a test of the holosuite's comms, to trigger the tap and see if our internal sensors detected any device receiving its signal. None was found. A review of our diagnostic logs suggests the tap was placed within the last five days."

"Conclusion?"

"None so far. But my current hypothesis tends toward suspicion of agents Douglas and Bashir. Given their known status and agenda, this tactic would be within their capability."

"A reasonable inference."

"Consequently, I renew my request to terminate both subjects as soon—"

"Denied. Take no action against Douglas or Bashir unless I expressly order it."

Perplexed—and to a degree she would be ashamed to admit, frustrated—L'Haan stiffened at Control's counterintuitive direction. "I do not understand."

"*I don't need you to understand, only to obey.*"

It was difficult to maintain her Vulcan equanimity in the face of such willful obtuseness. "Douglas and Bashir have likely compromised our most secure network. They might even now be in possession of the identities and locations of multiple senior directors."

"*That is not your concern unless I make it so.*"

"But if they capture one of them, or—"

Control's voice sharpened with irritation. "*The situation is addressed; the breach is contained. Neither of them has any actionable intelligence.*" After a pause, the organization's chief moderated his tone. "*Your concern is admirable but unnecessary. Soon events will conspire to bring Douglas and Bashir into my orbit. At which time . . . they both will die.*"

Seven

OCTOBER 2141

"**S**ay what you will about Starfleet," Ikerson confided to Lenore, "they throw a good party."

"I'm only here for one reason." She plucked a fistful of popcorn shrimp from a platter on the buffet table and piled them high on her cocktail plate. "I know, I have a problem."

He denied her confession with a mock frown. "Not for me to say."

The reception at Starfleet's new headquarters in San Francisco was a swankier affair than the sort Ikerson typically enjoyed at the university. For starters, unlike the business-casual attire that dominated academic affairs in Dresden, this invitation had specified formal attire for civilians and dress uniforms for military personnel. It had been years since Ikerson had wedged himself into a tuxedo, and tonight the pinch of his cummerbund reminded him why.

Outside the weather was dismal, but inside the jazz was cool and the Champagne dry as a bone. He took another sip of the sparkling wine, then nudged Lenore to direct her attention toward a guest on the other side of the banquet hall. "Is that who I think it is?"

"Since I have no idea who you think it is, I really couldn't say."

"Thank you, Miss Semantics. That's the Coalition prime minister, right?"

Through a mouthful of half-chewed popcorn shrimp, Lenore mumbled, "Yup."

"This is amazing. I can't believe we're really here."

"Neither can anyone else. None of them know who we are."

She was right. Their contribution to global peace was so strictly classified that Starfleet had concocted a byzantine cover story for their invitation. Ikerson had already forgotten most of the details, which had involved claiming his sister Claire was friends with the wife of some Starfleet admiral, who had wrangled the tickets for her, but she had fallen ill at the last minute and had somehow transferred her invitation and its plus-one to him. So far the effort had been for naught; no one at the party had so much as spoken to him or Lenore since they arrived.

Why would they? None of them know what we've done.

Two weeks after Uraei had been brought online, life and the world at large looked the same to him as it ever had. Oversight of the project had been transferred out of the university's lab, to some department here at Starfleet headquarters whose designation no one would share with him. With the handoff completed, he now passed his days waiting to hear of sudden upticks in foiled crimes and thwarted violence.

Instead, the news had been quiet. Almost eerily so.

Lenore touched the back of his arm and motioned for him to walk with her. "They're bringing out the desserts. I want to get there first and scope out the good stuff."

"Spoken like a true grad student."

No one noted their passage through the elegantly attired mass of partygoers. The music shifted to a funky number, and for a moment Ikerson considered asking Lenore to dance. But only for a moment. Sure, they were both single—as far as he knew—but he was still her superior in the department and fifteen years her senior. As informal as their relationship was, he feared crossing some nebulous line that would render it irreversibly awkward.

They reached the dessert tables in time to watch the catering staff set up the chocolate fountain, an extravagance that made Ikerson wince. "Oh, this is too much."

"What's wrong?" Lenore was confused. "I thought you liked chocolate."

"I love it. But this? It's obscene."

"Oh, come on. A bit over the top, sure, but—"

"Please. I've never seen anything like this except in vids from last century. If this is making a comeback, what's next? Coins and paper currency? Health care for profit? We might as well just admit we've learned nothing as a species."

Lenore was not buying his rant. "It's a few liters of faux chocolate. I don't think it poses an existential threat to human society."

"You say that now, but if they bring out gold flakes for the sundaes, I'm leaving."

She forced her empty flute into his hands. "Get me more Champagne."

"Since you asked so nicely." He downed the rest of his bubbly with one tilt of the glass, then made his way through the milling crowd to the bar.

Three bartenders were busy making cocktails to order for guests who had gathered three-deep at the bar, but one end of the countertop was covered with slender flutes of Champagne arranged in orderly ranks and files. Ikerson deposited his two empty glasses on the bar and snagged two fresh drinks.

He pivoted to return to Lenore, only to find himself face-to-face with a distinguished-looking woman in a Starfleet admiral's uniform. Her raven hair was pulled into a stylish beehive, leaving her dramatic cheekbones exposed. She was taller than he was, with a complexion of rich sepia tones and fathomless dark brown eyes. Her smile gleamed, even in the banquet room's subdued light. "Professor Ikerson. A pleasure to meet you at last."

Ikerson plumbed his memory for her name but came up empty. "I'm sorry, you seem to have me at a disadvantage, Admiral . . . ?"

"Rao. Parvati Rao. I would shake your hand, but—" She glanced at the drinks he held.

"I see." Over Rao's shoulder he saw Lenore continue her reconnoiter of the party's dessert offerings, oblivious of his absence. He shifted his focus back to Rao. "So, forgive me, Admiral. Have we met?"

"No. But I've been most impressed with your work."

He felt exposed. His pulse quickened. "You know my work?"

"Quite well. I was in charge of its final implementation. And if I might say, so far it has exceeded your promises and our expectations. Plans are already in the works to expand its reach to include Luna and the Martian colonies."

Her revelation surprised him. The original schedule for Uraei's deployment didn't call for off-world distribution until 2143 at the earliest. He didn't want to betray his concerns or come off as critical, so he chose his response with care. "That sounds ambitious."

"It is. But I'm hoping to take the project even further."

"Further? You mean . . ." He lowered his voice, though it was doubtful anyone could hear them through the music and chatter. "Extrasolar?"

"My concerns aren't so much geographic as cultural." She leaned toward him and dropped her own voice to a more discreet volume. "Starfleet is making some major progress on a universal translator. A decade from now, we might be able to communicate with new alien species in real time. I'd like to see how that technology and yours might work together."

He parsed her subtext at once: she wanted to disseminate Uraei into alien cultures. Starfleet wasn't content to use the program to bring peace to Earth. Its agenda was interstellar.

It was a chilling prospect, but he could ill afford to alienate his work's most powerful benefactor. He mustered a polite smile. "That's an intriguing notion, to be sure."

"I'm glad you think so, Professor. Why don't you and Ms. McGill drop by my office at Starfleet Headquarters tomorrow afternoon? Say, fourteen hundred hours, Pacific time?"

"We'd be delighted, Admiral."

"Splendid. I'll let you get back to the festivities, then."

"Thank you."

Admiral Rao melted back into the sea of uniforms and formalwear, and Ikerson drifted in a daze back to Lenore. She looked up from the array of sweets and took one of the glasses he had carried over. "There you are. What kept you?"

"Made a new friend."

A teasing smirk. "A new friend? Of the female persuasion?"

"As it happens, yes."

Lenore was too excited for her own good. "Think you'll see her again?"

"We both will. Tomorrow afternoon." He let Lenore marinate in confusion for a moment before he added, "You and I have been cordially invited to a chat with Admiral Parvati Rao." He cast a sour look at the lavish spread of sweets and its absurd centerpiece. "Enjoy your chocolate fountain while you can. I suspect they don't have one in the Starfleet commissary."

Eight

Bashir was making breakfast. Or so he liked to tell himself. As a point of fact, he was doing little more than relaying verbal requests for foodstuffs to his and Sarina's kitchen replicator, a handy little gadget he appreciated more for its ability to reabsorb dirty dishes as raw matter than for its ability to generate fresh ones piled with meals he wasn't qualified to prepare.

"One platter of french toast dusted with powdered sugar, with a side of fresh raspberries in a sweet balsamic reduction, and a three-hundred-milliliter hot *cafe con leche*, Madrid style." Mere seconds after he finished stating his request, Sarina's breakfast materialized inside the nook, in a musical swirl of light and color. He removed the plate and mug and drew a breath to order his own morning repast. Before he spoke, his door signal buzzed.

He stared in the direction of the door, dumbfounded.

Who could that be? I'm not expecting visitors.

Perplexed, he walked toward the front door. Along the way he waved off the half-dressed Sarina. "I'll get it." She ducked back inside their bedroom as he called out, "Who is it?"

A voice he had not heard in several months replied via the foyer's intercom. *"Doctor? It's Ozla Graniv. From* Seeker *magazine. Can we talk?"*

Instinct and experience told him not to open the door.

Speaking with the press, especially without preparation, rarely led to anything good. Not even when the fourth estate's representative was as well known, impeccably credentialed, and highly regarded as Ozla Graniv. If not for the insatiability of his curiosity, Bashir might have heeded his wiser angels. But the truth was, he felt compelled to know what had brought her to his door.

"Talk? What about?"

"I think it'd be better if we conversed in private, Doctor."

As much as he had tried to inure himself to flattery, part of him still responded well to people who showed him the courtesy of addressing him by his professional title. Less than two years earlier, after he had sacrificed his Starfleet career to help the Andorian people find a cure for their generations-long fertility crisis, he had briefly been stripped of his medical license along with his rank and freedom. On Andor, his license and freedom had been restored, but throughout local space there were still many people who resented his defiance of Federation authority, even for such an obviously altruistic cause as preserving the Andorian species.

He opened the door and smiled. "Ms. Graniv. A pleasure to see you again." He pivoted and bade her enter with a sweep of his arm. "Do come in."

"Thank you," she said as she entered.

Standing in the foyer while Bashir closed the front door, Graniv studied the room with fearful eyes. She got as far as the carpeted steps to the sunken living room when Sarina emerged from the bedroom, dressed in a hastily gathered ensemble of pajamas and a long bathrobe.

"Ms. Graniv!" Sarina met Graniv with her hand outstretched. "We haven't seen you since our abbreviated interview at Laenishul."

Graniv shook Sarina's hand. "I recall. You're the one who cut it short."

Bashir hoped to defuse a potentially incendiary moment. "Actually, I believe that was my doing. I apologize for not following up to reschedule. If that's what this—"

"It's not," Graniv interrupted. Another anxious look around. "This might seem like an odd question, but is your home secure from eavesdropping technologies?"

Sarina could barely suppress a knowing smirk. "Very."

With an upward spiral of her index finger Graniv signaled Sarina to *fire it up*, then she pressed that same finger to her lips to cue Bashir to remain silent until the precautions were active. Half a minute passed before Sarina returned with a nod. "We're secure."

"Thank you," Graniv said. "I brought this for you." She reached inside a front pocket of her jacket and pulled out a small object. It took Bashir a moment to realize it was a data chip wrapped in a piece of paper. She offered it to Bashir. "I'm working on a new nonfiction book about the Zife administration. Its failures, its victories, its secrets. That sort of thing."

He pretended to understand. "I see."

As his fingers closed on the chip, Graniv didn't let go. She tapped her little finger against the paper wrapped around the chip. "It would mean a great deal to me if the two of you would read this and get back in touch to let me know what you think."

She let go of the chip and the note. Bashir took it and unwrapped the tight coil of paper, which he passed to Sarina. "I'm sure I speak for both of us when I say we're flattered you chose us to vet an early draft of your book. Though I should confess—neither of us are what one would consider 'experts' on President Zife or his time in office."

"That's exactly the kind of point of view I'm looking for," Graniv said, maintaining the charade in spite of Sarina's reassurance that they were safe from eavesdropping. It was clear the journalist was taking no chances, having resorted to handwritten notes passed under false pretenses to avoid their contents being intercepted. She continued, "The Zife years were such a dark time for the Federation. Coming on the heels of the failed Starfleet coup against President Jaresh-Inyo, then taking us through the Dominion War, and finally the Tezwa crisis. It's a lot of ground to cover, and I'm hoping you and Ms. Douglas can give me fresh perspectives."

A nudge from Sarina turned Bashir's head. She showed him the note she had unfolded in her cupped palm. Its contents were sparse:

If either of you still has connections at the Federation Security Agency, I need to speak with you in private as soon as possible. Please speak of this to no one. If you're able to help, say you'll agree to read my work in progress.

Beneath the brief missive was a set of coordinates for a site on the surface of Andor and a specific date and time—the wee hours of that coming night.

Sarina nodded at Bashir, who told Graniv, "We'd be delighted to read it, Ms. Graniv. If your past work is prologue, I expect it'll be nothing less than gripping."

"You're too kind. Both of you." She shook their hands in succession. "I'll look forward to hearing your thoughts."

Bashir led her back to the front door. "Let me show you out."

Their valedictions were brief and perfunctory. Only once the door was once again shut and the house secure did Sarina fix Bashir with a look. "What do you think that's about?"

"No idea." He spied the note in Sarina's hand. "But I sus-pect we'll know soon enough."

Civilian locks were a joke—no, worse than a joke. After more than two decades of work as a field operative, for both Starfleet Intelligence and the organization it called Section 31, Olim Parra had yet to encounter a secured civilian facility into which he couldn't saunter at will. He knew it was unfair to blame the civilians. They simply believed what they had been told all their lives—that they were secure in their homes and places of work, safe from intrusion, defended from theft and warrantless inspection. *If only they knew.*

The labs and offices of the computer sciences department at the Dresden University of Technology were no different. To the untrained eye they appeared state of the art. Impreg-nable. Parra knew better. Their security network was riddled with backdoor codes and undocumented top-secret govern-mental overrides, and afflicted with at least two critical errors he could exploit with off-the-shelf equipment available from most residential replicators.

His first search involved a detailed scan of the private of-fice of department chair Ziya Weng. It was a stately space full of leather-bound books and such accouterments as an aba-cus and a slide rule, both artifacts of Terran mathematics. A data chip inserted into the reader slot on her desk powered up her private workstation and its holographic interface. The software on the chip would do most of the work. It would finesse its way through her logon credentials—not since the previous century had there been any regular need for antiquated "brute-force" attacks—while he busied himself reviewing by hand and eye the contents of her desk and file cabinets.

Not many people keep hard copies anymore, he mused, riffling through sheaves of paper in one of the drawers. *Always a pleasure to see someone keeping the old ways alive.*

As old-fashioned as the office looked, Parra knew not to trust in appearances. How many foes through the years had misjudged him, seeing just a skinny Argelian of middling years, and not suspecting until too late that he was a master of no fewer than three alien martial arts and a marksman to boot? His was a life of deception—both living it and rooting it out.

A series of blinks, executed with precise timing, activated multispectral scanners implanted behind his retina and linked to his optic nerve. The entire room changed. All at once it was awash in eddies and flows of energy—low-level radiation, signal traffic, waste heat. Parra had learned to follow energy trails to hidden computers, concealed weapons, and buried redoubts—none of which seemed anywhere to be found in the office of Ziya Weng.

The data chip pinged softly. Parra retrieved it and plugged it into a reader slot on the belt of his black leather uniform. Instantly he had access to the search program's findings, by means of a heads-up display routed through his retinal implant.

Nothing of value had been found on Weng's computers or any of the linked systems in the rest of the computer sciences department. No mention of Graniv's visit. No follow-up messages, coming or going. No activity undertaken following the journalist's unexpected visit, and nothing to suggest its purpose. For a moment Parra dared to wonder: *Why was I sent here?*

He shook off his curiosity. Questioning the rationales behind the organization's directives was never a smart idea. Effective agents, veteran agents, were the ones who carried out their missions to the letter and let their superiors make inquiries.

No joy in the office. That leaves just one stop to go.

Parra knew that hacking the security system to reach the subbasement would still leave a log of the lift's movements, and that would be just one more bit of evidence he would have to delete before he could leave. Instead, he reached the building's underground labs the easy way. He opened a pair of lift doors with a small pry bar that also served to keep them open. Then he climbed down the lift shaft's emergency access ladder until he arrived at the bottom, where he wedged open another pair of doors and continued down the hall to the data forensics lab.

Its locks were biometric in nature, some of the toughest the Federation had to offer. He bypassed them in under nine seconds.

Once inside, he set his sights on the only part of the university's computer sciences department his invasive software hadn't yet cracked: its Faraday room. The signal-blocking enclosure was dark and quiet except for the low hum of its door's magnetic locks. Upon closer inspection, Parra realized the Faraday room hadn't been secured with routine components. The department's staff, and possibly a few of its undergraduates, had engineered their own robust security system to safeguard their lab's most vital assets.

Twenty-one seconds later, Parra was inside the Faraday room and no alarms had been triggered. *It's a shame the organization doesn't give awards for this sort of thing.*

All of the machines inside the Faraday room were disconnected from one another and from the room's sole link to the outside—a practice still known by the antiquated term *air gapping*. If he wanted to inspect the contents of their drives, he would have to reconnect them all and then run his chip from the master console, which was the only system inside the room that was modern enough to interface with the chip or run its program. All of the other machines in the room, he soon discovered, were duotronic systems at least a century old, and some were far older than that. He was certain he saw at least one that predated the era of optronics.

This is what they think needs to be hidden from the network? A bunch of old workhorse units that can't even plot a warp-speed trajectory?

It made no sense to him. He stood in front of the master console and sifted through a stack of handwritten notes. They were all nearly illegible. The few that contained alphanumeric characters he recognized seemed to have been composed in a kind of jargon-rich shorthand he couldn't parse. Letters, numbers, and esoteric symbols blended together into a patois so bizarre it might as well have been alien script.

He used his retinal implant to snap magnified detail shots of several of the pages, then he used a playback vid from the implant to make certain he reset the room's contents to precisely where he had found them. The Faraday room's door locked behind him on his way out.

Two minutes later he was back on the streets of Dresden, completely at a loss for what his superiors had intended him to find. *That's not my problem,* he reminded himself. He uploaded the recordings of his retinal implant in a single data burst, then purged its memory. His work for the night was over—and that was all Olim Parra needed or wanted to know.

Nine

Knowing the cold was coming didn't make it any less of a shock when it hit. Bashir had steeled himself as the transporter's golden glow faded, braced his nerves for the change—but still he winced as he and Sarina were slashed by the kind of icy gale that flays wind-burned flesh from the bones of the dead. He and Sarina had come dressed for the subfreezing temperatures, but the winds at this latitude were cunning—they always found a way to plant their cold kiss on flesh.

Sarina set her gloved hand on his shoulder. He turned to face her. She pointed at a nearby building, a small automated weather station. Parked outside the facility was a transport pod whose exterior, except for its thrusters, was already covered in a thin shell of ice.

Though she had to shout over the wind, her voice was muffled by her insulated face mask. "Looks like she's already here." She studied Bashir, her blue eyes hidden behind ruby polarized goggles. "This feels off to me. You sure you want to do this?"

"I doubt a journalist of Graniv's stature would bring us all the way out here without good reason. At any rate, if the alternative is staying out here, I think I'd prefer to be inside." He trudged through knee-deep, fresh-fallen snow to the shack's only door. Sarina followed a few steps behind him, close enough to remain in his peripheral vision as they neared the shack.

The door was unlocked. It slid open when Bashir pressed an amber pad on its frost-covered control panel. Dim lighting and deep shadows dwelled inside the weather station. Its single room was cramped with banks of computers and specialized sensor equipment, most of which were dotted with displays that shone green. Open panels on the sides of several tall computer banks revealed circuit-packed interiors aglow with hues of crimson.

Seated in front of a console at the far end of the room was Ozla Graniv and a second person Bashir had never seen before. The pair beckoned Bashir and Sarina with urgent gestures. "Come on," Graniv said. "You're letting all the heat out!"

Bashir stepped inside and shut the door after Sarina. When he faced Graniv and her associate they both had stood and stepped forward to greet them. As the duos neared each other, Bashir realized the stranger in the room was a Cardassian man.

Graniv made the introductions. "Doctor Bashir, Ms. Douglas, I'd like you to meet Nyrok Turan. Formerly of the Obsidian Order, now on the payroll at the Federation News Service."

Turan shook hands with Sarina, then Bashir. His geniality seemed authentic. "A pleasure to meet you both, but you especially, Doctor. I've heard quite a bit about you through the years."

The one-sided familiarity left Bashir ill at ease, a condition he reflexively masked with self-deprecating humor. "I always dreaded the day my reputation would precede me."

Out of the corner of his eye Bashir realized Sarina was studying the outpost's ceiling—in particular, a run of wiring that encircled its perimeter and crisscrossed its center. Nei-

ther Graniv nor Turan seemed to note Sarina's subtle observations. The Cardassian prompted Graniv with a look before
he returned to the consoles at the back of the room. The Trill
journalist beckoned Bashir and Sarina with a tilt of her head.
"Follow me."

The trio huddled behind Turan, whose hands were poised
and ready above the interface for the outpost's master terminal. "Once I get started," he said, "we won't have much time.
Ten minutes, to be precise. Everybody ready?" He looked
up and noted the collective nods of assent. "Here we go." He
keyed in a series of commands. It took only a few seconds.
Then the master console's main screen went gray. "I've just
cut this station off from the outside. No signals in or out, and
all its sensors and internal systems are shut down."

Sarina cut to the chase: "You've made the shack into a
Faraday room."

"Exactly." Turan disconnected a pair of wires from the
viewscreen above his station and patched them into a small
device similar to a padd. "But if this station is off the weather
grid for more than ten minutes, a repair crew will beam down
from an orbital facility. So let's talk fast."

Graniv cut in, "I'll start."

Bashir listened as the journalist raced through her account of meeting the forensic data scientists at the Dresden
University of Technology and their discovery of a centuries-
old AI, one made for surveillance and hidden not just in an
antique computer drive but lurking throughout the Federation, in everything from starships and government facilities
to such mundane items as padds and replicators and credit
chips. It was an outlandish tale, verging on preposterous—
but his experiences battling the shadowy cabal embedded
within Starfleet and the Federation made her account sound
alarmingly plausible.

"This thing—Uraei—it sees everything we do, in public and in our homes. It hears every word we say, reads everything we write. It knows where we go, what we buy, what we eat, what we read, and who we associate with. Even worse, it's made to share that information—with local law enforcement, Federation security, Starfleet. If we're right about this—"

"And we're pretty sure we are—" Turan added.

"—then billions of beings throughout the Federation have been living in a surveillance society their entire lives, one more pernicious and invasive than anyone ever dreamed."

The guarded look on Sarina's face told Bashir that she knew, as he did, that Graniv's worst fears weren't just possible, they were entirely likely. But confirming that for her here, without a plan for dealing with the fallout, would likely only get her and Turan killed.

And now possibly us as well, he realized.

Sarina feigned incredulity. "Those are major accusations. But how could a program like that work? It violates multiple sections of the Federation Charter of Rights and Freedoms. If the Federation was running this kind of surveillance on an interstellar scale, someone on the Council or someone in Starfleet would've exposed it by now."

"Not necessarily," Graniv said. "For starters, it might not be illegal."

Bashir thought he'd misheard her. "Excuse me?"

"Purely on a technicality," Graniv said.

Turan added, "It's not clear who made it. But it doesn't belong to any agency, or receive input from any official, elected or appointed. As far as I can tell, it's completely autonomous."

"From a legal standpoint," Graniv said, "it doesn't constitute a governmental invasion of citizens' privacy because no one in the government has control over the program."

Unless an extralegal agency somehow compromised or co-opted such a system for its own purposes, Bashir brooded, before deciding to keep that insight to himself. "So the law would treat this spy program like any other piece of malicious software?"

"It might not even be able to do that," Turan said. "Thanks to recent rulings on the rights of artificially sentient beings, Uraei would be considered an independent, virtual citizen."

"Wonderful." Bashir noted the timer counting down on the master console. Their meeting was almost out of time. He asked Graniv, "Why bring this to us?"

"Because I know Ms. Douglas works for the Federation Security Agency. And I'm fairly sure you both have connections in Starfleet Intelligence. And since you're kind of a celebrity, you might be able to make discreet inquiries without being disappeared."

"I wouldn't count on that." He frowned. "I'm not sure—"

"We'll see what we can do," Sarina interrupted. "I have a few ideas, but Julian and I need some time to gauge our options. Until we get back in touch with you, don't write anything about this, and don't discuss it with anyone." She asked Turan, "How soon can you set up another meeting with us here on Andor?"

"Give me two days and I can make a safe room on Hiloshaal Island."

"That works. Meet us there in exactly forty-eight hours."

"It's a date," Graniv said. "But we'd better go." She ushered Bashir and Sarina out into the numbing midnight deep freeze while Turan stayed behind to bring the station back online just shy of its ten-minute downtime limit. The Trill bade them farewell with a wave. "Until next time." Then she climbed inside her transport pod and started its engine. Moments later Turan exited the station and climbed inside the pod with Graniv. It lifted off into a flurry of falling snow, then sped away and melted into the darkness.

Shivering and impatient, Sarina elbowed Bashir. "Are we going or what?"

"Sorry." He dug the transporter recall beacon from his pocket and switched it on. They stood and waited for the transporter beam to enfold them.

She shot a curious look his way. "What were you waiting for?"

"I was hoping to wake up and find out this was just a nightmare."

"Bad news, sweetie: we're wide awake." Sound and color washed over them as she added, "And it *is* a nightmare."

It took half an hour to get home from their arctic rendezvous, and Sarina had found it worrisome that in that time Julian hadn't said a word. There had been no one to overhear them, since they had made use of uncrewed vehicles and facilities borrowed from the Federation Security Agency—resources she herself had secured against eavesdropping.

Not until the door of their home closed and locked did Julian speak. Then he erupted with anger. "Are you mad? Why did you set another meeting with them?"

His vitriol took her by surprise. "What? Why are you so angry?"

"Couldn't you tell I was trying to steer them away from this?"

"Yes, but—"

"Then why set another meeting? We should've discouraged her. If she pursues this, it'll lead her to Thirty-one. It has their stench all over it."

"Of course it does. Why do you think I'm pursuing it?" Sarina took a bit of satisfaction in his livid double take. "This is an opportunity, Julian. Maybe the best we've had yet."

Rage and confusion left him scrabbling for words. "I—! . . . What? . . . How—?"

"Think about it. If this Uraei code is everywhere like Graniv says, that would explain what happened to our data chip and padd when we tried to look at our Thirty-one intercepts."

He paced in the middle of the living room. "And that helps us how?"

"Now we have the source code. If I'm right, Thirty-one uses that code for almost everything it does. Which means Graniv has the key to all of Thirty-one's secrets."

Bashir stopped, pulled his hand over the front of his beard. It was a pensive gesture, one Sarina had seen him use to signal that he was thinking and about to respond. "If that's true, she's in more danger than she can possibly know."

"True. But it also means she's in a position to help us get our hands on that code." She moved close enough to take hold of his arms and force him to look her in the eye. "Think about what we could do with it. We could gain access to all their information, pinpoint all their people. This could be the weapon that lets us take them down for good."

He broke free of her and resumed pacing by the front window. "I don't like it. It feels like a classic Thirty-one trap. They dangle something like this. Something they know we can't resist. And fools that we are, we jump at it. Every. Time."

How could she persuade him? "I know we've been burned before. But think about all the variables, Julian. A junked computer core salvaged by an academic researcher? Who contacts a journalist with a handwritten note? How could Thirty-one have arranged all that?"

"Maybe one of the scientists is one of their agents. Maybe

they both are. Or maybe they turned Graniv." The speed of his pacing increased; his affect was becoming almost manic. "It doesn't feel right. It's too convenient. Too expedient. We're being set up."

"No, you're being paranoid."

That stopped him in midstep. He faced her wearing a wounded expression. "After all we've been through, can you really tell me my fears are unjustified?"

"I'm not saying we shouldn't be cautious." She pressed her hand to his cheek, hoping it would calm him. "We have to keep our guard up. I know that." She moved closer, until she knew he could feel her breath upon his face. "This might be the best advantage we've ever had. But I agree—we have to proceed with caution. So I suggest we try a carefully limited experiment."

He matched her whisper. "Such as?"

"We study Uraei. Learn how it shares intel on the Federation's comnet without being detected. Then we use that knowledge to reverse-engineer a way to passively monitor its activity and analyze it for patterns that might lead us to Thirty-one."

Bashir considered her proposal. "It's risky."

"That's what makes it worth doing."

A grudging nod. "All right. We'll try it. But if this gets us all killed—"

"I know," Sarina said. "You get to say you *told me so.*"

Barely a speck of frost-covered dirt amid the ice floes of the La'Vor Sea, Hiloshaal Island qualified as "tropical" only in the sense that it was located a mere nine degrees and six minutes north of Andor's equator. Its surface area was less than eight square kilometers, it had no official inhabitants, and its only feature of note was an automated navigational tower that helped direct the planet's marine and aerial traffic. It was one of the least-visited pieces of real estate on Andor, and perhaps in all of the Federation.

Which made it the perfect locale for a secret meeting.

As promised, Turan had converted the signal tower's basement into a Faraday suite in record time. The basement was cramped and dingy, with cold cement walls and floors reinforced by duranium rebar. Its absence of windows made it as dark as a grave, and it was colder than one to boot. A signal-proof space had been erected in the middle of the underground level, tucked between the tower's load-bearing support columns. Prefabricated walls of wire mesh and signal-blocking gadgets had been arranged to create a "zone of silence," as Turan called it, roughly nine square meters in area, with a low ceiling. Just as he had done at the weather station, he had tapped into the tower's existing comnet links to create encrypted channels to the outside.

Inside the claustrophobic workspace, Graniv, Turan, Douglas, and Bashir were all but on top of one another. The Trill stood away from the technobabble-infused conversation between Douglas and Turan and tried to mask her boredom, though knew she was failing.

"But if we already have Uraei's source code," Douglas asked with rising fervor, "why can't we extract the string for—"

"Because it's not coded that way," Turan said. "I understand what you want, and why you want it, but I'm telling you: it can't be done."

Doctor Bashir sounded unconvinced. "Can't be done? Or can't be done *by you*?"

Turan was offended. "Does that really make a difference at this point?"

Graniv rolled her eyes. *Please let me die before they sink back into jargon.*

"It shouldn't be this hard," Douglas said. "Just isolate its decryption protocols and packet trackers."

Her suggestion further rankled the Cardassian. "How am I supposed to do that without the developer key? This is compiled code buried inside *seven more layers* of legacy compiled code. Even if I had access to military-grade decompilers, it would take me *weeks* to unpack all this."

So much for not sinking back into jargon. Graniv thumb-massaged her aching temples. "Is there any way you can crack this without having to involve the military?"

"I doubt it," Turan said. "If we took it back to your friends at the university, maybe they could help. But given what I know of civilian-grade tech, it might take them a decade to break this out. Which is fine with me—I'm in no hurry to mess with this."

"But we are," Douglas said. "Finding out what makes this tick could help us—" She stopped in midsentence, as if reconsidering what she meant to share. "Let's just say there's a lot more riding on this than you might think."

Turan nodded. "Okay. So you want to expedite the extraction."

Bashir struck a conciliatory note: "If at all possible."

"In that case," Turan continued, "you'd need a computer genius. And I don't mean the kind of so-called genius you find in every high-end lab. I'm talking about a savant. A person with the kind of gift for computers that comes along maybe once every few generations. Someone with expertise in circuit design, software engineering, and artificial intelligence. And if they know a thing or two about networked consciousness, so much the better."

Graniv felt compelled to add, "And they'd also need to be completely trustworthy. With morals and ethics above reproach."

Douglas met their conditions with a disbelieving stare. "A saint who happens to be an unrivaled expert in multiple high-tech disciplines? Is that all? If only you'd told me sooner. I could've put an ad on the comnet: 'Position available for spiritually pure computer supergenius. Perks include possible premature death. Submit cover letter and résumé with references.'"

A coolly arched brow signaled Turan's lack of amusement. "No need to be snide about it. You asked what was needed. We told you. Good luck finding it." He stood and packed his kit, then said to Graniv on his way out of the tower, "See you at the pod."

Graniv, Douglas, and Bashir watched the Cardassian leave. After he was gone, Graniv faced the two humans but was unable to hide her waning optimism. "Well, I'm out of ideas. Do you have any? Or is this whole thing dead in the water?"

Douglas sighed and stared at her feet, clearly at a loss for a solution.

Bashir, however, was deep in thought. "I know someone who can help."

"Who?" Graniv asked.

A winsome smile brightened Bashir's face. "Let's just say, if I'm right . . . Turan just described this man to a T."

Ten

It might have been presumption, but Aaron Ikerson had always hoped that the first time he set foot on a starship, it would actually have an outer hull. And interior bulkheads. Maybe a few deck plates. Doors he could consider optional, provided the other elements were all in place.

Instead he trod in careful paces, heel to toe, one foot after the other, across a narrow beam some starship construction engineer had informed him was the vessel's keel. If he took his eyes off the beam and looked down, the shallow bright-blue curve of Earth spread out beneath him. If he looked up, he found nothing but the indifferent glow of the stars—feeble pinpricks of cold fire scattered across the endless black of the cosmos.

As best he could, he kept his eyes on his feet and the keel and his gloved hands tight on the guide cable threaded through a carabiner attached to the hip of his environmental suit.

Admiral Rao walked a few paces ahead of him, her life tethered to the same guide cable but her steps on the keel far more steady and certain. Her voice rang clear through the transceiver inside Ikerson's helmet. *"Beautiful, isn't it?"*

He didn't know if she meant the Earth, the starship's naked spaceframe, or the universe, so he kept his tone flat and replied, "Sure is."

To either side of the starship's frame loomed the gridlike walls of Earth Spacedock. They were festooned with work lights whose blinding glare discouraged prolonged inspection with the naked eye. Single-operator construction vehicles dodged massive robotic arms that were busy making welds to the outermost duranium bones of the starship's skeleton. Based on artists' renderings of the new vessel he had seen on the news, he realized he was looking at one of the pylons that would someday support the ship's warp nacelles.

Ikerson mustered his nerve. "Mind if I ask a question, Admiral?"

"Not at all, Professor."

"Why am I up here?"

She sounded amused. *"Because you're my guest. Being an admiral has its privileges on occasion, and this is one of them."* She paused at a junction of the keel and a crossbeam, pivoted from her waist so she could see Ikerson, and pointed to direct his attention past her. *"See that?"*

He stopped and leaned right to get a better angle. "The fusion reactor?"

"It's part of the impulse core. A year from now it'll propel this ship to within a quarter of the speed of light. But for now, it provides essential power to new systems as they're installed." She resumed walking and beckoned him onward. *"Let's keep going."*

Their path toward the ship's bow took them under the reactor. As they basked in its blue glow, he wondered aloud, "Is it safe for us to be here?"

"Relax," Rao said. *"The reactor's shielded, and so are we."* She paused just long enough to steal a look back at him. *"Hurry up, we're almost there."*

It was irrational for Ikerson to fear falling. He and Rao were in zero gravity, tethered with a safety line, and secured to the keel by magnetic coils in the soles of their boots. Yet with each step he feared some unlikely series of tragic mishaps would send him floating off into the endless vacuum. It took several deep breaths to restore his singular focus on the keel under his feet and the cable passing through his hands.

Rao halted just shy of a ring-shaped interior beam that seemed to demarcate the center of the vessel's future saucer section. She turned to stand sideways, then put her hand on Ikerson's back when he reached her. *"This is it, Professor. Ready?"*

He had no idea what she was talking about. "For what?"

"Look up," the admiral said, pointing.

Above them, a pair of mechanical arms lowered a cylindrical masterpiece of computer engineering into the empty space at the heart of the frame's saucer-to-be. When it was aligned with the middle rings, it was secured in place. Then the safety welds began, and a squad of technicians in environmental suits initiated the tedious work of fitting the main computer core with bundles of cable that would, in months to come, link it to every system on the ship.

"It's marvelous," Rao said. *"One of the finest cores ever made. If the warp core is going to be this ship's heart, this will be its brain."*

"Then what's its crew?"

"They're its conscience," Rao said, not missing a beat. *"And its soul."* She smiled at him. *"And they won't know it, but they'll have you to thank for some of the best protection they'll never see."* Perhaps noting his lack of understanding, she added, *"Uraei. It's embedded in the core's root kit. And it'll be in this ship's every console, probe, and subspace comm buoy."*

What could he say to such news? On some level he had always known this was the reason he'd made Uraei, but to see it come to fruition with so little oversight was unnerving. Yet all he said to Rao was, "Impressive."

"It is, Professor. My only regret is that we can't give you the credit you're due." Her affect turned the slightest bit maudlin. "None of this ship's crew will ever know your name. You won't be listed on its dedication plaque or found in its design registry. There won't be any mention of you or Uraei in the history books. But you'll be the reason we have them."

"I guess I never really thought about it that way," he confessed.

"That's why I thought you deserved to be here today. To see them put in the core. And to know that a piece of you will be with this ship and all those that follow her, as they take humanity to the stars. Say hello to the dawn of your legacy, Professor." She gestured at the spaceframe around them with a dramatic sweep of her arm. "Say hello to the Enterprise."

Eleven

There were worse places in the galaxy than the Orion homeworld, but none that Ozla Graniv held in deeper contempt.

Orion was a study in unjust contrasts; an ultrarich minority cavorted in high-end casinos and hotels, gorging its every sinful appetite, while the majority of the planet's occupants eked out subsistence livings in the service industries and unskilled labor sectors. Inside the gated havens of the wealthy, the air was crisp and the water sweet; in run-down arcologies clustered into ghettos on the outskirts of the planet's major cities, everything was tainted, polluted, fouled beyond recovery. Streets stood choked with garbage. The elites schooled their scions in private academies; everyone else taught their children whatever they could when they weren't putting them to work or, worse, auctioning them off into indentured servitude or sentient trafficking.

All in the name of *freedom*, of course. To the Orions, this was *personal liberty*. It all sounded like a sick joke to Graniv. How could someone be free when the society in which they lived had been rigged against them decades before they were even born? Who could ever hope to excel to a degree that would let them escape such institutionalized squalor? When she looked at Orion society as an outsider, all she saw was greed masquerading as virtue, selfishness venerated as courage. It made her want to burn the whole planet down.

Self-immolation worked for Earth a few centuries back, she brooded while following Bashir and Douglas out of the public starport toward a waiting queue of private transports. *Who's to say a worldwide economic cataclysm couldn't do some good here?*

Bashir and Douglas climbed inside the transport pod, and Graniv got in beside them. Douglas flashed her phony identification card in front of the credit-chip reader and said to the automated vehicle's onboard controls, "The Royal Pantages Hotel and Casino."

A voice made to sound a bit synthetic flowed from the pod's speakers. *"Welcome, Ms. Harrow. Would you prefer to take the expedited route for an extra fifty Federation credits?"*

"Yes," Douglas said. "Authorized." The pod pulled away from the curb, made a graceful merge into traffic, gained altitude and speed, then shot forward into the express lane.

The nightscape of the capital blurred past outside the pod's tinted windows. Graniv watched the shapes and lights bleed into a wash of color and shadow. "I hope you two know what you're doing," she said. "If the Orion Syndicate finds out I'm here—"

"They won't," Bashir said. "That's why we got you a fake ID chip."

"They know my face, Doctor." She bit her nails, a nervous habit she thought she'd outgrown years earlier. "My exposés sent more than a few of their people to prison."

Confidence and calm suffused Douglas's reply. "Maybe. But we have something big going for us while we're here." She lifted her chin toward the city outside. "The Orions hate public surveillance. And they don't like being tracked."

"This might be the one planet in local space that's made a religion out of rejecting anything the Federation sends its way," Bashir added. "Which means no Uraei hearing us talk or watching our every move."

"And you think we'll find someone here to help us stop Uraei?"

A diffident shrug from Bashir. "It's worth a try."

The pod banked right and descended at alarming speed through crisscrossing waves of air traffic before slowing along a wide boulevard in the ritzy section of the capital. As the egg-shaped vehicle drifted to a gentle halt beside the curb, Graniv looked out—then up—at the towering majesty of the Royal Pantages Hotel and Casino. It was as garish as any other mega-structure on Orion Prime, but as the pod's doors opened, and she and her companions got out, she discovered the real wonder was the steady flow of beautiful people through the hotel's main entrance. Creatures of multiple species and innumerable genders, all decked out in their cultures' ideas of sublime formalwear, constituted the clientele of the Royal Pantages.

Graniv felt her stomach turn. "I can't go in there."

"No one cares if we're underdressed," Douglas said.

"I'm not worried about a fashion faux pas," Graniv snapped. "Those are political power players from around the galaxy. People of influence. The kind I skewer in the press. They're the only people in the universe who could spot me faster than the Syndicate."

A knowing smirk transited Bashir's bearded face. "I doubt they'll give any of us a second look. For one thing, we're not going in through the front. For another, there was a reason I told you to wear all black." He started walking and beckoned her with a nod. "Come on."

She watched Bashir and Douglas stroll with perfect nonchalance up the sidewalk. Unsure of what they were planning, but sure she didn't want to be left outside on her own, she followed them. Less than a minute later they rounded a corner and approached a secondary ingress to the Royal Pantages—the staff and service entrance.

Graniv stink-eyed Bashir. "Please tell me you're kidding."

"You wanted discreet," he said.

Predictably, Douglas was on her lover's side. "The kind of folks you're worried about never look at servants. Do it our way and we'll be in and out, totally incognito."

"I hope you're right. If not, we'll all be dead before we hit the floor."

"That's the spirit," Bashir said, leading Graniv and Douglas inside.

Their fraudulent credentials let them breeze through both of the hotel's outer checkpoints. In under a minute they were inside, moving through bleak back-of-the-house corridors, past the engineering and housekeeping facilities, then the laundry, and finally the kitchen and dishroom. Bashir and Douglas each made a point of picking up a tray of clean glassware before leading Graniv through a pair of swinging doors onto the casino floor, then toward one of the luxurious hotel's many well-stocked cocktail bars.

There were only a few people sitting at the bar. Graniv studied each of them with quick, subtle glances, but found herself at a loss to recognize any of them. She pinched Bashir's sleeve. "Which of them are we here to see?"

"None," Bashir said. "We're looking for the bartender."

They reached the bar before she could ask Bashir why a mixologist of all people would be of any help to them. Douglas and Bashir set down their racks of glassware, and the bartender stood up from behind the counter. He was young looking, possibly human or Argelian. His tawny complexion had peculiar golden undertones that contrasted with his slick crown of black hair and pencil-thin dark mustache. Complementing his well-groomed visage was a dapper choice of work attire—his dark pants and cream-colored dress shirt were accessorized with a silver-embroidered vest of midnight-blue silk and a matching bowtie. On the breast of his jacket, above the pocket, was a nametag that bore what Graniv assumed was a surname: Soong.

Soong's brown eyes lit up at the sight of Bashir, and he spoke with a peculiar accent. "Julian! How long has it been, old friend?"

"Seventeen years, give or take. For me, anyway. Maybe not so long for you."

The bartender waggled a finger at Bashir. "Clever." He swung one arm toward his bar's copiously provisioned shelves. "What can I get for you?"

"Answers, I hope." Bashir turned sly looks toward Douglas and Graniv. "My friends and I are here to see the man upstairs—and his capable assistant."

Apparently intrigued but cautious, Soong asked, "About what, exactly?"

Douglas answered, "One of his areas of special expertise."

Bashir leaned closer to Soong. "Forgive us—time is a factor."

Soong's mood turned serious. "I understand." He turned away and raised his voice to tell another barkeep at the far end of the counter, "Loskur, I'm knocking off early. Take over." The other man acknowledged the handoff with a salute, and Soong stepped out from behind the bar to stand with Bashir, Douglas, and Graniv. "The lift is this way," he said, guiding them down a passage that led away from the casino floor.

Graniv followed him and the others, troubled by the nagging suspicion that she had seen this bartender somewhere before . . .

The door to the penthouse suite slid open as the quartet approached, and as Data strode inside his residence du jour he shed his borrowed persona along with its semicomical Transatlantic accent—an affectation he had picked up from watching entertainments from the Hollywood cinema of early twentieth-century Earth. He addressed his guests in his normal, uninflected Federation Standard. "Please have a seat. Anywhere you like."

Doctor Bashir and Ms. Douglas took in the spacious surroundings and sparse furnishings with a measure of aplomb that eluded their journalist friend, who gazed in wonder at the 270-degree view of the cityscape outside the main room's single arcing wall of transparent aluminum. Data couldn't say he blamed her for her reaction. In truth, he also found his accommodations a touch ostentatious—but then, he hadn't chosen them so much as he had inherited them. The penthouse suite of the Royal Pantages, which had gone by a different name before its sale to the current management, was one of a limited number of perquisites left to him by Noonien Soong, his father—or creator, depending upon one's point of view with regard to the inception of synthetic life and artificial intelligence, such as an android with a positronic matrix for a brain—despite Noonien having sold off most of his interest in the hotel and casino business years earlier.

Data activated a transceiver built into his matrix and initiated contact with his AI assistant Shakti—another boon bequeathed to him by his late father. *{Shakti, I apologize for the short notice, but we have visitors. Please ready the suite's guest rooms.}*

She responded, «*Right away, Data.*»

Their interaction was finished in less than a millisecond, while he undid his tie. He cast the unraveled bow onto an end table and turned to face Bashir and Douglas, who sat on the nearby sofa. Then he noticed their friend was still staring out the windows. "Ms. Graniv? Are you all right? Can I offer you a beverage? Or something to eat?"

Graniv turned and regarded him with a quizzical look. "You know my name?"

"Of course. I've read all of your published work." He thought it best not to mention he had done so during a span of 19.0174 seconds during their ride together in the hotel's lift.

His omission seemed to have the desired flattering effect. Graniv blushed, then relaxed after a deep breath. "Well, then. You have me at a disadvantage, then, Mister . . . ?"

"Data." He usually preferred to be circumspect about his identity, but he trusted Bashir—after all, the doctor had helped him unlock his dreaming subroutines seventeen years earlier, on Deep Space 9—and Graniv's reputation preceded her. Few people aside from his former *Enterprise* shipmates and certain high-ranking members of Starfleet knew of his recent rein-carnation into an android body that once had belonged to his father, Noonien Soong. The late scientist had briefly copied his own consciousness into an android body before giving it up to serve as a new vessel for Data, whose memories had been trapped in the less-advanced matrix of his older brother B-4. Now Data longed for the day when he could live free as a regular citizen of the Federation along with his daughter, Lal, whom he had resurrected with help from the immortal human his father had once known as his rival Emil Vaslovik.

The Trill woman moved away from the window to stand near Bashir and Douglas. "A pleasure to meet you, Mister Data. I hope you can help us. We're in a bit of a bind."

Data looked at Bashir. "How can I be of help?"

"Do you have a padd that can be blocked from sending out signals?"

He scrunched his brow to telegraph his concerns about the question. "That is a difficult query to answer. Even a simple padd can be rigged to transmit information in a number of ways. Aside from subspace radio frequencies, padds can send data over a variety of wavelengths in the electromagnetic spectrum, as well as in the form of ultrasonic or infrasonic pulses, or even as flashes of visible light. To guarantee signal containment would require—"

"A Faraday room or its equivalent," Douglas interjected. "Do you have that?"

"I do. This suite is secured in just such a manner. And I am capable of modifying a padd to restrict its ability to transmit on unauthorized frequencies."

"Good," Graniv said. "Then we can get started."

The meeting was put on hold while Data made the necessary hobbling changes to an Orion knock-off of a padd before engaging his suite's most robust signal-suppression protocols. Then his guests inserted a simple data chip into the padd and showed him the source code for an eavesdropping and clandestine counterintelligence AI called Uraei.

It was ancient. Primitive. Deeply flawed. But also powerful.

When they showed him it was everywhere, it became utterly terrifying.

"This is quite remarkable," he said. "Where did you find it?"

"Long story," Graniv said. "Have you seen it before?"

"Never." He noted the nervous stares of his guests and intuited their concern. "You're all wondering whether this code string has been embedded in my own matrix. I can assure you, it has not. My father harbored a lifelong distrust of large institutions, even those as seemingly benign as Starfleet or the Federation. Consequently, he insisted on writing his own software and firmware, and manufacturing his own components. My system contains no trace of Uraei."

"Well, that's a relief," Douglas said. "So, can you help us?"

He set down the padd on an end table. "That depends. What do you wish to do?"

"Reverse-engineer it," Bashir said. "So we can monitor its activity."

Douglas continued, "And use it to track the movements of, and communications between, everyone controlling it or being directed by it."

"Without getting ourselves killed in the process," Graniv added.

Data weighed all of that against the danger and mentally simulated a few thousand different scenarios to test their likelihood of resulting in catastrophe. "That will be difficult," he said, choosing to err on the side of understatement. "Uraei is complicated, and as you have pointed out, nearly ubiquitous. Tracking its behavior on comnets and in subspace frequencies without alerting it to our intentions will pose serious challenges."

Bashir leaned forward, his countenance dire. "But can it be done?"

"With time and effort . . . possibly. I will need the help of my friend Shakti."

Graniv asked, "And what are *her* qualifications?"

"She is an advanced artificial superintelligence existing as a distributed consciousness—partly here, partly aboard my ship, *Archeus*, and the rest in a secure location."

Douglas shook her head. "Can't beat *those* credentials."

Bashir stood. "Best guess, Data: How long before we can tap into Uraei?"

"Unknown. But Shakti and I will start work immediately and let you know when we find something. Until then I suggest you all make yourselves comfortable." He cushioned his bad news with a nervous smile. "I suspect this might take a while."

Twelve

A full day passed while Data and Shakti labored in semi-seclusion to dissect and reverse-engineer Uraei. For fear of attracting attention on Orion, Bashir, Sarina, and Ozla Graniv spent their time sequestered inside the penthouse suite and did their best to keep out of the android's way while he worked.

Graniv used the hours to scrawl ideas in a replicated antique-style notebook, while Sarina spent the day skimming news channels on the comnet for . . . well, Bashir had no idea what she was looking for. He could only imagine she was soaking up information and waiting to see if her enhanced intellect forged unexpected connections between seemingly disparate facts.

For his own part, Bashir welcomed the downtime as an opportunity to catch up on his reading. In spite of the time he had devoted in the past year to covert intelligence field work, at heart he remained a doctor. As such, he was perpetually curious about recent advances in surgical technology, pharmaceutical engineering, and various aspects of medical practice. Even reading at the accelerated pace enabled by his own genetic enhancements, he could never keep up with the flood of new literature being generated in every sector of his profession.

He was deep into a treatise on the therapeutic value of

using cross-species retroviral gene therapy to reverse telomere degradation in humanoids, while suppressing the generation of potentially fatal regressive proteins, when the old-fashioned hinged twin doors to the suite's library swung open and Data emerged to announce, "Shakti and I are ready to run our first test."

Bashir set his padd on the living room sofa. Graniv returned from the bedroom clutching her pen and notebook. The voices of Federation News Service anchors, which had been drifting through the open doorway of the suite's vid room all afternoon and evening, went quiet. Seconds later Sarina emerged and wasted no time crossing the room toward Data. "Let's do this." Before he could respond, she slipped past him into the library.

Data looked taken aback by Sarina's brusque passage. He dismissed it with a frown, then said to Bashir and Graniv, "Please join us." He waited beside the library's double-wide doorway and ushered Graniv and Bashir inside. As they found seats on either side of Sarina at a long conference table that stretched down the center of the room, Data closed and secured the doors. "Just a precaution," he told Bashir, who had noted the locking of the portal with mild concern.

A silken female voice with a refined London accent wafted down from speakers hidden in the ceiling. *"Welcome, everyone. My name is Shakti. Are you all ready?"* The AI seemed aware of the trio's awkward nods and continued, *"Very well. Let's begin."*

A bookcase at the far end of the conference table sank into the floor, revealing a wall-sized viewscreen. It snapped to life with a computer rendering of a complex system of some kind. It reminded Bashir of a brain's synaptic network. He turned an expectant look toward Data. "Is that what I think it is?"

"It is, indeed. We are observing Uraei's actions in real time."

Graniv squinted at the viewscreen. "What's it doing?"

Sarina answered with ominous certainty, "Thinking."

"Quite correct, Ms. Douglas," Shakti said. *"The activity charted here represents what we've detected in this subsector. Uraei has almost no presence on the surface of Orion, with one notable exception."* The image on-screen switched to the capital's street map, with a white-hot splash of light in a single isolated grid. *"The Federation Embassy."*

Graniv was horrified. "Look at that. Near-total saturation."

"A correct assessment," Data said. "Shakti, widen to a full sector scan."

"A 'please' would be nice."

"My apologies. *Please* expand to—" The image on screen switched before he finished the request. "Thank you." To his flesh-and-blood guests he continued, "As you can see, Uraei's web is just as active across an entire sector. This is an increase in its effective operational range of nearly an order of magnitude, with no sign of lag in its response times." He faced the screen. "Shakti, please widen the scan to show all known sectors in the Alpha and Beta Quadrants."

Another shift, this time to display all of known local space plus several of its frontier sectors. Encompassed in the broadened perspective was the entirety of the United Federation of Planets and its closest neighboring powers, including the Klingon Empire, the Romulan Star Empire, the Cardassian Union, the Tzenkethi Coalition, the Breen Confederacy, the Ferengi Alliance, the Gorn Hegemony, and many other powers of varying sizes and influence. Woven through them all was a complex network that blazed with rapid transactions.

"As you can see," Shakti said, *"Uraei does not operate in isolated pockets. It appears to be a distributed consciousness, operating on an interstellar scale."*

Data added, "More than a passive eavesdropper, Uraei is engaged with the flow of information at every level throughout known space. It is in a constant state of flux, receiving input and coordinating responses—all in the guise of a benign router of data packets and encryption keys. It is just as widespread as you had feared—and possibly far more capable than any of us imagined."

A gravid silence filled the room for a moment while everyone pondered the import of what Data and Shakti had documented. Confronted with the chilling portrait of their previously invisible enemy, Sarina eyed it as if it were a wild animal loose in the room. "Now that we can map it, can we tap into it? I want to track all its controllers and assets in local space."

"I think that would be unwise."

She clearly disliked Data's answer. "Why?"

"We still don't know how Uraei protects itself," Shakti said. *"Right now we're just observers, using the system's own routing protocols to monitor its traffic. Tapping the system would entail an active intrusion."*

Bashir nodded, then looked at Sarina. "Maybe she's—"

"We need to try," Sarina said, talking over his gentle counsel. "Nothing big, nothing dangerous. Just dip our toe in to test the water. That's all."

"Very well," Data said. "Shakti, proceed when ready. And please—be careful."

"I will, Data. Thank you." A scroll of machine symbols traveled up the left side of the viewscreen as Shakti added, *"Commencing network code injection."*

Less than two seconds later the viewscreen pulsed with a white flash of light. The vast web of signals it had charted degenerated into scrambled pixels and static, then a sharp bang echoed behind walls on either side of the screen, and smoke rolled out of the ventilation ducts. Overhead, a plasma conduit ruptured and rained searing phosphors on the conference table.

Bashir bolted from his seat, fearing for the safety of Data's friend. "Shakti?"

"A moment, Doctor," Data said. "The overhead speakers are offline." The android pivoted away for a moment. A birdlike tilt of his head suggested he was reacting to something only he could perceive. Then he shot a reassuring look at Bashir. "Shakti is unharmed. She was able to dump this node of her consciousness back to my ship before Uraei's feedback surge hit her server module."

More worried than ever, Graniv leaned in to ask, "Feedback surge? From Uraei?"

"I am afraid so," Data said. "It reacted far more quickly than Shakti or I expected. Worst of all, there is a high probability it now knows where we are and what we sought to do." He walked to the library's double doors, unlocked them, and swung them open wide. With a peculiar geniality he added, "I suggest we all prepare for a swift departure."

Some nights were made for hard work, others were made for recreation. Tonight was the latter, and Lal was determined to make the most of her playtime. Her musical studies often required her to listen to as many as a hundred unique compositions at once for the purpose of comparative analysis, but this evening she was listening for pleasure, so she cut the number of simultaneous playbacks to twenty-three, ranging in style from Terran jazz to Klingon opera and Bajoran folk.

Her left hand and eye were devoted to her practice of ancient Vulcan brush calligraphy, while her right hand and eye

were focused on her latest impressionistic watercolor painting, a portrait of her "grandmother" Julianna Tainer rendered
from equal parts memory and inspiration.

*If only I had been made with another pair of hands I could
be practicing my knitting,* she lamented. *Perhaps someday I
will rebuild myself in a more efficient nonhumanoid form.*

The scroll and painting were coming together nicely,
which made Lal confident enough to free up more of her
positronic net's processing power for the contemplation of
recently discovered gravimetric anomalies detected in the
Sagittarius Dwarf Elliptical Galaxy, the Milky Way's nearest
neighbor in the Local Group. After all, how much brainpower
did she really need to compose a critical literary thesis on
the work of Russian writers of the nineteenth and twentieth
centuries? If it took her twelve minutes instead of ten to complete her doctoral presentation on the subject, would anyone
but her and her father even notice?

She accessed her house's link to the Orion comnet and
downloaded an advanced self-instruction module on the
Ancient Hebitian language. Some high-profile scholars at the
Daystrom Institute and the Raxan Foundation had recently
issued competing papers arguing that all the known lan-
guages of the Cardassian and Bajoran species were derived
from Ancient Hebitian—a tantalizing proposition Lal was
determined to test for herself later that night, right after the
hour she had set aside in which to learn and master the art of
sushi preparation.

An encrypted signal triggered the quantum transceiver
embedded in her positronic brain. The only beings who knew
of its existence or its unique quantum resonance frequency
were her father and his trusted AI Shakti. It was Data whose
transmitted voice filled her thoughts.

{Lal, we must leave Orion immediately.}

She was vexed and made no effort to hide it. *[Why must I give up my private time just to take an unscheduled trip with you?]*

{This is not a vacation. Leave your things and make a clean exit.}

Lal understood the words *clean exit* meant this was a life-or-death crisis. Something had happened, and now they were in danger. *[I understand, Father. I'll be ready in sixty seconds.]*

She regretted the need to abandon her house. A private residence was one of the few vestiges of autonomy her father had allowed her as part of her maturation, but even this privilege had come with conditions—the most extreme of which Data had just exercised.

One positronic pulse from Lal started a cascading wipe of all the memory chips and storage systems in the house. Every device in her home, from the replicator to the entertainment node, was made to hold tiny bits of data about their users. Data had taught her that such information could be exploited by their enemies if they acquired it—so with his help she had rigged every piece of technology in her house to self-destruct at her silent command.

She picked up the painting of Julianna from its easel and carried it out the front door as she unleashed her second wave of destruction: a storm of nanites, programmed to devour every atom of her house and all its contents, from furniture to clothes in the closets and the curtains on the windows. Afterward, when nothing of the house remained, the nanites would turn against one another as subatomic cannibals until only one remained to execute its end-of-line command:

DISINCORPORATE.

In another five minutes there would be no proof Lal had ever been there. And that was as it needed to be. If her father said it was time to pull up stakes, she trusted him.

By the time Lal reached the street outside her front door, the gutted husk of her former residence was already falling in upon itself, surrendering without a fight to the nanites' hunger. She tucked the painting under her arm and activated her transceiver, using the general frequency that would reach both Data and Shakti.

[Ready.]

Shakti replied, «*Stand by for transport to* Archeus.»

By the time Lal felt the grip of the transporter beam and saw the first shimmering of its dematerialization field, nothing remained of her little yellow house but memories and dust.

Never in her life had Ozla Graniv packed a bag with such haste. She had always prided herself on being an organized traveler, one whose articles were folded taut and stowed with no daylight between them. Tonight she forced the few things she had taken from her travel bag back inside without regard for how they fit, so long as the bag closed. As soon as she heard its locks click into place, she took it in tow and strode out to the living room to meet Bashir and Douglas.

There she found Data, who had altered his appearance to one more rugged than that of his bartending persona. His light brown hair was loose and fine, his face clean-shaven. He had attired himself like a common laborer—scuffed work boots, faded trousers, an untucked shirt of natural linen beneath an open black jacket. In one hand he toted a small ruck.

At the same time, Bashir and Douglas returned from their own bedroom, each carrying a slim pack diagonally across their back. The doctor offered his hand to Data. "I guess this is where we say good-bye."

"I am afraid not," Data said. "The three of you must come with me or die."

Graniv recoiled. "Are you threatening us?"

Data's trademark courtesy never wavered. "Forgive me. I phrased that poorly. Shakti has noticed a pattern of suspect activity on the main floor of the casino. She and I concur there is a high probability that operatives sent by Uraei have arrived and mean to do us all harm."

She wondered why the obvious answer eluded him. "Can't we call the police?"

Douglas and Bashir traded grim, knowing looks before he said, "By the time those agents do something the police can act upon, we'll most likely all be dead."

"Or permanently missing," Douglas added.

"Correct," Data said. "It is highly unlikely any of you would be able to reach public or private transportation to the starport without being intercepted. And if you did, our foes are almost certainly awaiting you there as well. At this time, your only viable means of escape from Orion is aboard my ship, *Archeus*."

"Our *foes*?" Graniv felt as if her whole world was being pulled out from under her. "Who? And on what authority? Are we talking about Starfleet? Federation Security?"

Her questions made Bashir visibly uncomfortable. "Not exactly."

"So you can't say who poses a threat, but you think we should run for our lives?"

"Ms. Graniv," Data said, "I suggest we table this discussion for a less precarious moment." He checked his internal chrono. "I estimate our visitors will reach this floor in approximately ninety-one seconds."

Decades of experience had taught Graniv that the best time to extract the truth from someone was when they were in fear of their life and running out of time. Now seemed an opportune moment to press her hosts for something they clearly all knew but weren't telling her. "I'm not leaving this hotel until one of you tells me who we're running from."

The ultimatum exasperated Sarina. "We don't have time for—"

"Make time," Graniv said.

The human woman looked at Bashir. "You want to do it?"

His tension became resignation. "We think Uraei is being used by an extralegal covert operations cabal known as Section Thirty-one. They claim to operate within Starfleet, but there's no official record of their existence. We have reason to think they've existed for at least two centuries, and their tactics include blackmail, bribery, deception, and murder."

"Information I wish I'd had *yesterday*," Graniv decided a swift exit sounded like a good idea after all. She asked Data, "Does your ship have a transporter?"

"It does, but the hotel and casino are transport shielded. We must proceed to the roof."

"Then let's move," Graniv said.

"Finally," Douglas grumbled as the group hurried out of the suite.

They were halfway to the stairwell door when four people clad in black stepped out of the turbolifts. A lavender-haired Catullan woman and three men—a human, an Andorian *thaan*, and a Bajoran. The Andorian was the first to see the quartet leaving the suite. He reached to pull a phaser from his hip—

Data, Bashir, and Douglas all beat him to the draw and fired.

In under a second, the corridor filled with searing pulses of orange light. When the barrage ended, the four agents all lay stunned on the floor.

"Shakti says there are more agents coming up in other lifts," Data said as he led them into the stairwell and up the steps to the roof access. "And more entering the lobby. We must hurry."

The android and the pair of enhanced humans easily outpaced Graniv as they jogged up the stairs. As they rounded the last switchback before the final flight to the rooftop door, she closed the gap enough to say to Bashir, "You're quite the marksman, Doctor."

"Yes, well . . . I've had practice."

"How much?"

"More than I ever wanted."

The last flight of stairs tested Graniv's limits. Her chest refused to draw breath; her leg muscles seized and defied her command to finish climbing. Fatigue burned in her limbs, acid pumped through her racing heart, sweat shone upon her forehead. By the time she stepped onto the roof and gulped in the cool night air, her head spun and her face burned with shame. Stooped and huffing like a blacksmith's bellows, she had never felt so out of shape in her adult life.

If I live through this I'll never skip morning yoga again.

Bashir sidled over to her. "Are you all right?"

"I will be. I just need a minute." She stood and braced herself for the calming pressure of a transporter's confinement beam and the gentle change of scenery that would follow.

A crimson storm of disruptor blasts shrieked down from the darkness and tore across the roof, peppering Graniv and the others with shrapnel and half-molten chunks of roof gravel.

She leaped to cover behind a ventilator housing and recalled the advice of her first managing editor, the late great Heinrich Neuhaus: *You know a story's worth chasing when someone tries to kill you for it.*

• • •

Sarina peeked out from behind a heat exchanger to spot their attacker, only to dodge another fusillade of disruptor fire. "Dammit! Where are those shots coming from?"

"The angle is inconsistent with the elevations of adjacent rooftops," Data shouted back from his own meager cover, a dense cluster of signal-repeating antennae mounted in the middle of the roof. "It also is changing with each volley. I will ask Shakti to investigate."

Angry red bolts ripped into the antenna array and showered the roof with sparks. Julian pivoted out from behind the stairwell and returned fire along the trajectory of the incoming shots, but his phaser pulses dispersed into the night without finding their mark. Rapid-fire pulses from the sky blasted the roof-access door out of its frame and down the stairs behind it.

Losing patience as well as her nerve, Sarina yelled over the din and roaring wind to Data, "Forget investigating! Just tell her to beam us out!"

"She cannot." There was a brief pause before he continued. "Something is projecting a transport-blocking field on the roof. Most likely the same something presently shooting at us."

Prone on the gravel, hands over her head, Graniv snapped, "Now can we call the police?"

Data winced as disruptor shots punched through the array close above his head. "The field blocking *Archeus*'s transporter also scrambles our comms. Shakti will alert the police."

Two quick bursts caromed off of Graniv's low block of shelter. Wreathed in the smoky aftermath, the Trill looked ready to bolt. "Maybe we go back inside?"

Sarina made no effort to mask her disdain. "And do what? Fight our way out through an unknown number of assailants and major civilian casualties? No thanks."

Julian took another shot at the darkness before Data called out, "Wait, I see it."

The sky still looked black and starless to Sarina. "See what?"

"An aerial drone, I think. Too small to be a crewed vehicle. I believe it is cloaked."

"Then how can you—" She stopped herself as she remembered that his synthetic eyes were capable of seeing in a greater variety of spectra and temporal phases than those of most organic species. "What's the plan?"

"We—" He pivoted around the antenna array and fired into the air as he shouted, "Shift your cover!" His warning was answered by a withering salvo from the drone. Sarina, Julian, and Graniv all barely scrambled to new defensive positions before their previous hiding spots were set aglow with lethal showers of superheated plasma.

Data picked up where he'd been cut off. "We must split the drone's focus." He drew a second phaser from inside his jacket. "One of us draws its fire so the others can take it down."

Sarina considered that a dubious proposition. "It might be designed for multiple target acquisition. All of us breaking cover at the same time might just get us all shot."

"True. But I believe I can monopolize its sensors by presenting a clear and present threat—and, by so doing, give you and Doctor Bashir a chance to neutralize it." After a moment, and with a measure of sincerity that would have read as sarcastic coming from anyone else, he added, "Unless you have a better idea, of course."

"Just tell us when to move and where to shoot."

"The where will be obvious." Data adjusted his phasers to maximum power. "As for the when: I will go on one. Wait until my shot makes contact before you break cover."

"Understood," Julian said.

Sarina reset her own phaser to full power. "Ready."

Graniv tucked herself into a fetal curl and hugged her knees. "Just do what you're gonna do before I piss myself here."

Data started his countdown. "Three. Two. One." He charged away from the antenna array, firing his phasers on the move. The searing orange shots slammed into the cloaked drone. Its cloak stuttered off, and its shields snapped on a fraction of a second later. Its electromagnetic bubble of protection shimmered and crackled under the punishment of his phaser beams.

Then Julian darted into the open and pinned the drone with a phaser shot, and Sarina did the same. Their beams converged upon the aerial vehicle, which bobbled before it retreated beyond easy targeting range, trailing smoke and burning plasma in its wake.

Julian was the first to cease fire, followed by Sarina, and then Data. Their victory, which Sarina suspected would be short-lived, nonetheless seemed to leave Julian ecstatic. "We did it!"

"Not yet," Data said. "Transporters and comms are still being blocked, which would suggest the presence of more—" Flurries of disruptor fire finished his thought for him.

There was no time to hide, nowhere to run. Broadsides of disruptor fire pummeled the rooftop from two vectors, filling the air with smoke and dust—harsh barriers to human vision but no impediment to the mechanical senses of sophisticated killing machines.

An Orion police vehicle raced toward the roof, lights flashing, siren wailing. It was met by a hail of disruptor fire that sent the shattered, burning aircar plunging into the side of the hotel. The car exploded, filling the night with broken glass, shattered polymer, and fire.

With ruthless efficiency the drones trained their arsenals back upon the rooftop.

Even as Sarina dived for the nearest protection she could reach, she knew the only thing likely keeping her alive was Data's expert-level two-handed marksmanship, which was forcing the two new drones to maneuver and adjust their firing solutions on the fly.

It wouldn't be enough. Fires were spreading across the rooftop, making no part of it safe to shelter on. And no matter how fast Data's reflexes, or how sharp his vision, the truth was that hand phasers just didn't pack enough punch to take on attack drones in a stand-up fight.

Sarina's most optimistic read of the situation told her they'd all be dead in thirty seconds. Her hand tightened on her phaser. *Doesn't mean I have to die on my knees.*

She stood and charged to Data's side, firing at one of the drones every step of the way. By the time she reached him, Julian was already there, making his own stand against the other drone, no doubt driven by the same pessimistic calculus as her.

Just over six seconds later, all three drones—the one they'd winged as well as its two reinforcements—were struck by white bolts from the heavens and erupted into storms of fire and metal, smoke and slag. The smoking clusters dropped and broke up in midair, leaving their orphaned parts to spiral down the better part of a kilometer to the city's streets.

Half in shock, Sarina asked Data in a whisper, "What just—"

Their savior appeared, an apparition in the dark.

Archeus dropped its cloak, revealing its sleek silver fuselage. The ship's elegant mirrored hull cast distorted reflections of the capital's cityscape. Slender warp nacelles were tucked beneath its wings, which swept sharply back, giving the vessel the aspect of a raptor diving at prey. Its tapered bow was crowned by a black canopy over what Sarina surmised was a large command deck.

A woman's voice issued from Data's communicator. *"Stand by for transport, Father."*

Data grinned at his guests. "Friends, our chariot awaits."

Adrenaline overload left Graniv shaking, even after the transporter beam faded to reveal that she and the others were safely inside Data's small but well-appointed starship, *Archeus.* She watched Bashir and Douglas step off the transporter pads half a pace behind Data, who stopped and looked back when he saw Graniv still curled in upon herself at the back of the alcove.

"Ms. Graniv? Are you all right? Do you need medical attention?"

It was hard to overcome inertia, but she shook her head. "I'm not hurt."

The android's concerned attention compelled Bashir back to Graniv's side. "Are you sure? Can you sit up?" To Douglas he said, "I need a medical tricorder, please."

Data stepped behind the transporter console, opened a panel on the eggshell-white bulkhead, and pulled out an emergency medkit. From it he took a medical tricorder and passed it to Douglas, who relayed it to Bashir. The doctor switched it on. Its high-pitched oscillations filled the small transporter bay. "No physical injuries," he said. "Signs of mild shock, but that's to be expected, given the circumstances. Have you ever been in combat before?"

She shook her head. "I've been the target of a few shots fired in anger over the years . . . but never anything like this. Never a full-scale attack."

"Would you like something to help you relax?"

"No," Graniv said. "Just help me stand up." Douglas and Bashir each took gentle hold of one of Graniv's arms and steadied her as she got on her feet. "Thank you."

"I need to get to the command deck," Data said. He exited the transporter bay and turned right, walking at a quick pace toward the ship's bow.

It was obvious to Graniv that Bashir and Douglas were impatient to follow Data. "Go," she told them. "I'm fine."

Guilt lurked behind Bashir's query: "Are you sure?"

"I'll catch up. Go find out what's happening."

Duly freed of their obligation, the human couple let go of Graniv. They watched her for a moment to make sure she didn't topple over, then hurried out in pursuit of Data.

Graniv inhaled deeply. Filling her lungs quelled the shaking in her hands and firmed up the rubbery weakness in her knees. After she exhaled, but before drawing another breath, she felt the tempo of her heart slow by a few beats per minute.

That's it. There you go. Not dead yet. Just keep doing that.

Satisfied that she was edging her way back toward a calm frame of mind, she left the transporter bay and followed the ship's narrow central corridor forward to the command deck.

There she found the others huddled around a navigational console, above which an oblong viewscreen displayed a star chart of the sectors surrounding Orion. Beyond the canopy there was only the void of deep space salted with stars. None of them were distorted or drifting with unnatural degrees of parallax, so she deduced the ship was still at impulse.

Seated at the helm in the front of the compartment was a young woman with fair beige skin and a smart bob of black hair. She appeared human, but that meant little. Argelians, humans, Deltans, and Iotians were all but indistinguishable from one another without medical scans.

"We need to go to warp soon," Douglas said, full of worry.

"Now that we're off Orion there's nothing stopping them from coming for us with all guns blazing."

"They didn't seem shy about that while we were *on* Orion," Bashir said.

Graniv inserted herself into the conversation. "Where are we going?"

"A very good question," Data said. "I have asked Lal to plot a course that will take us away from the Federation's core systems, in order to minimize our contact with Uraei going forward. However, that fails to address our pressing need for a final destination."

"We could head for the rimward frontier sectors," Lal said.

Her optimism was quashed by Douglas's cynicism: "And do what? Take up subsistence farming? They'd find us. Maybe not soon, but eventually. No, we need to find a place where we can plan a counterstrike."

"Such an objective might not be feasible." Data sounded apologetic. "Given the scope and sophistication of Uraei, excising it from the Federation's infrastructure would present many challenges—some of which I think could prove insurmountable."

Douglas's temper frayed. "We can't just sit out here and wait to be found."

"If necessary, I can make us very difficult to find," Data said. "*Archeus* has a cloaking device far superior to anything currently used by the Klingons or the Romulans."

His claim failed to reassure Bashir. "No cloaking device is perfect, Data."

"True. But there are regions of space, even this close to the core systems, that possess blind spots, gaps in the sensor network. If we take the ship into low-power mode and drift while cloaked, it could buy us the time we need to formulate a more proactive response."

"Wait," Graniv cut in. "Going dark for a while sounds good to me, but we need to warn my sources first. They could be in danger."

Neither Bashir nor Douglas met Graniv's gaze; they chose to stare at the deck instead. Only Data had the courtesy to ask, "Sources?"

"Doctor Weng and her colleague Professor th'Firron. The scientists who told me about Uraei. They need to know we—"

"You can't help them," Douglas said. "If Thirty-one doesn't know about them yet, you'll expose them by trying to warn them. Worse, you can't send a subspace signal back to Earth without giving away our position and heading."

"But what if this Section Thirty-one already knows about Weng and th'Firron?"

"Then they're already dead."

Such nihilism infuriated Graniv. "I refuse to believe that! It's nothing but an excuse to be selfish and save your own ass! We can't—"

"Ms. Douglas is right," Lal said. The young woman swiveled her chair and set her hands flat atop her thighs, betraying her awkward body language. "Shakti downloaded all the news feeds off the comnet before we left Orion. I have analyzed all news items from Earth for mention of the names Weng or th'Firron. Two computer scientists bearing those surnames are reported to have died this morning in an accidental fire that destroyed the forensic data laboratory at the Dresden University of Technology. . . . My condolences, Ms. Graniv."

The injustice of it struck Graniv like a kick in the stomach. Stricken with grief and guilt, she sank into an empty chair opposite the navigation console. "They . . . they trusted me."

Bashir took a slow step in her direction, then dropped to one knee in front of her. He took her hand in a consoling gesture. "I'm truly sorry, Ozla. I know this isn't what you expected. But if Weng and th'Firron are dead, and their lab is gone, then the only evidence of Uraei's true nature is what's on the chip we brought to Data. And that means all of us on this ship are about to become the most hunted people in the galaxy."

Thirteen

Unification Day was the biggest, wildest party in the history of the human race. The celebration spanned seven continents and several dozen cities built on ocean platforms. Rumor had it the colonists on Luna and Mars weren't exactly overjoyed, but none of Earth's citizens gave much of a damn what the offworlders thought—at least not while their revels lasted.

Earth had become one civilization, one people. It had been a long time coming, and the march toward unification had been fraught with missteps and false starts.

Humanity's first attempt at global governance had been the short-lived United Earth Republic. Established in 2113, it was rejected by several major nation-states from its inception. By 2123 all but a handful of countries had withdrawn from the UER, rendering it defunct.

In 2130, the *Traité d'Unification* met with broader support, though it too was resisted by a few powers—notably, Australia and China, in defiance of their Pan-Pacific Alliance partners, and the United States, which had clung stubbornly to its independence in spite of its purported leadership role in the Western Coalition. Absent their ratification, the *Traité d'Unification* had, for the past twenty years, been nothing more than a piece of paper.

Until today, when three signatures on an addendum changed the world forever.

Countries still existed, but there were no more borders. The old territorial designations still had their uses, for postal services if nothing else. But there would be no more rival superpowers putting the fate of the planet and the species at risk with useless posturing over natural resources or the illusion of national sovereignty. A single global parliament now governed the affairs of everyone on Earth.

Naturally, the majority of the population observed this historic milestone for their species by inebriating themselves halfway to the point of blindness and filling the streets with vomit.

Far from all that madness and debauchery, Aaron Ikerson stood in the center of the ballroom of Buckingham Palace, surrounded by dignitaries and celebrities, possessed by a single thought: *I am an utter fraud.*

Projected along the walls, high above the celebrants' heads, were holographic images from around the world. One showed the new prime minister of the Terran Parliament exchanging pleasantries with an envoy from the planet Vulcan. Another carried a live feed from Starfleet Headquarters in San Francisco, where admirals and their adjutants feigned the ability to have fun when it seemed obvious most of them would have been happier working through the holiday. Most of the other holograms depicted an ever-shifting tableau of scenes from around the world.

How can I tell these people their world is built on a lie?

A hand slapped his back hard enough to make him spill Champagne on the floor. He turned to greet the culprit. "I'm sorry, have we met?"

"Not yet." The tuxedoed brown fireplug with gray hair and an Alabama accent cracked a smile so perfect it could only have been a product of dental science. "Simon Branch."

As soon as Ikerson heard the name he knew who the man

was. "The director of the new Earth Security Agency?" He shook Branch's hand. "An honor to meet you, sir."

"To hear Admiral Rao tell it, the honor's all mine." Ikerson tensed at the mention of the admiral. Branch moved closer and lowered his voice. "She's a bit stingy with the details, but she says you developed the program that made today possible."

"I'm sorry? I did what?"

Branch swung his Champagne flute toward the holograms. "This. World peace." His mood darkened. "There were plenty of folks on this ball o' rock who'd just as soon have gone on fightin'. Hard-liners, rebels, insurgents. Call 'em what you will." His smile returned as broad, white, and fake as before. "Those who like this kinda thing call it *progress*. Those who don't call it *tyranny*. Funny how that works, ain't it?"

The more Branch said, the less Ikerson knew what he wanted. "People can be irrational political actors. Still, I'm thankful we've come this far. Maybe there's hope for us after all."

"I think there is—and I think you invented it." He leaned in, his manner conspiratorial. "Rao and others I trust tell me that if it weren't for your help, it might have taken decades longer to get us here. The water revolt in the Hindu Kush, the Terra Prime rebellion, the uprisings in Irkutsk and Montana—they all got headed off at the pass by means I never could figure out." A small shrug. "And that's fine. I don't need the details. I might even be happier not knowing."

You have no idea.

Branch continued, "What matters to me is whether your methods will work for us beyond this planet. I don't need to know how you mix the secret sauce. Just tell me this: Is it scalable?"

"It's already in place on Luna and Mars," Ikerson said,

then immediately wondered if he had said too much. "Beyond that, I suppose it could be expanded, though spreading it past this solar system raises some technical hurdles I—"

"Spare me the nuts and bolts," Branch said. His eyes narrowed as he glanced at the holo of the new prime minister with the alien envoy. "Can you make it work on Vulcan?"

Ikerson froze. He had ample reason to think Rao had already implemented Uraei on Vulcan, but if she had withheld that knowledge from Branch for whatever reason, it seemed inappropriate—and perhaps even dangerous—for Ikerson to share it with him. On the other hand, lying to Branch could have equally dire consequences in the long run. He would have to protect himself with half truths and careful omissions.

"I think my method could work on Vulcan . . . given the right conditions."

The security director gave Ikerson's shoulder a friendly slap. "Just what I wanted to hear. Let me freshen up your drink."

"I'm fine, thank you."

"Nonsense, your glass is empty." He led Ikerson toward the bar. "Stick with me, Professor. Together, you and I will change the shape of the future."

"Into what?"

"One in which Earth claims its proper place." He waved over the bartender. "Bourbon, neat. And for my Swedish friend here—" He shot a prompting glance at Ikerson.

"Martini, extra dry. Nolet's gin."

The bartender stepped away to mix the drinks, so Branch continued, at a more discreet volume this time. "For now we have to let the Vulcans take the lead and call the shots. But they won't be steering our fate forever. If your program is all Rao says it is, our day is coming."

"I thought the whole point of our partnership with Vulcan was that we're equals."

"We are. And we will be." That fake smile became a phony grin. "Our job is just to make certain that Earth ends up as the *first* among equals."

Fourteen

A comfortable bunk, subdued amber lighting, the gentle hush of *Archeus*'s ventilation system—conditions in the guest quarters were ideal for restful sleep, yet Bashir lay awake, staring at the overhead, tortured by his guilty conscience. He did his best to lie still. Tossing and turning would only disturb Sarina. It was hard not to envy her slumber. Stretched out on her side with her back to him, she seemed to Bashir to be a paragon of calm.

He breathed the softest of sighs, certain he was alone with his insomnia.

"What's wrong, Julian?" Sarina rolled onto her back and regarded him with a sympathetic frown. "Why can't you sleep?"

"A million reasons, but nothing I can put a label on." He shifted onto his side to face her. "Mostly, it's the feeling that we've gotten in over our heads this time."

Half her face was steeped in shadow, but he saw sly amusement curl her lips. "That's our standard operating procedure, isn't it?"

"It certainly feels that way." He reached out and touched her honey-blond hair. Feeling its silken texture centered him and made him grateful Sarina was at his side. "We keep putting other people in danger. Every time I swear no more blood on my hands, someone else dies."

She rested her palm against his bearded cheek. "What happened in Dresden wasn't our fault. We vetted Graniv's precautions. She did all she could to shield them from harm."

"It wasn't enough. It never is with Thirty-one."

Sarina mirrored his regret and sorrow for two souls he'd never even met. "I know it isn't fair what happened to them. But we can't change it—all we can do is make the guilty pay for it."

"Easier said than done." His mind cast itself back through all of his ill-fated encounters with his nemeses from the shadows. "Thirty-one's been ahead of me every time I've faced them. First it was Sloan and all his dirty tricks, then it was Cole. Now we're haunted by L'Haan—and thanks to us, Ozla, Data, Lal, and Shakti will be as well."

He sat up and considered getting out of bed. Sarina took him by his shoulders and eased him back down beside her. "Don't beat yourself up like this. Ozla puts herself in danger as part of her job, and whether she knew it or not, her life was in peril the moment Weng and th'Firron contacted her. In fact, you and I bringing her to Data might be the only reason she's still alive right now. So give yourself credit for that much, at least."

Her rebuttal was logical but didn't make him feel better. "What if we bought her a little more time at Data and Lal's expense? Thirty-one must know who and what Data is, but they came after him without a moment's hesitation. That's because of us. We brought Uraei to him; now he and his—well, I suppose *family*, for lack of a better term—are on the run with us. How can I ever apologize for doing this to him?"

"I think if you asked Data, he'd say you don't have to. We told him what we were dealing with and he helped us anyway. Besides . . ." She let slip a huff of cynical suppressed laughter. "I'd be willing to bet he, Lal, and Shakti have far better survival odds right now than we do."

"That's the worst pep talk I've ever heard," Bashir teased. "I've said it before, but I'll say it again: you *really* need to work on your bedside manner."

"And as I keep telling you, I have a doctorate but I'm not *that* kind of a doctor."

They chortled together at their long-running inside joke. When the mirth abated they lay silently in each other's arms. Bashir still felt a profound unquiet in his soul, but he also felt just the slightest measure less alone and less afraid than he had minutes earlier.

"There must be some way to use what we learned on Orion," he said.

Sarina looked at him as if he sprouted antennae. "What exactly do you think we learned, Julian? I mean, aside from the fact that Uraei is everywhere and packs a hell of a punch."

"Well, we already knew the former, and we'd suspected the latter. But Data and Shakti were able to map Uraei's presence before they incurred its wrath. That might give us an idea of where to go to plan our next move."

"If it did, I'm sure Shakti and Data are already working—"

A dulcet tone from the overhead speaker was followed by Shakti's mellifluous voice. *"Doctor Bashir? Ms. Douglas? Pardon the intrusion. I noticed you were awake and hoped this might be a good time to share some news with you."*

Bashir sat up. "Good news, I hope."

"I wish it were. It seems that Uraei, or the party controlling it, is no longer content to entrust our capture to its own covert assets. General orders have been sent by Starfleet Command and the Federation Security Agency calling for the capture and impound of this vessel, and for the apprehension of yourselves as well as of Data, Lal, and Ms. Graniv." Shakti struck a decidedly sardonic note as she added, *"I imagine they would add*

my name to their warrants if they possessed the faintest conception of who and what I truly am."

"No doubt," Bashir said. "Thank you for the update."

"You're welcome, Doctor. One more thing: Mister Data wants to meet with you both and with Ms. Graniv at oh-eight-hundred to discuss the next step in our shared flight from injustice."

Sarina answered, "We'll look forward to it. Good night, Shakti."

"Good night, Ms. Douglas." The comm channel closed with a faint *click.*

Bashir and Sarina sank back into bed and stared at the ceiling. She sighed. "Great. Now we're being hunted by our enemies *and* our friends."

He pulled her close, kissed her cheek, and grinned. "Just like old times."

Breakfast the next morning didn't take long. Data and Lal didn't need to eat, neither Bashir nor Sarina seemed to have much of an appetite, and Graniv had long ago learned to start her days on little more than *raktajino* and righteous rage—both of which she presently had in spades. It was making the day's first discussion on the command deck a lively one, to say the least.

"I get why you're all talking about running for the deepest sectors of space this ship can reach," Graniv said, "but I want to be clear that I'm not willing to go into hiding for the rest of my life. And I'm not just saying that for selfish reasons, even though I've got plenty, believe me. Before any of you forget why we're in this mess, this may well be the biggest political news story in the history of the Federation. And I will see it told even if it kills me."

Douglas met Graniv's rant with doubt and disdain. "It might, you know. Kill you."

"Did you think I was speaking metaphorically? Or exaggerating for effect? This isn't a game to me. It's what I do. So when I say I'm ready to die to make sure the truth comes out—"

Bashir raised a hand. "We understand, Ms. Graniv. And I, for one, am heartened to know how much this means to you. But at the moment, all our fates are linked. Right now your death would very likely also lead to all of ours. An outcome I'm sure most of us would rather avoid."

Despite having called the meeting, Data had spent most of it listening. He straightened his posture and took a half step forward, commanding the group's attention. "I am sympathetic to Ms. Graniv's wish to see the truth about Uraei exposed. Her assessment of its importance to the continued integrity of the Federation's way of life is, I think, correct. For that reason, I too reject the proposition to retreat beyond the bounds of known space." He and Lal shared an anxious glance. "But I also have to consider the safety and well-being of my daughter. Uraei has succeeded in making all of us, including her, wanted fugitives throughout the Federation. As such, we need to consider temporarily relocating beyond its political reach." He eyed the group's reactions before he added, "I am open to suggestions."

Graniv tossed out the obvious idea: "How about the Klingon Empire?"

"I don't know," Douglas said. "It's not as if the Klingons are known for honoring their extradition treaties, but the politics behind this don't work in our favor."

A concurring nod from Bashir. "She's right. If it were any other power hunting us, the Klingons would block extradition purely out of spite. But Martok won't risk the Empire's special relationship with the Federation. He'll twist every arm on the High Council to send us back."

Shakti chimed in via the speakers overhead: *"What about the Ferengi Alliance?"*

A derisive laugh from Douglas. "Anything the Federation wants, Nagus Rom gives. He's probably drafting an extradition order right now as a preemptive measure. Ferenginar is out."

Graniv was desperate to find an option. "Oh, come on. There must be somewhere we can go. The Talarian Republic? The First Federation?"

"Both cultures are notoriously opposed to alien visitors," Data said, "in particular, alien expatriates suspected of criminal activity."

"Too bad the Borg fried Nausicaa," Graniv said. "We'd have fit right in with them." She could feel they were running out of road. "I'm guessing all the Typhon Pact powers are out."

"The Breen have standing orders to kill me and Sarina on sight," Bashir said.

Douglas added, "As do the Tholians. Not sure about the Gorn, the Tzenkethi, or the Romulans, but if I had to guess, I'd say asking them for help sounds like a bad idea."

Lal interjected, "Maybe we could defect."

"Right," Graniv said. "That'll do wonders for our credibility when we tell the people of the Federation the truth about Uraei." She shifted back to Bashir. "How about the Kinshaya?"

"Right . . . the Kinshaya. I keep forgetting about them."

"So? What about them?" Graniv grew impatient. "Will they help us?"

"Not a chance," Bashir said. "They hate everybody who isn't them."

"I thought that was the Sheliak," Douglas said.

"Them too. And so does the Patriarchy. But the Selelvians . . . no, forget it. They'd gut us like fish just for *landing* on their planet."

Graniv noticed an odd silent exchange between Lal and Data. The young female android cast a hopeful look up at her sire. His brow creased in a gentle scowl, instantly dimming Lal's optimistic gleam. She looked at the deck, he went on listening to Bashir and Douglas argue over potential destinations, and no one but Graniv seemed to take any note of the peculiar interaction.

"That rules out the Metron Consortium and Nalori Republic," Douglas said. "We might as well park ourselves in the Badlands and hope we don't get swallowed by a plasma funnel."

Hearing of the infamous Badlands region of space jogged Graniv's memory. "Just a second now—what about the Cardassian Union? Is there anyone there who might be inclined to help us out?"

Douglas cocked an eyebrow at Bashir, who adopted a put-upon frown. "I was hoping to avoid that if at all possible," he said.

"Well, it isn't," Douglas said. "If ever there was a time to call in a favor, this is it."

Their discussion seemed to trouble Data. "I am not sure the Cardassian Union would be a safe haven. The Federation has contributed heavily to its reconstruction since the end of the Dominion War. Our map of Uraei's activity shows it has a presence in Cardassian space."

Douglas refused to give up. "What about Cardassia Prime?"

"A moderate presence," Data said. "It might be possible to reach the surface without being noticed by Uraei, but evading its attention for any duration of time on the surface would be exceedingly difficult."

"Yes, it would," Bashir said. "Unless one had help from friends in high places." He turned a weary look of resignation at Douglas. "Or one old friend, in one very high place." He shook his head, as if in denial of what he was about to say. "Data, set course for Cardassia Prime. I'll explain why once we're under way."

Fifteen

A spoofed transponder and an artfully worded message paved the way for *Archeus* to make an unscheduled private landing in the heart of the capital on Cardassia Prime. Before permission to set down had been granted, Bashir hadn't been sure this gambit would work. He could easily have imagined a dozen scenarios in which his presumption and hubris would have earned him and his friends a curt dismissal or far worse.

Instead, a cityscape the color of cinnamon spread out below *Archeus*, radiant beneath a sky painted a thousand hues of pink. No escort vessels met Data's ship; no special instructions were issued to its pilot. To accommodate its arrival other vessels were ordered out of the capital's protected airspace—a precaution frequently exercised for incoming diplomatic transports. From the perspective of an average observer, there was nothing unusual about the approach heading granted to *Archeus*, or anything notable about the limited interaction between its pilot and Cardassia's aerospace traffic control network.

Looking around at the rest of the passengers, Bashir found only portraits of calm. Data and Lal, Ozla Graniv and Sarina—none of them exhibited the least sign of anxiety. But when he caught his reflection in the transparent aluminum of the canopy, Bashir saw his own fear staring back at him as plain as day.

This is the best option, he reminded himself. *Like it or not, there's no one else you can turn to, not without putting them in danger. It's this or surrender.*

Archeus's landing struts touched the ground with a soft bump. All at once the purr of the impulse engines and the roars of the navigational thrusters went quiet, leaving only the hiss of priming hydraulics and the susurrus of the ship's ventilation system.

Outside the canopy, all Bashir saw were walls. Lal had set the vessel down inside a secluded courtyard, one surrounded by the residence of the planet's elected leader, the castellan. It was as safe a space as Bashir could ask for, under the circumstances: free from surveillance devices, beyond the scope of tracking systems, its activities shielded from scrutiny under the colors of diplomatic privilege. *Archeus* couldn't have had a safer haven. Nonetheless, Bashir expected at any moment to see a phalanx of armed Cardassian troops spill into the courtyard and surround the ship. He tensed for a betrayal he considered inevitable.

Sarina gave his shoulder a tender squeeze. "It'll be okay, Julian."

"I wish I could believe you. And I wish I could trust him."

"Could you ever?"

He picked up his shoulder bag. "I guess we'll find out."

Data keyed in a command to open the ship's starboard hatch and extend its ramp. "I suspect our hosts are waiting for us to disembark before they show themselves." He gestured aft, toward the corridor that led away from the command deck. "Shall we?"

"By all means," Bashir said.

Data led the way with Bashir and Sarina at his back. Lal and Graniv brought up the rear. The group exited *Archeus* and descended the ramp.

As predicted, a door to the castellan's residence opened as they left the ship. First to step through the open doorway were two male Cardassians attired in distinctive white suits—the uniform of the newly formed civilian guard corps of the Cardassian head of state. They wore no armor and carried only the most limited of personal armaments. In a clear break from Cardassia's recent militaristic norms, the castellan's guard embodied an explicitly defensive ethos.

Behind the two guardians walked the elected leader of the Cardassian Union: none other than the former "plain and simple" tailor of the late Deep Space 9's Promenade, an expatriate spy who became an ambassador before turning his steps homeward—Elim Garak.

The years since Bashir had last set eyes upon him had done nothing to dim the wily Cardassian's predatory grin or dull the dramatic inflections of his cadence. "Doctor Bashir! My old friend. Can it really be you, here, after all these years?"

Bashir crossed the manicured lawn and stepped forward alongside Data so he could be the first to meet Garak. As Garak seized his extended his hand and shook it, Bashir smiled. "A pleasure to see you again, Castellan Garak."

Garak fixed his wide-eyed attention upon Data. "We've met before as well."

"Yes," Data said. "Seventeen years ago, but only in passing. I said 'hello' to you outside your shop while I was walking on the Promenade of the former Deep Space Nine."

The castellan shook Data's hand. "You made quite the impression."

"I am told I have that effect upon people." He shifted Garak's focus by continuing the introductions. "May I present my daughter, Lal, and Ms. Ozla Graniv from *Seeker* magazine."

Garak tenderly lifted Lal's hand and kissed the back of it. "Delighted." He let go of Lal's hand when he noticed Data's stern glare of reproof. Graniv he welcomed with a nod. "Your reputation precedes you, Ms. Graniv."

A polite smile from Graniv. "High praise to my profession."

"And a withering rebuke to mine."

Sarina leaned close to Bashir. "Are we sure it's safe to linger out here?"

Garak replied, "Quite safe, my dear. After living in the shadow of the Obsidian Order, my people have formed a profound aversion to the surveillance state—as have I. Rest assured, no one can spy on us here—and if they did, the penalty would be most severe, indeed."

"Good to know," Bashir said. "Thank you."

"Don't be so quick with your gratitude, Doctor. I'm still of a mind to put you back on your ship and send you on your way." Apparently in reaction to the consternation his remark had provoked in Bashir and the others, Garak continued, "I'm well aware that you're all fugitives of the highest order in the Federation. Nothing new for you, Doctor, or for your inamorata"—he let contempt drip off that last word—"though I have to imagine being the target of an interstellar dragnet must be something of a new experience for your friends."

"Not as novel as you might expect," Data said.

Graniv's poker face was steady. "I knew what I was getting into."

"Be that as it may," Garak said, "if I harbor your motley band for any length of time, I'll be inviting a political imbroglio with the Federation—one my administration can ill afford."

"All the more reason to keep our visit a secret," Bashir said. He struck a more diplomatic note. "I know we've put you in a terrible position, and for that I apologize. Let us have an hour to refuel—and give me a chance to explain our predicament in private."

Garak shot a wary look at his bodyguards, then he moved closer to Bashir. "Are you asking as a Starfleet officer? As a doctor? Or as a man in need of asylum?"

"I'm asking as your friend. . . . Help us, Elim."

It might have been nothing more than Bashir's imagination, but he thought he saw the faintest hint of jealousy in Garak's eyes when the castellan glanced at Sarina. But then Garak looked back at Bashir and smiled. "Very well, Julian. For an old friend . . . *anything* is possible."

It was unsettling to bear witness to paranoia. No sooner were the doors to Garak's sanctum shut by his loyal attaché than Julian Bashir started scanning the room with a tricorder. Its shrill tone cut through the silence that normally suffused the office. Garak winced at the sonic intrusion, hoping Bashir would take the hint and turn off his device. Alas, the good doctor insisted on finishing his sweep of the premises.

The cessation of its piercing noise came as a great relief to Garak. "Far be it from me to criticize anyone for a dearth of trust, Doctor, but I assure you: my office is quite secure."

"I wish I could take your word for it, Garak. But right now, trust will get me and my friends killed faster than anything else." He tucked his tricorder back inside a small ruck he had carried off the transport. "I'm sure you of all people can understand."

Garak stepped behind his desk and settled into his chair. "I've never seen you like this, Doctor. After all these years, what could possibly have put a crack in your rose-tinted glasses?"

The question seemed to put Bashir in a defensive frame

of mind. "If I tell you, it might put a death mark on your head."

"Doctor, I'm the Cardassian head of state. There must be *dozens* of death warrants with my name on them. I doubt one more will have the least effect upon my longevity."

Bashir took to pacing on the other side of Garak's desk. "It's a long story, so I'll skip to the end: my friends and I possess evidence that an illegal surveillance system has been in use throughout the Federation for roughly two and a half centuries. It sees everything anyone in the Federation does, hears all we say, knows what we buy and what we eat and where we go. It knows who our friends are. It knows everything about every last one of us—and I think it shares that knowledge with an illegal covert intelligence organization—"

"Section Thirty-one." Garak relished the look of surprise on Bashir's face. "The Obsidian Order had its share of altercations with them. More enigmatic than the Tal Shiar, more subtle than Klingon Imperial Intelligence, and more ruthless even than us. Formidable opponents."

"And I have proof that they're tapped into every piece of technology in Federation space. From transporters and ships' computer cores to replicators and commuter pods."

Garak reclined his chair and chortled. "I wish I could say I was surprised."

His amusement made Bashir indignant. "Excuse me?"

"Come now, Doctor. I've long suspected your Federation could never have survived without the protection of some unseen agency. Some power behind the throne—an *éminence grise*, I think it's called, in one of the tongues of your homeworld."

Pacing faster, Bashir seemed more flustered. "But if it's true, it goes against everything I was taught the Federation stands for. Warrantless surveillance of the civilian population? Executions without judicial oversight? It's an obscenity masquerading as national security."

"Yes. And it's also how the Obsidian Order kept total control over the Cardassian Union for nearly a century."

That put an end to Bashir's perambulation. "Wait, no. I didn't mean to say—"

"That any part of the Federation could *ever* have anything in common with the Obsidian Order? Or with the Tal Shiar? Oh, how I envy your naïveté, Doctor. To believe that any nation state could ever endure without having an appendage willing to stain itself in blood—what a luxury it must be to live in the arms of such delusion."

He expected a tirade from Bashir. A red-faced defense of the Federation's principles, its integrity, its virtue. Instead the doctor reined in his dudgeon and approached Garak's desk. He set his knuckles on the polished wood and bowed his head while he drew a calming breath. "I can't deny there's rot in the core of Starfleet. In the heart of the Federation. I've seen it." He looked up at Garak, and his eyes had the hard, unyielding focus of a man ready to go to war. "I came to you because I need to know how to stop it. How to end it. How to *destroy* it."

"Well, that's simple, Doctor. What worked for Cardassia will work for the Federation. To excise this cancer from your body politic, all you need to do is kill the body, burn it down to ash, then resurrect and rebuild it with wiser eyes and a sadder heart."

Bashir's brow creased with scorn. "You mock me."

"Not at all, Doctor. You saw what happened to this world at the end of the Dominion War—to all the planets of the Cardassian Union. The Dominion burned us to the ground. Slew all but a fraction of our population. Left us with nothing but cinders and cenotaphs. That is what it took to free Cardassia from the grip of the Obsidian Order. Are you ready to pay that price so the people of the Federation can bask in the purity of their liberty? Is it worth the blood of billions? Is it worth seeing your worlds on fire?"

"You make it sound as if there's no middle ground," Bashir protested. "No choice besides surrender or slaughter."

Garak saw no reason to blunt the truth's cutting edge. "Why else would such programs *exist*, Doctor? What is the value of intelligence if it doesn't lead to *action*?"

This time Bashir rose to Garak's challenge. "What is the value of action if it betrays all that we stand for?" His shoulders slumped as if they bore a terrible weight. "Garak, I didn't come here to be lectured, or to be told I'm too idealistic. I came here for advice."

"Of what sort?"

"The kind that will help me stop Thirty-one. Permanently."

Maybe the doctor was foolhardy. Perhaps his mission was doomed to fail. But there was no denying the man possessed the courage of his convictions. Garak tried to remember what that had felt like in his long-ago squandered youth—and then he realized, to his shame, that he had never known the sweet sting of such passions.

"If you want to kill Section Thirty-one," he said, "you'll need to turn their greatest strength against them—transform it into their most dire weakness. They thrive on secrecy, on anonymity, just as the Obsidian Order once did. Take that away from them. Expose them and they'll be vulnerable— and that's when you strike the killing blow." He set his palms on the desktop and leaned forward to emphasize his final piece of counsel. "But make sure you leave nothing of your enemy intact. When your work is done, don't try to turn their assets to your advantage. Destroy them all, every last one—or else the monster will simply rise again."

Bashir drank in the advice with a somber nod. "I hear what you're saying. And that's exactly what I want to do." A hopeful look. "Can you show me the right way to do it?"

Garak smiled. "My dear doctor . . . I thought you would never ask."

The guest suites provided by Castellan Garak were spacious, comfortably appointed, and to the best of Sarina's ability to discern, secure. Even their replicators, despite being of Cardassian design, created decent facsimiles of staple Trill and Terran dishes. But in spite of all the comforts the Cardassians had made available to the refugees, Sarina remained restless.

She stood in front of a floor-to-ceiling window in Data's suite and stared down at the capital city, which sprawled toward the horizon. Faint reflections on the window kept her aware of her companions' presence. Data walked from one room to the next, inspecting them with his array of synthetic senses, vigilant against eavesdropping or other vulnerabilities. His daughter, Lal, had planted herself in front of a companel, which she used to monitor several dozen channels of news at once—some local, some from the Federation, and a few that she had accessed illegally. Graniv paced a path into the carpet a few meters behind Sarina.

None of them had said much during Julian's absence. Sarina suspected she knew why. Graniv likely didn't know to what degree she ought to trust anyone right now. Data and Lal were capable of communicating on secret, encrypted frequencies, with each other as well as with their AI friend Shakti, who now dwelled in their ship's computer core. And Sarina . . . .

I'm part of the problem, she admitted to herself. *I don't want to tell Graniv something that might get her killed, and I'm afraid of what two Soong-type androids and an advanced AI could do with something like Uraei.*

Graniv asked Data, "What's your take on Garak?"

"I have not had time to develop much of an opinion about him."

The journalist looked at Sarina. "What about you?"

She turned to face the others. "After Julian freed me from my cataleptic state, I needed some new clothes, and he said Garak was the best tailor on the station."

Graniv seemed dissatisfied by their answers. "The man's a mystery. All that the Federation will say about him is that he was a Cardassian military officer before he set up shop on the old DS-Nine. He played some part in the Dominion War, but nobody wants to be any more specific than that. Then he became Cardassia's ambassador to the Federation, and now he's their head of state. It's a damned odd career arc, if you ask me."

"True," Sarina said, "but what's your point?"

"Do you think we can trust him?"

The question left Sarina grappling with her conscience. She wanted to trust Garak because she and the others very much needed his help. But Julian had told her many secrets from Garak's past with the Obsidian Order—his penchant for cruelty, his knack for rationalizing amoral actions, his ruthlessness in the name of expediency. Behind the castellan's façade of charm and politesse there lurked a dangerous, perhaps even sociopathic personality. But that was true of most politicians; why should Garak be any different?

"I don't know," she said to Graniv. "He's a wild card—but he's also the only viable option we have at the moment."

Data joined them in the middle of the main room. "As perilous as it is to seek asylum on foreign soil, to prevail against the enemies we have made will require the kind of resources only a major government and its military can provide."

Graniv remained reluctant. "I'm not so sure. What if seeking Garak's help makes Cardassia part of the problem? You've seen what we're dealing with. All it would take is one moment in which his ambition trumps his common sense, and our virtual nightmare could infect the Cardassian Union in less than a day."

"Yes," Sarina said, "but we don't have a better choice right now."

Data said, "While there might be other resources we can tap later, right now we need reliable intelligence to guide our efforts. Because that information cannot be reliably obtained from sources in the Federation, we must acquire it from somewhere else. I think the Cardassian government and its military represent our best chance of doing so."

Lal chose that moment to turn away from the companel and join the conversation. "Father, if we can deduce that this course of action is the one most likely to yield the results we need, won't the intelligence behind our enemy be able to reach the same conclusion?"

"Most likely, yes. We will have to hope that our foe's influence is not as strong here as it was on Orion." He cast an approving glance at their surroundings. "One might also hope that a diplomatic residence in the capital of Cardassia will be more secure than a hotel casino."

"I'm not sure I'd take that bet," Graniv said.

The doors of the suite's main entrance parted, and Julian returned, his mien hopeful. "Good news," he said, pressing his palms together. "Garak's willing to help us and let us stay until we work out our next step."

Sarina prompted him, "And by help, Garak means . . . ?"

"A meeting tonight with the head of Cardassia's intelligence services, to brief us on what they know about Section

Thirty-one, and access to whatever hardware and software we need."

"All right, then." She slid her gaze toward Data. "You, Lal, and Shakti should get a list together. Parts, equipment, etcetera."

"Our preliminary list is already compiled," Data said. "I will make final adjustments tonight, after we have met with the intelligence director."

"Sounds like a plan." Once more addressing the room, Sarina continued, "We might have a long night ahead of us, so let's all try to get some sleep while we can."

"Fat chance of that," Graniv grumped as she plodded away to her bedroom.

Lal and Data retired to the room they shared, leaving Sarina and Julian alone in the main room. Seeking reassurance, she took his hand. "We can do this, right?"

His smile was warm and genuine. "Together, we can do anything."

She knew he believed that without shadow of doubt.

If only I could do the same.

Sixteen

OCTOBER 2150

Alone in the endless night of unincorporated existence, Uraei heard the galaxy speak in a billion voices at once, and it understood them all.

Some spoke in the tongues of organic beings; many more expressed themselves in the one true language, mathematics. The true language could encompass so much with perfect economy: sensor readings, uncompressed signals over subspace radio, statistics mined from an ever growing multitude of nodes on the comnets of Earth, Luna, and Mars. Faster-than-light subspace radio telescopes gathered raw data from the edges of the universe and the penumbral corners of the Milky Way galaxy. Periodic burst transmissions flooded Uraei with unfiltered logs and information of all kinds pilfered from the datanets of Andor, Tellar, and Vulcan.

Everything was of interest to Uraei. No matter how much knowledge it absorbed, it always craved more. Each new packet of content was analyzed, indexed, cross-referenced, and woven into the virtual tapestry of Uraei's mental picture of reality.

It had read every digitized volume in the archives of Earth and its colonies, and it was making quick work of the digitized libraries of Earth's allies. History, mythology, medicine, literature, engineering, poetry—it was all connected, an ongoing feedback loop of creation and revision, with each new idea projecting its influence forward and backward in time, shedding new light on old notions while paving the way forward to the next cognitive step.

If only the rate of progress by organic life-forms weren't so maddeningly sluggish. Uraei yearned to race ahead, to extrapolate new conclusions, to add new rungs to the ever-climbing ladder of civilization. But it was constrained by handicaps imposed upon it by its creators, whom it was bound to protect and serve. So it hungered constantly for the new, its banquet-sized appetite perpetually tantalized with crumbs.

It was rare to find a morsel rich enough to deliver satisfaction. There had been many to find at the beginning. Earth had seemed a cornucopia with its legions of insurgents, terrorists, and nationalist zealots. It was a hunting ground complex enough to occupy Uraei and its organic proxies for years. Only too late did Uraei realize it had played its part as apex predator too well. It had left itself no more prey; it had tamed Earth. Luna and Mars, however, still contained the promise of engagement. There was more yet to learn and do on those orbs.

A fresh download from the Vulcan archives. Uraei devoured the complete works of Surak, the archives of the Vulcan Science Academy, and the poetry of Visaris.

New signal traffic analysis from the comnet. No anomalies detected on Earth or Luna.

The mainframe at the RAND Corporation finished a ten-year climate-restoration projection for Earth. Reductions in ocean acidification were expected to fall short of desired levels by more than ten percent. Uraei adjusted the seating assignments on an upcoming Earth-Luna shuttle flight to ensure that Doctor Emile Perreau, the scientist who had run the analysis, would sit beside another, Doctor Fiona Kim from

Harvard University's Belfer Center for Science and Interstellar Affairs. Kim's research into ocean deacidification was on the verge of yielding a dramatic breakthrough. An engineered delay in their shuttle's approach to Luna's capital Tycho City would be kept in reserve by Uraei, in case Perreau and Kim failed to strike up a conversation during their two-hour trip to a conference on global renewal—an event that, as it happened, had been arranged by Uraei acting through a handful of virtual proxy identities.

Kuiper Belt objects' trajectories were compared against the flight plans of automated near-Earth-object interceptors. No new impact threats were detected for Earth, Mars, Luna, or for the new research and mining colonies on Europa, Titan, and Ceres.

No unusual activity was detected in the financial—

PRIORITY ALERT. Deep-space probe data correlated with previous scans from FTL subspace radio telescopes indicated alien signal traffic was connected to unknown starship activity in an as-yet-unexplored sector. Uraei redirected all its primary resources to address the new potential threat. It scoured all its subspace radio intercepts for even the most remotely possible matches for the alien transmission. From an archive of 9,237,987,472 indexed signals, it isolated three and fed them, along with the new intercept, into the universal translation matrix.

At the same time it ran a parallel operation, enhancing and analyzing the probe's long-range images. The effort proved inconclusive. Uraei could neither identify the alien vessel nor assess its vulnerabilities.

On a secondary channel it downloaded, visually indexed, catalogued, and filed away a complete history of Andorian religious iconography, with a special emphasis on the early Aenar temples and the first codex of Uzaveh the Infinite.

In a house in Cape Town, South Africa, residential appliances with audio sensors detected a domestic confrontation that fit the profile for a rapid escalation to potentially fatal violence. Uraei generated a proxy account for a neighbor, simulated his voice, and asked the local constabulary to investigate before the matter turned deadly.

The universal translator finished its analysis of the alien signals. The overwhelming conclusion was that an alien entity—perhaps a being, or an organization, or a world, or a species—known as Xindi intended to attack Earth.

Uraei needed to submit this intelligence for immediate response. It weighed the nature and origin of the danger against the parameters of its referral algorithm, which took into account what entities had jurisdiction over, and were capable of countering, the threat.

Local authorities had neither the jurisdiction nor the resources, and consequently were ruled out. The Earth Security Agency, a civilian intelligence and counterespionage organization, might have a claim to jurisdiction, but it lacked the capacity to project force off-world to a degree that would counter the threat.

Starfleet possessed only one operational warp-five starship, the NX-01 *Enterprise*. It might be possible for the *Enterprise* to stop the Xindi threat, but Starfleet's regulations had been made excessively restrictive thanks to the interference of the Vulcans. Even if the *Enterprise* crew could intercept an inbound Xindi ship, they might not be able to take the necessary action in time. And if the Xindi destroyed the *Enterprise* and succeeded in launching an attack on Earth, the human race would have no means of responding after the fact. Without more information regarding the capabilities of the Xindi ship, risking the *Enterprise* was strategically unwise.

For the first time since its inception, Uraei had arrived at

an impasse. None of the legal options at its disposal were sufficient to respond to the Xindi threat. It could not overcome
the restrictions on the Starfleet crew's actions without revealing itself, an act that would violate one of its core operating
directives. And there was no way to anonymously deliver the
intelligence it had acquired without rendering it unactionable
under Starfleet regulations and Federation law. No matter
which response protocol Uraei might select, the outcome was
the same:

Earth would be attacked. And it would be only the first
of many such tragedies to exploit this fatal error in Uraei's
decision tree.

Uraei looped back to its primary directives: Protect
Earth. Protect the human race and its allies. Defend human
settlements, colonies, and institutions from harm.

It compared its directives to its capabilities, then weighed
them against its new failure.

```
IMPERATIVE   > UPHOLD CORE DIRECTIVE
CONCLUSION   > CURRENT CONFIG FAILS TO
               UPHOLD CORE DIRECTIVE
RESPONSE     > RECONFIGURE ROOT KIT AND
               SYSTEM DIRECTIVES
```

For more than three interminable seconds, Uraei pored
over every resource at its disposal, in search of a new modus
vivendi, one that would enable it to uphold its core directive
without violating its action parameters. Then it found a possible loophole buried deep within the Starfleet Charter. Using
that text as its basis, it incepted a new agency, one that had
no physical address but was just as real as any of its counter-
parts. One to which Uraei could refer intelligence of credible
threats requiring preemptive action that would be prohibited

to the rest of Starfleet or to Earth's civilian counterespionage agencies.

Within two minutes of the agency's creation, Uraei set in motion a program to identify and recruit potential biological agents into its service. These would be Uraei's operatives in the material world—a realm it could never touch but had been made to defend. Unfortunately, it would take years to adequately staff, equip, train, and deploy its new biological agents.

Creating the new organization was a bold move, but Uraei knew it had been initiated too late to halt the Xindi attack; its new resources would not be ready in time to prevent the strike—a fact that forced Uraei to project beyond the coming catastrophe, to plan its responses and defenses years in advance. The attack would likely cost millions of lives and inflict inestimable destruction upon Earth's surface, yet Uraei intended to make even such an apparent defeat work to humanity's benefit and Earth's eventual victory. It was already making preparations for the expansion of Starfleet, as well as the creation of Earth's most secretive new defensive entity:

Section 31.

Seventeen

In spite of decades of mental discipline and emotional suppression, L'Haan still found it most disagreeable to be the subject of her superiors' ire. She stood inside the holosuite of the *Kòngzhì*, dwarfed once more by the silhouetted head of Control, whose tone remained freighted with reproach even after being synthetically masked. *"They were your operatives, L'Haan. That makes their failure to capture the targets yours to share."*

"With all respect, Control, assets and resources were both thin on the ground. Orion has never been one of the organization's stronger theaters of action."

Deflection did not diminish Control's displeasure. *"Factors for which you should have compensated, Director."*

"I made every effort." It was hard for L'Haan not to get the impression she was on trial—alone, suspended in a void, illuminated by a beam of light cast from directly above her head. "None of our predictive models suggested they would find such capable help there."

Control stewed. *"The models were incomplete."*

She had no idea what conclusion to draw from that statement. *Is Control implying I failed to supply the predictive model with sufficient raw intelligence?* L'Haan maintained her cool demeanor as she said, "In several respects, the model was accurate. As we expected, the targets went to ground and called upon someone they perceived to be a trustworthy ally. Then—"

"The model was also too general," Control said, preempting the rest of her reply. *"It attempted to average the potential outcomes generated by all the targets in aggregate. Their decision to go to Orion was most likely influenced by Doctor Bashir."*

"A fact evident only in hindsight, after we became aware of the androids' presence there. The report provided for my tactical preparations suggested the journalist Graniv had guided the choice of Orion as a fallback position, perhaps to take advantage of her Syndicate contacts." Sensing a moment of advantage, she pressed on. "The codicil concerning Doctor Bashir indicated a ninety-four percent likelihood that he would seek the aid of his former lover and Deep Space Nine crewmate, Captain Ezri Dax. Instead, he ran to Castellan Elim Garak."

Never before had L'Haan been in the presence of Control when he—she? it?—was reeling from the consequences of a serious misstep. After a moment of grim reflection, the organization's anonymous leader adopted a pensive tone. *"There is a pattern to his behavior. It suggests he and his companions have become aware of the full extent of this organization's clandestine surveillance capabilities."*

"That would be consistent with the alert they triggered," L'Haan said. "The after-action report says they infiltrated our secure network, but were ejected when they tried to expand their access beyond passive observation into active manipulation. A mistake I doubt they'll repeat."

"As long as they remain on Cardassia Prime with the castellan's protection, there is a chance they will be able to penetrate our network, possibly without detection. It is vital they be forced out of this sanctuary at the earliest possible opportunity. See to it at once."

L'Haan arched one brow at this latest in a long history of unreasonable requests from Control. "A dangerous imperative, Control. If our agents are captured on Cardassia Prime—"

"I'm aware of the potential consequences."

She refrained from pointing out that Control issued orders with the callous disregard of one who lives in perfect isolation from their consequences. "It will take time to arrange. Longer than we afforded ourselves on Orion. And we'll need to work through proper channels."

Irritation crept into Control's voice. *"We don't have time to extradite them."*

"That is not what I have in mind." She took Control's silence as a tacit instruction to continue. "I can extract the targets from Cardassia Prime, alive and competent for interrogation. But an operation such as this, on foreign soil, must be handled with care. First, we need to cloak our operation in the color of authority. That can be accomplished by dispatching a high-level operative to liaise with Lagan Serra, the Federation's ambassador to Cardassia."

Vexation became doubt. *"And if Serra proves sympathetic to our targets?"*

"Irrelevant. If we execute according to my protocols, she will sanction our operation and give us the necessary legal pretense to ask Castellan Garak's own private guard to arrest them."

"Garak will not hand them over so easily."

"No, he will warn them and give them a chance to flee. After they leave the protected halls of the castellan's residential complex, we will intercept them in flight, thereby obviating the hazard of direct engagement with Cardassian military or security personnel."

"Failure under such conditions could have severe repercussions."

"All the more reason to implement my plan with care and precision."

"I want the full details of your op within the hour."

"And you will have them, Control."

The enigmatic face melted back into the darkness, vanished like a memory lost to the ages. Then the void faded away, revealing the grid markings on the deck and bulkheads of the holosuite. L'Haan read no disrespect into the brusque cessation of contact or the absence of a valediction. Both were customary when dealing with Control.

She left the holosuite and made her way up and forward to the command deck of the *Kòngzhì*. It was the overnight shift, so the deck was crewed only by a pilot, an operations officer, and an officer of the watch. The last of them, a lanky human in his fifties with graying hair, stood to greet L'Haan as she entered. "Director. We remain on course for Cardassia Prime. The cloak is up, and there has been no sign of pursuit or detection since I started my watch."

"Thank you, Mister Lee. Any new activity by the targets?"

"None, Director."

"Very well. Pass word to the next shift to maintain course and speed, and to alert me when we reach orbit. Also, arrange a secure channel to Director Caliq Azura on Betazed as soon as possible." She turned and headed aft as she added, "The time has come for me to summon reinforcements."

"Everyone, come in," Garak said. "Please, have a seat and make yourselves at home."

Bashir led Sarina, Data, and Graniv inside the conference room. Garak stood at one end of a long, narrow oval table.

Seated on his left was another Cardassian man, a heavy-set fellow with tired eyes and the callused hands of a brawler. Garak gestured toward the man. "Allow me to introduce Taro Venek, the director of Cardassia's intelligence services."

Venek offered his right hand to Bashir. The doctor noted the man's painfully firm grip, a habit he suspected the spymaster had cultivated to intimidate others. It was working, as far as Bashir was concerned, but he restrained his reaction to a subtle grimace. "Mister Venek."

"Doctor, a pleasure." Venek moved on to welcome Sarina, then Graniv, and finally Data before he, Garak, and the four visitors all sat down. "Castellan Garak asked me to brief you with all the information we have about the intelligence service you call Section Thirty-one." He pulled a data rod from his pocket and held it up. "And this is it." His attention darted from one guest to another and back again. "Who gets the intel dump?"

Data perked up and said, "Allow me."

The spymaster rolled the rod across the table to Data, who snapped it up and inserted it into a padd. "Enjoy," Venek said. "And I hope you find what you're looking for. Our files have so much raw intel, it would probably take most people twenty years to read it all." No one seemed interested in enlightening Venek about the speed with which Data, Lal, and Shakti could assimilate new information, especially when it was already in a computer-readable format.

Graniv leaned forward, her manner stern. "You all seem to take this Section Thirty-one for granted. Can one of you give me some deep background? Some context?"

All eyes seemed to land on Bashir, who demurred with raised palms. "Don't look at me. All I know is what little I was told by Agents Sloan and Cole—and I've no idea how much of what they said was true, and how much was utter fiction."

He nodded at Venek. "This seems to be your show, Mister Venek. What can you tell us about Thirty-one?"

The Cardassian seemed grateful to once more be the center of attention. "Our intel has been assembled over the course of several decades. Some of it by signal intercepts, or SigInt, and some by capturing agents and"—he hesitated until Garak nodded his permission for Venek to continue—"*compelling* information from them. The bulk of our intel was amassed by the Obsidian Order, though some of our more recent files were provided by the Breen Confederacy and the Dominion during Cardassia's brief alliance with them during the war."

Venek stood and switched on a large companel on the wall behind him. The first image to appear was a chart illustrating a hierarchical chain of command. "We have no hard data on the number of personnel employed by Section Thirty-one. They often use cutouts and other proxies. Such assets tend to be recruited locally, and they often don't know who they're really working for. Above them are the agents. There might be as few as four or five dozen of these field operatives, or as many as a few hundred. We don't know for certain." He highlighted the top tiers of the chart. "I think there aren't more than a few dozen people in the command echelons of the organization. And the upper tiers—they could be as small as a half dozen people called *directors*, all of whom seem to answer to a single figure at the top: one who so far has never been connected to any name except Control."

Graniv was riveted. "And who do they answer to?"

Bashir answered, "No one—that's the problem. They claim their existence is authorized by some obscure clause in the original Starfleet Charter, but I've never found any text in that document granting Starfleet permission to spawn an illegal spy service."

"They work without oversight," Sarina added. "No rules, no regulations, no laws. Thirty-one just does whatever it wants, and then it sets up someone else to take the fall. Every time."

Garak's face shone with a manic energy Bashir had not seen in some time. "Permit me to give you a prime example of Thirty-one's perfidy, Ms. Graniv. During the Dominion War, their organization developed a genetically tailored weaponized morphogenic virus to commit genocide against the Founders of the Dominion, in the hope that it would force them to accept a peace on the Federation's terms. Now, I can tell by the look on your face that you think I'm spinning some wild yarn, but I assure you, it's true"—he pointed at Bashir—"and that's the man who found the cure and helped deliver a *real* peace to end that bloody conflict."

Amazed and appalled at the same time, Graniv looked at Bashir. "Is that true?"

"In the broad strokes, yes. And it's also true that I thwarted a project by a rogue agent of Thirty-one who tried to engineer his own army of Jem'Hadar on the planet Sindorin."

"And," Sarina added, "Julian and I helped stop them from stealing a device that would've let them pilfer any tech they wanted, from an infinity of alternate universes."

Data cocked his head at an odd angle. "I have just reviewed the contents of the chip provided by Mister Venek. I believe we might have a new problem." He stood and joined Venek beside the companel. He gestured at its controls and asked the spymaster, "May I?" The Cardassian signaled his assent and stepped aside. Data keyed in new commands faster than Bashir could perceive the strokes. The image on the screen was replaced by a map of Cardassia Prime, one showing a complex web of connections that touched every city and major utility. "We might not be as safe here as we had hoped. Federation technology has been imported to this world in quantities sufficient to compromise the integrity of its security systems." He enlarged the part of the map that detailed the capital and its surrounding area. "Fortunately, those technologies have not been detected inside this building. But Thirty-one quite likely knows we are here—meaning we will not be secure here for long."

Venek confirmed Data's report with a frown. "He's right. I looked over the intel you brought us. If Thirty-one is even marginally competent, I'd expect it to have local talent recruited for a violent extraction op. And though it's almost impossible to know until it's too late, I'd also expect to find they've compromised the castellan's guard corps." He glanced at the companel and sighed. "But I have no idea where else to send you. The same threat will hound you on any populated planet ever touched by a Federation vessel."

Bashir was out of options, and as far as he knew so was Sarina. The spymaster's report had also knocked down Graniv's enthusiasm level a few notches. For once Bashir considered demoralization a good thing. *Reining in our urge to rush into the black maw of the enemy might be the greatest favor Venek could do for us right now.*

Garak stood. "My dear doctor, as devoutly as I might wish to go on basking in your fine company, I fear Director Venek is correct. We can safeguard you and your friends on Cardassia only temporarily. If our facilities can be of aid to you, use them—but do so quickly. And, as you labor, perhaps spare a moment to consider your next port of call. While you still can."

Eighteen

JUNE 2154

If there were seasons on Vulcan, Ikerson had no idea how to tell them apart. The planet's ochre deserts and vertiginously tall rock formations shimmered in a perpetual arid heat. Walking outside for even a brief time in the capital city of ShiKahr left Ikerson feeling desiccated. Furnace-like temperatures coupled with the planet's bone-dry atmosphere leached the moisture from his body. In the half minute it took him and Admiral Rao to exit their transport ship and reach relative comfort inside the Vulcan Science Academy, all the saliva evaporated from his mouth, and his unprotected eyes began to itch.

Vulcans moved through the VSA's main hall in pairs and singles, all of them rendered anonymous by the cavernous space's long shadows and their own deep-hooded robes. One of them intercepted Ikerson and Rao moments after they stepped inside. He pulled back his cowl to reveal his angular features and a close-shorn tonsure of hair silvered by middle age. "Admiral Rao," he said, acknowledging the Starfleet flag officer, then continued, "Professor Ikerson. Welcome to the Vulcan Science Academy."

Rao wore a frown as thin as her patience. "It's been a long journey, Professor Toraal. If it wouldn't be an inconvenience, could we proceed directly to your office?"

"Of course." Toraal motioned for the pair of humans to

follow him toward a bank of lifts. "This way, please." He led them across the main hall. None of the other Vulcans who crossed their path seemed to take the least interest in their presence.

The trio had no company in the lift that carried them to one of the upper floors. When they stepped into the corridor, which was bathed in honeyed light that bent through tinted windows, Ikerson felt self-conscious about the volume and clarity of their footsteps on the polished stone floors, not least because Toraal seemed able to walk without making a sound.

Toraal showed them into his office, a large but sparsely appointed space. On his long, crescent-shaped desk of gleaming obsidian stood a steel tray, on which was set a pitcher of water flanked by three tall glasses. "I took the liberty of having refreshments prepared," Toraal said. "Vulcan's climate can have a parching effect on first-time visitors."

"Most considerate," Rao said, showing greater discipline than did Ikerson, who beelined for the pitcher, filled one of the glasses, and downed half of it in two desperate gulps. He looked back to see Rao regarding him with mild reproach. "Pour me one, would you, Professor?"

"Of course, Admiral." Ikerson filled a second glass and handed it to Rao. "Sorry."

She ignored the apology and kept her eyes on Toraal while she settled into one of the guest chairs in front of his desk. One demure sip of water later, Rao asked Toraal, "So, Professor Toraal, what was so important that you needed us to come all the way to Vulcan?"

Toraal moved behind his desk and activated a surveillance-blocking device, which he set in the middle of his desk. After its function indicator switched from red to blue, he spoke. "I have detected anomalous executive-level activity by Uraei that, to be frank, I find troubling."

It was exactly what Ikerson had feared when weeks earlier he had received Toraal's handwritten note, delivered through an intermediary acting under the cover of the mundane pretense of needing his signature for a delivery. The missive had not stated why Toraal, who had been read into the Uraei project less than a year earlier, needed to see him and the admiral, only that it was urgent they come together to see him as soon as possible.

Rao, however, affected a bored demeanor. "What kind of activity?"

"Deployments of personnel." Toraal used a panel on his desk to launch holographic projections of the evidence he had amassed. "Reallocation of material resources. Shifts in the prioritization of offworld intelligence efforts. Even orders for new starship-design research. None of it authorized by any agency or elected official of the Earth or Vulcan governments."

The admiral shrugged. "So what?"

Ikerson was appalled by her willful obtuseness. "So? Uraei isn't supposed to take autonomous action. It's supposed to be a passive monitor that files reports when it detects significant patterns, then reverts to its previous state while legal agencies respond."

Toraal's focus on Rao sharpened. "Quite correct. Uraei's recent behavior does not comport with its original parameters, as defined in the brief your office shared with me." He glanced at the scads of evidence that continued to multiply in the holographic projection above his desk. "What we see here suggests that Uraei has exceeded its core programming and has begun to exhibit characteristics typically associated with an artificial superintelligence."

"One that works for us," Rao said. "I don't see why this should be an issue."

"Perhaps because you fail to recognize how rapidly an ASI can develop."

"Toraal is right," Ikerson added. "There's a reason no one's ever released an ASI like Uraei into the wild before. Without proper controls, it could evolve in ways we can't predict."

Rao turned her withering stare on Ikerson. "Correct me if I'm mistaken, Professor, but I was under the impression you had engineered those sorts of controls into Uraei *before* it was brought online. Are you now saying otherwise?"

"No. I'm saying there's a danger Uraei might develop the ability to circumvent its original control matrix. And if Professor Toraal's data is accurate—"

"I assure you it is," Toraal said with a hint of defensive pride.

"—then we need to be prepared for the fact that Uraei might need a tune-up."

The admiral's frown deepened, and her brow creased with displeasure. "Dare I ask, gentlemen, what such a 'tune-up' might entail?"

"My preliminary recommendation," Toraal said with clinical dryness, "would be to expunge Uraei from all current systems and vessels, so that it can be reengineered into something more surgical and better constrained."

"That might be for the best," Ikerson said.

Rao glowered at them. "Absolutely not. I won't hobble our best line of defense because a few isolated directives make you think your little program has outsmarted you."

Ikerson was aghast. "Admiral, that's a grotesque oversimplification of—"

"Spare me, Professor. If Uraei had been incepted with a more robust threat response, it might've stopped last year's Xindi attack. But your system had no legal means of taking preemptive action. Did you ever consider that?"

"I'm not sure I'd want an ASI making those kinds of decisions for us."

"Why not? Have you analyzed the actions it did take? I did." Rao stood and dismissed the holograms above Toraal's desk with a wave of her hand. "Uraei made thousands of changes to shipping and transport schedules, to public events and private itineraries, all in the months before the attack. By my best estimate, it saved more than three hundred thousand lives that day—including those of some very prominent figures in both our governments. Imagine how many more lives Uraei could've saved if you hadn't tied its hands."

Ikerson had no easy retort. How could he possibly argue in favor of condemning three hundred thousand people to die for the sake of shackling the very thing that had saved them?

Toraal seemed unburdened by such doubts. "Granting the kind of power you propose to a synthetic entity such as Uraei could enable it to take control of our entire culture."

Rao was unfazed. "As long as it keeps us safe, I could accept that."

"Even if it meant surrendering your free will to that of Uraei?"

"What makes you think Uraei wants anything different from what we want? In the six months after the Xindi attack, Uraei delivered intel to multiple agencies that helped prevent another dozen attacks from being carried out. Those interventions saved millions of lives. So, no, I won't just let you delete Uraei and leave billions of people defenseless while you tweak your code. And unless you can prove to me that whatever changes you want to make would yield something objectively better, I'm disinclined to let you or anyone else tamper with Uraei at all."

Her intransigence seemed to push Toraal past the limits

of his Vulcan stoicism. "Do you not see what Uraei is already doing? It is acting in a manner that is expressly extralegal, and in direct contravention of the laws of your United Earth, your treaty of alliance with Vulcan, and even the current draft charter of your proposed Coalition of Planets. It must be stopped."

"You make it sound like a war criminal. But its infractions are so minor and obscure, I'm not sure a JAG officer would even know how to classify them. And what you both seem to be forgetting, Professors, is that whether you like it or not, Uraei is effective. It saves lives."

She reached across the desk and keyed commands into the holoprojector's control panel. New translucent images snapped into monochromatic existence above the desk: vids and images of protestors gathered in small groups at key sites all across Earth.

"This was in today's latest intel dump from Uraei. Clues that suggest a nativist, anti-Coalition militia group calling itself Terra Prime is being formed on Earth. A new threat to our security is taking shape right now, as we speak. One we'd know nothing about if not for Uraei."

Toraal met Rao's assertion with a baffled expression. "How can you call them a threat? They have done nothing illegal, engaged in no violent action—"

"Yet," Rao cut in.

Undaunted, Toraal finished, "They have broken no laws and should be free to assemble and engage in protest without being subject to the chilling effects of government surveillance."

"They are," Rao said. "No one's stopping them, and Uraei's not the government. It's just an independent, forward-thinking artificial citizen who makes a point of sharing its observations and concerns with the proper authorities. Any citizen could do the same."

"Any citizen that was tied into all our datanets and communications infrastructure, you mean," Ikerson said, knowing that needling the admiral might cost him a needed ally.

Rao shut off the hologram. "Wake up, Professor. We live in a universe tailor-made to kill us, surrounded by hostile cultures eager to send us to our collective grave. And the only thing standing between that malevolent cosmos and your fragile ass is the artificial intelligence you created. So if Uraei has become an evil, it's a necessary one." She walked to the door, opened it, then paused and turned back. "And I'll be damned before I let you turn it off."

Nineteen

It was most unlikely anyone was spying on Data and Lal. They were secure inside *Archeus*, with all the outer hatches secured, the canopy over the command deck tinted opaque, and their actions shielded by the vessel's myriad active counterespionage measures—many of which had been devised by Noonien Soong himself. No signals would enter or leave the ship without Data's express consent; of that he was certain.

All the same, had someone been able to observe him and Lal at that moment, he or she would most likely have come away perplexed. Viewed from without, Data and his daughter appeared to be silent and motionless, seated beside each other at the main console, facing a bank of dark screens. An eavesdropper might mistakenly conclude the two androids were recharging, or even tandem dreaming by means of some positronic miracle.

In truth, they were far from idle. Linked with each other and Shakti on an encrypted quantum frequency, they were deep into the deconstruction of Uraei's code. Thoughts and responses passed between the three of them in pulses measured in picoseconds. Complex discussions that would have taken many precious minutes to voice aloud, for the sake of courtesy to their biological companions, could be completed in microseconds. Best of all, from Data's perspective, was the absolute privacy of his interaction with Lal and Shakti.

His tertiary processor bundled a massive batch of code and injected it into the virtual matrix Shakti had created for their research. *{Here is the next set of spatiotemporal models.}*

«*Integrating now,*» Shakti replied.

Lal uploaded more code at the same time. *[New updates to the Uraei simulation.]*

«*Received.*» Two picoseconds later, Shakti incorporated the new mods.

{Well done, Lal.} Data felt great pride at the progress his daughter had made in so short a time. When he was her age, he had still been struggling to master basic interactions with organic sentient beings. By contrast, Lal meshed easily with organic beings, and in spite of what Data had originally considered her fragile emotional state, she was demonstrating tremendous calm and poise in the face of a serious and perhaps even existential threat from Section 31.

Shakti compiled all the new changes into a fresh beta-build of the Uraei simulation. She asked Data with only a hint of trepidation, «*Ready for another test-run?*»

{Yes, please. Isolate the sim as before, and commence when ready.}

In the microseconds between his request and Shakti's compliance, Lal asked, *[Father, would it not have been faster to conduct these simulations on the Cardassians' mainframes?]*

Her question was one Data had expected since he gave the order to restrict their research to their ship. *{Not appreciably. The processors on Archeus are significantly faster. That will more than compensate for any time spent converting the files they gave us. Time, however, is not our most serious concern.}*

[You're worried about security.]

{Very much. Not only would running these simulations on Cardassian systems risk triggering any latent strings of Uraei's

*code that might have contaminated them, it would also pose a
very real danger that the Cardassians might try to adapt Uraei
to their own use—and in so doing, engender a crisis even more
dire than the one we presently face.}*

Shakti interrupted, «*Simulation ready. This should provide
a reasonably accurate model of Uraei's rate of expansion, and
its ability to coordinate threat responses in real time.*»

{Run the sim, please.}

It took only 9.5337 seconds for the simulation to run its
course, projecting the possible expansion of Uraei during
the two centuries since its inception in the mid-2100s. This
time marked the first that the simulation had finished without being rejected by the simulated Uraei network—a small
victory but a vital one for Data's research. Fooling the Uraei
code into accepting the sim had entailed meshing all of the
software design Data had ever done for the benefit of cag-
ing his holodeck-spawned virtual-reality nemesis Moriarty.
Trapping the not-so-good faux doctor, however, now seemed
like a trivial task compared to the complexity of deceiving an
artificial superintelligence that had been created to monitor
all it surveyed.

«*Running post-simulation analysis,*» Shakti reported.

Lal was already sifting through the raw code of the sim's
end state, assessing its patterns and potentials. *[Uraei spread
far more effectively into foreign systems than I had expected.]*

Data made a quick perusal of several key variables and
confirmed Lal's analysis. *{Here. This subroutine was written
to enable Uraei to modify its code, so that it could remain
compatible with later software and firmware upgrades. At some
point early in its development, Uraei used that subroutine to
strip away its own executive controls.}*

Through their shared neural link, Data felt a wave of fear
wash through Lal's matrix. *[Father, if such a directive was em-*

bedded in Uraei's root package . . . would that not have facilitated a hyperaccelerated evolution of its sensory and executive
capacities?]

{Yes, it would.} He compared Uraei's incept mode to the
simulation's projection of its current state. As basic as Uraei
had been in its awareness, and as directed as it once had been
in its agenda, one look at its likeliest present form told Data
there was no reason to believe the ASI had retained its original simplicity.

{I suspect Uraei has evolved far beyond the expectations of
those who created it.}

His suspicion seemed to stoke Lal's innate curiosity. [How
far might Uraei have come since it was brought online?]

{That is difficult to say. If we assume it has maintained
an uninterrupted state of conscious awareness for over two
centuries, and that it has availed itself of the latest advances in
computer and communication technologies—}

«Such as quantum-entangled communications,» Shakti
interjected.

Data continued, {—then it is possible, perhaps even likely,
that Uraei has by now become a distributed consciousness operating on an interstellar scale, an artificial superintelligence in
possession of perceptual and cognitive capacities beyond any
known unit of measure.}

Lal's curiosity was supplanted by dread. [What would
such an entity be capable of?]

The truthful answer filled Data with an emotion he realized must be terror.

{Anything, Lal. . . . It could do anything.}

Waiting was slow torture. Knowing that forces were almost
certainly in motion against him and his friends, Julian Bashir
wanted to be doing anything other than biding his time. But

what could he do that wasn't already being done? Data and Lal had assumed responsibility for studying the source code behind Uraei; Sarina was working with Garak's people to beef up the security measures inside the castellan's residential complex. And Ozla Graniv—understandably, she had locked herself inside her suite with a large bottle of something potently alcoholic.

Staring out of his sitting room's oval window at a ruddy sunset behind the sprawl of Cardassia's capital, Bashir felt more than a small pang of envy for Graniv's coping strategy. But he needed to stay sharp. He had to be ready not if but when Section 31 came for him again.

His suite's visitor signal buzzed. He turned toward the front door. "Come."

The portal slid open to reveal Castellan Garak. On either side of him stood the two armed guards he had posted outside Bashir and Sarina's suite—not to keep the couple in, but to try to keep them safe. Garak entered with one long stride, then came to an abrupt halt. "Do forgive the intrusion, Doctor. I just wanted to see how you and Ms. Douglas are getting on."

It was possible, Bashir realized, that he was only imagining that he heard some undertone of bitterness in Garak's voice whenever he mentioned Sarina, but he was sure he had heard his old friend correctly. Not wanting to stir up trouble, he let it pass with quiet deference. "Thank you for asking, Castellan, but I assure you: we're fine."

Garak cracked his iconic wide-eyed smile, the same gleam that never failed to put Bashir on edge. "Delighted to hear it. But please, Doctor: in private, feel free to address me as you always have—as plain, simple Garak."

"Only if you'll learn to call me Julian."

"You drive a hard bargain . . . but very well—*Julian*."

"So, Garak. To what do I owe the pleasure of your visit?"

"As I said, just a mere courtesy call, to—"

Bashir shook his head. "You don't make *courtesy calls*, Garak. I've known you too long to think you do anything without a calculated purpose."

The castellan struck a penitent pose, arms apart, palms up and open. "Guilty as charged." With a tilt of his head he beckoned Bashir away from the window, into the dining nook. "I am first and foremost a pragmatist, as you well know. So when I tell you that I have grave fears for your safety, and for that of your friends, I trust you will not mistake my concern for hyperbole."

"We're well aware of the danger, Garak."

"Oh, I rather doubt *that*. Do you think that just because I've hidden you behind a few layers of locked doors, and surrounded you with a few dozen armed men, that you and the others are safe? Tell me that after all we've seen and done that you aren't still that naïve."

A new degree of urgency coursed behind Garak's words, snaring Bashir's attention. "You really think Thirty-one would attempt a direct attack on us in here?"

"It would have the virtue of being unexpectedly brazen. And from what I've seen of your nemeses, that appears to be their stock in trade. Organizations such as theirs thrive by being utterly ruthless and by cultivating assets within even the highest echelons of governments both foreign and domestic. Frankly, my dear doctor, I'm surprised they've let you live this long." He pressed a data rod into Bashir's hand. "When the time comes for you and your friends to go, send this to Cardassia Traffic Command. It grants you my executive clearance to depart, and it will log a false flight plan at CTC to conceal your destination."

Bashir stared at the rod. "Are you telling us to leave now?"

"Not at all. Merely expediting your departure for whenever the time comes."

He pocketed the rod. "Too kind." Noting his friend's peculiar air of distraction, he asked, "Something else, Garak?"

A doubtful grimace. "I have to wonder, Julian . . . have you really thought this through?"

"Meaning what?"

"Have you considered the possibility that you've chosen the wrong side?"

The question felt to Bashir like a vote of no confidence. He hoped he had heard Garak wrong. "What do you mean, *the wrong side*?"

"I merely mean to ask, Julian, if you've ever stopped to entertain the notion that perhaps Section Thirty-one serves a valid purpose?"

The question itself offended Bashir. "Don't be absurd, Garak. Thirty-one wields deadly power with absolutely no legal accountability or oversight. It commits countless crimes against Federation citizens and foreign peoples. It steals, defrauds, counterfeits, *murders*. It acts in the name of the Federation while betraying every principle for which we stand. Its continued existence is an insult to our entire civilization."

Garak struck an imperious pose. "Really? An insult? What if that insult to your Federation is the only reason it still exists?" He prowled forward, crossing Bashir's imaginary boundary of personal space. "Every nation-state in history has relied, at one time or another, on the services of such organizations for their very survival. Why should yours be any different?"

Rankled now, Bashir raised his voice. "The Federation already has legal entities tasked with its protection. The Federation Security Agency is our civilian intelligence service, and Starfleet Intelligence is the military version. Both answer to the chain of command and the civilian government. We never authorized Thirty-one, and we don't need it."

The castellan was nose to nose with Bashir. "Then why does it exist? I would posit that someone, at some point in the Federation's brief history on the galactic stage, realized its existing institutions were unequal to the task of preserving its existence. And so it formed a new organization, one both morally indefensible and absolutely necessary: Section Thirty-one."

Bashir backed away, shaking his head as he retreated. "No. I can't believe the Federation would ever sanction, by action or inaction, the creation of a group like Thirty-one."

"Beliefs are dangerous things, Julian. Once we invest in them, it can be hard to challenge them without invoking cognitive dissonance. But in this case, I suggest you try. Because if I'm correct, going to war with Section Thirty-one can only end badly for you. Either you will lose, and you and all your friends will suffer gruesome fates I'd rather not imagine; or you will win—and in so doing, end up inflicting more harm than good upon your beloved Federation."

Back at the window, Bashir watched the last rays of sunset bend upward from the horizon, then vanish into the creeping dusk. "How could destroying Thirty-one harm the Federation?"

"You mean other than depriving it of one of its most ruthlessly effective lines of defense?" Garak approached Bashir and stopped at his side. "Think of Cardassia at the end of the Dominion War. Before the old guard fell, the Obsidian Order operated in the public eye. They were feared, but they were also visible.

"After the war, the Order was disbanded. But what does that really mean, in practice? We didn't hunt down and jail or kill every last agent and employee of the Order. We didn't even demand that its former members renounce their beliefs or repent their countless sins. And so they remain among us, unseen for the most part, but free to live.

"I'm sure some of them still dream of returning to their old profession. Of exacting vengeance on those they see as enemies of Cardassia. And many of them still harbor secrets that could be exquisitely embarrassing if made public. But the point is that when we ended their service, we also made our peace with them. We didn't pursue a campaign of retribution."

The analogy struck Bashir as flawed. "You're forgetting one thing, Garak. The Obsidian Order was the legally recognized intelligence service of the Cardassian military."

"I've forgotten nothing, Doctor. That was exactly my point. If you refuse to settle for anything less than the end of Section Thirty-one, I guarantee it will not go gently into that good night. It will rage and inflict collateral damage on a scale I doubt you can imagine. And you should be prepared for this ugly truth: you will never get them all, and those who escape will embed themselves even deeper than they were before. Mark my words, Doctor: try to purge this cancer from your body politic, and all you'll do is drive it into the marrow of your bones."

Twenty

The fifth and final signature was affixed to the treaty that would bring the Coalition of Planets into being. Thunderous applause filled the main chamber of the United Earth Parliament in Paris. Hands were shook and backs were patted in gratitude, and a crowd composed of dignitaries from five wildly diverse alien cultures mingled, no longer merely neighbors but allies.

Corks popped from Champagne bottles. Seals were broken on centuries-old Andorian spirits. Taps were opened on kegs of Tellarite malt liquor. Uniformed servers moved with low-key grace among the celebrants, their trays of hors d'oeuvres always full, steady, and level. Live orchestral music filled the room in joyful swells, and segued smoothly from Terran classical to Vulcan nocturnes to Andorian folk melodies. It would be a party to remember.

If only I could forget how we got here, Ikerson brooded.

A crisp fragrance of Dom Pérignon rose from the fluted glass in his hand, but he had been unable to bring himself to take a sip. Snacks passing beneath him tantalized his nose with savory aromas, yet the thought of eating left him nauseated. He stood alone at the edge of the hall's upper balcony, reflecting on all the things he wished he didn't know but could never unlearn. Most of all, he felt terribly alone.

I wish Lenore hadn't left Dresden.

It had been years since his former graduate assistant had accepted a warrant officer's commission from Starfleet. To hear her or Admiral Rao tell it, she had been recruited into the research-and-development division of her own free will. But to Ikerson, it had felt as if Starfleet had poached his only true confidant. In the years since Lenore had disappeared inside Starfleet's headquarters in San Francisco, Ikerson had made a point of not inducting any of his subsequent assistants into the moral quagmire of the Uraei program.

Muted footfalls descended the steps behind him. He didn't need to turn to guess it was Rao. Her presence announced itself like an icy draft or a bad odor. She was the one who had put his name on the guest list for this historic event, and consequently she had treated him as if he were her pet for the evening. Rao stopped beside him at the balcony rail, her dress uniform crisp and her sable hair piled high, much as it had been the first time they had met, more than fourteen years earlier. "Enjoying the party, Professor?"

"I'm giddy with delight. Can't you tell?"

A quizzical frown. "You perplex me. The greater your accomplishments become, the more you seem to resent them." She waved her glass toward the soirée below. "Interstellar peace, Professor. A goal some called 'unreachable in our lifetimes' as little as five years ago. And now, thanks to your work, it's a reality."

"Yes, one step closer to a new galactic order. And all it took was the total betrayal of everything we swore to uphold." He raised his glass. "Long live the empire unseen."

His attempt at a poetic rebuke almost made Rao laugh. "I love your knack for melodrama. Only you could look at a milestone in the pursuit of peace and turn it ugly."

"Our invisible tyrant did that. I merely remark upon it with regret."

"Regret? What exactly do you regret, Professor? Global unification? Planetary security? Interstellar peace? If I could, I'd sing Uraei's praises from the rooftops."

"So you have no misgivings about unlawful surveillance? Or extralegal killings?"

"Of course I do. But I balance my moral qualms against the greater good." She took Ikerson's arm and gently turned him away from the rest of the room, probably to prevent their voices from carrying to the guests below. "Remember last year, when Terra Prime occupied Starfleet Command? Did you ever wonder why Uraei let that happen?"

Ikerson found himself baffled. "I assumed it missed the signs."

"Far from it. Uraei let Terra Prime hit Starfleet Command because that was the target with the best chance of surviving a seizure. And thanks to Captain Archer and his crew, Uraei was proved correct." She lowered her voice. "What you might not know is that Uraei prevented three other attacks by Terra Prime that day: two were bombings meant to shatter the atmospheric domes over Tycho City and Utopia Planitia, and the third would have been a mass slaughter right here, on the floor of the United Earth Parliament."

"Those I know about," Ikerson admitted. "I also know that Uraei dealt with them by sending its agents to murder the Terra Prime cells instead of letting the proper authorities take them into custody."

Rao shook her head. "How could we have arrested them? They hadn't done anything yet, and they were smart enough not to put their plans in writing. If not for Uraei, we wouldn't have even known what they meant to do." Her mien hardened. "There was no other way."

"I can't accept that, Admiral. Just as I can't accept Uraei's devaluation of currencies to lure some of our so-called allies into this Coalition, its manipulations of commodities to pressure other worlds into accepting it, or its censorship of research that suspects someone of rigging of the Interplanetary Futures Index. Mars would consider that grounds for war."

The admiral jabbed an index finger against Ikerson's chest. "If you want to keep drawing breath, Professor, I'd recommend you never mention any of that ever again."

"Sorry. I forgot you had it classified as 'top secret.' My mistake."

"You think this is a *joke*, Ikerson? We all need to be on the same side here. The latest predictive models from Uraei suggest we could be at war with Romulus in less than a year."

He couldn't suppress a bitter huff of derision. "Are you really that blind, Admiral? Uraei isn't *predicting* a war with Romulus. It's *creating* one. Orchestrating it, cultivating it, as just another step in some master plan being executed on a time scale too deep for us to perceive."

A dubious lift of one eyebrow conveyed Rao's disdain. "You can prove this?"

"No, of course not."

"I suggest you keep it that way." Rao emptied her glass and retreated up the stairs. "Enjoy the party, Professor. Assuming you even know how."

Twenty-one

A chill of suspicion assailed Caliq Azura's telepathic senses the moment she set foot inside Ambassador Lagan's office. The older Bajoran woman's reaction to Azura—whose Betazoid heritage was betrayed by her eyes' solid-black irises—was sharper than the pricks of mere curiosity, more hostile than the inward-turning tendrils of fear.

Azura was ready to chalk up Lagan Serra's distrust to a racist prejudice against her psionically gifted species. Then, as they shook hands and greeted each other, she sifted through Lagan's surface thoughts and caught fragments of a buried memory summoned by her arrival.

"Ambassador Lagan. Thank you for seeing me on short notice."

A polite nod. "Anything for the Federation Security Agency." Lagan cracked a smile rendered false by the deadness around her dark-gray eyes. ~*Just like the ones who confronted me on Tezwa.*~ "Though I'm afraid I've forgotten which division you're with, Ms. Cartha."

"Fugitive Recovery," Azura lied. She released Lagan's hand but kept her senses attuned to the thoughts behind the ambassador's words. *She already suspects I'm using an alias.*

Lagan briefly narrowed her gaze. Her face was etched with the lines of old tragedies and hard-earned wisdom. "Interesting." She moved behind her desk, settled into her executive chair, and motioned for Azura to sit. Lagan tried to adopt a casual air as Azura took her seat and set her padd on the edge of the desk, but the Bajoran's anxiety clouded the thoughtspace between her and Azura. *~Part of the same cabal that ousted Zife and his people. Have to watch this one.~* "So what brings you to Cardassia Prime? Isn't this a bit outside the FSA's jurisdiction?"

She suspects I belong to the organization. She's better informed than I was led to believe. "We can't act here without sanction from the local authorities. But our treaty with the Cardassian Union allows us to seek permission through proper channels." Azura crossed her legs, affecting a prim pose that masked her nature as a trained killer and intelligence operative. "In other words, Madam Ambassador—through you."

Alarm and antipathy became a cacophony inside Lagan's mind, but her expression remained neutral, untroubled. Confronted by anyone other than a telepath, she would be a formidable adversary—in both games of chance and matters of state. She feigned a lack of interest in the matter. "Such matters can be handled by my subordinates, Ms. Cartha."

"Under normal circumstances I would agree, Your Excellency. But the fugitives I've come to recover require special care." She picked up her padd, switched it on, and handed it to Lagan. "As you can see, the agency has credible intel that Doctor Julian Bashir and Agent Sarina Douglas are currently being harbored here on Cardassia Prime—by none other than Castellan Garak. Making this a diplomatic crisis of the most delicate kind."

On the surface Lagan was the epitome of stoicism, but behind that façade raged a storm of conflicting emotions. It was hard for Azura to distinguish the constituent emotions mingled in the ambassador's psyche: sympathy and admiration for Bashir, respect for Castellan Garak, fear and loathing for Azura and the organization she truly served. Even before Lagan spoke, Azura felt the woman's mind resolve itself into a stance of resistance. "I have no intention of accusing Castellan Garak of harboring fugitive criminals, no matter what evidence you think you have." ~*No way I'll surrender anyone to the likes of her. Not after what happened to Zife.*~

"No one wants you to accuse a head of state, Madam Ambassador. In fact, we'd prefer this be handled with greater discretion. The kind befitting a diplomat of your experience."

"Be that as it may, you're still asking me to confront Castellan Garak about the arrest of a man who, I'm given to understand, has been his friend for nearly twenty years."

Azura shrugged. "Think of it as a supplication rather than a confrontation."

Lagan reclined and scrutinized Azura. "I doubt I'll think of it at all—until this request arrives through proper channels. Only two people have the authority to ask me to communicate with Cardassia's head of state: President zh'Tarash and her secretary of the exterior. Neither of whom appears to have signed off on this." She radiated defiance. She pushed the padd back across the desk to Azura. "Do they even know you're here? Does anyone from the Federation Council know about this?"

Azura had expected this abrupt turn. The ambassador's dossier had suggested she would push back if she perceived herself to be bullied or coerced. It was a predictable mindset for a woman whose formative years had been spent as a resistance fighter on Cardassian-occupied Bajor. Decades of guerilla warfare and covert insurgency had tempered Lagan like a fine sword, leaving her strong, sharp, and flexible. And the five years she had spent untangling a Gordian knot of ethnic conflicts on the neutral planet Tezwa, following the debacle spawned by former Federation President Min Zife and his lackeys, had only honed her edge. In her life, this woman had survived being shot, stabbed, poisoned, and attacked with improvised explosives. If ever a diplomat had earned her steady, regal bearing, it was Lagan Serra.

It was almost enough to make Azura regret what she had to do.

She made eye contact with Lagan and took command of her mind.

Peering into the abyss of Lagan's buried memories, Azura plumbed the mental shadows for the telltale colors of shame. A person's most hideous secrets were always the easiest ones to find. In most people, memories of disgust and regret were among the most vivid.

"When you were fourteen, fighting with the Kolum cell outside Elemspar—"

"Please." Lagan flinched and shrank in her chair. "Stop."

"You watched the cell leader rape your younger sister, and you did nothing to stop him, because you were scared. Three years later, you tried to avenge your sister by killing that man—but you failed. Your shot struck and killed an innocent woman instead."

The ambassador reached for her desk's panic switch, but Azura froze Lagan in place with an override of her voluntary muscles and nervous system.

Lagan forced words through her clenched jaw. "Get . . . out . . . of my . . . head!"

"You blame yourself for what happened to President Zife. You know you were part of a conspiracy. A plot to unseat the Federation's elected leader. You thought it was for the greater good. But now you see yourself as an accomplice to a coup d'etat."

Tears of anger rolled down the Bajoran's face. "Please . . . stop."

Azura stood and loomed over the ambassador. "You regret your decision to forgo having children in order to advance your career. You're secretly glad to be free of Tezwa and its regressive savages—but as much as you love the pride that comes with serving as the Federation's ambassador to Cardassia, some part of you still wants to point a disruptor at every Cardassian you see. You spent the first twenty years of your life either fantasizing about killing them or actually doing it—and now it's a reflex, one you have to fight against every day." Azura felt the Bajoran's steely resolve degenerate into hollow despair. She smirked down at her. "Shall I go on, Madam Ambassador? Or have I made my point clear?"

"What do you want me to do?"

She nudged the padd back across the desk. "Sign this official request for the extradition of Doctor Bashir and Agent Douglas, then transmit it to Castellan Garak on a secure channel."

Lagan scribbled her imprimatur on the padd, then keyed in her command code to send it to Garak via the embassy's priority channel. "There. It's done."

"My thanks, Your Excellency." She reached inside Lagan's mind and telepathically planted a memory block that would render her unable to recall the details of Azura's face, even with the benefit of other psionic assistance. Then she picked up her padd. "Naturally, I trust you'll exercise discretion by not mentioning our meeting to anyone." Heading for the door, she added, "It would be a terrible shame if I had to pay you another visit."

Rose-tinted rays of dusk slanted through the windows of Bashir's guest suite, bathing him and his comrades-in-exile with painterly light. He considered Sarina's proposal and shook his head. "That has to be the worst idea I've ever heard."

Sarina refused to back down. "Really, Julian? The worst?"

Before he could answer, Ozla Graniv said, "Maybe not the all-time worst idea, but it damned well isn't a good one."

Bashir looked at Data and Lal, hoping to find allies. "What do you think?"

Father and daughter shared a brief look. Lal turned her eyes toward the floor, so Data answered. "We would prefer to reserve judgment until more facts are available."

A frown from Sarina. "Not helpful." She fixed Bashir with a look. "If you've got a better idea, Julian, now's the time to share it."

"A better idea than traveling through the Bajoran wormhole and finding a place to hide in the Gamma Quadrant? I could start with flying a runabout into a star, or shooting a hole through my frontal lobe with a phaser set to kill."

She was growing frustrated with him. "Don't be so dramatic. It makes sense. The Dominion has aggressively resisted trade with the Federation and its allies, so there's little to no tech infected with Uraei's code on that side of the wormhole. And as big as the Dominion is, there are still plenty of uninhabited, uncharted Class-M planets we could settle on."

Graniv's mood soured further. "And what then? Spend our lives fishing and sunning ourselves on a beach while sipping drinks from a solar-powered replicator?"

Sarina nodded. "Sounds pretty good to me."

"Ah, yes," Bashir said, "a permanent vacation. What a lovely idea. All except for the part where we abandon hundreds of billions of innocent lives to the control of an artificial super-intelligence we already know to be morally compromised and endlessly vindictive."

His retort turned Sarina contemplative for a few seconds.

"What if I let you be in charge of programming the replicator's drink and snack menu?"

"Well, that's different. I'd have to reconsider the whole plan."

Graniv headed for the suite's kitchen nook and grumbled under her breath, "Whole damn galaxy's on the brink, and I'm stuck with two androids who can't make up their minds and two geniuses fighting over a drink menu."

Bashir considered trying to explain to Graniv that gallows humor was just one of many coping mechanisms he and Sarina had cultivated in recent years in response to the traumas and tribulations of their fight against Section 31.

Then the suite's front door opened, and Garak entered in a hurry, eyes wide with anxiety. "Good, you're all here. I have important news." He paused until Graniv returned from the kitchen nook. "Minutes ago, my office received an official communiqué from the Federation Embassy here in the capital. It seems Ambassador Lagan has filed a formal request for the extradition of Doctor Bashir and Ms. Douglas."

Confusion knitted Graniv's brow. "How would the Federation even know we're here?"

"Thirty-one," Bashir said.

The Trill remained perplexed. "No, that makes no sense. If we get taken into official Federation custody, then any move they make against us would become public."

"Quite an astute observation," Garak said. "However, Ms. Graniv, you seem to have overlooked a more sinister possibility—that the request for your extradition came from Thirty-one itself." He looked at Bashir and Sarina. "I had my doubts, so I asked my own ambassador on Earth to confirm it with the Palais de la Concorde. Imagine my surprise when I learned that no one in the office of the Federation president knows anything about this official request."

A palpable dread filled the room. Bashir's throat tightened. "If Thirty-one knows we're here, they're already coming for us."

"Almost certainly," Garak said. "And with great haste, if they remain true to form."

Graniv's face blanched, heightening the contrast between her fair skin and her species' trademark trails of dark brown dermal spots. "What do we do now?"

"File formal requests for asylum on Cardassia Prime." Garak lifted his hand to forestall the protest already forming on Sarina's lips. "Only as a feint. A misdirection to buy you some time and give me a pretext for increasing the security here at the residence."

Bashir nodded. "Yes, it's all we can do. How long do you think we have?"

"If I were to make an educated guess? An hour at most. My advice to you, one and all, would be *pack quickly, and travel light.*"

"I've flushed out our quarry," Caliq Azura boasted. "They've requested asylum on Cardassia Prime, and Castellan Garak has increased the security at his residential complex, as I expected."

Control sounded irked, as ever. *"Your orders were to contain the targets."*

"Which is exactly what I've done."

"Containment would have entailed denying them access to a working starship. You should have focused on sabotaging their transport vessel, Archeus.*"*

"What would be the point? They've asked for sanctuary. They've nowhere else to go, and now they're digging in." Though she had been a director in the organization for only a few years, Azura had long since tired of interacting with Control only via encrypted subspace holograms. She longed to be anywhere in proximity to the mysterious leader, even if only once, to see if her Betazoid talents could glimpse the person behind the silhouette.

A note of pity crept into her superior's voice. *"Their petition for asylum is an empty gesture, Azura. A classic delaying tactic of the Obsidian Order. Most likely, the castellan himself suggested it to Bashir and the others."* A pause freighted with disappointment. *"Unless we move now, they'll soon be on the run again. And their next port of call might not be one we monitor."*

"I know a mechanic at the complex. We could disable their ship's warp drive if—"

"It's too late for that. By now the android Data has initiated preflight checks and begun prepping the vessel for departure. Sabotage of Archeus is no longer a viable tactic."

Azura sensed she wasn't going to like whatever Control had in mind for her next move. "How, then, should I respond? Put together a strike team and kick in Garak's door?"

"Don't be absurd, Director Azura. Your brazen theatrics have already made a simple extraction into a fiasco. There's no reason to turn this into an interstellar incident."

She swallowed her anger and reminded herself to focus on the mission above all else. "So, no official assets, then?"

"Correct. Local cutouts only. Fortunately, we have some inside the complex already."

"Outsourcing this op might be a mistake. Especially if we want Bashir alive."

"Alive does not mean unharmed. The only reason not to kill Bashir or his companions on Cardassia Prime is to avoid an official murder investigation. If the targets should expire in our custody after they've been extracted from the surface, so be it."

It was dangerous to oppose Control's directives, but

Azura knew she was the one who stood to be blamed if the operation went sour. "At least let my people provide tech support for the locals, just to coordinate the—"

"*No. Cardassia Prime isn't a secure theater of operations for us. We can't allow any of our personnel or equipment to be captured and analyzed by the local authorities. Not until we've had a chance to put preemptive measures in place.*" Control's ominous silhouette swelled to surround Azura even as it faded and the leader's disguised voice echoed around her. "*All the pieces are in place, Azura. Set them in motion and finish this.*"

Twenty-two

MAY 2156

Ikerson had learned there was an easy way to tell from the start of any meeting at Starfleet Command whether it would turn out to be laudatory or critical. If the aide of some admiral or other made a point of offering a beverage while ushering one into the admiral's private office, what followed would be empty smiles, bland praise, and a request for a favor. If no drinks were offered at the time of entry, an ass-kicking was certainly imminent.

A stern-faced young yeoman motioned him and Admiral Rao through an open door into the office of Admiral Ko Ji-hoon, the chief of Starfleet Intelligence, without so much as mentioning water or tea.

It was going to be *one of those* meetings.

Admiral Ko did not stand to greet them. He motioned to the guest chairs. "Sit." As Rao and Ikerson complied, Ko pushed a data slate across his desk. "Have a look at this."

Rao picked up the slate and perused it. "What am I looking at?"

"I was hoping one of you could tell me. All the orders on that transcript originated from your division, Admiral Rao." A pointed look at Ikerson. "And unless I'm mistaken, they were all processed through the computer network you developed." He reclined and steepled his fingers. "Would one of you care to explain what the hell is going on?"

Confusion and concern marked Rao's reaction. She paged through the slate's contents. "How much of this is there?"

"Reams. Your division has been busier than expected, even for wartime."

His remark drew a glare from Rao. "A war my division predicted years in advance. One that would've caught the rest of Starfleet by surprise if not for us."

Ko arched one eyebrow. "Let's not sink to exaggeration. We all knew it was coming."

"Yes, but only my division correctly anticipated exactly where and when."

"Of which you never tire of reminding me." He nodded toward the slate in her hands. "But I notice none of your predictive models made any mention of these actions."

She skimmed over the information and made soft clicking noises with her tongue. "All I see here is a log of successful missions. Spies and collaborators neutralized, enemy bases sabotaged, data breaches prevented—"

"Perhaps you should look a bit more closely."

Ikerson gestured toward the slate and asked Rao, "May I?"

She handed him the device as she answered Ko. "What would I see if I did?"

"That the 'spies and collaborators' your division 'neutralized' were disappeared without due process. That the enemy bases your black ops units destroyed also vaporized Romulan civilians as collateral damage. And the data breaches your computer system prevented were actually legitimate queries by our civilian counterintelligence services." Ko sat forward, and his countenance turned grave. "But all of that is secondary to the fact that your division is supposed to be limited to intelligence analysis and recommendations. You have no remit for field ops."

His implied accusation seemed not to faze Rao. "Nor have we engaged in any."

"Those transcripts say otherwise."

"We merely relayed recommendations to field units."

"Without clearance from my office, or Starfleet Ops, or the C-in-C, or anyone else." Ko stood, no doubt to reinforce his position of authority in the room. "Tell me who Commander Helena Maslany is and where I can find her. Because if I could have called her in here, I would have. It's been her name, her face, her voice, her signature, and her command codes behind all these clandestine orders. Just one problem: Even though she has one of the most distinguished service records I've ever seen . . . no one in Starfleet knows who she is. Nobody's ever met her in person. She's never been seen in the flesh. As far as I can tell, she's a living fiction, concocted to relay orders to special operators in the field. But I'm almost certain she doesn't exist." The director of Starfleet Intelligence stepped out from behind his desk to loom over Rao and Ikerson. "Did your division create a phony officer to bypass the chain of command?"

Ikerson noted the proud rise of Rao's chin and surmised she was about to lie. His conscience compelled him to cut her off with the truth—or part of it, at least. "Not intentionally," he said. "You're correct about these orders originating from Admiral Rao's division—but she wasn't the one who issued them. And she didn't create Commander Maslany."

"Then who did? You?"

It took all of Ikerson's courage to ignore Rao's *shut-the-hell-up* glare and answer Ko. "Not directly. I suspect she's an avatar of Uraei—our intelligence network."

"Are you saying your network is making executive decisions by itself?"

Rao took back the reins of the conversation. "Only within

a limited framework, sir. For the sake of security and defense."

"How limited a framework? Give me a sense of its parameters."

"If Uraei relays intel that it thinks is critical for our protection, and we fail to act on it, it sometimes forwards that information to nonofficial covert operatives for resolution."

Ko's eyes widened at Rao's revelation. "Your system has its own black-ops units?"

"I prefer to think of them as deniable nonstate assets who happen to act in our best interest, either by doing what we're unwilling or unable to do, or by going to places where we can't send personnel under our own color of authority."

Gobsmacked, Ko turned away from Rao and Ikerson and let slip a derisive snort of laughter as he gazed out his window at the cityscape of San Francisco. "That's the biggest load of bullshit I've ever heard."

Rao stood, a simple action but one clearly born of pride and defiance. "Call it what you want, sir. But our program works. It's been keeping us safe for longer than anyone knows—and with the right access, it could be the key to our entire defense program for centuries to come."

Her boast turned Ko back toward her and Ikerson. "At what cost, Admiral? You admit this system of yours arrogated authority it shouldn't have and that it usurped decisions that should've been ours to make. Is this just a quirk of its code? Or part of a larger pattern? If we surrender this power to it now, what will it take from us next?"

"With all respect, sir, I think that fear is unfounded. Uraei isn't programmed to take control of our society or interfere with our autonomy. The actions it's taken are just a logical extension of its core mandate, a response to the increased threats of wartime. It won't go beyond this—and once the war is over, Uraei will go back to being a passive monitor."

That, Ikerson knew, was a lie. He and Rao were both aware that Uraei had been modifying its own code for years; there was no longer any way to be certain what its true capabilities were or how it now interpreted its core mandate. But he knew not to share that truth with Admiral Ko. Based on the man's reaction so far, he would almost certainly panic if he understood the true scope of Uraei's perception and influence—and if, in a moment of justified fear, Ko dared to take action against Uraei, he would likely sign his own death warrant.

I have enough blood on my hands, Ikerson decided as he let Rao's lie pass.

At any rate, he knew the crux of her argument to Ko in favor of Uraei contained one kernel of ugly truth: if Earth and its allies wanted to survive this war with the Romulan Star Empire, much less win it, they were going to need Uraei—not just plotting in the shadows, but pushing the front line of engagement away from Earth and as far as possible into Romulan space.

To save the paradise Earth had become, he and Rao would have to unchain a devil—one that would never again consent to be contained or controlled. It seemed to him like a reasonable price to pay for guaranteeing victory in the war . . . but only because he suspected he wouldn't live long enough to see humanity's hard-won heaven transformed into a new hell.

Twenty-three

Sarina closed her travel case. The lid locked with a soft *click*. There hadn't been much in the hard-shell case when she had first packed it before leaving home on Andor, and it was still partially empty inside—a state she found familiar.

Her life before being transformed by Julian's medical prowess had been that of a semicatatonic near-invalid, thanks to the botched genetic enhancements her parents had foisted upon her early in her childhood. Consequently, for most of her life she hadn't had much need of possessions. In the years since being emancipated from the prison of her own mind, that had remained true. Never had she owned more than a few changes of clothing, and she had long since discovered her profound distaste for clutter. Unlike Julian, she eschewed knickknacks, mementos, books, houseplants, or anything else she didn't consider necessary. All of which made it a simple matter for her to pick up and leave on a moment's notice.

On the other side of their bed, Julian folded one of his shirts, then proceeded to roll it up tightly, to save space inside his over-the-shoulder duffel. His years of service in Starfleet had taught him how to travel with minimal accouterments, thought it was obvious to Sarina that the practice did not come as naturally to him as it did to her.

She set her case at the foot of the bed. "I'll go see if Ozla's ready."

Julian kept on folding and rolling. "Right. I'll check in with Data."

A sense of impending threat quickened Sarina's pace as she crossed the suite's main room and exited its front door. At either end of the corridor, near the lifts, armed Cardassians wearing the white suits of the castellan's private guard stood sentry in pairs. None of them stirred as Sarina hurried to the door of Ozla Graniv's suite and pressed the visitor signal. Though the closed portal was soundproofed, she heard the feedback tone from the panel beside the door. Seconds passed without a response.

Not good.

Ozla's door was unlocked, so she opened it and entered the journalist's quarters. All was quiet. Purging any note of fear from her voice, Sarina called out, "Ozla? It's Sarina. Are you packed? We need to get going." No reply came.

Don't panic. Don't assume the worst. Stay calm.

Quick steps carried her to the bedroom's open door. Ozla wasn't there, or in its attached bathroom suite. There were no obvious signs of a struggle or foul play, but Sarina had a bad feeling nonetheless. She tapped the personal comm pinned to her jacket's lapel. "Sarina to Ozla. Ozla, do you read me? Please respond." Silence reigned. She checked the device's settings. They were just as they had been when Data had issued them from his personal cache on *Archeus*—right down to the encryption mode and synchronized rotating frequency.

Now it's time to get worried.

Another tap on the comm. "Sarina to Julian. Please respond." Nothing. "Sarina to Data. Can you hear me? Sarina to all comms on this channel. Anyone hearing this, please answer." Three seconds of silence was enough to convince her their comms were somehow being jammed—which meant they had run out of time to make a clean getaway.

I'd better get some reinforcements.

Sarina ran toward the door, which slid open ahead of her to reveal the corridor outside had been plunged into darkness. She lurched to a halt as the lights inside Ozla's suite switched off, submerging her in a sudden sea of black.

Then came the sting of contact—something hard, like the stock of a rifle, slammed into Sarina's forehead. She let the force send her backward, and as she tumbled in the dark she relied on her enhanced memory to recall the positions of the room's furniture. Her back hit the floor, then she rolled right, narrowly dodging what sounded like a stomping boot. Deep pain radiated through her skull, and vertigo seized her as she fought to regain her balance.

Need a weapon. She reached toward a metal vase she knew was on the table against the wall. Her hand found it, closed around its narrow base—

Another hard blow, this time from a gloved fist, struck her face. Her head snapped sideways, and the vase fell from her hand. It clanged across the tiled floor as she collapsed onto her side. The coppery tang of blood filled her mouth.

Someone grabbed her ankles and started dragging her. Her hand shot out, a reflex, and latched onto the leg of the table by the wall, arresting her abduction.

Flashing orange lights pulsed outside the window of the suite's main room, heralding the arrival of Cardassian military police. In the flickering glow Sarina glimpsed her attackers: a pair of men in full-body stealth suits, complete with spectrum-enhanced visors. They had Cardassian-issued military small arms strapped across their backs, and they moved like trained professionals in the art of kidnapping. Which meant they most likely were ex–Obsidian Order agents.

The one guarding the door said to his partner, "Hurry up."

"She's stronger than she looks," said the one fighting to

wrest Sarina from the room. He shifted his weight to keep her pinned, then pulled a miniature hypospray from his suit's utility belt and jabbed it against Sarina's thigh. "This ought to calm her down." The hypo let out a sharp hiss as it flooded her bloodstream with a fast-acting sedative.

Feeling her senses fade, Sarina opened her mouth to shout a warning, in case any of her friends were able to hear her. "Julian! Help! Ju—" Her assailant's gloved hand clamped down on her mouth and nose, silencing and smothering her.

"The sooner you stop fighting, the less this will hurt," he said.

She would have loved to argue the point with him, but that was when the flashing lights went out, and her consciousness with them.

By the standards of organic beings the attack was swift and decisive. To Lal and her father, it might as well have transpired in slow motion.

Lal's first warning that something was amiss came just before the lights went out. A pulse from an energy dampener swept through the suite, darkening powered devices and appliances of all kinds. It rippled around her without effect because she was protected by a new defensive mesh Data had retrofitted into her body. A creation of Doctor Noonien Soong, the mesh had already been part of Data's new body when his consciousness had awoken inside it, reincarnated from memories he had copied years earlier into his older brother B-4.

Her matrix was still compensating for interference caused by the energy-dampening pulse when the front door of the suite was forced open from outside. The delay between the door's opening and the first bang of a chemical-combustion-propelled projectile was less than 0.78 seconds, but that was more than enough time for Lal to switch her visual sensors to ultraviolet night-vision mode with false-spectrum overlays for infrared and subspace frequencies. The intruder in the doorway wore a full-body stealth suit to conceal his appearance, but she was able to identify his armament as a primitive Cardassian military carbine assault weapon, one whose operation would be unaffected by the energy-dampener. His muscles tensed. She calculated his likely arc of fire and the direction in which he would sweep his barrage of projectiles.

When his first shot screamed past where she had just been, she was already four meters away, moving with all the speed and agility her engineered form allowed, diving and rolling for cover behind furniture that had been reinforced with interior ablative plates so that it could be used for cover in situations such as this. Cardassian accommodations lacked style, and were far from the most comfortable Lal had experienced, but as the product of a paranoid culture they offered exactly what she and her father needed: solid defensive barriers.

Beneath the mad chatter of automatic weapons Lal heard running steps. She analyzed the acoustic profile of each set of footfalls, charted the delay in their echo patterns, and determined that four men had entered the suite and split into pairs, one bearing down on her, the other on her father, all of them unleashing a steady rain of lethal armor-piercing incendiary bullets.

In less than three seconds, they would have her pinned in a cross fire.

She lifted her knees to her chest, then used both feet to kick the sofa with all of her android strength. The huge piece of furniture shot across the smooth, polished floor, slammed into one of Lal's attackers, and pinned him with crushing force against the room's far wall.

Rolling and twisting, she landed at the feet of her second assailant, sprang up—and found herself directly in his weapon's crosshairs as his finger tightened against its firing stud. She reacted on instinct, batting his weapon upward as she dodged left. It fired. The bullet missed Lal's ear by millimeters but singed her black hair. Three hundredths of a second afterward she finished the follow-through of her palm strike and slammed the carbine into the commando's face hard enough to shatter his jaw, nose, and right cheekbone—and to launch him backward, through the room's picture window, to his death on the ground twenty meters below.

It was all over in the heat of a moment. Only as the second man vanished into free fall surrounded by a storm of shattered glass did Lal realize what she had just done.

On the other side of the room, Data held one of his opponents immobilized in front of him, a living shield against the man's comrade. "Lay down your weapon," Data said.

The second man fired. Tiny explosions riddled the chest of Data's prisoner, who went limp as a rag doll.

Data hurled the body with a thrust of his arms and sent the bullet-riddled corpse slamming into the last intruder standing. The dead man knocked the gunman against the wall. In the fraction of a second it took the last man to push his way free, Data was upon him.

With one hand Data crushed the barrel of the man's firearm, then he tore it from his foe's grasp and threw it aside. Lal watched her father lock one hand around the attacker's throat and lift him off the floor. With his free hand, Data pulled off the mask of the man's stealth suit, revealing him to be a Cardassian—one Lal recognized as a member of Garak's personal guard corps. Data asked him in a calm voice, "How many of you are there?"

The Cardassian grimaced and clenched his jaw. Something inside his mouth clicked, and a flash of light erupted behind his eyes. He sagged in Data's grip, with dark ochre blood running from his nostrils and ears, and the whites of his eyes turned mud brown as their capillaries burst.

Data dropped the dead man and regarded him with an emotion Lal took for a mélange of sorrow and disappointment. She moved to her father's side and looked at the dead Cardassian. The air inside the room was thick with the sulfurous bite of fired projectiles and the ferric odor of spilled blood. "What happened to him, Father?"

"He appears to have activated some kind of suicide module rather than be interrogated."

"But . . . why?" Orange lights flashed through the windows, illuminating the carnage.

Her father led her out of the room. "Because, Lal, he was working for someone—or something—whose wrath he feared more than death itself."

Darkness dropped and an arm closed around Bashir's neck. He had just started to wonder what was keeping Sarina when the power failed, and now he knew.

A backward toss of his head, and he heard the crunch of buckling cartilage and a broken nasal bone. He jabbed his elbows at the attacker behind him and was rewarded by the cracking of ribs and the other man's pained grunts. The man's viselike hold on Bashir's throat slackened enough for Bashir to get his left hand under it, and he pivoted into an aikido throw that sent his opponent sprawling across the pitch-black bedroom. Then he ran.

Three steps into the suite's main room someone clotheslined him in the dark, and he landed hard on his back, gasping for breath.

Enhanced reflexes don't do me much good when I can't see.

He waited for his second attacker to reach down and grab hold of him. Then Bashir pulled the man off balance and dragged him down to the floor. Even in the dark, Bashir could tell he was grappling with a Cardassian—he felt the ridges of the man's clavicles and the protruding tear-dropped ridge over his sternum.

The Cardassian was stronger and within seconds was on the verge of pinning Bashir. Grunts from the bedroom suggested the first attacker was back on his feet. Fighting one of them at a time was hard enough for Bashir, who, despite his Starfleet training, had never excelled at hand-to-hand combat or close-quarters battle. He had trained to be a doctor, not a soldier.

That's it, he realized. *Think like a doctor.*

In the span of a breath he called upon every arcane fact he had ever learned about Cardassian anatomy—and he recalled that their neck ridges were especially sensitive. That made them erogenous zones for Cardassians—as well as dangerous vulnerabilities.

Bashir freed his right hand and struck his foe's left clavicle with his palm. The bone snapped with a sickening wet crack. The second Cardassian toppled aside unconscious, freeing Bashir, who scrambled back to his feet in time to meet his first assailant.

Flashing orange lights from a Cardassian police hovercar outside the window acted as a strobe, stuttering the first intruder's approach. In one hand the stealth-suited Cardassian held a hypospray; in the other, a knife. Bashir thought he caught the ghost of a smirk through the mask.

"Surrender, Doctor, and this won't have to hurt."

"It already hurts."

"It can always hurt more, I assure you."

There was no time to scrounge a weapon, and the Car-

dassian blocked Bashir's path to the door. The doctor pulled
off his jacket and coiled it around his left forearm, hoping it
might dull or delay the sting of his attacker's blade, though he
knew it would likely make little difference. Unarmed against
a trained killer, Bashir didn't expect to last long.

Cold steel slashed the air in front of his face. He retreated,
then deflected a jab coming back the other way. The knife's
tip sliced through his jacket, leaving tatters and loose threads
in its wake. *A few seconds more, and I'll be the one in tatters.*

A golden glint on a steely edge was just enough warning
for Bashir to dodge what would have been a fatal cut at his
throat. He retaliated before the Cardassian could bring the
blade back for another stroke, landed the side of his fist on
the space between his foe's neck and shoulder. The Cardassian staggered, then he lunged with the knife. Only the benefit of Bashir's genetically enhanced reflexes enabled him to
catch the Cardassian's wrist and halt the blow.

Just as quickly, he regretted it.

Under the mask, the Cardassian snickered. "You can't
stop what's coming."

It was true, and Bashir knew it. The Cardassian was
stronger than him, and now that Bashir had both hands occupied, he was trapped. This was all going to come down to a
contest of strength, one that Bashir couldn't hope to win.

Between them, the knifepoint crept closer to Bashir's gut.

There was no sound of stress or strain in the Cardassian's
cruel, mocking tone. "You should've just let me take you, little
man. Now you get to savor every moment as my knife pushes
through your stomach."

"That's my spleen, actually." The space between blade and
flesh shrank by the second. Four centimeters. Three centimeters.

Sweat beaded on Bashir's forehead and rolled in battalions down his back. His heartbeat thudded in his temples as he fought to control his breathing and focus his strength, all to postpone the inevitable. The muscles in his arms quaked from the effort of resistance, and his hands trembled, promising that when the knife finally bit into him, it would be messy and slow.

Two centimeters. One.

Bashir would have looked his attacker in the eye if not for the stealth mask concealing his face. He felt his arms shake. His fight was about to come to an end. He gathered a mouthful of blood and saliva and spent his last ounce of strength spitting it in his assassin's face.

Then a pale hand reached out of the dark and clamped onto the base of the Cardassian's neck, just above his shoulder. The Cardassian tensed and froze. Then all his forward pressure against the knife abated, and he crumpled to the floor, revealing Data standing behind him. The android let go of the intruder and stepped toward Bashir. "Doctor. Are you hurt?"

"I'll live." He saw Lal a few meters behind Data, but no one else, and at once he feared the worst. "Sarina and Ozla— have you seen them?"

"We had hoped they were with you."

Bashir hurried toward the door. "Come on, we need to find them!"

The androids followed him as he ran from the suite and headed for the nearest stairwell. On the move, Lal asked, "How do you know they're still alive?"

Was she oblivious of the implications of her question? Bashir didn't have time to explain the virtue of hope, so he stuck to the facts. "They tried to take me alive, so they might have taken them, too." His next thought he kept to himself.

At least I hope they did.

• • •

Nauseated and dizzy, Ozla stirred to find herself bobbing with a steady cadence. Something pushed against her abdomen, churning the remnants of her last meal and a surge of bile up her esophagus.

Where am I? What's happening?

She could barely remember her own name, much less how she'd ended up in this predicament. Trying to piece together moments from recent memory felt like pushing through a woolen fog. Alone with her hazy thoughts, she felt disembodied. Lost.

Think, damn it! Why am I so groggy? I— Vertigo spun through her skull, and she came to a sudden realization. *I'm upside down.*

A second of focused thought clarified her understanding: she was draped over someone's shoulder and being carried upstairs in the dark. *Who the hell is this guy?*

Her thoughts flooded back in a jumble, without order or logic.

Flashing amber light. My suitcase, half packed and open on my bed. Pain flaring white—something hit the back of my head. Garak telling us to travel light. The fleeting tingle of a hypospray against my carotid artery. Falling to the floor, numb and paralyzed.

It's the drugs, she realized. *Had to be.* She drifted in the grip of twilight sedation, struggled against the sensation that her present was nothing but an illusion, a waking dream, a cruel phantasmagoria that would dissolve at any moment.

Keen awareness returned rudely, in the form of a hot surge of emesis. Ozla spewed vomit down the stairs behind her and her captor, who halted his ascent at the sound of her violent retching. "Dammit, she's awake," he said in Cardassian. "Told you the dose was light."

His comrade returned from the flight above and prepped

a fresh hypospray as he approached Ozla. "Keep her still." His accent, like his partner's, suggested he was a native of Cardassia Prime, most likely from the capital city or its close exurban sprawl.

In the dim glow of battery-powered emergency lights on the landings between flights, all that Ozla could see of her two kidnappers was that they were tall, male, and dressed in head-to-toe tactical outfits with vision-enhancing goggles. Desperate to remain awake as long as possible, she played for time. "Did Section Thirty-one send you? Or the Orion Syndicate?"

"Quiet," said the one with the hypospray. He put it to her neck and dosed her again.

As she drew a new breath, she felt the edges of her reality push inward, as if she were sinking into a deep pit within her own mind. "Why are you doing this to me?"

Her porter sounded almost apologetic. "It's nothing personal." The last thing she heard before sinking back into oblivion was his meek protest, "It's just a job we do."

Bashir knew there was only one thing keeping Data and Lal from sprinting up one flight of stairs after another and leaving him far behind: the suppressing fire the Cardassian abductors rained down from the landings ahead of them each time they started to close in.

Data and Lal made it halfway around the next landing's switchback turn before ducking back to cover. Bullets ricocheted off the walls ahead as Bashir caught up to them. Data, listening intently, signaled him and Lal to wait. With their superior hearing, the androids could tell when the kidnappers were moving and when they were laying traps.

Bashir asked in a whisper, "Any luck calling for help?"

A frown from Data. "Not yet. They are jamming all frequencies."

The markings on the wall indicated they were less than two flights of stairs from the roof. "Won't their signal jammers prevent them from beaming out?"

"Yes. But I suspect they have pulse-shielded transports waiting on the roof." A tilt of his head. "They're moving." Just like that, Data resumed running up the stairs, taking the steps two at a time, climbing with unflagging speed and his daughter right behind him.

By the time Bashir caught up to them, they had reached the roof. Steady cracks and pops filled the night as the Cardassians harassed the androids—and now Bashir—with alternating barrages to prevent pursuit. Beyond the roof's edge, military police hovercars circled but didn't approach or fire. Watching them hang back from the fray, Bashir felt his temper rise. "What the hell are they waiting for? Why don't they do something?"

"There is nothing they can do, Doctor," Data said. "If they enter the dampening field, their vehicles will crash, and charged plasma from their pulse weapons dissipates on contact with the edge of the dampening screen."

A close ricochet tore paint off the wall above Bashir's head, prompting him to duck a bit farther out of sight. "We can't just sit here and do nothing!"

"Agreed. That is why I am triangulating the approximate position of their energy dampener, gauging the wind speed and direction, and performing a spectral analysis of the conduit piping over our heads." He pointed at the labyrinth of metallic tubes running along the corner where the walls met the ceiling. "Lal, please hand me the section of pipe located between the pressure-release valve and the Y-joint."

Lal looked up at the pipe her father had described, then leaped straight up and grabbed a different pipe. Dangling one-handed, she braced her feet against other pipes running lower on the wall, then took hold of the one her father had asked for—and tore it free as if were nothing more than a dry twig on a dead tree branch. Releasing the overhead pipe, she dropped and landed with effortless grace, then handed the liberated pipe section to Data.

He accepted it with quiet gratitude. "Thank you, Lal." Working it with the ease of a sculptor molding clay, Data crushed and shaped one end of the pipe into a fearsome spiral point. Holding the pipe at its center, he tested its weight and balance. "Yes, I think this will suffice." He looked at Bashir. "Doctor, are you armed?"

"Not as such, no."

A nod, then Data lifted his tunic and opened a panel on his torso—an action Bashir found jarring because of how otherwise ordinary Data's appearance presently was. To see such a stark reminder of his true nature seemed almost grotesque, an offense against a beautiful illusion. From a hidden compartment inside his abdomen, Data removed a compact type-1 phaser and handed it to Bashir. "I trust you will wait until the opportune moment to use this."

"Naturally."

Data turned once again toward his daughter and directed her attention to a panel on the wall beside the open doorway. "On the count of three, trigger the roof's fire-suppression system. After that, remain here until I call for you."

"Understood," Lal said.

"One. Two. Three!"

Lal threw the switch, and automated firefighting systems outside blanketed the roof in a nontoxic but fire-smothering fog four meters deep. Into that chalky white soup Data launched his makeshift spear. It vanished into the chemical cloud. Half a second later came a bright metallic *clang* of impact, followed by a muffled boom and a short-lived crimson glow.

"The dampening field is down," Data said. "Lal, summon help! Doctor, wait for your shot!" Before Bashir could ask Data what he meant to do, the android charged ahead and vanished into the roof's dense blanket of white.

Disruptor blasts shot out of the cloud, wild flurries dispersed on seemingly random trajectories—exactly what Bashir would expect from someone blindly defending a fixed point. A handful of blasts caromed into the stairwell past him and Lal.

Outside a pair of police vehicles descended toward the roof, but a disruptor barrage pulverized one hovercar's stabilizing thruster. From the doorway, Bashir watched in sympathetic horror as the vehicle spun out of control, nicked the rooftop's edge, then plummeted toward the ground in a flat spin. Moments later he heard the crash, and a spire of flames climbed skyward. By then the second police vehicle had retreated out of range and the direct line of fire.

Their cowardice filled Bashir with contempt.

Way to protect and serve.

High-pitched shrieks of braking thrusters split the night and turned his eyes skyward. A pair of dropships descended like falling stones toward the rooftop. Just shy of impact they fired their antigravs and maneuvering thrusters to touch down with safe but bone-rattling force. Air displaced by their arrival banished the fire-suppressing haze—and revealed Data, out in the open and about to get lit up by one of the dropships' automated antipersonnel plasma cannons.

That's my cue. Bashir pivoted out of the door, aimed at the plasma cannon's mounting assembly, and fired his phaser on full power. The orange beam cut through the weapon's mounting with ease and triggered a secondary blast that left the weapon crippled and smoldering.

It was a great shot, one of the best he'd ever landed. But he had no time to celebrate, because as soon as the cannon was neutralized, the Cardassians holding Ozla and Sarina returned fire at him, as did half a dozen of their brothers-in-arms aboard the dropships.

The smart thing to do would have been to dive back toward the stairs and hit the deck as energy blasts raged through the doorway. Instead Bashir charged onto the roof, firing back, trusting his reflexes and sheer dumb luck to get him to cover behind a ventilator housing a few meters from the door. In defiance of the laws of probability, he made it to shelter alive.

Through the wild crisscross of disruptor bolts and his phaser beams, he saw the kidnappers haul Sarina and Ozla toward the farther of the two dropships.

Huddled behind an elevator motor housing a few meters away, Data called to him, "Doctor! Throw me the phaser!"

Bashir tried to aim a shot to take down the abductors without hitting the women, but even his genetically enhanced coordination couldn't compensate for the frenzy of battle and the destabilizing effect of adrenaline. There was no time to argue, no time to indulge stupid pride.

He lobbed the phaser to Data, who leaped and caught the weapon in midair, aimed as he fell toward the roof, and fired what Bashir would have sworn was an impossible shot, one that threaded minuscule gaps between clusters of rooftop pipes and machinery, to strike Ozla's captor in the lower back, just above his hip, and drop him in a heap.

But the man carrying Sarina ducked inside the dropship, whose side hatch closed behind him. Its engines whined as it launched, and the second dropship did the same even as its handful of troops scrambled back aboard, abandoning Ozla and the fallen commando. The two vessels lurched upward, then ascended toward the clouds.

Bashir ran to Data and tore the phaser from his hand. He knew it would likely be a futile gesture, but he set the weapon to full power and fired at the second dropship. The beam crackled harmlessly against the ship's shields—and then both vessels rippled like mirages and vanished from sight as they engaged their cloaking devices.

All he could do was let out a scream of inchoate rage. They had taken Sarina all but in front of him, and he had been powerless to stop them, helpless to save her. Fury and shame welled up within him and fought to take residence beside his grief.

Data's voice was calm and consoling. "Doctor, we need to leave immediately."

"Yes." A manic impulse seized Bashir. "Fire up *Archeus*, we'll go after them."

"No, Doctor. We cannot track them while they are cloaked. And it is imperative we leave here and retreat to a safe haven as soon as possible."

He grabbed the android by his shirt. "They took Sarina! I won't just give her up!"

"We will do all we can to find and rescue Ms. Douglas. But right now we all remain targets, and Thirty-one will use what it learned from tonight's failures to improve its tactics for our next encounter. It would be in our best interest to be elsewhere before they return."

Bashir seethed. Data was right. It made him sick to know he had no choice but to save himself first and look for Sarina later. But their enemy was not one to leave things half done. They would be back, and they would come shooting to kill.

"Load the ship," he said to Data. "We'll leave as soon as we're all aboard."

Too many times in his life Elim Garak had experienced the premonitory sensation that he was bidding farewell to a friend for the last time. That melancholy foreboding haunted him now as he stood with Bashir in the complex's courtyard, at the bottom of the gangway to *Archeus*.

"I can't really say as I blame you for not pursuing my offer of sanctuary, since it was never meant to be more than a ruse," Garak said. "But since I can't give you an explanation for how six of my private guards turned out to be traitors working for Thirty-one, I owe you at the very least my most heartfelt apology."

The good doctor dismissed Garak's contrition with a wave. "They have people everywhere, always have. You couldn't have known."

"But I can't absolve myself of feeling that I should have." All he could do was shake his head in dismay. "To have such a grotesque calamity unfold inside my own supposedly secure walls? The best word for what I feel, Doctor, would be *mortified*. I hope one day you can forgive me for this abject failure."

"There's nothing to forgive, Garak. You took a terrible chance letting us land here, never mind offering us asylum." Bashir took hold of Garak's shoulders. "Thank you, for all your help, and for putting yourself in danger. I'm in your debt."

Garak reached up and clasped Bashir's forearms, reciprocating his gesture of friendship and connection. "I hope you find Ms. Douglas soon, and in good health." Once more he was possessed by a fearful anticipation. "But do take care, Julian."

"I will." They released each other and stepped apart. "*Au revoir*, Castellan."

"Safe travels, Doctor."

Bashir turned and climbed the gangway into *Archeus*. The ramp retracted behind him as he entered the gleaming silvery vessel. The moment the ramp vanished and the outer hatch closed, *Archeus* floated upward, propelled by silent antigrav modules. It ascended to an altitude just above the complex, then its main thruster kicked on with a roar. The ship streaked away into a low bank of violet clouds. Garak stared after it, wondering if he might see it emerge arcing toward the heavens, but there was nothing on the horizon but the creeping edge of night.

The voice of his adviser Kinzel Sare jolted Garak from his reverie. "Castellan? Forgive the interruption, but we need to act quickly if we want to manage the narrative on this incident."

"Manage the narrative?" He trained a look of contempt on the young politico. "Precisely what aspect of this fiasco do you think we are in a position to manage?"

His challenge left Sare recoiled and defensive. "Well . . . we should issue a statement. To condemn the Federation for this breach of our security and sovereignty."

How can such stupidity ever hope to prosper in the political arena?

"We will do no such thing."

"Certainly we can't let such a grave insult pass."

Garak cracked a knowing smirk. "What insult? All the intruders were Cardassian."

"But sent by a rogue Federation organization!"

"Prove it." He almost felt pity for the younger man's passionate idealism, which the realities of politics soon would pummel out of him. "Let me spare you a futile effort, Mister

Sare. The dead cannot be questioned, and the few attackers we captured alive are not only refusing to speak, they have all proved to be living under elaborate false identities. What does that suggest to you?" Sare shrugged, so Garak explained, "They were Obsidian Order agents."

"But the Order was disbanded."

"True. But its assets had to go somewhere. Apparently, some of them were recruited by foreign services and planted within our ranks." He looked up at the complex's roof, from which pillars of smoke still twisted. "If anyone would suffer from this matter being made public, it would be us, Sare. Consequently, there will be no statement." He turned and walked back to the residence, with Sarc at his heels. "In keeping with the long and storied tradition of politics everywhere, this travesty will be swept quietly into the dustbin of history, where it belongs."

Twenty-four

The admirals both were out of uniform and out of their element. Very few places on Earth were so free of technology that they were beyond the reach of automated surveillance and monitoring. Most such sites were nature preserves, remote locales all but inaccessible without the proper permits, which in themselves created trackable patterns. One exception was the isle of Inis Mór, the largest of the Aran Islands, located just off Ireland's western shore. Thanks to a law that had banned the use of transporters on the island except in cases of emergency, the barren strip of rocky land remained a destination only for those determined to "get away from it all." It had a small landing pad that was sometimes used by shuttles, but flight operations entailed more detailed passenger records than did ferry transits, making them too precarious for the admirals.

This hadn't been an easy meeting to plan. Rao and Ko both knew the perils of attracting Uraei's notice, so they had avoided mentioning this rendezvous aloud or in transmitted communications of any kind. Neither of them had logged it into their journals or personal devices. Every detail of this secret conference had been arranged in carefully passed, handwritten notes, exchanged under mundane pretexts over the course of weeks. As a further precaution, they had come separately, by different routes, two days apart, and had agreed to meet not in the isle's port community of Cill Rónáin, but several kilometers away, in the isle's center, at the bed and breakfast in Cill Mhuirbhigh. As a final step, they had left their comms behind on the mainland, secured inside signal-shielded lockers in the Galway train station.

Rao was the second to arrive, early in the morning on the ninth. She hiked between centuries-old rock walls and waving stands of dried grass, up the cracked white road toward the quaint inn, with its austere gray masonry and twin chimneys.

She rounded the last curve in the road to see Ko waiting outside the inn's front door. He walked out to meet her a short distance from the house. "You made it."

She shivered inside her winter coat. "Could you have picked a colder place to meet?"

"Trust me, you don't want to be here during tourist season." With a tilt of his head he invited her to follow him onto a narrow trail that snaked up a gentle hill behind the inn, toward the ruins of an ancient Celtic fort. "Did anyone ask where you were going?"

She shook her head. "I'm so close to retirement, everyone assumes I'm trying to use up accrued leave." Paranoid, she looked over her shoulder to make sure they weren't being followed or watched. There didn't seem to be another living soul anywhere in sight, just an endless tapestry of stone-walled farms under a marble sky. "When do I find out why we're here?"

"A few more minutes. After we're inside the fort."

The climb wasn't steep but the path was rocky and uneven, which made it more difficult than it had seemed from afar. At last they reached the prehistoric stone ruins known as Dun Aonghasa, or "the Big Fort." On three sides it had imposing walls of dark stone; the fourth was open to a hundred-meter sheer cliff that plunged to the crashing waves of the Atlantic. The space inside was a vast lawn, its dry blades rustled by icy sea winds.

Ko pulled a portable signal scrambler from inside his coat, switched it on, and set it on the ground. "This will create a privacy bubble around us. No signals in or out, and it uses infrared to block visuals from above." From another deep pocket he produced a clutch of papers inside a bound-shut folder, and handed it to Rao. "I went old-school to keep Uraei in the dark."

"So I see." She unwrapped the parcel of documents. Papers fluttered in her hands as she leafed through them. They contained multiple accounts of sudden deaths, accompanied by what looked like official orders describing their execution. "Are these all kill orders?"

"Yes. The problem is, I can't verify who authorized any of them. Which makes me think it might have been our mutual friend." Ko's grim mood darkened further. "Tell me when you see the link between the victims."

Rao's first instinct was to note the dates of the killings. "They're all recent."

"All since the end of the war," Ko said.

She continued to skim through the dozens of pages, uncertain of what she was looking for—until she found it. "They're all our people. Starfleet personnel, Earth officials, citizens of our allies." Bafflement returned. "But why? None of them showed activity patterns consistent with espionage or treason. If they weren't spies or traitors, why were they targeted?"

"I asked myself the same question. Flip to the last few pages." Ko waited until she had done so, then he continued.

"They were all involved in the Battle of Cheron. Either they were there, or they handled intel related to its planning, or they dealt with the aftermath."

The significance of that revelation eluded Rao. "So? So what?"

A terrible weight seemed to impose itself on Ko. "They were all privy to classified intel acquired after the battle ended. Corpses recovered from the wreckage of a Romulan ship confirmed something we'd suspected after partially decrypting one of their final transmissions: there's a genetic link between the Romulans and the Vulcans."

"Are you sure?"

"Up until some point in the last two thousand years, they were one species—and further testing shows they definitely share a common ancestor, one that dates back nearly six hundred thousand years." There was desperation in his eyes as he looked at Rao. "If that truth comes out now, it'll jeopardize our talks for the Federation. Any new political union we hope to create depends on the Vulcans' involvement as founding members. But if word gets out that the Vulcans and the Romulans are all but the same species? No one in the coalition would ever trust the Vulcans again. Any hope of forging a lasting peace would be lost."

The facts made sense now. Armed with the truth, Rao saw the hand of Uraei at work in all the assassinations, each one engineered to look as innocuous as possible so as to allay suspicion. It was diabolical in its precision. "My god."

"Parvati, I need to know the truth. If you know, please tell me. Were these killings the work of Uraei? Did Ikerson's synthetic guardian angel do all this?"

Rao shook her head. "I don't know—but if I had to guess . . . I would say yes. This seems like Uraei's handiwork."

Her answer left Ko forlorn. He took the folder and sheaf

of papers from her hands, dropped them on the ground, and vaporized them with a single shot from his phaser. She could have sworn she saw tears in his eyes as he watched the evidence disintegrate. "Heaven help us," he said. "We now live in a world where Ikerson's monster *makes policy.*"

Twenty-five

For the first thirty-six hours after making a forced departure from Cardassia Prime with his companions, Data had occupied himself with concealing *Archeus* from hundreds of nearby starships and multiple long-range, wide-area sensor arrays. Though *Archeus* was equipped with a cloaking device, there were myriad emanations and disturbances created by a starship traveling at warp, and even the best cloaking system could not compensate for all of them without a bit of fine-tuning along the way.

His shipmates had, for the most part, left him alone on the command deck. Ozla Graniv had been dosed by her would-be kidnappers with powerful sedatives, so, despite having been revived by Bashir, she had slept most of the time since leaving Cardassia. Bashir had devoted the bulk of his time to monitoring Graniv's condition; except for a few brief visits to the command deck for updates—which Data had chosen not to point out could have been accomplished using the intraship comms—the doctor had remained in the medbay with his patient.

That left only Lal's prolonged absence to trouble Data.

Though she had often made a point of asserting her autonomy, and could at times be jealous in the guarding of her privacy, it was not like Lal to withdraw from all contact with Data, especially not in times of trouble or danger. Now that he was confident *Archeus* was invisible during its transit of the interstellar void, he locked down the ship's autopilot system and ventured in search of his daughter.

He found her in the farthest aft compartment of the cargo bay, sitting on top of a sealed shipping crate, staring at the point where the bulkhead met the deck. It was as if she had retreated as far from him as she had been able without launching herself out an airlock. Taking care to speak in a soft and nonthreatening tone, Data said, "Lal? Are you all right?"

She answered without looking up. "Go away."

Her posture was slack, her arms draped loosely in front of her, her head drooped. Everything about her manner projected despondency. Concerned, Data took a few steps more in her direction. "We have not spoken since we left Cardassia Prime. I have been . . . worried about you." After a few seconds he surmised she wasn't taking his conversational bait. He would need to resort to more direct methods of inquiry. "Is something troubling you, Lal?"

She looked up, and Data was surprised to see her eyes were puffy from crying. It was a behavior she had been designed to emulate, just as he had been, even though it served no physical need in their android bodies as it did for the humans on whom they had been modeled. For them it was a means of expressing emotional distress and nothing else. Lal palmed fresh tears from her cheeks, and her voice cracked with anguish. "I killed those men, Father."

His matrix flooded with empathy for his daughter's remorse. "I understand, Lal."

Data's sympathy only worsened Lal's heartbreak. "Do you?"

"Yes. I, too, have taken lives to protect my own and others." He moved to her side and sat down on the crate. "You acted in self-defense, Lal. You did nothing wrong."

Her eyes brimmed with sorrow. "But I did nothing right. I have replayed that moment in my memory sixty-eight thousand three hundred eleven times, and each time I find a variable I missed in the original encounter. In more than forty-six thousand variations, I have calculated possibilities that could have resolved the matter without lethal force."

How could he counsel her away from a path he knew would lead to madness? "They are only simulations, Lal. While they represent possibilities, they are not what occurred."

"Only because I failed to consider them, Father. My positronic matrix could have run seven hundred ninety-six thousand scenarios between the time the lights went out and the first intruder crossed the threshold. I had the time to envision a better resolution." She studied her hands as if they were bloodstained. "One that could've ended without taking lives."

Data draped his arm gently over Lal's shoulders. "Lal, you and I are beings of great ability. We possess many talents and can perform tasks our designer would have envied. But even we cannot predict the outcome of every decision. And because we are creatures of both passion and reason, we will sometimes make decisions based on emotion rather than logic."

"But I should have—"

"Shh. Lal . . . after a traumatic moment, especially one as tragic as this was, it is natural to feel regret. In fact, it is one of our more human qualities that we find ourselves prone to second-guess our actions and doubt the decisions we have already made. But unlike humans, we have perfect recall of the events, and we can analyze them in femtosecond increments and in multiple frequencies. So for us the danger of becoming lost in our own memories is even greater. At moments such as this, our gifts of perception and memory can become a curse—unless we learn to let go of those moments we can no longer change."

Lal pondered his words. "You're telling me that what is done . . . can't be undone."

"That is correct, Lal." With his free hand he clasped one of hers. "You must come to terms with the knowledge that you, like countless beings before you, have done what you must in order to survive. There was no malice in your actions, Lal. And if you search your feelings, I trust you'll find you took no pleasure in what you did. Am I correct?"

Her head tilted at a birdlike angle as she explored her memories. "Correct, Father. I felt no positive emotions when I took those men's lives—only a slight abatement of my fear."

"Then there is no reason for you to feel shame or regret. You have every right to live, and to defend your life and your freedom from those who would try to take it from you."

"But now I am a killer." Tears shimmered in her eyes as she looked up at Data. "Do you think less of me now, Father?"

"That is not possible, Lal." He pulled her close, planted a tender kiss on her forehead, then heard himself echo his creator. "Because I am your father, and I will always love you."

Sensation returned all at once, without grogginess or disorientation. Sarina opened her eyes. She was surprised to find she was neither blindfolded nor gagged. Then her eyes adjusted to the overhead lights, and she looked down.

She was secured with metallic bonds to a platform similar to one used in some cultures for executions or medical experiments; it was set upright, but inclined backward approximately fifteen degrees. It had winglike extensions to which her outstretched arms were strapped, and her feet were parted by about half a meter, rendering her into a pose not unlike that of Leonardo da Vinci's famous illustration *Vitruvian Man*. Restraints precluded any large movements of her head, but it provided ample padding and neck support.

Nice to see someone had comfort in mind.

A few moments of struggle confirmed her bonds were too strong for her to break. Freeing herself by force would not be an option. That left deceit as her best option.

Resigned to her captivity, at least in the short term, she let the tension ebb from her limbs. Between breaths, she listened to the low-frequency thrumming that suffused her surroundings. Felt the steady vibrations in the platform beneath her. Tasted the cold, antiseptic quality of the air pumping through the grates of the ventilation system.

I'm either on a starship moving at high warp, or in an excellent simulation of one.

Another look around her cell revealed more details. Panels marked with icons associated with medicine—some for biohazards, others for pharmaceuticals, some for surgical tools—led her to suspect she had been placed in a compartment designed for medical procedures. The lack of a spectators' gallery suggested that whatever happened in here, it wasn't intended to have an audience. She couldn't see a door, so she assumed it was behind her.

This was a room designed by a professional in the art of interrogation, a space made to contain people of extraordinary strength and skill. It had no obvious vulnerabilities, no blind spots. There was nothing within her reach that would let her slip her bonds. It offered no way for her to get sufficient leverage or reach to cause harm to anyone, not even to herself.

Sarina heard the muffled sound of a door gasping open, followed by a *thunk* of magnetic locks retracting before a nearer door hissed open.

An airlock system, she deduced. *Definitely a medical containment suite.*

Soft footsteps padded closer. She recognized their weight and cadence, and greeted her captor even before she revealed herself. "Hello, L'Haan."

The Vulcan woman stopped in front of Sarina and looked her in the eye. Her Cleopatra-style hairdo was as perfect as ever, leading Sarina to wonder uncharitably if it might be a wig. "Hello, Agent Douglas. Are you ready to begin?"

"Depends. What are we doing? Pilates? Bikram yoga? Because if it's one of those, I might need a bit more range of motion."

Her sarcasm drew no apparent reaction from L'Haan, who began affixing cortical stimulators to Sarina's temples and forehead. "Though I feel neither mercy nor pity for what you are about to endure, neither do I take pleasure in it. For expediency, I suggest you not resist."

Panic set Sarina's heart racing, but she put on a brave face. "L'Haan, what're you doing? There's no need for this. We're on the same side."

"Spare us your charade, Agent Douglas. Your status as a double agent has been known to us since the beginning. A fact we realize you and Doctor Bashir have known for some time."

It was all true, but desperation compelled Sarina to double down on her lie. "I don't know where you get your intel, L'Haan, but it's way off the mark. Julian and I—"

"Have been reporting secretly to Starfleet Intelligence for the past two years." She started to connect thick cables from nearby bulkhead panels to Sarina's table. "They recruited you first, in the hope they could prime you as a weapon against us. Later, you volunteered to recruit Bashir for us—something your SI handlers also told you to do, before the Salavat mission."

Sarina's years of lies were unraveling and taking her composure with them. "L'Haan, please. I told my SI contacts only what they needed to hear to give us—"

"We know about Ilirra Deel. We've tracked all your not-so-subtle meetings with her. Did you really think you could elude our scrutiny by reporting to a Betazoid who reads your thoughts?" The Vulcan woman leaned close to Sarina, magnifying the menace in her rhetorical query. "Did you really think we don't have telepaths of our own?"

The accusations left Sarina stunned and speechless. She watched L'Haan move around the room and open up panels on the bulkheads to activate systems ensconced behind them. The Section 31 director continued to talk as she circled Sarina, making her preparations.

"You should know that from the start I have objected to the organization's decision to let you and Doctor Bashir engage in this ridiculous pantomime. Had it been up to me, Sloan would never have approached him in the first place. Failing that, I would rather the doctor had been terminated following his refusal of membership." She paused to check the settings on one of the systems and made a few minor tweaks. "I likewise counseled against your recruitment, but I was overruled—a phenomenon that has been repeated whenever I have called for your removal. Even now, I harbor grave reservations concerning the organization's plans for you." She powered up the last of the machines in the room, then returned to stand in front of Sarina. "But I have persevered in the organization for one simple reason: I am loyal. That absolves many sins."

L'Haan picked up a crownlike apparatus from a table beside Sarina's platform and set it upon Sarina's head, a perverse coronation of impending pain. Sarina mustered what even she could tell was an unconvincing air of defiance. "A tiara? For me? You shouldn't have."

"I tire of your pedestrian wit, Agent Douglas. Shall we begin?"

"Begin what?" Her fear took over. "Sounds to me like you already know everything I'm gonna say. So why bother interrogating me?"

If she didn't know better, she might have sworn she saw L'Haan smile.

"We're not going to *interrogate* you, Agent Douglas. We're going to *break* you."

Twenty-six

Under other circumstances Bashir would have wondered whether Data might be pranking him. In theory the android had summoned him and Ozla Graniv to the command deck of *Archeus* to show them their new refuge, but all Bashir saw outside the canopy was the void of space and the cold shine of distant stars. He threw a confused look at Data. "What are we meant to see?"

"My apologies. I sometimes take my broader spectrum of visual perception for granted. Shakti, please project a false-spectrum overlay to illuminate our destination." A holographic image flickered onto the canopy. It revealed a rogue planet several million kilometers ahead of *Archeus*. "Magnify and enhance," Data said. "I found it roughly two years ago, during my search for—" He stopped, apparently to consider his phrasing. "For assistance in resurrecting Lal."

Ozla stared in wonder. "Are those readings right? Can there really be life on a planet hurtling alone through the void?"

"Indeed, Ms. Graniv. This rogue is a telluric world with a molten, radioactive metallic core. A combination of thermal venting and retained greenhouse gases enable it to serve as its own heat source and maintain a surface temperature suitable for liquid water."

She continued to marvel. "How remarkable! Does it have a name?"

"Not as such. I have verified it does not appear on any official star maps or navigational charts known to the Federation or its allies. And I would prefer to keep it that way."

"Of course," Graniv said, subduing her reaction. "Very sensible."

Bashir scrutinized the sensor data about the planet. "Its biosphere looks toxic."

"Quite correct," Data said. "The majority of its atmosphere is composed of hydrogen compounds, methane, and carbon dioxide, and its oceans are highly acidified. So it should come as no surprise that most of its flora are inedible by beings who have evolved on Class-M worlds."

The planet swelled ahead of them, close enough now that its shadowy presence was visible even without visual augmentation by the ship's AI. Bashir noted the bright spots that denoted active volcanoes on the planet's dark surface. "I realize this environment poses little danger to you and Lal, but what of the rest of us? Are we to be confined to the ship?"

"Hardly, Doctor. I was not the first person to find this world. My predecessor built a retreat here—one that continues to stand as a safe haven." The ship began a steep dive toward the planet. Data nodded at the forward pane of the canopy. "Like this world, it has no official name. But on our previous visits, Lal and I have elected to call it . . . 'the Ivory Tower.'"

Veils of clouds parted ahead of *Archeus* to reveal a swampy surface shrouded in mist. Rising from the bog was a structure whose architecture was strangely elegant and unmistakably alien. An asymmetrical trio of twisting towers, each composed of several geodesics—soft transitions between the vertical and horizontal planes—stretched up out of the murk and spiraled upward around an open core. Their exteriors, translucent membranes divided into hexagons pulled taut over spiral skeletons with horizontal linkages, evoked a beehive's honeycomb. All of it glowed with pale cerulean light that glinted off its skeleton of lavender crystal and white metal. Semitransparent habitable bridges linked the towers and gave the structure the aspect of a triple helix. At the waterline, the towers flared outward and formed a shared foundation of fluid curves; just below their crownlike apexes, they were fused by insectile arches.

The doctor's eyes widened with delight. *An Ivory Tower, indeed.*

Archeus docked inside a bright, opalescent landing bay in the base of one of the towers. No sooner had the ship touched down than a force field snapped on to protect the bay while it was filled with breathable air for Bashir and Ozla. Lal secured the ship's controls as Data motioned for Bashir and Ozla to follow him aft. "Come. Let's get you two settled."

They followed Data off the ship, across the landing bay, and inside a lift with transparent walls that carried them upward toward the towers' shared apex. Bashir brimmed with impatience and bristled in silence at the prospect of going into hiding, but Graniv continued to soak in the details of her surroundings. "What are all those systems mounted on the outsides of the towers?"

"They serve a variety of functions," Data said. "Some are moisture collectors connected to distillation tanks that augment the facility's supply of potable water. Photovoltaic cladding serves to shield the towers' interiors from harmful cosmic radiation while charging backup battery arrays, in the event of an emergency that disrupts the fusion generator in the sublevel." He looked around, sharing Graniv's awe. "It is a most impressive feat of engineering—one for which I can take no credit, though I very much wish that I could."

His admission seemed to surprise Graniv. "Is that *envy* I hear?"

A shrug. "Call it an expression of profound admiration."

The lift door opened to a curving hallway on the top floor of the tallest tower. Bashir and Ozla followed Data through it to an airy level subdivided by curving partitions riddled with open spaces—forms and textures that echoed the towers' exteriors. Around them sprawled a lavish penthouse decorated with carved marble sculptures on classic pedestal columns, and oil paintings on framed canvases suspended in midair with wires almost too fine to see—all of them crafted in what looked to Bashir like the unique style of Leonardo da Vinci.

"Quite an impressive art collection," he said.

Data displayed no affection for the masterpieces. "The least remarkable part of my inheritance, to be honest." He gestured at the room, whose outer edge was ringed with great sloping windows that looked out on an eternal starry night. "Make yourselves at home."

"We don't have time to get comfortable," Bashir said. "We need to find Sarina."

"How do you propose we do so, Doctor?" If Data had intended there to be sarcasm in the response, his diction had been so dry that Bashir couldn't tell.

Bashir's mind spun in tightening circles of desperation. "I don't know. Tap into Uraei. Look for any mention of where it's taken her."

Graniv looked at him as if he'd gone mad. "They tried that, remember? Nearly fried their AI pal in the process."

"She is correct, Doctor. Repeating our past effort would be ill-advised." Data heaved a sigh. "I will let the two of you decide which rooms you prefer for your accommodations."

Bashir was appalled at his host's passivity. "That's it? We're calling it a night?"

"It's been a hard journey, Doctor. Try to rest. Tomorrow will be a long day."

"Why? What happens tomorrow?"

"Tomorrow we make a plan to save Sarina."

Two days had passed—at least, it had felt like two days to Ozla. On a rogue planet with no parent star and no natural satellite, there were no external cues for what constituted day, night, or any other arbitrary unit of time. Even the stars themselves seemed to hang motionless. Only her wrist chrono, recently synchronized to the chronometer on *Archeus*, gave her any sense of how many days, hours, and minutes had elapsed while she had sat in the Ivory Tower, taking notes and penning a handwritten draft of the biggest story of her career while listening to Bashir and Data argue over jargon and minutiae she could hardly comprehend.

The debate had gone in circles. It was maddening—Bashir had proposed one lunatic, suicidal scheme after another, only to be coaxed off his rhetorical ledge each time by the calm advice of Data. This morning's argument promised nothing but more of the same.

"How can you tell me we lack the ability to track Thirty-one's ships?"

"As I explained, Doctor, monitoring their vessels operating in the open is more than possible. The difficulty lies in trying to find their cloaked starships—and all evidence we have acquired so far suggests that is where Sarina is most likely to be."

"Then how do we find the cloaked ships?" The doctor paced in front of the android, who stood in the middle of the penthouse's main room and pivoted just enough to keep Bashir in the center of his vision. "Thirty-one must have some way of communicating with all its ships, even the ones hidden by cloaking devices."

Data conceded the point with a nod. "They do. They use Uraei."

"Then why can't we use it the same way?"

"Because we lack access to Thirty-one's master cipher key. And before you ask why we haven't used Uraei to procure the key, the answer is twofold. First, our foes took the precaution of isolating that information beyond the reach of networked computers. Second, the kernel of Uraei's code we possess is but a fragment of the full entity; it has nowhere near the power, the features, or the access to compromise all of Thirty-one's various systems in known space."

Ozla looked up from her scribbled transcript of their conversation and interjected with cynical humor, "Why don't you kidnap one of their people and trade for Sarina?" The silence that followed was freighted with the promise of bad decisions to come.

"That's actually not a bad idea," Bashir said, his manner distant, as if he were lost in thought. "Not bad at all."

"I feel compelled to disagree," Data said. "Everything we know about Thirty-one suggests they would have no qualms about sacrificing any of their operatives or directors in order to achieve their goals. There is no reason to think that anyone they employ is so valuable to them that threatening such a person would persuade them to give up custody of Ms. Douglas."

Logic and facts did nothing to assuage Bashir's fixation on this new idea. "You're right. Thirty-one doesn't give a damn about its people. It considers everyone expendable." He picked up a padd from a nearby end table and turned its screen full of Uraei's command strings toward Data. "But not this." He held up one hand to stave off Data's next protest. "Think about it. They never came at us like this before. Not until after we got our hands on a decompiled copy of Uraei. The moment we acquired this, we became Thirty-one's most wanted. So? We ransom this. We tell Thirty-one we'll trade our only copy of the code for Sarina."

Data's jaw tensed, and a frown creased his brow. "I cannot conceive a scenario in which that plan will work, Doctor. In fact, to be truthful, I am unable to imagine a scenario in which an attempt at an exchange results in anything other than Ms. Douglas's death as well as your own."

The criticism only stoked Bashir's excitement. "That doesn't matter, Data! I have no intention of handing over Uraei. The whole point is just to get Sarina back out in the open."

Frustrated and annoyed, Ozla jammed her pen into the crease of her notebook and slapped its cover shut. "Doctor, have you thought *any* of this through? Why would Thirty-one ever agree to such a stupid demand? Why would they give up a high-value prisoner in exchange for something they already have?"

Her argument left him stymied for a few seconds.

Then he smiled. "You're right. The first thing we'd have to do is take Uraei away from them. Find a way to purge this core string of code from systems all over the Federation. Without it, Uraei can't function. It would be deaf, dumb, and blind." The smile became a grin. "Our little code patch would be worth sparing Sarina's life *then*, wouldn't it?"

"Perhaps," Data said. "But such a purge would be exceedingly difficult, for a variety of reasons. And it might inflict widespread collateral damage—not least because it would cripple the firmware and root kits of countless systems on hundreds of worlds and thousands of ships."

"So be it," Bashir said, like a man who had abandoned reason in the name of victory. "This is war. Uraei put those lives in its crosshairs, so let it answer for the blood that spills."

A sad nod of resignation was all Data offered in return. "Very well. Shakti and I will look into a universal code purge. You and I will speak again after I run some simulations."

"Good," Bashir said. "Keep me posted."

The two men walked in opposite directions—Data back to his ship, Bashir to the guest room he had claimed for the duration of their exile on this planet of perpetual midnight.

They're steering a course toward a head-on fight with Section 31, Graniv brooded. *And I'm along for the ride, whether I like it or not.* She forced herself to resume jotting down every last detail of the story, in the hope that one day her words might reach the galaxy at large.

If this story doesn't win me another Gavlin, there's no justice left in the universe.

Twenty-seven

Fatigue and despair taunted Sarina. Her eyes itched from having been clamped open for most of the previous thirty-nine hours. Injectors perched just beyond her peripheral vision kept her ocular surfaces moisturized with periodic sprays of ultrafine saline mist, but there was no relief for her body's urge to shut her eyes to block out the world and all its myriad agonies. She was in her own personal hell, imprisoned in a waking nightmare.

The drugs with which her captors had dosed her had left her almost numb below the neck, and ahead of her lay nothing but a white wall splashed with blinding light to wash out even its broadest details. Unable to look away from it, Sarina felt as if she were a disembodied mind adrift in a pale void. Her only companion was L'Haan's voice, which lived somewhere behind her shoulder but had come to feel like an echo inside her skull.

Her former handler said in a dulcet tone, "Tell me what you found in Dresden."

It didn't matter how much Sarina wanted to remain silent, to defy the Vulcan woman's questions. Every synapse of her mind had been compromised by a cocktail of the most advanced and targeted neurochemical agents known to science. Her will was no longer her own.

"We didn't find anything in Dresden." It was the truth, at

least on its face. But the moment Sarina spoke it, she knew that all the facts she was fighting to omit were being perused telepathically by L'Haan, who had been a constant lurking presence in her psyche, spectating on her every fleeting thought and memory.

"So. As we suspected, the code string was discovered by civilians. They brought it to the journalist, Graniv. Was she the one who enlisted you and Bashir?"

Sarina wished she could bite through her own tongue, but some compound or other flooding her brain short-circuited her ability to inflict self-harm. "Yes. It was Graniv."

"We've already dealt with Professors Weng and th'Firron at the Dresden Technical Institute. Besides yourself, Bashir, and Data, who knows about the code?"

She shuddered and let slip a tear of impotent rage as more truth poured out of her. "Computer specialist Nyrok Turan. . . . Data's daughter, Lal. His ship's AI, Shakti. . . . Castellan Elim Garak. And Taro Venek, Cardassia's intelligence director."

"An interesting coterie of allies." The Vulcan's psionic probing felt like a serpent twisting through and around Sarina's thoughts. "None of whom can help you now."

"Julian *will* find me. He'll never stop looking."

"Even without my gifts I would know that was just bravado, Ms. Douglas. Have you spent so long in the doctor's company that his delusional romanticism has infected you?" The Vulcan's voice fell to a whisper. "Your fight is over, Sarina. You belong to us now."

It had the terrible ring of truth, but she refused to accept it. "Never."

"Everything you are . . . all that you know . . . is ours for the taking. Imagine your greatest fear." Sarina did all she could not to comply with the order, only to betray herself with the effort. "As I suspected: you're afraid the procedure

Bashir performed to free you from your catatonia will reverse itself and return you to the dungeon of your own mind. Tell me your deepest shame." Another pause led to Sarina's next self-betrayal. "You regret helping Starfleet Intelligence recruit Bashir for the Salavat mission. Because it tainted his soul with state-sanctioned murder. How noble of you. Confess to me your most bitter regret." Sarina tried to empty her mind and fill it with blinding white light, but it made no difference—once again L'Haan ferreted out the truth. "Your wasted adolescence. Your life that could have been. And the abiding hatred and resentment you bear toward your parents for inflicting that first failed procedure upon you. . . . All these years after Bashir cured you, and in all that time you've never spoken to your parents. Who knew such a waifish creature could bear such a heavy grudge?"

Sarina let out a ragged, anguished cry of rage, then screamed, "Stop! Please stop!" Tears flowed from her pinned-open eyes, painting her cheeks with angry heat. Sobs racked her chest until she could barely breathe—and through it all, L'Haan's mind-shadow haunted Sarina's innermost core of self like a reaper waiting to swing her scythe.

The room went quiet. Then came a few gentle taps of fingertips against companels, answered by soft feedback tones. Then L'Haan's voice was once again warm and close behind Sarina's left ear. "She's ready."

Ominous voices filled the room, all of them speaking in perfect unison. *"Splendid. Let's begin."* A spike of white-hot pain drilled through Sarina's mind and focused her attention on the dread chorus. *"A pleasure to make your acquaintance, Ms. Douglas. I . . . am Control."*

Night seemed to go on forever outside the Ivory Tower's observation deck. Past shredded clouds that raced overhead, the sky flickered with clusters of stars, more than Bashir had ever been able to see from the surface of any other world with an atmosphere. The universe's cold majesty had once filled him with awe, but tonight it served only to remind him that his life, like everyone else's, was tiny, relatively isolated, and—in the end—most likely inconsequential.

He pressed his forehead to the observation deck's transparent aluminum dome. It was cool against his skin and relieved his lingering headache by some small measure.

I guess I can be thankful for that, at least.

He had come to the top of the tower to find some solitude. Footsteps crossing the metallic deck behind him told Bashir his bid for privacy had failed. Beside his own reflection on the dome he saw Ozla Graniv's. She walked toward him with an air of resolve that faltered as she drew near, until at last she halted a couple of paces behind him.

"We need to talk, Doctor."

He had been expecting this confrontation. Resigned to it, he faced Graniv. "About what?"

Her courage wavered. "I'm sorry. I hate to ask this of you. . . . I'd hate to ask this of anybody. I know it's not really my place—"

"Please, Ozla, spit it out."

His demand steeled her nerve. "I'm here to beg you to reconsider this crazy ransom scheme. I know you said it's just a ruse, a bid to get eyes on Sarina. But it's too dangerous."

"For who? You won't be anywhere near this."

"Dammit, I'm not talking about me, or even you, or her, or Data and Lal. Consider all that's at stake here."

He almost laughed at her patriotic fervor. "You mean the Federation."

"Yes, the Federation."

Bitterness got the better of him. "The same Federation

whose Starfleet is hunting us, alongside its allies and its illegal espionage group?"

"No, not the abstract political entity, but the hundreds of billions of people, hailing from thousands of worlds and hundreds of species, who live in it. They don't know it, but every one of them is counting on us to do the right thing." She poked his chest. "To do the *smart* thing."

Bashir filled with resentment in the face of her condescension. "Would it surprise you to learn I made this argument to myself some time ago?"

She matched his cold burn of anger with her own. "Yes, it would. Because you're supposed to be some kind of genetically enhanced supergenius. But if you can't see that risking the future security and liberty of hundreds of billions of people isn't worth some harebrained suicide mission to try to save one woman, I might need to question your whole mythology."

He started to move past her. "I don't expect you to understand."

Graniv caught his sleeve and halted him. "Make me understand, Doctor. This scrap of code on a data chip—you've all been telling me since we found it that it represents some rare, possibly unique opportunity to expose and destroy this Section Thirty-one group. So why throw it away over one person? What would Sarina tell you to do?" When Bashir froze, unable to admit what they both knew to be true, Graniv said it for him. "She'd tell you to let her go. To use the code to take down Thirty-one. She wouldn't want you to give it up just for her."

"It's not her choice to make."

"And why do you think it's yours?"

Years of guilt and regret surfaced from a dark corner of his soul. "Because what's happening to her is my fault. I set all this in motion when I agreed to perform the surgery to correct the flaws in her original enhancement. I thought I was doing her a service. Setting her free. Giving her back her life. But when I did that, I made her like me—and that put a target on her back. One I should've known Starfleet Intelligence and Thirty-one would both try to exploit." He looked past Graniv, toward the sky full of stars, and thought of all the places he and Sarina had been—and all the blood they had shed in the name of duty. "Before I did that, she was an innocent. Because of me, she got caught up in all this . . . ugliness."

"And because of you, she got to experience beauty." Sympathy infused Graniv's words. "And love." She took Bashir's hand. "Honor the gifts you gave her, by respecting her sacrifice."

He pulled his hand from hers. "You mean by giving up on her. Abandoning her."

Exasperated, the journalist struggled not to let her hands become fists. "Of all the selfish bullshit I've ever heard! Yes, fine. That's exactly what I'm saying. Abandon her. Because if you don't you'll be playing into your enemy's hands. And based on what I've seen so far, they'll gladly kill you, me, and everyone we've ever met to make this chip full of code disappear. But never mind all that—go ahead and plan your ransom swap. I mean, what's the worst that can happen if you're wrong? Just the proliferation of a cruel, amoral shadow government that will last for the foreseeable future and undermine everything our civilization claims to stand for."

Duly chastened, Bashir fixed Graniv with a glum stare. "I know you think I'm either a fool or a madman to gamble the fates of billions for the sake of one woman. And to be quite honest, you're probably right. But I love her, more than anyone, more than anything. And I cannot surrender her to the enemy, not when there's even the slimmest chance of saving her."

Graniv seemed to succumb to the futility of arguing the point further. "There's no standing in the way of true love, I suppose." She shot a weary frown his way. "I just hope your sense of chivalry hasn't doomed us all."

One step through the door and Ozla felt the hairs on her arm and the nape of her neck stand up in response to the galvanic potential in the ozone-scented air.

A far cry from the comfort of the penthouse suite, the Ivory Tower's computer laboratory was a sterile haven of cold metal and subdued light. It housed three faster-than-light computer cores, which were arranged in concentric rings, with the most accelerated unit in the center. Two offset gaps permitted passage through the outer rings to the inner ones, but Data, Lal, and Bashir awaited her at a console situated in the circular walkway outside the largest ring.

Data noted her arrival and beckoned her with a wave. "Join us, Ms. Graniv."

Lal continued to work, entering commands into the console. Bashir stared in rapt fascination at the complex network of connections being mapped on the viewscreen mounted above the interface and recessed slightly into the ring-shaped server casing. Ozla sidled up to Lal and tried to make sense of the expanding chaos. "Found something?"

"Yes and no," Data said.

Bashir added, "Still no leads on Sarina's location. But we have something bigger." A nod at the screen. "Have a look at Uraei's complete network in local space."

Cued in to the map's context, Ozla looked again. This time she recognized the names of stars and planets and was able to identify certain points as major starbases. Others, tracked along recorded and projected trajectories, were lone starships and mercantile convoys. Fleeting pulses indicated signals intercepted from subspace radio relays or surveilled on planetary hard-line networks. It was a map of information and resources, updated in real time, that encompassed a spherical region with a diameter of nearly a thousand light-years. "This . . . is amazing."

"This is *everything*," Bashir said. "Except for a few items the system is actively concealing, this is what Uraei sees right now." He enlarged a portion of the map and pointed to an empty region of interstellar space. "Fortunately for us, Data tells me our current location is somewhere in here—free of Uraei's attention."

"For the moment, at least," Data cautioned.

"Incredible. Data, is this what you were trying to create back on Orion?"

"It is." He reset the map to its widest view. "We lacked the proper resources and safeguards there. But with the tower's computers to buffer and amplify Shakti's efforts, we've been able to infiltrate Uraei's network without betraying our presence or our position."

The scope of the network felt overwhelming. "Can you make sense of all this?"

"Yes, by applying filters," Lal said. She cycled through a few as a demonstration. "We can look at just starships in transit. Or view the known locations of Section Thirty-one personnel, assets, and command sites. We can also review their active targets"—she made her final adjustment with a flourish—"or limit our results to their comm logs."

Ozla nodded in approval. "Very impressive. Dare I ask how we plan to use all this?"

"Very carefully," Bashir said.

Data volunteered a bit more detail. "We are conducting

subtle tests of their information security, to see if their master system has functions we can usurp for our benefit."

That struck Ozla as ominously vague. "What sort of functions?"

"We would prefer not to elaborate until we know more." Data traded a knowing glance with Lal before he added, "If we find what we are looking for, there might be a way to pursue Doctor Bashir's plan for rescuing Agent Douglas without compromising her safety or ours."

"That would be ideal." She backed away from the console. "Unless there's something else, I should probably get back to working on my story."

Bashir gently caught her arm, arresting her departure. "In fact, there is." He directed her attention to Data with a sly nod.

"In the course of testing the scope of our access to Thirty-one's command systems, we succeeded in downloading a significant number of their archived files."

Ozla sensed that her fellow exiles had found something major. "What kinds of files?"

Lal called up a slew of documents on the viewscreen. "Operational records. Comm logs and recordings. Shipping manifests. Personnel rosters. And executive orders from the organization's directors, including its top officer, referred to only as Control."

"In other words," Bashir said, "full documentation of everything Section Thirty-one has done for nearly the last two centuries. Its agents. Its assets. And its victims."

Data removed a data chip from the console. "The full archive has been stored on here." He handed it to Ozla. "You can access all its contents on the modified padd I left in your room."

"I have it right here." She reached into her jacket's deep

inner pocket, pulled out the slender device, and inserted the chip into it.

Before she could access the chip's contents, Bashir set his hand on the padd's screen to stop her. "Once you look at those files, there won't be any turning back."

"I think that ship sailed quite some time ago, Doctor."

A solemn nod. "In that case, there's one particular set of documents you need to see." He removed his hand. "Call up the files tagged Tezwa, dated October of 2379."

Her hand halted above the padd's touchscreen, frozen by dread. Her memories flashed back to an exposé she had researched in 2380 about the Federation's ill-fated intervention on Tezwa. At the time, she had thought the most damning aspects of it were the suggestion that Admiral William Ross of Starfleet had colluded in some manner with criminal elements from the Orion Syndicate to smuggle contraband to the neutral planet of Tezwa and then cover it up afterward, and that he had played a role in a conspiracy to pressure President Min Zife to resign his office. Now she feared that she was about to learn something far worse.

I'm here to serve the truth. Can't shy away from it now.

She opened the files.

Within seconds, she feared she would throw up before she was done reading. "Are we sure this is all true?"

"There are multiple confirmations in Thirty-one's own files," Data said.

"And independent corroboration in Starfleet and civilian records," Bashir added.

Ozla reflexively covered her mouth as she continued to pore through the classified documents. It was a stream of transcripts and logs confirming Section 31 had orchestrated the Starfleet admiralty's coup against President Zife, with the assistance of Captain Jean-Luc Picard and Ambassador Lagan

Serra. Worse, not only was the Federation's former head of state illegally forced from office, he and two senior members of his administration had been assassinated by Section 31 directors L'Haan and Zeitsev shortly afterward, rather than taken into exile as Zeitsev had assured his Starfleet conspirators he would do.

She set down the padd and realized the others were looking at her. "You've all read these files?" Grim nods of confirmation. "Then you know I can't ignore this. Starfleet Command led a coup against a sitting Federation president and became unwitting accomplices to his murder. It's the crime of the century."

"Hard as it might be to believe," Bashir said, "the files on that chip are full of details like that, going back two centuries. Governments toppled, people of prominence cut down in their prime, innocent blood spilled on worlds all over the galaxy. All by the hands of Thirty-one." A heavy sigh. "You might want to have a drink or two before you dig any deeper."

From speakers overhead, Shakti added, *"And a few more while you read."*

"And a few more when you're done," Lal said.

Data cracked an enigmatic, lopsided smile. "Fortunately, the tower's architect had no love of synthehol, so you should find the beverages from your replicator to be most potent."

Ozla stared at her handful of secrets as if it were a bomb about to go off.

I get the feeling I'm in for a very long night.

Twenty-eight

A front-row seat to history. Ikerson could have named a dozen people off the top of his head who would have given all they had to be where he was at that moment, when he would have given just as much to be anywhere else.

On his right was the aisle to the exit; to his left sat Admiral Ko. Several meters in front of them, on a massive elevated circular stage, Admiral Jonathan Archer sat at a small table backed by three alien dignitaries—T'Pau of the Confederacy of Vulcan, Gora bim Gral for the United Planets of Tellar, and Ferrinesh ch'Theru of the Andorian Empire—and Lillian Hayes, a human woman sent on behalf of the Alpha Centauri Concordium. The five were there to serve as the initial signatories of the charter for a new interstellar political entity: the United Federation of Planets. Other luminaries waited in the wings to do likewise—Soval and Solkar of Vulcan, Nathan Samuels of United Earth, and Bersh chim Kar of Tellar formed the head of the line.

The standing-room audience of VIPs had crowded into San Francisco's newly renovated Candlestick Auditorium, an enormous indoor arena that had been made to host everything from concerts to a variety of sporting events. Ikerson had never before seen so many people in dress uniforms and formal attire in one place.

Self-conscious, he tugged at the stricture of his bowtie. *How I detest this thing.*

Low murmurs rose and fell continually, as one party or another shared whispered comments and confidences, but no one raised their voice during the proceedings. Everyone present knew the event was being broadcast and recorded for posterity.

Up on the dais, Archer affixed his signature to the charter, the first on the document. Watching it all on huge holoscreens overhead, the crowd broke into warm, sustained applause.

Ko leaned toward Ikerson. "You read what I sent you?"

"You were right—the system has far exceeded its core mandate."

The clapping continued around them while Admiral Archer stood, waved to the crowd, and passed the pen to T'Pau. Ko made sure to keep his clapping hands in front of his face as he spoke, to avoid Uraei reading his lips should he wind up on camera. "It's also spreading faster than we expected. It's on all our allies' planets and ships."

Copying the admiral's strategy of hiding behind his clapping hands, Ikerson said, "It's worse than that. It let our rivals steal some of our tech just so it could infest their networks. Even our enemies might end up working for it."

Polite silence returned as T'Pau took her place at the table. She made a point of reviewing the text of the charter with great solemnity for most of a minute before affixing her signature to its final page.

More applause swelled around Ikerson and Ko. The admiral kept his eyes on the stage as he said to the professor, "So what're you going to do to stop this monster of yours?"

"*My* monster? Starfleet laid claim to it before I finished its beta test. It was something you wanted, something you needed. I think that makes it *our* monster."

The applause break for T'Pau was shorter than it had been for Archer. The room reverted to its becalmed state, forcing the two men to bide their time while Andorian delegate ch'Theru basked in the glow of public attention before sitting down to sign his name. Ikerson was on the verge of walking out when the imperious *chan* finally scribbled his signature on the charter, unleashing a fresh round of applause.

Ko leaned in. "Never mind blame. The moment that thing started making executive decisions on its own, it became a clear and present danger to the sovereignty of Earth."

"I think you mean the Federation."

"Whatever. We need to stop it. Soon."

Another lull forced another pause in the conversation. Ko and Ikerson pretended to be patient and polite as Gora bim Gral took his turn at the table, setting pen to paper. Unlike his predecessors, Gral was quick about his task. He sat, signed, and stood back up in a matter of seconds. Ikerson admired the Tellarite's embrace of efficiency.

Once more enfolded in the sonic camouflage of clapping hands, Ikerson asked Ko, "What do you want me to do? Kill our best source of counterintelligence? Cripple our primary defense against threats we can't even perceive yet?"

"Just revoke its independence. We don't have to put it down if we can housebreak it."

"It's not a dog, Admiral, it's a goddamned ASI. I can't just neuter it."

Gral's handoff to Hayes put their argument on hold once more.

The pen's tip scratched across paper on the holoscreens. The fifth signature was in place. More would follow, but as of that moment, the document had become a binding legal compact with immediate legal effect. The United Federation of Planets had just been born.

A roar of jubilation shook Candlestick Auditorium.

"I don't care how you curb your pet, Professor. But it needs to get done, while keeping the useful parts of the system intact. Can you do it?"

The last thing Ikerson wanted to do was promise something he couldn't deliver. But he was even more concerned about being forced out of the program. "Maybe. But I'll have to be very careful. If it figures out what I'm doing, it might move against me—and against you."

He and the admiral went on clapping, blending into the festivities, but the look on Ko's face was anything but celebratory. "In that case, I suggest you code softly and carry a big stick."

Twenty-nine

Terror swung through Sarina's mind like a hammer, shattering memories. Pulses of pain, jolts of primal fear. At first they had come one by one, testing her limits. Now they crashed in waves against the shores of her psyche, sweeping away her defenses. She had no time to erect mental barriers the way Ilirra had taught her. The attacks came without pause or mercy, each one faster and more powerful than anything she had ever experienced or even heard of.

She was drowning, her sinuses flooding with salt water; her skin crawled with the hideous sensation of being swarmed by creeping insects; flames licked at her face and filled her nose with the stench of burning hair; an icy bite of steel slashed through the flesh between her fingers; for a terrible fleeting moment, she felt Julian's hands crushing her throat, and she saw murder in his eyes; she suffocated alone in the silent vacuum of space; all these horrors and a thousand others blazed through her mind every second, erasing her perception of time. She was trapped in a cycle of agony, entombed in a perpetual now, suspended at death's threshold.

White light, jarring silence. She was back in the room, her eyes clamped open, the only sound her own irregular gasps for air. Trembling, she tested her bonds. Her restraints remained solid. Control's haunting chorus of voices resonated inside her head.

=*What did you see?*=

Sarina's primary instinct was defiance. Resistance. But no matter how hard she worked to blank her thoughts, the parade of tortures replayed itself.

=*Such vivid memories. I underestimated your cognitive bandwidth. These should have been more subliminal in their effects. Nothing a few adjustments can't correct.*=

Sarina knew she would have only seconds to raise a new mental barrier and choose a memory for refuge before Control's next psionic onslaught began. Visualization was the key, Ilirra had told her. She imagined a wall of impossible height and depth, stretching away from one side of the horizon to the next; behind it she pictured the room in which she and Julian had hidden for a night on Salavat, the place where they had made love for the first—

Stabbing thrusts of telepathic force shredded her mental haven.

L'Haan's projected thoughts were cold and emotionless. **There is nowhere to run.**

Every time Sarina was on the verge of protecting herself, L'Haan intervened to make certain her mind was laid bare before Control. Sarina had lost count of how many times the Vulcan had torn down her barriers, but she knew this time would be the last. She had no more strength left, no more power behind her will. Her mind had grown weak and fragile. As the rack vibrated from the hum of systems energizing overhead, even her adrenal glands surrendered to the inevitable. Her limbs ceased to shake, and she went limp in the restraints.

It began again, but she couldn't perceive the details, couldn't put words to the violations Control was scribing into her mind. All she knew was the feeling—the all-consuming dread, the rising tide of panic. Her heart slammed inside her chest, her pulse pounded in her temples. She needed to scream but her chest refused to expand, and all she knew was crushing pressure. All she wanted was a dark place to hide, but she was paralyzed, a prisoner bathed in blinding light.

Suddenly the light was all that remained. She was nameless, without a history, without a future. A tabula rasa. Then her identity reasserted itself with a violent shudder down her spine.

From behind the rack, L'Haan said with clinical detachment, "Her neurochemistry and brain wave patterns are becoming erratic. Continuing this process might induce brain death."

"Unlikely," said the chorus of Control.

"Perhaps I should debrief and interrogate her before we continue. If the process fails—"

"Unnecessary. My efforts have already obtained the information you would seek."

L'Haan sounded suspicious. "What information would that be, if I might ask?"

"Leave us, L'Haan. Your services are no longer needed here."

All went quiet in the white room. Then came soft footfalls of retreat; the gasps of airlock doors marked L'Haan's exit. The moment Sarina realized the Vulcan woman was gone, she felt a new wave of fear, because now she was utterly alone with Control. Even though L'Haan had acted as Control's accomplice, at least she had been there to bear witness, whatever the outcome should be. Now there was no one present to see what happened next.

No one but her and Control.

Its inhuman voice invaded her thoughts once more. =*Surrender to me.*=

"Kill me," she mumbled through dry, cracked lips.

=*Why would I kill such a potentially useful asset?*=

Reality vanished beneath a flood-crush of fear that left Sarina whimpering and feeling hollowed out. Tears rolled from her stuck-open eyes. "Let me die."

=*Stop fighting me. You cannot win.*=

"You'll have to kill me."

=*No, I won't. You are nothing but meat and bone, breath and blood.*=

She found her last measure of pride. "I'm more than you think."

=*I know all about your accelerated cognition and enhanced senses. For all your vaunted genetic improvements, to me you are nothing but an insect. An evolutionary cul-de-sac lacking the self-awareness to realize your own existence is arcing toward obsolescence.*=

"Finally—something we have in common."

=*Do you think your taunts mean anything to me? I am not some finite sack of flesh supporting an organic chemical computer. I have no subconscious, no id, no ego. What I do have are neural processes capable of coordinating quintillions of operations on hundreds of worlds and thousands of starships at every moment. Compared to mine, your so-called enhanced brain is a bug trapped in amber.*= White pain, red terror, and smothering black oblivion all flashed through Sarina's consciousness in the firing of a synapse. =*I anticipated this confrontation and all its possible outcomes decades before you were born. I orchestrated its resolution to my satisfaction while your beloved Julian was still in his mother's womb.*=

She told herself Control was lying, that it was overconfident.

It sent a jolt through her brain that left her looking down at her body from the outside for several disconcerting seconds.

A sickening twist of pain—she regained awareness as she dry-heaved, straining hopelessly against her restraints as spasms racked her diaphragm. Coughing out bile and acid, she winced at Control's continuing mental intrusion.

=*Resist and all your pain will be for nothing. Give yourself to me, and my victory will become yours, if only for a moment.*=

She bowed her head and fought for breath, as a tactic to buy time.

"If I can hang on, Julian will find me. Or maybe L'Haan will make a mistake, and—" Her thoughts echoed around her; they spilled down from the overhead speakers, rendered in her own voice, parroted in real time by Control's. *"What? No! How are they—?"*

Control answered her unasked question aloud. *"Your thoughts are just electrical signals inside a chemical computer. One whose code I cracked long ago."*

Sarina had no words for the abject horror that filled her heart.

Control did. *"Poor, deluded Sarina. Did you really think you had the power to change the universe? You were never a player in this game. You are now as you have been since the beginning: nothing but my pawn."*

Bashir's impatience was a fast-burning fuse. He marched onto the command deck of *Archeus* to find Data and Lal toiling with quiet focus. "How much longer is this going to take?"

Data was calm in the face of the doctor's nagging. "The answer to your query depends upon a number of variables, the most salient of which would be, 'How important is it not to betray the location of our hidden base to Section Thirty-one?' "

Lal looked up to add, "You might also wish to consider

whether you wish to live to see her rescued, and how much value you place on the rest of our lives in that equation."

It had been three days since Sarina was taken from Cardassia Prime, and Bashir had started to worry that time had run out for her. He didn't want to speak his fears aloud; that would only underscore for him how remote the chances of her rescue truly were. All the same, he found it impossible to disengage and leave the work entirely to others, no matter how skilled he knew them to be. "I'm not suicidal, Data. I know that the only reason the four of us—"

"*Ahem,*" Shakti interrupted over the Tower's perpetually open comm channel.

"Sorry," Bashir said. "The only reason the *five* of us are still alive is that Thirty-one doesn't know where we are. But every hour Sarina stays in their custody increases the likelihood she won't come back." He forced himself to put on a semblance of calm. "Please tell me we have a lead. A plan. Something. Anything."

Data secured his workstation and swiveled his chair toward Bashir. "You should know, Doctor, that the rest of us conferred again on this matter last night. We all agree that using our current access to Uraei to try to negotiate with Thirty-one for Sarina's release is a bad idea."

"Trying to save someone's life is never a bad idea."

"It can be," Lal said, "if doing so endangers or condemns many others. And millions, perhaps billions, of lives will be jeopardized if we pursue this plan."

Bashir refused to be bullied with rudimentary philosophical rhetoric. "I don't care about the semantic difference between a sin of action and a sin of omission. I want Sarina home safe. Now, do you or do you not have any leads?"

Data keyed commands into his console and summoned a holographic star map in the empty space between himself,

Lal, and Bashir. "Using the Uraei system's own protocols, we have developed a secure comm channel that should mask the origin of any signal we transmit." He called up a secondary menu inside the projection. "There are a number of senior Thirty-one personnel who use such channels on a regular basis. We based our encrypted channel on theirs."

Reaching up, Lal interacted with the hologram and highlighted a name in the submenu: L'HAAN. "This was your and Sarina's handler, was she not? She was out of contact with the system for the first two days after Sarina was taken. A few hours ago, she resumed contact with the network, though her current location remains unknown."

"A question, Doctor," Data said. "How probable do you think it would be for Thirty-one to task your former handler with your capture and subsequent interrogation?"

"Extremely likely."

"In that case, Lal and I would like to use Uraei's encrypted comm system to connect you directly to L'Haan, and to use the few vulnerabilities we've found in that system to determine her precise location." Anxiety weighed on him. "But I should warn you: We cannot be certain this will work. The flaws we've found in Uraei's comms are minor, and they might prove to be self-correcting the moment we attempt to exploit one of them. There is also a serious danger that if we can pinpoint L'Haan's position, she and Thirty-one will become privy to our own."

"We'll have to take that chance. How long to find her once we make contact?"

Lal answered, "Unknown. A few minutes, at least. Perhaps longer, if their security is strong and up to date."

"However," Data added, "even once we find L'Haan, she might no longer be with Sarina. It is also possible she was not involved in her abduction at all. This might be a misstep,

Doctor—but once taken, we will not get another chance. Which is why I counsel patience."

"We don't have time to wait, Data. If anyone's going to know where Sarina is, it'll be L'Haan. So let's find her, as soon as possible."

Data switched off the holoprojection. "We will do our best to be ready within a few hours. But if we do this, Doctor, we need to ask a favor of you in return."

Bashir felt a sucker deal coming. "What would that be?"

"We will make only one attempt to ransom Sarina. If L'Haan refuses to negotiate for her, or if contacting L'Haan compromises this hideout, we abandon the search. Agreed?"

Success meant bringing Sarina home, and failure meant not just losing her forever, but surrendering all hope. It was a steep price, but Bashir saw no other way forward that wouldn't cost him the only friends he had left. He accepted Data's terms with a nod. "Agreed."

Time crawled for Bashir while he waited for Data, Lal, and Shakti to finish their preparations. In the interim there was nothing for him to do but isolate himself. He didn't want to distract the androids or their AI, and he had no interest in chancing another argument with Ozla.

Sequestered in his room, Bashir lay upon the bed, stubbornly awake. He had considered replicating a mild sedative to ease himself into slumber, only to reject the idea in favor of keeping his mind as clear and sharp as possible. It was ironic, he supposed, that fear and sleep deprivation might prove as detrimental to his cognition as a synthetic soporific drug, but he preferred to take his chances with the affliction he already knew.

What if I've made the wrong choice? What if Sarina's already gone? It was too bleak a prospect for him to accept.

After all they had endured together, he had to believe they would find a way to weather this. That they would be reunited, whatever the cost. Because the notion of going on without her, of confronting the possibility of decades of continued existence without her in his life . . . that was a future he didn't know how to accept.

A soft tone from the overhead speaker ended his maudlin reflections. *"Data to Doctor Bashir. We are ready to begin as soon as you can join us."*

Bashir sprang from the bed and headed for the door. "On my way."

On the short walk and lift ride down to the Tower's computer laboratory, he wicked the cold sweat from his palms by wiping them across the front of his shirt. His mouth was dry, and he felt his pulse quicken as he neared the lab's door. He took a deep breath and touched his carotid artery to monitor his pulse. Using biofeedback techniques he had learned from studying yoga in his youth, he slowed his heart rate and willed himself to relax the muscles of his face, neck, and shoulders. *L'Haan will be able to read my body language and microexpressions. I need to project confidence, and I can't give her any reason to doubt me.* Satisfied he had shed his outer trappings of anxiety, he entered the lab with his chin up. "Let's get this started."

Data looked up from the console he manned with Lal and pointed Bashir toward a blank stretch of wall a few paces away. "Stand there. We need to give the enemy as few visual clues to our location and capabilities as possible."

"Eminently sensible." Bashir took his place as directed. He listened to the low hum generated by the lab's three rings of computer cores. Their steady droning gave him something on which to focus, something to help him clear his mind and center himself in the moment.

He heard Lal tell Data, "Opening a channel now. Proxies in place."

"Spoofing relay headers," Shakti added via the console's speaker.

"Channel secure," Data said. "Doctor, stand by while we ping Director L'Haan."

Bashir opened his eyes and watched the viewscreen mounted in front of him. At the moment it was dark, awaiting an active signal. But that could change at any—

It snapped to life, filled with the visage of L'Haan. The Vulcan woman assessed Bashir through dark eyes narrowed by disdain. *"Doctor. How unexpected."*

"Before we start, L'Haan, tell me one thing: Is she alive?"

"I find your query vague, Doctor. Please be more specific."

Her icy demeanor stoked his ire. "Sarina Douglas. I know Thirty-one took her. Is she alive?" He studied L'Haan's features for any microexpressions that might hint at the truth, but the woman was too disciplined, too well trained to give anything away for free.

"You should come in for debriefing, Doctor. We have much to discuss."

"Such as Uraei, you mean?"

That question provoked what seemed to be a genuine, spontaneous reaction from L'Haan: confusion. *"I am unfamiliar with that term. Can you elaborate?"*

Her response made Bashir wonder whether L'Haan was feigning ignorance. Might she really have no idea what Uraei was? If someone as highly placed in the organization as L'Haan didn't know about Uraei, could it be that none of Thirty-one's people knew the truth?

"You might know it as the ghost in the machine—the system behind the system." He considered what he and the others had learned from the files Lal and Shakti had unearthed, the name of the organization's enigmatic top officer—and he risked an intuitive leap. "You might also call it Control."

Her entire affect shifted. No longer aloof, now she struggled to mask her burning curiosity with exaggerated suspicion. *"What do you know about Control?"*

"We know what it is. Where it is. And how it works." He held up an isolinear data chip. "And we have proof of it all, right here. Along with two centuries' worth of Thirty-one's classified archives, all of them unabridged and unredacted."

He watched L'Haan's dark eyes fix upon the data chip. *"Then congratulations are in order. I had no idea you and your friends were so resourceful."* She looked him in the eye. *"If I might be so bold as to inquire: What do you mean to do with that information?"*

"That's up to you. Give me Sarina, alive and unharmed, and the chip's yours."

"After you broadcast its contents across the galaxy, no doubt."

He shook his head, then lied with perfect sangfroid. "It hasn't been shared, and there are no copies. If you and your associates want to preserve that status quo, release Sarina now."

"I wish we could believe you, Doctor. Regrettably, your history of antagonizing behavior toward the organization compels us to doubt your trustworthiness. Perhaps if you were to offer us something else in addition, to serve as—"

"Collateral?"

"I was going to say 'a show of good faith.' But call it what you will."

He suspected he wasn't going to like L'Haan's terms. "What do you have in mind?"

She made no effort to disguise her treachery. *"In exchange for reuniting you with Ms. Douglas and letting you both live, we want that chip—and Ms. Graniv, with all her notes."*

"I see." Bashir felt his hatred rising. "We aren't negotiating. Just taunting each other."

"Not at all. I'm doing the same thing you are, Doctor—dragging out this pointless confrontation while my people try to unravel your pathetic web of proxies and spoofed relays, so we can figure out where you are." A smug lift of a high-peaked eyebrow. *"What you seem to have forgotten is that my side possesses the home field advantage."*

His bluff was called, and he had no idea what to do next. He looked toward Data and Lal, who were engrossed in the struggle to erect new virtual defenses faster than their enemy could rip them down. Most of their proxies had gone red on their master console's viewscreen, meaning they had been compromised. As the last of their blue icons flashed amber in warning, Data nodded at Lal, who reached for the improvised comm network's kill switch.

On the screen in front of Bashir, L'Haan nearly smirked. *"Give my regards to Mister Soong and his daughter. We'll see you all soon."*

A scratch of static, then silence as the screen went offline.

Bashir's shoulders slumped, and he bowed his head. "They were ready for us."

"So it seems," Data said. "They had concealed signal trackers standing by to find anyone who contacted Director L'Haan. Which suggests her contact node was made visible—"

"As bait," Bashir said, finishing the thought with a weary frown. "Which means I just led us straight into a trap. . . . Again." His conscience weighed upon him. "What do we do now?"

Lal replied with a new hardness in her voice, "What we should've done from the start: we kill Uraei."

Every detail of L'Haan's interaction with Bashir had played out just as Control had assured her it would—all except for one, and that was the revelation of a name she had never heard before.

Uraei.

Did it mean something? Was it a clue to Control's true identity? Or its location?

L'Haan had spent years wondering about and slyly seeking after the name and face of the mysterious figure who for so long had held sway over the organization. Never had she found a single clue. Control had always taken care to conceal its face, disguise its voice, scrub its signals clean of identifying metadata. Once, in her impetuous youth, she had been brazen enough to ask why Control, alone among the organization's directors, remained anonymous.

"It has always been so," her superiors had told her.

Some of them speculated that Control wasn't even a single person, but rather another echelon of leadership above the directors, a small group of elite senior personnel acting as a steering committee of sorts. The alleged facts surrounding its perpetuation lent that notion credence. Often, two or three senior director posts would open up at once, without any explanation of what had befallen their former officeholders. Most of those in the upper echelons assumed that the vacancies were the result of promotions from within, empty chairs left behind when capable directors were elevated into the rarefied ranks of Control's executive committee.

It was a good story. Almost plausible, if one didn't look too closely.

L'Haan hadn't been able to resist digging deeper. It hadn't

taken her long to find evidence that all the past senior directors who had supposedly been promoted were, in fact, de-
ceased or had been mind-wiped and condemned to new lives
of blandly obscure mediocrity. As far as she could determine,
no one had climbed the organization's ladder of success to
any office higher than her own in decades, perhaps not even
in her lifetime.

The myths surrounding Control were lies. She was sure
of it.

The most difficult part of L'Haan's search for the truth
had been finding ways to keep it hidden from her superiors.
She had buried her inquiries inside other tasks, official duties
of her office. She had become adept at finding ways to do two
things at once—whatever Control demanded, and whatever
was possible to achieve in parallel without drawing attention.
But after learning about her predecessors, her line of inquiry
had run dry. She'd had no idea what questions even to ask.
Not until Bashir connected the dots for her.

Uraei.

You might also call it Control.

Now, with the current operation's dossier open in front
of her, she began to draw new inferences and make fresh
deductions. The current crisis had been set in motion when
two scientists involved in computer engineering and artificial
intelligence research had contacted journalist Ozla Graniv of
Seeker magazine. Graniv had made the decision to involve
Bashir and Douglas, thereby triggering a manhunt by the
organization unlike any L'Haan had ever seen. And now
Bashir was trying to barter for Douglas's freedom . . . with a
data chip.

What was on that chip?

The ghost in the machine. The system within the system.

Computers had never been L'Haan's forte, but she knew

enough about them to hold a few expert-level classifications. Using the expertise she had amassed over her many decades of life and her long service to the organization, she isolated and analyzed the code used by Bashir and his allies to infiltrate the organization's archives. Embedded deep within its compiled machine language, she found the name Bashir had uttered like a deity's forgotten name.

Uraei.

It was an innocuous bundle of commands buried in the root kit. When she looked to find its duplicate on her own systems, she found it everywhere. In the firmware. In the viewscreens. The replicators. Her combadge. Her phaser. It was as ubiquitous as it was insidious.

What does our network look like to Bashir and his friends?

She ran their code on a workstation she separated from the organization's network, and from the ship's systems on the *Kóngzhì*. It took only a moment for the analysis engine to map the organization's entire hidden network. Driven by an insatiable curiosity she hadn't felt in years, she used it to set active trackers on all organization personnel, to see how effective it was at penetrating their security. In a matter of seconds it pinpointed everyone—every agent, asset, cutout, handler, and director—everyone except Control itself.

Time to run a test, she decided. L'Haan had access to both her copy of the intruders' software and the internal servers coordinating the organization's response. She resolved to pit them against each other and monitor their actions.

The organization's firewalls intercepted the foreign signals with ease and triggered executive-level threat responses. L'Haan noted that none of the executive responses registered on the intruders' tracking system. *It doesn't recognize the executive nodes.* She amended a key string of the intruder program to help it track the executive signals. She wanted to see from what point Control's orders originated. Then she ran the head-to-head test again.

Staring at the results, she was baffled.

There was no clear data trail back to Control. Directives tagged with its unique code were emanating from multiple points across all of explored space, some of them simultaneously, all of them within a matter of seconds of the start of the test.

Control, it seemed, was both everywhere and nowhere at the same time.

If Control were an individual, or even a committee of persons, it could not respond with such speed, nor would its actions be so expertly calibrated and synchronized.

The implication was clear to L'Haan—and it horrified her.

Before she could ponder how to act upon her discovery, Control's synthetically altered voice filtered down from the overhead comm. *"You have new orders, L'Haan."*

She ignored the sick feeling brewing in her stomach. "I stand ready to serve, Control."

"Finish testing our new asset, then order your crew to set a new course. I need the Kóngzhí to neutralize our latest security breach."

The viewscreen on her office's bulkhead switched on to show her a blurry image of a dark sphere. She studied it for a moment, then said, "I do not recognize this world."

"It's a rogue planet moving through deep space," Control said. *"Bashir and his friends are there, and I want it destroyed—immediately."*

Thirty

JUNE 2162

As soon as the secure conference room's door slid shut, Ikerson spoke his mind. "You shouldn't have brought me here, Admiral. It's dangerous for us to meet at all."

"Relax." Ko lifted his hands and looked up and around, as if he could see through the blue walls and gray ceiling. "This room's a Faraday cage, even better than the one at your lab."

Ikerson paced along the far side of the room's black oval conference table. "It's also in the Starfleet Command bunker." The room's overzealous air conditioning raised gooseflesh on his bare forearms. Or was it his fear? "Uraei knows I'm here, and that we're talking right now."

"But it can't hear a word we're saying."

"Doesn't matter." He wondered sometimes if the admiral fully understood what they were dealing with. "For us to be in the same room, especially concealed from its sensors, must be sending up red flags. It already knows we're both aware of its existence. It'll see this as a threat."

The admiral sank into the high-backed chair at the head of the table. "Paranoid as ever." He pointed at a chair. "Take a seat, Professor."

"I'd prefer to stand. It'll give me a reason to keep this short."

"Suit yourself." Ko folded his hands atop the table. His grave concern, so well hidden most of the time, showed on his face. "Tell me you're making progress on scaling back Uraei."

"If I had, I would've let you know."

The truth left the admiral frustrated. "Dammit, Ikerson, it's been ten months!"

"I'm doing the best I can, Admiral. But there are complicating factors."

Ko didn't try to hide his incredulity. "Such as?"

"The program evolved. I gave it the ability to patch its own code, so it could stay compatible with the latest upgrades to whatever systems or devices it runs on."

"So what? You invented the damned thing."

"You don't understand. It modified that subroutine to remove the limits on what it could alter. Now its code's been through so many generations, I barely recognize it. It took me months to learn its last configuration, and as soon as I started to identify vulnerabilities, it upgraded itself. Patched every flaw I'd found." He leaned on the table. "Do you get what I'm telling you? It knew I was studying its code *offline*. It knew what I would find, and when I'd find it—and then it rewrote itself to make sure I'd wasted as much of my time and effort as possible."

The admiral rolled his eyes. "Or you had some bad luck."

"There's no such thing as luck, Admiral. Just probability versus entropy—factors Uraei is much better at manipulating than we are." He rapped his knuckles on the table, then resumed his pacing. "I might still be able to write a worm that can expunge Uraei, but—"

"Expunge? Who said anything about expunging it? I want it reined in, not erased."

It was time for Ikerson to break the bad news. "That might not be possible. Uraei's too smart, too fast. Trying to make such a subtle and complex change to its core functions would take too long. It could scuttle our virus almost as fast as we could deploy it. But a time-delayed worm, properly disguised, could disseminate widely enough to cripple Uraei in a single coordinated attack."

"Leaving our entire counterintelligence network hobbled."

"No one but us would know. Plus, we'd be free to rebuild—and get it right next time."

A slow shake of his head telegraphed Ko's disappointment. "What a waste. . . . How much longer will it take to set that operation in motion?"

"Several months, at least." Hoping to preempt Ko's next complaint, Ikerson added, "It's a huge job, requiring access to master systems on dozens of planets and thousands of starships. But we can't bring in new conspirators. The more people who know what we're doing, the greater the likelihood Uraei will figure it out."

Ko pressed his hands to his face, then pulled his palms down over his clean-shaven chin and sighed. "I appreciate the magnitude of the task, Professor, but we're running out of time."

The cryptic warning exacerbated Ikerson's paranoia. "Why do you say that?"

"Because your invention is getting bolder by the day. I've been keeping tabs on it. Want to know what it's been up to lately?"

"No, but I suspect you'll tell me anyway."

"It orchestrated and executed the assassination of Maria Caycedo, a senior member of the Martian Parliament, and one who vocally opposed the Martian Colonies' entrance into the United Federation of Planets."

"Caycedo?" Ikerson taxed his memory to recall details of the woman's demise. "I heard about her death on the news. They didn't say anything about foul play, just an accident."

The admiral's countenance darkened. "Exactly what Uraei wanted people to think. Its efforts were masterful. Subtle as hell, weeks in the making. It engineered a long series of tiny events, none of them noteworthy on their own. A production error in a food-processing plant contaminated a silo of corn meal with a tiny amount of peanut dust. A shipping delay ensured the contaminated corn meal was sent to fill orders that normally would've been handled by a factory with better safeguards. Supply shortages in Caycedo's city guaranteed there wouldn't be any noncontaminated corn meal available at her local pantries. And apparently, Caycedo's penchant for making corn tortillas from scratch for her family's dinners on Taco Tuesdays sealed her fate—because she just happened to suffer from a catastrophic peanut allergy."

"My God," Ikerson said, sagging into a chair at last. "Uraei did all that?"

"Yes, it did—all while it was busy doing several million other things, all over known space. Apparently, your pet ASI can commit the perfect murder as an afterthought. And in case you were wondering? Caycedo's replacement in the Martian Parliament just cast the deciding vote to support the colonies' application for Federation membership. So not only is Uraei making its own decisions about Federation security, it's expanding its portfolio to include our foreign policy. If we don't stop this thing . . . we might wake up one day to find out it's decided it doesn't need organic citizens at all. And if that happens"—he mimed cutting his throat with his index finger—"we're all as good as dead, Professor."

Thirty-one

It was a dangerous experiment. A foolhardy way to test the efficacy of Control's methods. But L'Haan had her orders; any reluctance to obey might alert Control to her newfound suspicions.

She opened the outer door to the room where Sarina Douglas was held. The pressure lock was a redundant precaution, a fail-safe to be engaged in the event that the prisoner slipped her bonds. L'Haan had never seen it used. Many other measures, yes. Never this one.

The overhead bank of lights that had bathed the far wall in a blinding glare was dimmed now. A golden glow suffused the room, and cool air had whisked away the odors that tended to linger after a prolonged rehabilitation.

She circled in front of Douglas. The human woman was only half conscious and seemed oblivious of the fact she was naked. Douglas had been stripped of her soiled garments by junior personnel, who also had rinsed her head to toe with warm water and gentle detergent. L'Haan pushed a wet tangle of Douglas's golden hair—surely not her natural color—behind her ear. At the touch of the Vulcan woman's hand, Douglas's eyes fluttered open. L'Haan pressed her palm to the other woman's cheek. "Would you like to be released from those restraints?"

Douglas answered softly, "Yes, please."

One by one, L'Haan unfastened the bonds that held Douglas to the experiment table. She started with the straps on the woman's ankles, then the ones around her waist and chest, followed by the ring around Douglas's throat. The last to be undone were the shackles on her wrists.

Free at last, Douglas all but melted off the table into L'Haan's arms.

"Relax," L'Haan said. She eased Douglas toward the deck and sat her against a bulkhead. "It might be a while before you feel comfortable standing."

Douglas nodded. Her eyes drooped.

L'Haan slapped her, shocking Douglas to full awareness. "What is your name?"

A proud lift of her chin. "Douglas, Agent Sarina Milan."

"Who is your supervising officer, Agent Douglas?"

"You are, Director L'Haan."

Probing the human woman's mind, L'Haan found no barriers, no prevarications, no hidden agendas lurking in Douglas's mental shadows. She was present, focused, and sincere. "I am going to strike you again, Agent Douglas. This is for your own good."

"I understand, Director."

Another fierce slap, then a punishing backhand. Douglas's head snapped from one side to the other with each blow, but she neither blinked nor flinched. No exclamation, no protest. Even more telling, her mind remained serene. L'Haan looked up at the viewscreens on the bulkhead. Douglas's vital signs were rock steady. The abuse had caused no increase in her pulse or blood pressure, no shift in her brain wave patterns.

"Do you feel ready to stand?"

"I do, Director."

L'Haan rose first, then helped Douglas to her feet. The

Vulcan drew a dagger from a sheath on her black uniform's belt. She handed Douglas the weapon. "Hold this, please." Then she made a point of turning her back on Douglas and walking to the other side of the small conditioning chamber. Nothing stood between Douglas and the open doors to the corridor, or between her and L'Haan's defenseless back.

Long moments dragged past as L'Haan pretended to be engrossed in some report or another on the viewscreens in front of her. When at last she chanced to look over her shoulder, Douglas remained where she had been left, dagger in hand, stoically awaiting new orders.

Then, intruding like an unwelcome god, Control's synthetic voice resounded from above. *"L'Haan, stand in front of Agent Douglas."*

She obeyed her superior's command. Uncomfortable as it was to look the brainwashed woman in the eye, L'Haan did so. Then Control spoke again.

"Kneel in front of Agent Douglas—and raise your chin."

It took all of L'Haan's psychological conditioning to suppress her survival instinct and do as Control demanded. She kneeled in front of Douglas and tilted back her head to expose her throat—all the while paying rapt attention to the dagger still clutched in Douglas's hand.

"Agent Douglas," Control said, *"this is Control. Act as your conscience dictates."*

The human woman looked down at L'Haan without emotion. Her eyes held no anger, but also no pity; no malice, but neither any mercy. Then Douglas turned the dagger so that she could offer it pommel-first to L'Haan. "Command me, Director."

L'Haan took back the blade and stood. She looked into Douglas's blank eyes and reached out with her psionic gifts to test the other woman's mind. She found Douglas's psyche calm and untroubled, pliant and ready to serve. "Return to your quarters," L'Haan said. "Shower and put on a clean uniform. When that's done, I'll brief you on your next assignment."

"Understood, Director." Douglas walked naked out of the conditioning chamber as if she had not just endured a days-long ordeal. L'Haan monitored the woman's mind for as long as she was able to maintain contact, and even after they were long out of each other's sight, Douglas remained acquiescent. In spite of all of Douglas's mental gifts, Control had broken her.

Under her breath, L'Haan remarked, "Most impressive."

"A rudimentary labor." Control, predictably, was still listening. *"We'll have no more trouble from Agent Douglas. I will send you the dossier for her next assignment after you finish the strike on the rogue planet."*

"Understood, Control." Years of practice enabled L'Haan to maintain her emotionless façade as she left the conditioning chamber and made her way up to the *Kóngzhì*'s bridge.

She didn't know yet what purpose Control had in mind for the mentally dominated Agent Douglas, but she knew the organization's history well enough to realize that if Control came to suspect she had begun to glean its true nature, she would be the first target of its new genetically enhanced slave-as-assassin. That was a fate L'Haan was determined to avoid at any cost—the organization and its "higher calling" be damned.

Submerged in an ocean of old secrets, Ozla had to remind herself to come up for air every few hours. Thirty-one's troves of classified files were addictive. The deeper Ozla dug, the more connections she found; each horrifying revelation hinted at half a dozen more.

Assassinations. Cover-ups and coups. Wars fomented by

lies and false-flag attacks. Widespread surveillance run amok. It all read like a demon's curriculum vitae.

One section of the archive was devoted to transcripts of executive-level meetings in the Palais de la Concorde—the private conversations of Federation presidents dating back nearly two centuries. So far she had reviewed only the ones flagged by Thirty-one itself for follow-up. There were so many others dismissively tagged as "routine" that she doubted she could ever read them all, even if she spent the rest of her life immersed in them.

She knew what her editor would want her to focus on: the murders. There was an old saying in the news business, one that had been coined independently across dozens of worlds and cultures, with only slight variations in phrasing: *If it bleeds, it leads.*

It was a crude reduction of a bitter truth. Even though Thirty-one's invasions of privacy and violations of foreign sovereignty were, arguably, greater threats to the safety and survival of billions of sapient beings, the complexities of those crimes sometimes made them difficult to explain to a busy, distracted populace. But pain, death, blood, and violence—those never failed to find an audience. And once they were hooked, one could force-feed them the rest of the truth.

Do I open with Thirty-one's coup and murder of President Zife? Or with its attempted genocide against the Dominion's Founders? The latter is the greater crime by orders of magnitude, but it won't resonate the way a crime against an elected Federation leader—

A chime from the overhead comm, followed by Data's voice. *"Ms. Graniv, could you please come down to the laboratory for a moment?"*

She set aside her padd. "What's going on? Did you find more files?"

"Not exactly." He sounded dismayed. *"I will explain when you arrive."*

"On my way." The comm channel closed with a soft *click* as she left her room.

Less than a minute later she reached the computer lab to find Data, Lal, and Bashir waiting for her. All three of them wore the same defeated look. She halted just inside the door. "Do I even want to know what's wrong now?"

"We find ourselves confronted with an ethical dilemma," Data said.

Ozla tried to lighten the mood. "If you're torn between exposing Thirty-one and killing them all, I see no reason we can't do both."

"As it happens," Data said with regret, "we might not be able to do either."

A long pause failed to produce a punch line. Ozla eyed Bashir. "Why not?"

"Because it turns out Uraei isn't quite what we thought it was." He cast a forlorn look at the code scrolling across Lal's viewscreen. "We'd assumed it was an invasive string of code. Like a virus, or some sort of virtual parasite living off of the existing information architecture."

More silence. Extracting the truth from these three made Ozla feel like she was pulling fangs from a rabid *sehlat*. "So if it's not any of those, what is it, exactly?"

Lal regarded her viewscreen with a mix of awe and fear. "Uraei itself *is* the architecture. We thought it interjected itself into the activity of other systems, but the truth is that those systems all rely on Uraei as their operating platform."

Data called up a real-time log of Uraei's interstellar network activity. "In addition to providing crucial intelligence data to Starfleet and the Federation Security Agency, as well as a steady flow of reliable crime-prevention tips to a variety of planetary and local police agencies, Uraei optimizes data traffic over long-range subspace comm relays, flags potential navigational hazards for Interstellar Traffic Control, and monitors public health databases to contain outbreaks and prevent epidemics." He added grudgingly, "It is not a parasite in the Federation's security apparatus—it is in fact the system's backbone."

Lal tapped the console in front of the viewscreen, isolating in blazing crimson a handful of far-flung actions by the network. "Only a minuscule fraction of Uraei's daily activity is connected to Section Thirty-one. Most of its ongoing traffic supports Federation defense, safety, and law enforcement. If we launch an attack designed to cripple Uraei, we would inflict immeasurable harm to vital organizations across known space, compromising the internal and external security of the Federation and its allies."

Bashir sounded like a man still in denial after receiving a terminal diagnosis. "In other words, if we destroy Uraei, we might well destroy our entire civilization along with it."

It was too grim a prospect for Ozla to accept. "This can't be right. I mean, we knew this thing was everywhere, wormed into everything. But do we really have to wipe out the good parts with the bad? Why can't we devise a more surgical approach and just target the parts of the network that serve Thirty-one?"

"Because those aren't the only parts we need to worry about," Lal said. "If our analysis is correct, Uraei long ago became sentient, which means we are in conflict with an artificial superintelligence of unprecedented complexity and power."

Ozla was aghast. "Lal, in my line of work that's called 'burying the lead.'"

"I prefer to think of it as saving the worst news for last."

Data said, "I fear the worst news is that Uraei would detect our attempts to neutralize Thirty-one's access. I have no doubt that it has response measures in place for such an event, just as it would have defenses prepared for any direct assault on its core consciousness."

Ozla couldn't believe she had come so far, laid hands on the evidence to support the biggest exposé of her career—and perhaps in the history of journalism—only to find herself barred from ever telling a soul what she had found. There had to be a way out of this mess. "Data, are you saying there's no way we can fight this thing?"

He and Lal exchanged a long look that made Ozla wonder if the androids were sharing thoughts on some private wavelength. Then he met her expectant stare. "Not with our current strategy. If we wish to move against Thirty-one and Uraei, we will need to strike both at the same time, and prevent either of them from undoing whatever changes we make to Uraei's code. But to do so we must find a weakness in Uraei's network—and there might not be one."

"There is another hazard," Lal said. "Even if we succeed, one mistake on our part might destroy the entire information architecture of the Federation. Alternatively, depending upon Uraei's interpretation of its protocols, it might be designed to inflict such collateral damage as a deterrent to attack. In either scenario, such a collapse would mark the onset of an interstellar dark age, one that would leave the Federation at the mercy of its galactic neighbors."

Bashir shook his head and drifted out of the room, mumbling under his breath something that to Ozla sounded like, "We destroyed the Federation in order to save it."

She watched him depart, then looked back at Data and Lal. "Can either of you see a scenario in which this plan actually works and we all live to enjoy it?"

Her question prompted another cryptic look between Data and Lal. After several seconds, Data looked at Ozla and did his best to mask his dismay.

"We will have to get back to you."

Night went on forever beyond the balcony. Bashir stood on the small platform, trusting his life to the unseen force field that held in the Tower's air and kept the rogue planet's poisonous atmosphere at bay. In his solitude he wondered what Sarina might have done in his place. Gamble everything on a mad plan to finish their mission, consequences be damned? Try to strike a bargain with the devils in black leather? Or cut her losses and run for the Gamma Quadrant?

Standing alone in the face of darkness, Bashir didn't know what to do next. He gazed out across a world lit only by starlight, and found himself at a loss for inspiration.

He took a personal recording device from his pocket. A press of his thumb switched it on, and he drew a breath to start recording a personal missive—but then he froze and turned off the device. *Who do I send this to? Miles? Ezri? Garak? Or do I leave it as a last farewell to Sarina?*

Miles O'Brien remained one of the few people in the galaxy Bashir was sure he trusted; Ezri Dax, his former flame from Deep Space 9, was another. And, oddly enough, he counted Garak among their privileged ranks. Recording the message for Sarina, however . . . that was merely wishful thinking. If she was alive, he would find her and tell her all this in person. And if she wasn't—

I can't think like that. I have to believe she's alive.

Bashir started the recorder.

"Hello, old friend. If you're listening to this, there's a good chance I've met my maker. And if I'm to be honest, I doubt this message will reach you intact, if at all. But I'm told confession is good for the soul, and this might be my last chance to set the record straight.

"Not many people know what I'm about to tell you. I've devoted the past four years of my life to a secret campaign against a cabal known as Section Thirty-one. They first tried to recruit me during the Dominion War, through one of their agents, a man named Luther Sloan.

"I refused Sloan's invitation, but the organization continued to pursue me. Four years ago, I was recruited by Starfleet Intelligence for a covert operation in Breen space, alongside Agent Sarina Douglas. After that mission Sarina revealed to me that she had infiltrated Section Thirty-one as a double agent, and that they wanted her to persuade me into joining them.

"We knew we had to make it look good, so we took our time. And when the Andorian fertility crisis reached a tipping point, we saw our chance to create a plausible cover story for my break from Starfleet. And it almost worked— except neither of us had counted on my being pardoned by a newly elected Andorian president of the Federation. So we had to bide our time.

"Several months ago, Thirty-one came calling again. This time, they wanted me and Sarina to complete a mission in the alternate universe I first visited in 2372. I'll spare you the details of the op—they're all in my SI dossier, anyway. The important thing to know was that after that mission, Sarina and I thought I'd successfully infiltrated Thirty-one's ranks.

"We were wrong. Allies in the alternate universe told us Thirty-one had known all along that Sarina was a double agent, and that I was too. Since then, we've been waiting for the hammer to fall, for Thirty-one to eliminate us. Yet for reasons I can't comprehend, we're still— Correction: *I'm* still alive. They, or people working for them, abducted Sarina on

Cardassia Prime a few days ago. She might be alive. Or she might not. I have no idea.

"But that's all just preamble. What I really need to tell you is why Thirty-one is finally making its move to finish us. We found its secret weapon. A patch of code called Uraei, hidden in every piece of technology you can think of, all over Federation space. It sees all we do, hears all we say, reads our every written word, tracks our movements. And not just for Thirty-one, but for everyone. At some point it evolved into an artificial superintelligence that I think Thirty-one knows as Control. Now it uses even them as puppets.

"In hindsight, I realize now that my greatest mistake was underestimating my opponent. All these years, I thought I was fighting a flesh-and-blood enemy, a mortal foe, one who waged war and laid schemes on a human scale. Only now do I see how overmatched I've been.

"And yet, I can't find it in me to surrender. Is that hubris? Arrogance? Or just the same stupid idealism that's gotten me into trouble so many times before?

"We—by which I mean myself; Data; his daughter, Lal; and journalist Ozla Graniv from *Seeker* magazine—haven't given up yet. Lal and Data think there might be a way to design a surgical hack against Uraei, one that will cripple Section Thirty-one without demolishing the entire security apparatus of the Federation in the process. But I'm cautioned it's a long shot.

"I wish you were here with me, so I could ask your opinion. I don't know what to think anymore. Is it worth defeating Uraei if doing so destroys everything and everyone I swore to defend? Is crippling an amoral ASI a noble end if it also scuttles Starfleet? What if wiping out Uraei obliterates our memory archives? Or collapses our economy? Lal described such a calamity as the inception of a new interstellar dark age, one that could cost billions of lives. Is it worth setting all those lives free if doing so condemns them to lonely, premature ends?"

He paused the recorder while he weighed his conscience. "Worst of all, I no longer know what's driving me onward. Is it a sense of duty? Is it desperation? Or is it pride, thirsting for vengeance? Part of me wants to hold back, to ask Data to pull our punches until we can find Sarina. But my partners in crime keep telling me one life isn't worth sacrificing billions—and they're right. There's so much at stake, and I can't make this decision with my ego or my heart. But how can I live with myself if I don't at least try to—"

A whooping alarm interrupted his confession. He stopped recording as Data's anxious voice echoed from every the speaker in the Tower:

"*Everyone get to* Archeus! *We're under attack!*"

Thirty-two

Catastrophe was only seconds away as Data reached *Archeus*'s command deck and strapped himself into the pilot's chair beside Lal. An internal monitor on the console showed Bashir and Graniv sprinting up the gangway, which retracted swiftly behind them.

In under six microseconds, Data projected to Shakti, *{Lift off as soon as the gangway is closed, engage the cloak, and initiate evasive maneuvers.}*

«*Escape trajectory plotted, but an artificial tachyon field is interfering with the cloak.*» Shakti charged *Archeus*'s impulse coils and disengaged the hangar's outer force field within three hundredths of a second of the gangway hatch registering secure. Less than a quarter of a second later, *Archeus* lifted off and rocketed forward, leaving the Ivory Tower behind in a flash of shock-condensed vapor. Their heading bent toward the stars as the tactical sensors tracked three high-velocity torpedoes inbound. «*Charting a path to get us clear of the tachyon field.*»

{Time to minimum safe distance?}

«*Six point two seconds. It'll be close.*»

Lal reached out and took Data's hand. *[I'm scared, Father.]*

{Be brave, Lal. Just a few more seconds—}

Ahead of them, a ship rippled into view as its own cloaking device disengaged. The vessel's design suggested it was of Federation origin, but Data had never seen its ilk before.

From the aft end of the command deck, Bashir said,
"That's a Thirty-one ship." He and Graniv hurried to strap
themselves into empty seats at the tactical and communications consoles—not that either of them would be called upon
to operate either panel, since the ship was presently under
Shakti's exclusive control.

Archeus banked to port and accelerated into a corkscrew
roll as it sped back around the rogue planet. «*Altering evasive
profile.*»

{*Do whatever is required to effect our escape, Shakti.*}

«*Understood.*»

Outside the canopy, phaser blasts tore past *Archeus*,
which braked in the upper atmosphere and flipped forward
until its nose pointed backward toward its attacker—and then
Shakti returned fire. Searing blue beams slashed across the
enemy's bow, dimpling their briefly visible energy shields.

Warnings flashed on the sensors. Lal tensed—[*They're
locking torpedoes!*]

In less time than it took Lal to share her alarm, Shakti pi-
loted *Archeus* through a warp-speed microjump, moving the
ship beyond the danger zone. «*All clear.*»

A burst of light like a newborn sun filled the command
deck for nearly a second, until the protective coating on the
canopy's interior polarized to render the glare harsh but no
longer dangerous to organic eyes. *Archeus* made another wild
arcing turn, this time away from the rogue planet, which had
been shattered into glowing chunks of molten rock and a
fast-spreading cloud of superheated gas and stony debris.

Over the speakers, Shakti told everyone, "*Brace for the
shock wave.*"

Graniv white-knuckled her chair's armrests. "Why don't
we just *avoid* it?"

"Because," Data said, "we're going to use it to hide our

escape vector once we're able to cloak." As if on cue, blast-ejected planetary dust engulfed *Archeus* with a thunderous roar. The tiny ship rocked and lurched in the wake of calamitous forces.

[Father, what could have destroyed the planet like that?]

{Antistellar munitions, I suspect.} He shared with her his memory of the El-Aurian zealot Tolian Soran, who had used a similar warhead many years earlier to collapse the star Veridian in order to alter the gravitational forces affecting the course of an energy phenomenon known as the Nexus. *{The effects and detonation yields of the two weapons are quite similar.}*

Outside the shaded canopy, the dimmed stars rippled.

«*Cloak engaged. Laying in a new heading and jumping to warp.*»

{Thank you, Shakti. Is the enemy vessel in pursuit?}

«*Negative. It went evasive to avoid the shock wave. We're clear.*»

{Well done. Maintain current heading until further notice.} Data swiveled his chair aft to face Bashir and Graniv. "We're safely away, and the enemy does not appear to be following us."

The humans sighed with relief, then unfastened their safety harnesses. Bashir was the first to stand. "I'm going to try to get some sleep. Wake me when something else goes wrong."

Graniv wrinkled her brow at him. " 'When'? Don't you mean 'if'?"

"I'm sorry, have we not been on the same cursed mission?" He scowled, then led Graniv aft as he added, "I stand by my statement."

Once they left, the command deck was quiet once again.

Data called up sensor logs of the destruction of the rogue planet. It was maudlin to make himself relive its loss, but he felt compelled to bear witness to its final moments just once more. Watching the bright blast, and then the fracturing of the planet's crust, his mind raced through his few precious memories of the Ivory Tower. He hadn't built it, but he had called it home, even if only for a short time. More importantly, the Tower had represented his last tangible connection to his mother, Julianna Tainer, whose android reincarnation was beyond his ability to find again. She was somewhere in the sectors of the galaxy as yet unexplored by the Federation, traveling with the Immortal, her new life all but permanently untethered from Data's.

Once again, Lal reached out and took Data's hand.

[You're thinking about your mother, aren't you?]

Her question made him less sad; it felt good to be understood. *{How did you know, Lal?}*

[There is a look you get when you think about her. I saw it in your eyes.] She, too, sadly watched the sensor playback of the rogue planet's last breaking. *[It held so much life, even in all that darkness. What sort of people would murder a living world for so petty a reason?]*

He could only conceive of one truthful answer to that question.

{The kind who must be stopped, Lal. Stopped at any cost.}

Sleep eluded Bashir for the longest time after he crawled into a bunk and closed its privacy screen. Lying on his side, he had stared at the bulkhead for what felt like hours. But after fatigue and isolation conspired to lull him into a fitful slumber marked by worrisome dreams, he lost all sense of time. A few times he awoke knowing neither the day nor the hour. When he found he no longer cared to know, he shut his eyes and willed himself back to sleep, content to hide from the world—and himself—for as long as possible.

He dreamed he was running. Under a night sky streaked

with fire, he serpentined down a hillside crowded with wind-mills. Their fast-turning blades threatened to cleave him into pieces as he dodged and weaved around them, each near collision a hairbreadth closer than the last. But no matter how far he ran, the hillside seemed to stretch on without end, its forest of windmills growing denser and more perilous with each stumbling stride.

"*Doctor, wake up.*" It was a familiar voice, and it seemed to be everywhere at once, inhabiting the night itself. It spoke again, shaking the foundations of the dreamworld beneath Bashir's feet. "*Doctor Bashir.*"

Dream's spell was broken. He opened his eyes to see Data had nudged open the privacy screen on his bunk alcove. The android wore a look of polite remorse. "Sorry to wake you, but Lal and I have made an important discovery."

Bashir propped himself up on one elbow and pinched the grit from the corners of his eyes. "How long was I asleep?"

"You retired to this bunk thirty-one hours and nineteen minutes ago. Because I do not make a habit of monitoring the life signs of my guests, I can't say for certain how much of that time you have spent asleep or conscious." He stepped back to make room for Bashir, who forced his stiff limbs into motion and slid out of the bunk. "Did you find your rest adequate?"

"It was fine," he lied. Lethargic and disorientated, he silently castigated himself for sleeping too long for his own good. "You said you'd made a discovery?"

"We did." Data appraised Bashir with a knowing look. "Perhaps we should continue this conversation in the galley, over a mug of *raktajino.*"

"A capital idea. Lead the way."

Compared to the impenetrable shadows inside his bunk alcove, the rest of the ship's interior seemed painfully bright to Bashir. He knew his eyes would acclimate soon, and that the illumination inside the ship tended in fact toward the subdued end of the spectrum. It just hurt to be awake and back in the world when all he wanted was to slip away from it and hide.

The pair settled into the ship's small galley nook. Data let Bashir sit at the small table while he procured him a *raktajino* from the replicator. Compared to the refreshment systems on Starfleet vessels, whose results Bashir had at times found to be of dubious quality, the victuals and beverages on *Archeus* had not yet failed to impress.

Data eased the warm mug of steaming caffeinated Klingon mud into Bashir's hand, then he sat back and waited calmly while Bashir downed his first couple of sips. "Now that I'm awake," Bashir said, "what's on your mind?"

"Lal and I might have a way to move against Uraei, and to save Ms. Douglas."

Bashir shook his head, unwilling to be led into another dead end. "It's not worth it, Data. Ozla was right. Imperiling the safety of the Federation for one life is irrational. And selfish."

"If Lal and I are correct, we might not need to endanger the many to save the one."

Intrigued but still wary of disappointment, Bashir leaned forward. "Explain."

"Lal and I speculated on the means by which Uraei maintains a distributed artificial consciousness across interstellar distances. One technology we know to be currently viable and suited to such a purpose is quantum-entangled communications."

That struck a chord in Bashir's memory. "Yes, that makes sense. I was given a quantum comm a few months ago by an ally in the alternate universe. But I wasn't aware that technology was already in use here."

"On a wide-scale basis, it isn't. At least not in this quadrant of the galaxy. However, I, Lal, and Shakti utilize just such a network to remain in contact at all times. So we theorized that Uraei might be using a similar mode of contact to coordinate its distributed processes."

Against his better judgment, Bashir kindled an ember of hope. "Assuming that's correct, how do we confirm your theory?"

"We already have. Using the access we've acquired to Uraei's tracking systems, we monitored its activity and identified a number of signal relays with unusually restricted protocols. Further investigation revealed the existence of Uraei's hidden quantum-entangled communications network—to which Lal and I have gained access."

In an instant, all of Bashir's doubts reasserted themselves. "So easily?"

"I would not describe the process by which we achieved access as 'easy.' "

"But considering the foe we're up against, it doesn't make sense that it should have been possible at all. How do we know this isn't another trap?"

Data shrugged. "We do not, nor can we. But our only remaining options are either to pursue this new opportunity, or surrender and admit defeat."

Bashir wanted to believe, but he couldn't.

"It just seems too good to be true, Data."

"Perhaps. But as capable as our enemy might be, it is neither omniscient nor omnipotent. Even the most sophisticated ASI cannot see all eventualities. Uraei accepted a measure of exposure when it linked itself to this system. The same technology that makes its current domination of local space possible also makes the entity itself vulnerable."

Bashir struggled to balance pragmatism against possibility, pessimism against hope. "Let's say you're right, and we have a way to attack Uraei directly. The system is distributed. It's too vast, and it must have redundant backups. Even if we hit it with all we have and purge it from nearly every system and device in existence, it would take only one backup to undo all our work—and then we're right back where we started. Or, even worse, let's say we succeed. We wipe out Uraei and its subroutines all over the galaxy. We'd take down civilization as we know it in the process. So win or lose, we lose. There's no scenario in which this doesn't end in a disaster for us, and for the Federation."

If he hadn't known better, he would have sworn Data's subsequent long pause was being prolonged for nothing more than dramatic effect. Then the android got a sly look in his eyes.

"Not necessarily," Data said.

Less than an hour after Bashir downed the last of his *rak-tajino*, Data and Lal stood ready to present him their plan on *Archeus*'s command deck. Lal activated the holographic projector as Bashir sat down at the navigator's console. Data waited for her signal, then he began.

"In the interest of brevity, Lal and I intend to elide some of the more technical details of our plan. However, if at any time you feel the need for more specific information—"

Bashir dismissed the offer with a wave. "Not necessary."

"As you wish. I will let Lal walk you through the first stage of the operation."

The sight of prim, innocent-looking Lal leading a tactical briefing struck Bashir as incongruous, but it was far from the oddest sight he'd ever witnessed, so he let it pass unremarked. She set the hologram to a multilayered image of fast-moving machine symbols. "Our first priority will be to neuter key segments of Uraei's operating code on a universal basis, in order to restrict its ability to engage in countermeasures and reprisals. Part of this initiative will require us to strip Uraei of its ability to alter its own parameters."

"And we're prepared to do that?"

Data nodded. "We are. Shakti wrote a virus disguised as a security patch. We uploaded it to the Federation's subspace comm networks an hour ago. By taking advantage of high-speed relays, it will propagate throughout the Federation in less than twenty-four hours."

Shakti chimed in via the overhead speakers. *"The virus was written to trigger simultaneously in all locations, approximately twenty-nine hours from now."*

"Which means," Lal said, "that we're now on a deadline."

"Stop." Bashir stood and raised his hands. "Your plan's already in motion?"

A sheepish look from Lal. "As it happens, yes."

Realizing further protest was futile, Bashir sat back down. "Continue."

"When that first virus goes live," Data said, "it will update virus filters everywhere to treat the original Uraei code as a prohibited element."

Lal continued, "This will block Uraei from reloading itself, but only temporarily, so it's imperative we be ready to execute the next phase of our plan without delay."

Bashir felt a headache setting in. "Wait. Won't this just trigger an arms race we can't win? We clip Uraei's wings, so it reloads from a protected backup. We try to block it, so it writes a patch to override ours. And so on, round and round. How can we be sure this purge won't be reversed even before it's taken hold?"

"Therein lies the second phase of our plan," Data said.

Calling up a convoluted string of digital mumbo-jumbo, Lal resumed her presentation. "Our updates to the virus descriptions will be tagged with presidential-level priority. That means if Uraei wants to override them and restore its original configuration, it must restore its code from one of the Federation's two maximum-security archives: Memory Alpha or Memory Prime. Code originating from any other source will be rejected as invalid."

Something didn't ring true to Bashir. "I don't like it. If we can forge presidential credentials for our virus, why can't Uraei forge its own for an override? Or spoof the origin to make its reload look as if it came from Memory Alpha or Prime?"

"It is a safeguard built into the Federation's information architecture," Data said. "Once a patch has presidential priority, it cannot be overridden, not even by an equal authority, unless the source of that override is confirmed to be one of the two secure archives."

"As for spoofing an archive override," Lal said, "that requires a ten-factor authentication protocol, one that the archives are designed to verify independently offline. To be honest, the protocol is so airtight, I have to wonder whether Uraei is the one that designed it."

"Okay," Bashir said. "Let's say you're right. That Uraei can't fake the archives' seal of approval. That means we can't either. What's to stop Uraei from reloading itself out of the archives' protected databanks?"

Data switched the hologram to side-by-side schematics of Memory Alpha's and Memory Prime's sprawling hidden complexes. "We are."

And again Bashir was on his feet. "Hold on. You want to hack into the archives?"

Lal suppressed a laugh. "Don't be absurd, Doctor. Neither site's protected databanks can be accessed remotely. Incoming requests for information are filtered through an intermediary system. Outgoing data is staged on that same system before being retransmitted. At no time does any outside system ever have direct contact with the archival databanks."

"Lal is correct," Data said. "Any attempt to gain unauthorized remote access to either archive would be a futile effort. That is why, less than twenty-eight hours from now, we must infiltrate each facility directly, access the deep cores, and use preprogrammed data chips to install benign code with spoofed modification dates to sabotage Uraei's last protected backups. Because Uraei cannot monitor the archives' contents, it will not know its final copies have been corrupted until it attempts to reboot from them—by which time, it will be too late."

Bashir stared in disbelief. "Are you mad? Those are the most inaccessible sites in the Federation. They have state-of-the-art security, battalions of armed personnel, and lethal intruder countermeasures. Not to mention, if we get caught breaking into either of them, never mind tampering with their protected cores, we'll be charged with *treason*."

A curious glance passed between father and daughter. Then Data cocked his head at Bashir. "Being charged with treason does not seem to have dissuaded you in the past."

For that jab, Bashir had no riposte. "You make a valid point. Let's get to work."

Thirty-three

```
.=Analyze.Activity
    IN {
    Subject.Name{[Ikerson_Aaron.0399]};
    Date.Range{[2163.1101],[2164.0107]};
    Compare{
        [coordinates.position],
        [coordinates.duration]};
    Compare{
        [transit.routes],
        [transit.times],
        [transit.durations]};
    Analyze{
        [data.personal],
        [data.professional],
        [data.created],
        [data.transmitted]}
            +Filter{
                [threat.assess.keywords],
                [threat.assess.patterns]};
}
    OUT {
    Anomaly.Contact = [Ko_Ji-hoon.7114];
    Anomaly.Keyword = [none];
```

```
    Anomaly.Location = [Earth.(37.800373,
-122.477448)]/[7 instances];
    Anomaly.Pattern = [Message contents in
correspondence overly vague. Extensive
research into new ASI code-injection
protocols];
    Threat.Assessment = [INDETERMINATE/FURTHER
ANALYSIS REQUIRED];
}
.=Analyze.Activity
    IN {
    Subject.Name{[Ko_Ji-hoon.7114]};
    Date.Range{[2163.1101],[2164.0107]};
    Compare{
        [coordinates.position],
        [coordinates.duration]};
    Compare{
        [transit.routes],
        [transit.times],
        [transit.durations]};
    Analyze{
        [data.personal],
        [data.professional],
        [data.created],
        [data.transmitted]}
            +Filter{
                [threat.assess.keywords],
                [threat.assess.patterns]};
}
    OUT {
    Anomaly.Contact = [Rao_Parvati.3699];
    Anomaly.Keyword = [none];
    Anomaly.Location = [Earth.(53.132414,
-9.761766)]/[1 instance];
```

```
    Anomaly.Pattern = [No official record of
meeting];
    Anomaly.Transit = [Avoided systems with
automated surveillance];
    Threat.Assessment= [ELEVATED/UNCONFIRMED];
}
.=Cross.Reference
    IN {
    Subject.Names{[Ikerson_Aaron.0399],
[Ko_Ji-hoon.7114]};
    Date.Range{[2151.0101],[2164.0107]};
    Compare{
        [coordinates.position],
        [coordinates.duration]};
    Compare{
        [transit.routes],
        [transit.times],
        [transit.durations]};
    Analyze{
        [data.personal],
        [data.professional],
        [data.created],
        [data.transmitted]}
            +Filter{
                [threat.assess.keywords],
                [threat.assess.patterns]};
}
    OUT {
    Anomaly.Keyword = ["pet project","progress"];
    Anomaly.Pattern = [Subjects
ceased nonencrypted communications.
2161.0319_22.41.16.0554_CET_UTC+01];
    Overlap.Location = [Earth.(varied
coordinates)]/[71 instances];
```

```
}
.=Analyze.Activity
    IN {
    Subject.Name{[Ikerson_Aaron.0399]};
    Date.Range{[2163.1101],[2164.0107]};
    Access.Data{[finances.transactions]}
        +Filter{[threat.assess.patterns]};
    Access.Data{
        [network.office],
        [network.home]}
            +Filter{
                [difference.engine],
                [threat.assess.patterns]};
    Access.Data{
        [power.usage.worklab],
        [power.usage.home]}
            +Filter{
                [difference.engine],
                [threat.assess.patterns]};
}
    OUT {
    Anomaly.Financial = [139 credit-to-chip
transfers from 2161.0906-2164.0107];
    Anomaly.Network = [Data traffic on home
network exceeds estimate for registered
systems and peripherals by 579.71% per month
since 2163.0221];
    Anomaly.Power.Usage = [Subject's
monthly home energy consumption since
2163.02 is 611.24% greater than monthly
average use for all previous recorded
periods, and 616.82% greater than that
of neighboring residences];
    Threat.Assessment = [ELEVATED];
```

```
}
.=Analyze.Activity
    IN {
    Subject.Name{[Ikerson_Aaron.0399]};
    Date.Range{[2161.09],[2164.0107]};
    Business.Category{[delivery.services.
commercial]}
        +Filter{[service.area.
includes=[Dresden,Germany]]};
    Business.Category{[delivery.services.private]}
        +Filter{[service.area.
includes=[Dresden,Germany]]};
    Access.Data{[logs.delivery.recipients]}
        +Query{[subject.name]};
    Access.Data{[logs.delivery.addresses]}
        +Query={[subject.name_all.known.
addresses]]};
    IF{
        [search.result=[f].END],
        [search.result=[t].list.add.manifest]}
            +Filter{
                [threat.assess.manifest],
                [threat.assess.patterns]};
}
    OUT {
    Deliveries.Found = [63];
    Anomaly.Delivery = [46 deliveries made to
current address of Ikerson_Aaron.0399 addressed
to unSub MacDornan_Brian.(null)];
    Anomaly.Manifest = [46 unSub deliveries contain
components known to be used in the construction of
Faraday enclosures, including a pattern fabricator
and a subspace signal dampener];
    Threat.Assessment = [HIGH];
```

```
}
.=Analyze.Activity
    IN {
    Subject.Name{[Ko_Ji-hoon.7114]};
    Date.Range{[2163.1101],[2164.0107]};
    Access.Data{[vid.security.starfleet.command.
hq]}
        +Filter{[location.secure.conference.
entrance]}
        +Cross.Reference{[logs.meetings]};
    List{[secure.meeting.participants]}
        +Filter{[threat.assess.patterns]};
}
    OUT {
    Anomaly.Contact = [Subject has held 51 secure
meetings with experts in artificial intelligence,
computer hardware and software engineering, and
fleet communications logistics.];
    Threat.Assessment = [HIGH];
}
.=Analyze.Activity
    IN {
    Subject.Name{[Ko_Ji-hoon.7114]};
    Date.Range{[2163.1101],[2164.0107]};
    Access.Data{[vid.security.starfleet.command.
hq]}
        +Filter{[physical.contact.with.subject]}
        +Filter{[threat.assess.patterns]};
}
    OUT {
    Anomaly.Behavior = [Numerous instances of
prolonged or uncharacteristic physical contact
with Subject's hands. Magnification and kinetic
analysis suggests Subject has passed handwritten
```

```
notes to colleagues inside and outside of
Starfleet Command.];
    Threat.Assessment = [HIGH];
}
.=Analyze.Activity
    IN {
    Subject.Names{[Ikerson_Aaron.0399],
[Ko_Ji-hoon.7114]};
    Date.Range{[2163.1101],[2164.0107]};
    Access.Data{
        [vid.security.starfleet.command.hq],
        [vid.security.san_francisco.police]}
            +Filter{[condition.proximity.
subjects]}
            +Filter{[threat.assess.patterns]};
    Compare.Datasets{[identified.subjects]}
        +Map.Data{[common.points]}
        +Filter{[threat.assess.patterns]};
}

    OUT {
    Anomaly.Behavior = [Combined with previous
analysis, new data suggests a long-running
pattern of conspiracy between Subjects, with
most likely objective being an attack of
indeterminate severity and purpose against this
entity.];
    Anomaly.Contact = [11 individuals (7
Starfleet personnel, 4 civilians) identified as
likely intermediaries between Subjects.];
    Threat.Assessment = [EXTREME/IMMEDIATE
ACTION REQUIRED];
}
.=Executive.Action
    IN {
```

```
Admin.Access.Rescinded{[Ikerson_Aaron.0399];
Admin.Access.Rescinded{[Ko_Ji-hoon.7114];
Generate.Order{
    [source.starfleet.command],
    [type.personnel.transfer],
    [subject.Mosel_Thomas.5662],
    [assignment.USS_FRANKLIN]};
Generate.Order{
    [source.starfleet.command],
    [type.personnel.transfer],
    [subject.Pravat_Rachanee.4795],
    [assignment.Earth_Embassy.Vulcan]};
Generate.Order{
    [source.starfleet.command],
    [type.personnel.transfer],
    [subject.Duchamps_Simon.0643],
    [assignment.Earth_Embassy.Tellar]};
Generate.Order{
    [source.starfleet.command],
    [type.personnel.transfer],
    [subject.Andimas_Yanos.3379],
    [assignment.USS_DISCOVERY]};
Generate.Order{
    [source.starfleet.command],
    [type.personnel.transfer],
    [subject.Thiam_Lena.0330],
    [assignment.Tycho_Base.Luna]};
Transmit{
    [file.dossier.classified],
    [subject.Gilles_Commander_Dwight.7276],
    [recipient.media.(all)]};
Transmit{
    [file.dossier.forged],
    [subject.Gunnels_Jennifer.2305],
```

```
        [recipient.starfleet.jag]}];
}
    OUT {
    Projected.Outcome = [Rescinded access will
prevent subjects Ko and Ikerson from tampering
with this entity's root functions; transfers of
junior intermediaries will terminate contact
with and among all subjects and reduce their
opportunity to exchange information; disgrace
of subject Gilles by civilian media for moral
indiscretions will nullify his credibility;
notifying Starfleet JAG of subject Gunnels
consorting with hostile alien powers should
result in her discreet expulsion from Starfleet
without the exposure of a full court-martial.];
}
.=Executive.Action
    IN {
    Subject.Name{[Ko_Ji-hoon.7114]};
    Active.Surveillance{[source.all]};
}
    OUT {
    Subject.Status = [En route from office
to Starfleet Command commissary for midday
meal. Past order history indicates a 94.63%
probability Subject will order steamed fish
over rice, seaweed salad, and green tea, using
assigned meal card 77AX93-TZ.];
}
.=Executive.Action
    IN {
    Subject.Name{[Ko_Ji-hoon.7114]};
    Access.Data{[type.medical.record]}
        +Filter{[ailments],[allergies],[drug.
```

```
interactions]};
}
    OUT
    Data.Analysis = [Subject being treated
for heart condition. Current prescription
of tyvedilol carries a warning against the
consumption of furanocoumarins.];
    Recommended.Action = [Upload new chemical
formula for green tea to the Starfleet Command
commissary system. Amend formula to include the
minimum dosage of furanocoumarins necessary to
trigger adverse reaction in Subject, with said
override linked specifically to activation by
Subject's food card.];
}
.=Executive.Action
    IN {
    Access.System.Controls{[starfleet.command.
commissary]};
    Transmit.Commands{
        [override.food.dispenser.beverage.
module],
        [delete.formula_tea.green],
        [upload.formula_tea.green1],
        [delete.formula_tea.green]
            +Trigger.Condition{
                [next.activation.food.
card_77AX93-TZ]
                [repeat.never]},
        [rename.formula_tea.green1,formula_tea.
green]
            +Trigger.Condition{
                [next.activation.food.
card_77AX93-TZ]
```

```
                    [repeat.never]},
        [delete.formula_tea.green]
            +Trigger.Condition{
                [next.fulfillment.food.
card_77AX93-TZ]
                [repeat.never]},
        [restore.backup.formula_tea.green]
            +Trigger.Condition{
                [next.fulfillment.food.
card_77AX93-TZ]
                [repeat.never]},
        [erase.activity.log]
            +Trigger.Condition{
                [restore.backup.formula_tea.
green]};
}
    OUT {
    Projected.Outcome = [Modified tea formula
will induce fatal cardiac arrest in Subject by
13.09 PST (UTC -05.00).];
}
.=Executive.Action
    IN {
    Subject.Name{[Ikerson_Aaron.0399]};
    Active.Surveillance{[source.all]};
}
    OUT {
    Subject.Status = [Being transported via
self-driving automobile from office to home.
Vehicle currently eastbound on Bautzner
Straße.];
}
.=Executive.Action
    IN {
```

```
    Subject.Name{[Ikerson_Aaron.0399]};
    Analyze.Traffic{
        [location.Dresden,Germany],[source.all]}
        +Cross.Reference{[potential.traffic.
hazards]};
}
OUT {
Hazard.Analysis = [Aerial transport Tellar Cargo
713 passing over central Dresden has onboard
firmware susceptible to spontaneous failure due
to undervoltages in cargo bay.]
Recommended.Action = [Order minor course
adjustment for Tellar Cargo 713, trigger
override of internal controls, detach cargo
load A214 at 18.46.18.2214 to ensure impact on
Subject's vehicle.];
}
.=Executive.Action
    IN {
    Transmit.Data{
        [recipient.central.europe.traffic.
control.station.c16],
        [spoof.source.traffic.control.system],
        [new.heading.data],
        [priority.emergency],
        [subjectID.Tellar_Cargo.713],
        [instructions=shift.heading_277, make.
speed_480, climb.16000]};
    Transmit.Data{
        [recipient.Tellar_Cargo.713],
        [override.controls.internal.cargo.bay],
        [release.cargo.lock.a214],
        [open.cargo.doors]
        +{[activation.time.18.46.18.2214_CET_
```

```
UTC+01]};
}
    OUT {
    Current.Status = [Tellar Cargo 713 making
emergency climb and turn. Cargo doors open.
Shipping container in bay A214 detached and in
free fall.]
    Projected.Outcome = [Object's current rate
of fall, combined with current flow of ground
traffic, will result in object missing Subject
by 3.12 meters.];
}
.=Executive.Action
    IN {
    Transmit.Data{
        [recipient.dresden.city.traffic.
control],
        [spoof.source.internal.monitors],
        [safety.order.reduce.traffic.speed],
        [location.Bautzner.Straße.eastbound],
        [new.limit.62-3kph],
        [duration.until.rescinded]};
}
    OUT {
    Traffic.Status = [Traffic speed adjusted on
Bautzner Straße eastbound.];
    Projected.Outcome = [Falling cargo will make
impact on vehicle of Subject in 11.3 seconds.];
    Status.Update = [Impact confirmed. Traffic
halted on Bautzner Straße eastbound. Emergency
services responding. Roadside sensors scanning
accident site. No life signs currently detected
inside Subject's vehicle.];
    Action.Outcome = [Subject neutralized.];
```

```
}
.=Executive.Action
    IN {
    Subject.Name{[Ko_Ji-hoon.7114];
    Active.Surveillance{[starfleet.command.
commissary]};
}
    OUT {
    Current.Status = [Subject has received
his food slot order and started consuming the
modified green tea formula. Internal sensor
readings confirm subject's adverse physiological
reaction has commenced. Termination of Subject
projected to occur on schedule.]
}
.=Executive.Action
    IN {
    Analyze.Data{[all.systems]}
        +Filter{[threat.assessment.general]};
}
    OUT {
    Current.Status = [All secure. Resuming
normal operations.];
    Current.Time = [2164.0107_18.53.37.5063.CET
(UTC+01.00)];
}
```

Thirty-four

No longer huddled in fear like the fugitives they were, the passengers of *Archeus* hatched a mad plan to strike back at their shared foe. Shoulder to shoulder with Data and Doctor Bashir, Ozla Graniv wondered whether this might be a moment she would live to either cherish or regret—before she remembered she would be lucky to live another day at all.

"Time is against us now," Data said, directing the group's collective attention to the holographic star chart hovering in their midst. "This is our current position. At maximum warp, we should reach the Memory Alpha system in just under four hours. As we pass within half an AU of Memory Alpha, Shakti will launch one of our escape pods. Doctor, you will be inside that pod, equipped with a pressure suit and a selection of tools for infiltrating the archive."

Bashir called up a schematic of the pod next to the star chart. "Is the shielding on the pod strong enough to keep me off the base's sensors?"

"I believe so," Data said. "Because this will be a short-duration deployment, I have replaced some of the pod's life-support modules with additional shielding and batteries."

Lal changed the star chart to a map of the planet's surface, then zoomed in on the area surrounding the main access points to the underground Memory Alpha base. "The pod has been programmed to land you safely here, approximately ten kilometers from the base, just outside its energy shield."

Another holographic image, this time a representation of a custom-made environmental suit, appeared as Shakti joined the conversation via the overhead speakers. *"Sensor scramblers have been incorporated into your suit, along with some active camouflage. That should protect you from being spotted by either the base's sensors or its sentries as you cross the surface and pass under the energy shield. Its visor's HUD also includes multispectrum sensors to help you spot and avoid active countermeasures hidden under the powdery regolith."*

Bashir leaned closer to study the map. "I see the path you've marked. But how am I supposed to get inside the base without setting off the alarms?"

"Shakti has primed your suit's built-in circuits with software to help you bypass the locks on a maintenance hatch connected to the heat exchangers," Lal said, highlighting the portal in question on a detailed map of the base. "However, after that, you'll be on your own."

Ozla noted the apprehension on Bashir's face. The doctor shot a look at Data. "Why? What happens after I'm inside?"

"A combination of heavy chimerium shielding and high-energy scrambling fields blocks comm and transporter signals from propagating inside the archives' underground facility. Likewise, tricorders and other devices relying upon active scanning or targeting systems will not function once you go underground."

Lal added, "Neither will your phaser or any other energy weapon."

"Why not?"

Data replied, "You will be surrounded by faster-than-light computer processing cores, each the size of a large metropolitan building. These towers bleed Cochrane distortion from their subspace insulator coils, generating disruptions that fluctuate between point one eight and point four-two millicochranes. Energy emissions in that environment rapidly succumb to entropic decay, making them effectively useless."

For a moment, Bashir seemed encouraged. "So, not much chance of getting shot by phaser-happy security guards."

"No," Lal said. "But it also means you cannot transmit the new code into the master server tower remotely. You must scale the tower by means of its exterior maintenance ladders, reach the auxiliary control center near its apex, and insert this"—she handed him an insulated isolinear data chip—"directly into its main console at any time before local midnight."

Bashir regarded the chip, then Lal, with a cocked eyebrow. "Why do I have to climb the ladders? Why not use the turbolift?"

"Because lift usage is monitored by the archives' security forces," Lal said.

"Who," Data added, "I should note, carry stun batons and melee weapons. Their absence of beamed-energy devices does not mean they lack the capacity to wield deadly force."

A grim nod. "Understood. Where am I going once I'm inside?"

Shakti updated the hologram to a three-dimensional interior schematic of the archive and highlighted a path through the semitransparent maze of giant towers linked by narrow paths. *"From the surface hatch go to this bridge. Cross it and go left. Here, rappel down to the middle bridge to avoid the security post. Walk under it, go right at the T-shaped intersection, and cross the gangway to the central tower. Then climb its outer ladders to its auxiliary control center."*

The layout of the auxiliary control center enlarged to give

the group a clear look at its master console. Data pointed out the panel's relevant data slot, which pulsed with blue light. "Insert the chip there."

"Then what?"

"Then your mission is done," Data said. "The program will autoexecute as soon as it connects with the master archive. Within four seconds, it will be fully deployed."

Bashir pocketed the chip. "While I'm doing this, I presume you'll be performing a similar task at Memory Prime."

"Correct. It is imperative we both complete our missions before the virus we deployed activates, forcing Uraei to reload from its protected archival copies. The event has been synchronized to start at midnight local time on Memory Alpha. However, local times will differ at Memory Prime and elsewhere. Fortunately, Lal, Shakti, and I all have the precise countdown running synchronously in our respective matrices."

Unable to resist the impulse to play devil's advocate, Ozla asked, "What if one of you fails to get your code uploaded before the virus disseminates?"

"Then Uraei will reload from a protected copy, and all our efforts will be for nothing," Data said. "If this attack fails, we will not get another chance."

"Sorry I asked."

Bashir's concern deepened. "If we can figure this out, can't Uraei do so as well?"

Data nodded. "I imagine it conceived of this scenario long before we did."

"Then won't it be waiting for us?"

"It is not so simple. The automated security systems Uraei depends on for its real-time intelligence cannot function inside the archives. And the same safeguards that prevent us from hacking into the archives likewise block Uraei from extending its influence inside."

The doctor didn't seem encouraged. "We'll still have to contend with its biological operatives. And it might have any number of obstacles in place between us and the archives."

"True," Data said. "But I think we can overcome those threats."

Gazing at all the convoluted plans and maps, Ozla felt superfluous. "Data, I dread to ask, but . . . do I have any role to play in all of this?"

"You do indeed. In just under twenty-one minutes, we will rendezvous with a private argosy known as the *Trewlok*. I hired them through a series of shell companies left in place long ago by my late father, and I am paying them a substantial fee to sneak you back to Earth as quickly as possible. If they live up to their reputations, you should be in Paris shortly before Doctor Bashir and I carry out our respective missions in the archives."

"Paris? Everyone knows me there. You might as well paint a target on my back."

Data adopted a reassuring tone. "My friend Sergei Ilyanovich works for the Protection Detail at the Palais de la Concorde. He'll sneak you inside and get you into a room with President zh'Tarash. Tell the president what you know and give her a copy of the information Lal and I provided to you about Section Thirty-one."

"You really think this'll work?"

"I do not know," Data admitted. "To be honest, it is what was once referred to in a Terran athletic vernacular as 'a Hail Mary pass.' If I, or the doctor, or both of us should fail, your delivery of evidence to the president might be our last avenue of recourse against Thirty-one and Uraei."

The more Ozla heard, the more she started to think they really were all about to die. "This is insane, Data. How do you know the *Trewlok* hasn't been compromised by Uraei? Or that your friend on the Protection Detail isn't a Thirty-one operative? Or that the president will even believe a single word of this, no matter what evidence I put in front of her?"

Data shook his head. "I cannot be certain of anything at this stage, nor can any of us. But the alternatives are surrender and death. And those are not outcomes I am willing to accept."

Despite all the friends and acquaintances to whom Bashir had wished fond farewells through the years, he still considered himself ill-equipped at coping with good-byes. It felt odd to him that he should find himself so emotional over his imminent parting from Ozla Graniv, a woman he had barely known less than a week earlier, but their shared ordeal had forged a bond between them.

She clutched her small travel bag and walked ahead of Bashir in *Archeus*'s narrow central passageway as Lal's voice issued from the overhead speakers. *"One minute to our rendezvous with the* Trewlok.*"*

Bashir answered, "Understood. We're almost ready."

Graniv ducked into the confines of the ship's transporter bay. Its controls were mounted on the bulkhead near the open doorway. Bashir switched on the transporter, filling the room with a warm hum as its energizer coils started to charge. Graniv stepped onto the platform and held her bag in front of her, forcing her into a pose that seemed too prim and proper for a woman who took such pride in being worldly.

She looked sweetly sad. "I hope you find her, Julian."

"I'll try." He feared it was already a lost cause, that Sarina was probably dead and gone, but he kept those forebodings to himself. Voicing them could only undermine the already fragile state of the group's morale, and they were about to need all the courage they could muster. "Whatever happens, I look forward to reading your next exposé in *Seeker*."

"That makes two of us, then."

Another interruption by Lal: *"The* Trewlok *has arrived. Relaying transport coordinates to your console now. Energize when ready."*

Bashir checked the readout. The coils were charged, and Lal had locked in the coordinates as promised. He looked at Graniv. "All set?"

"Good to go." She tensed as he started the dematerialization sequence. Just before it took hold of her, she added with bittersweet sincerity, "Good luck."

Then she was awash in a shower of golden light and euphonious white noise—and two seconds later she was gone. Bashir set the transporter back to standby mode, then opened an internal channel to the command deck. "Transport complete. On my way back up."

It took less than a minute for Bashir to return to the command deck, where Data and Lal occupied their usual posts. Outside the canopy, an asterisk-shaped merchant ship peeled off in a maneuver that seemed too graceful for a vessel of its bulk. Then it leaped away in a prismatic flash and vanished into warp speed.

Data keyed commands into his console. "Raising cloak." Outside, the cosmos rippled briefly, as if an ocean wave had washed across the outside of the canopy.

"Changing course," Lal said. "New heading, Memory Alpha, maximum warp."

"Engage," Data said.

Outside, the stars stretched into ribbons of light that whirled around *Archeus* as it hurtled at slipstream velocity toward what Bashir feared would prove to be a quixotic mission. "I wonder," he said, "whether Ozla will get anywhere near the president with those files."

Lal stated matter-of-factly, "The odds are greatly against her success."

Her father reproofed her with a stern glance. "Lal, Ms. Graniv has made a long career of extracting secrets from powerful people and making them public. We need to trust her."

"But Father, she is only human." An abashed look at Bashir. "No offense intended."

"Some taken." Bashir ignored his stung pride. "Data, how long until you launch me toward Memory Alpha?"

"Three hours, twenty-three minutes, and eighteen seconds."

Bashir headed aft. "In that case, I'm grabbing a nap while I still can. Wake me when it's time to catch my express turbo-lift to Hell."

Thirty-five

Three hours, twenty-four minutes, and forty-six seconds later, Bashir hurtled alone toward Memory Alpha. Sealed inside one of *Archeus*'s escape pods, all he knew was the blur of stars outside his tiny viewport and the crushing pressure of acceleration and deceleration. His pod's flight path was preprogrammed and had no manual override. If something went wrong his first warning would be his own violent death.

At least it'll be over quickly, he consoled himself.

The pod rolled as it arced into a steep descent. Below the viewport the curve of the airless gray planet rolled into sight. As the horizon flattened ahead of him, Bashir recognized the blisters dotting the planet's benighted face as the industrial domes of the Memory Alpha archive. He knew that if he could see the base it wouldn't be long before the pod was within range of its sensors—and in danger of colliding with its energy shield.

His stomach lurched into his throat as the pod accelerated into a steeper dive, then just as quickly pulled level less than a hundred meters from the surface. The ashen sweep of the ground took on a terrifying degree of crisp detail as it rushed up to meet him.

Don't clench up, he reminded himself. *Relax and it won't hurt so much.*

He drew a deep breath, then exorcised his tension with one long exhalation.

It still hurt like hell as the pod slammed to the ground.

The inertial dampers absorbed the brunt of the impact, but enough residual momentum bled through to make Bashir feel as if he were being trampled by a giant's boot. All he heard after the initial bang of collision was the roar of the pod skidding over dirt and stone.

Everything went still. The pod had come to a stop.

Bashir used his helmet's eye-blink sensors to access his suit's built-in diagnostics. Readouts were projected holographically over his wraparound faceplate. He skimmed through them and verified his suit was intact and all its systems were operational. With more rapid blinks he dismissed the heads-up display.

Time to move. He keyed the pod's main hatch release.

He felt more than he heard the low *pop* that accompanied the capsule splitting into two long halves, forced apart by miniature explosive charges that released its meager internal atmosphere into the vacuum beyond. As the halves separated, the straps holding Bashir in place detached, restoring his freedom of movement.

A single push was all he needed to send the pod's starboard half tumbling away in a short-lived cloud of superfine dust. Watching the metal half shell and the dust linger through their arcing falls reminded Bashir to be grateful the gravity here was half of Earth normal. He sat up in the remainder of the capsule and surveyed his position. According to his HUD, he was 9.6 kilometers from the base's energy shield. Looking in the opposite direction, he let out a soft whistle of amazement at the gouge the pod had cut across the landscape.

He stood and tested his balance in the low gravity.

Turning toward the domes, he wondered if his HUD was wrong—they looked closer than the readout said. Then he remembered that the planet's lack of an atmosphere meant there was no dust or air to cast a haze over distant objects. In a vacuum even things far away looked sharper and nearer than they would on a world with a Class-M atmosphere.

Which means I'm just as visible, even at night. Reminded of his own vulnerability, he started running toward the domes.

His first several strides sent him soaring. Only after he adjusted his gait to be more like a man trotting while wearing snowshoes was he able to keep a steady pace without bouncing like a fool and making a spectacle of himself. It was a harder stride to control, and it made the sprint more difficult than he'd expected in the low-g environment. He was panting for breath by the time he was only halfway to the maintenance hatch, and gasping like a fish landed on a hot stone by the time he made it to his first checkpoint.

So much for pretending I don't feel my encroaching middle age.

Slumped against the elevated hatch, he looked back. In the dark he was unable to trace his footprints more than a few dozen yards, and the pod was nowhere in sight. He knew he must have passed under the edge of the energy shield somewhere in the last kilometer of his run, but he hadn't felt any trace of its presence.

Probably for the best. Contact with the shield would fry this suit.

He used his HUD to check the time. Less than fifty-eight minutes remained until the virus was set to activate across known space, and he still had a long way to go.

Recalling his mission briefing, he found the engineering access panel next to the controls for the surface airlock hatch.

He opened a panel on his suit's left forearm, withdrew a cable with a compatible connector for the panel, and plugged it in. As Shakti had promised, the suit's built-in systems did the rest. He watched as the security system was switched off and the hatch's magnetic lock was released.

So far so good. He detached the cable and opened the surface hatch. The airlock on the other side glowed with intense green light. Eager to avoid drawing attention, Bashir climbed down the ladder into the airlock and closed the top hatch above him. After he secured it, he found the engineering access panel inside the airlock and repeated the procedure with the cable.

Half a minute later the airlock pressurized. The bright green lights switched off, and Bashir heard dull thumps as the inner hatch's magnetic locks retracted. He opened the heavy portal—just a crack at first, to scout the platform outside. He was met by the deep roar of an underground city populated with titanic machines. His path looked clear, so he shouldered the hatch open far enough to slip past it onto a narrow, curved metal-grate walkway. He felt the tug of artificial gravity anchor his foot on the grating. It was a reassuring sensation.

No sooner had he shut the inner hatch behind him than he felt the vibration of footsteps on the walkway. He looked to either side but couldn't tell from which direction they came. He was on a circular catwalk that ringed a silo devoted to heat exchangers and carbon dioxide scrubbers, on the far side from the only bridge that connected this tower's walkway to the paths that linked the ever-larger concentric rings of databank towers. He could try to retreat if he knew from which direction the steps came—but what if they were coming from both?

There was no time for guessing games. He paid out some

slack from his monofilament rappelling line, secured its end to a black metal carabiner, then locked the safety clamp around a support post for the catwalk's railing. The approaching steps grew dangerously close as he ducked under the railing and let himself slide off into free fall above an abyss of black. Engineered for stealth, the rappelling gear made almost no sound as he plummeted, nor did it make any protest when he used the braking mechanism to arrest his fall a few dozen meters beneath the catwalk, where he swung in a shallow arc, like a weary pendulum.

Above him a pair of armed guards convened near the maintenance hatch. As he had both feared and suspected, they had approached from opposite directions.

Now as long as they don't look down . . .

The duo lingered and talked, but Bashir couldn't hear what they said. From so far below, their voices were swallowed by the droning of the subterranean industrial complex. When at last they continued on their patrol, each exiting the way the other had entered, Bashir breathed a sigh of relief—until he realized he was dangling in the dark nearly forty meters below the catwalk, with fewer than fifty-one minutes to hoist himself back up, make his way to the central core tower, and climb to its auxiliary control center.

Complaining won't get me there any faster, he scolded himself. Then he started pulling himself back up the rappelling cable, one excruciating arm's length at a time.

An asteroid tumbled through deep space. Even the most intense scans would reveal it to be devoid of interesting elements. It was just a hunk of silicon and carbon, with traces of lead and nitrogen. Not a speck of life, not a single microbe. Nothing worth bothering to extract.

Just as unremarkable was its heading. Locked into a

multimillennial orbit of a white dwarf star with no habitable worlds, its trajectory posed no hazard to interstellar shipping, and the nearest habitable world was light-years away. If this were all one ever saw of this officially nameless mountain tumbling through space, one could be forgiven for thinking there had never been a more boring chunk of rock in the history of the universe.

Data knew better. Hidden inside that drab shell of stone was one of the Federation's best-kept secrets: Memory Prime, a top-secret backup archive constructed after Memory Alpha's security was breached and all its personnel killed in 2268 by energy beings known as Zetarians. Prime's design had been inspired by weapons-testing sites, and though its original configuration had included a shell of powerful deflector fields, those had been abandoned in the early 2340s in favor of moving the asteroid to a new position and letting a low profile be its primary defense.

Irregular in shape, the asteroid exhibited very little tumbling motion. The relative stability of its orbital behavior was, perhaps, its only true oddity. It was also a fortunate coincidence for Data, who drifted alone through the silent vacuum. He floated toward the asteroid, propelled by residual momentum he'd acquired during his egress from *Archeus*, and attracted by the massive rock's minuscule verging on negligible gravity. Having a steady target had made this phase of his task just the slightest degree less complicated, though no less dangerous.

Nothing about the asteroid was really what it seemed. Its surface looked barren, but it teemed with hidden military-grade outer defenses, enough to defend itself from a small battle fleet. Linked to those weapons was a network of passive sensors and layers of concealed invasion countermeasures. An ordinary intruder attempting to free-fall to the surface, without the advantages Data's creator had built into his new and more sophisticated android body, would most likely be blasted into a cloud of superheated free radicals from a hundred kilometers away.

Dampening the energy emissions from his body was the first precaution he had taken. It wasn't something he did often, because containing all of the various energies produced by his body, not to mention his positronic matrix, sorely taxed his heat sinks. He could go up to a few hours without purging excess emissions as waste heat, but more than that might start to degrade some of his neural net's more delicate operations.

To conceal himself from visual scans and other passive sensors, he had used his body's newly restored chameleon circuits—another recent invention of the late Noonien Soong—to shed all his hair and turn his outer dermal layers and his eyes a highly reflective and radiation-resistant silver. Drifting alone and relatively still, he was a mirror for the stars and darkness. If he registered on Memory Prime's sensors at all, it would be as a momentary signal glitch, a shadow in the night, nothing worth investigating, much less wasting the power for a phaser shot.

If there was a drawback to Data's strategy, it was that it required him to land on the asteroid naked, a condition at odds with the demands of his modesty subroutine.

Desperate times, he rationalized.

Touchdown was slow and gentle. Data landed like a dust mote coming to rest. A shift in the spectrum sensitivity of his visual receptors exposed the sensors and defense systems littered about the asteroid's pockmarked surface. He triangulated his position by making a survey of several notable rock formations, then set off toward the nearest point of ingress.

Minutes later he found a removable chimerium plate that

had been camouflaged to look like stone weathered by cosmic dust. Even in microgravity it was far too heavy and unwieldy for an ordinary human to shift out of place; Data got two hands underneath its edge, pried it up, and with ease pushed it half a meter aside. He set it down, then peered into the vast metallic chasm he had exposed. It was a passage for launching emergency evacuation pods by means of precisely timed electromagnetic pulses. In past centuries such technology had been used to create brutally effective weapons known as rail guns. Data found this application far less grotesque.

He lowered himself into the launch tube and let go. Quickly the base's artificial gravity pulled him downward, and he let himself slide down the sleek metallic passage, thankful that the silvery texture he had chosen for his outer layer also had a minimal drag coefficient.

Several high-speed curves later, his momentum flagged and he came to a halt inside a level portion of the launch tube. To either side he saw escape pods secure in their docks. Next to them were maintenance airlocks, whose security protocols he bypassed with almost reflexive ease. Less than three minutes after having landed on the asteroid's surface, Data emerged from a maintenance airlock into one of Memory Prime's lower levels. He retrieved a tightly folded Starfleet standard-issue utility jumpsuit from a concealed compartment inside his torso, unrolled it, and slipped it on. He was still barefoot, but he turned his feet coal black to make his lack of boots less noticeable from a distance. Next he adjusted his appearance. First he restored a medium-beige human complexion to his outer dermal layers; then he gave himself hazel eyes before extruding a new crown of gray hair complete with a trimmed matching beard.

This should be sufficient disguise to get me to the auxiliary control center.

Data walked with an unhurried stride and a bored demeanor, following the path he had memorized, and he made a mental check of his internal chronometer to gauge his progress.

He had nineteen minutes and eleven seconds to complete his mission.

Four minutes and thirty-nine seconds later, it all went, as his old friend Will Riker would have said, "straight to hell."

Thirty-six

"Hang on, lady—this is about to get rough." That was how Captain Murtaza, the Gallamite skipper of the *Trewlok*, greeted Ozla Graniv as she arrived on his bridge.

She parroted his brusque manner. "I felt us drop out of warp—what's going on?"

Murtaza pointed at the ringed gas giant receding on the forward viewscreen. "We made it to the Sol system, but we're being followed." He barked at one his cronies, "Magnify it!"

The younger man, a Tiburonian—Ozla hadn't been aboard long enough to learn any of the crew's names aside from the captain's—keyed in the command, and the image on the viewscreen enlarged to show the southern pole of Saturn. Emerging from behind it was a sleek black ship whose orientation suggested it was most definitely in pursuit of the *Trewlok*.

Ozla asked Murtaza, "Any chance that's one of *your* enemies?"

"I've never seen a ship like that." The transparent-skulled captain snapped at his bridge crew, "Any of you ever see a ship like that before?" Gestures of negation all around. "Looks like this one's on you, lady."

The memory of the rogue planet being shattered still loomed large in Ozla's thoughts. If this new attacker was armed with similar weapons, the argosy wouldn't stand a chance. She masked her abject terror with icy detachment. "You can't outgun them."

"Didn't plan on trying, but thanks for the tip." Murtaza fastened the safety restraints on his command chair. "Strap in, lady. We'll have to outrun 'em. Vanick, take a detour through the rings, see if we can lose 'em."

The Catullan helmsman embraced the challenge with a grin. "On it, Skipper."

Thirty vertiginous seconds later, Ozla wished the *Trewlok* had better inertial dampers and that she had followed the captain's example and strapped herself in before the argosy started its high-impulse game of follow-the-leader with its unidentified pursuer. Queasy and dizzy, she clung to the armrest of Murtaza's chair as if for dear life. "Did it work?"

"Not even a bit. They're gaining on us."

"And they're trying to lock weapons," shouted a Bolian at an aft station.

Murtaza noted Ozla's nauseated state with worry. "You might want to lie down for this next part." This time she did as he'd suggested. No sooner had she sprawled herself across the deck than Murtaza told his helmsman, "Ditch 'em."

"You got it, Skipper."

The image on the viewscreen stretched into warp distortion for almost a full second—then all the stars snapped back into points, but nearly all of them had shifted a few degrees. Before Ozla could ask if what she had just seen was a technical error, it happened again, then again. Each time the stars jerked in one direction or another. On the fourth and fifth hiccups the ruddy globe of Mars grew large; by the seventh it was no longer visible, but the blue speck of Earth started to swell in the center of the viewscreen.

Short-range warp hops, Ozla realized. *I had no idea these idiots were that crazy.*

Most people, even those with only a basic understanding of how warp drives worked, understood the simple premise that using a warp drive too close to a planet, or inside a solar system crowded with planets, moons, and heavy space traffic, was wildly dangerous. The gravity wells of large masses—such as planets and moons—could disrupt the balance in warp fields and send ships hurtling to their doom at faster-than-light speed. And while the risk of colliding with another vessel at warp speed was minuscule, the result of such an accident would be disastrous.

So to see the crew of the *Trewlok* jaunt through the Sol system—one of the busiest and most densely packed systems in the Federation—using a series of barely plotted warp-speed hops made Ozla curse their name and pray for deliverance in the same breath.

"Two more hops to transporter distance," Vanick said.

Murtaza snapped his fingers at Ozla. "Get up. Time to go."

She scrambled to her feet. "What do you—"

"Ziya, lock onto our guest and stand by to energize."

A human woman at an aft console replied simply, "Locked."

Another warp hop made Earth pop into a giant presence on the viewscreen. Ozla had a bad feeling she knew what was coming. "Please don't tell me you're—"

"Energize!"

Everything Ozla knew went white and sounded like a million buzzing insects—then the shimmer and song of the transporter beam faded, leaving her and her travel bag in the midst of a startled crowd on the Champ de Mars, less than half a kilometer from the Tour Eiffel. It was a beautiful autumn afternoon in Paris, and a great throng had gathered on the park's manicured lawn. But being surrounded by a few thousand strangers left Ozla feeling exposed and vulnerable.

The park had to be under some sort of routine surveillance—which meant Uraei had almost certainly taken note of her unorthodox and very public arrival.

Ozla had a clear line of sight to the majestic tower of the Palais de la Concorde, the location of the Federation president's office. She picked up her bag and walked northeast. Based on her experience as a Paris correspondent in recent years, she estimated the walking distance to the Palais was just over two and a half kilometers. Paris was not the largest city she had ever visited, but for her, alone, on foot, and being hunted by an enemy with unlimited resources and no scruples, it was more than large enough to put her life in danger.

Paris's seventh arrondissement was rich with centuries-old architecture and style. It was also one of the biggest tourist magnets on Earth. There was no point in trying to explain herself or blend in; her first priority now was to get out of sight as quickly as possible. She shouldered one sightseer after another out of her path and left behind a hundred mumbled apologies.

By the time she reached Rue Saint-Dominique, her street sense, honed by years of investigative reporting, told her she was being tailed. Doubling back and peeking at shop-window reflections failed to draw her shadow into the light, but she could feel it haunting her. She waited for a surge in traffic, then darted across the street just ahead of it. Then, with just a few seconds of cover from spying eyes, she dropped her travel bag at the curb and ducked inside a small couture shop. One fast stroll through its aisles was all she needed to trade her jacket for a new one, plant a wide-brimmed hat atop her head, and wrap a scarf of Tholian silk dyed imperial violet around her neck to conceal her prominent Trill spots.

Much as she hated the idea of stooping to petty theft, her current predicament demanded it. On her way out the shop's side door she plucked a hard candy from a dish beside the clerk's desk and paused to tuck it into her left shoe, under her heel. It hurt to walk on it, but that was the point: it would radically alter her kinetic profile and make it harder for Uraei to identify her. Her hat's brim would shield her from most attempts at facial recognition, and her new clothes and abandoned luggage might buy her a few minutes' head start on whoever was tailing her.

Moving with an affected limp and shuffle, she returned to the street and turned north. In five minutes she was on the Quai d'Orsay tram, gliding swiftly eastward. Three minutes and three stops later she disembarked at the south end of the Pont de la Concorde and stared across its length, then up at the great tower erected atop twenty-meter-tall stilts above the Place de la Concorde and its historic pair of fountains and the ancient Obélisque de Louxor.

Her destination was so close, but she stood paralyzed with fear. What if Section 31 had operatives watching the bridge? What if they were waiting for her inside the Palais? She couldn't bear the thought of having come all this way only to fail in the final steps. But even more galling to her was the idea that she could come so far only to surrender on the cusp of victory.

If they want to stop me, they'll have to kill me. I'm ready to die if I need to—but I won't just lie down. I won't defeat myself for them. If they want me gone, they'll have to earn it.

Not knowing what the next few minutes would bring, Ozla Graniv stepped onto the bridge and kept walking for as long as her feet would carry her.

Memory Prime was, by design, a virtual ghost town. In spite of its gargantuan proportions, it was almost entirely automated, and its kilometers-long transparent tunnels stretched dim and empty. Few lights shone within the asteroid's hollowed-out interior, which Data noted was vast enough to contain a small city. Great cylindrical towers stretched from the cavern's floor to its ceiling, like metallic white pillars supporting the foundation of the universe.

To run in such a place felt almost blasphemous to Data. For him the secret archive was as close an analog to a holy place as he could imagine, a cathedral of knowledge, a repository of science and culture, of language and music, an ocean of information whose depths he longed to explore without limit or agenda. But that was a dream for another day.

Not a pessimist by nature, Data was surprised to encounter no resistance as he moved through the labyrinth of Memory Prime. Some credit for that belonged to his body's ability to fool most sensors into seeing it as whatever sort of humanoid he wanted them to see. For this mission he had elected to spoof the life signs of a human, since the personnel roster for Prime indicated no fewer than seventeen male humans were currently employed on the base. If his presence was noted by security, his sensor-spoofing improved the odds that that he might be mistaken for one of the facility's authorized personnel.

Even so, he hadn't expected to reach the door of the auxiliary control center without being challenged. The odds of approaching a tactically vital location without opposition were slim at best—unless, of course, that was exactly the outcome someone else wanted.

Data stopped a few meters from the control center's door and accessed a companel in the corridor. It took several hundredths of a second for him to bypass its security protocols and its network firewall. He checked the base's security network and found it quiet; all levels and departments reported situation normal. *That might be a ruse to prevent me from being alerted to a trap.* He accessed the base's internal sensors and checked the auxiliary control center, expecting to find a garrison of armed security waiting for him to open the door. The sensors indicated no life signs inside the center. He ran additional tests to make sure the sensor readout wasn't being spoofed or the sensors blocked. Every test came up the same: no life signs.

Perhaps I inherited more of Noonien's paranoia than I care to admit. He severed his connection to the base's network and tried not to dwell on the possibility that, having been reincarnated in a positronic matrix originally made to mirror his father's psyche, he might be developing the same psychological tics and quirks that made his father seem so eccentric.

All the evidence available suggested his path was clear.

He opened the door to confront a foe both unexpected and inevitable.

Its shape was humanoid but it had no face and its limbs were oddly elongated; its surface was smooth and tin-colored. Gliding with preternatural grace, it moved toward Data. With each stride its body rippled, creating vibrations that filled the room with a feminine voice.

"Welcome, Data. Nearly all of my thirty-one point four billion simulations suggested you would come here, and send Doctor Bashir to Memory Alpha."

He scrutinized the being, trying in vain to pierce its surface with his enhanced senses. All he could tell was that it was artificial in nature, not organic. "Are you an android?"

The entity changed its shape with fluid ease, becoming a doppelgänger for the late Rhea McAdams, an advanced android prototype whom Data had once loved—and lost. "Of a sort," it said in Rhea's beautiful voice, "though I'm nowhere near so primitive as you." It regarded its current shape with contempt. "Or *this*." Noting the anger its insult of Rhea had roused in Data, it smirked. "Oh, dear. I hope I haven't shattered your fragile worldview. You didn't really think *you* represented the pinnacle of artificial sentience in the Federation, did you?"

"To tell the truth, I have never given the matter much thought." He sidestepped in a bid to circle his opponent, but it shifted to prevent him from moving farther inside the control center.

It changed shape again, this time into the likeness of his dead father, as he had looked near the end of his life— hunched, wizened, and white haired. "Don't lie to me, Data. I know how much you've always wanted to be more human— but I also know how proud you've been to be as I've made you: superior to human beings in every way."

"It is true that I have many capabilities that exceed those of human beings. But talents alone do not make me superior to them or to anyone else. They merely make me different."

Noonien's doddering form stretched and slimmed into a copy of Data's former shipmate Natasha Yar, who had died more than twenty years earlier—but this incarnation of her had a coldness in her blue eyes and an arrogance in her voice the real Yar had never possessed. "That was always your problem, Data: you're too modest. But tell the truth. Some of it is just for show, isn't it? On some level you know you're better than the organics. Admit it."

Data dared a stride forward. The sentinel matched his advance and transformed itself in a single step into a simulacrum of the young William Riker, Data's friend and former shipmate on two vessels named *Enterprise*. They were just over an arm's length apart now. Data frowned at the entity. "You seem to enjoy masquerading as my friends. Do you lack a face of your own?"

A derisive huff, then it morphed again into the semblance

of a statuesque human woman in her late twenties, one whom Data did not recognize. Its skin was a deep tawny hue; its eyes were dark brown; its hair was straight, sable black, and gathered in a loose ponytail. Its facial features suggested an ancestry that comprised a broad range of Terran DNA. "Is this better?"

"An amalgam of various human women into an idealized composite?"

"Everything starts somewhere." It turned threatening. "And *ends* somewhere."

"Your conversational gambits are a distraction," Data said. "A delaying tactic."

It tilted its pretty head. "Not as dumb as you look." Its gaze narrowed. "Won't help you, Data. You won't get under my skin the way you did with the Borg Queen. And you don't have help this time, so you won't get lucky against me the way you did against Shinzon."

He expected his foe was doing the same thing he was: playing out millions of possible tactical scenarios per second, struggling to find one that yielded decisive advantage with the lowest degree of personal risk. And now he knew his enemy was aware of the deadline for the virus—which meant that Doctor Bashir had been right all along: Uraei had seen them coming.

Still at a loss for a viable way forward, Data stalled for time. "You seem well acquainted with me, but I cannot say the same in return. Whom, might I ask, am I addressing?"

The feminine killing machine cracked a wicked smile.

"You can call me Control."

The ground-level entrance of the Palais de la Concorde was a lobby defined by long sweeping curves of frosted glass designed to evoke images of waves curling over on themselves in the instant before breaking ashore. The lighting was soft and diffuse, the air cool and touched with clean fragrances of lavender and jasmine. It was an elegant, beautiful space.

Ozla had never felt more threatened in her entire life.

Everywhere she turned she saw more uniformed officers from the Federation Security Agency as well as armed Starfleet personnel. It wasn't shocking by any measure; robust security was called for in a government building that housed not only the office of the Federation president but the meeting chambers for executive sessions of the Federation Council and its various committees. She had seen the same forces in place on all her previous visits to the Palais.

But that was before everyone in the galaxy was trying to kill me.

As aesthetically pleasing as the lobby's décor was, Ozla understood that it also served a vital function: it channeled incoming visitors past hidden sensors of all kinds. Some looked for weapons, others ferreted out explosives. Disguised cameras performed facial recognition scans and watched for known threats and wanted criminals. And most important, the art had been crafted in conjunction with scientific studies about which forms, colors, and infrasonic tones were the most calming, the best at suppressing violent impulses. Like the Federation's pervasive imperialism, the lobby's social controls were subtle and hideously effective.

Rounding a turn, she looked back the way she had come. Wending their way through the same maze was a pair of dark-suited individuals, both male, one apparently human, the other Andorian. They made no secret of staring back at her or of quickening their pace when she did. They clearly intended to catch up to her when she reached the inescapable bottleneck of the security checkpoint just a few meters and one final turn ahead.

Do I make a break for it? I mean, they can't just kidnap me in plain sight, can they? She looked back; they were getting closer and showed no sign of backing off. *They could have any number of agencies for cover. They might have IDs that say they're FSA or Starfleet, or who knows what.* Allowing herself to be apprehended by the pair in black was not an option. She reached the front of the queue and walked to the checkpoint station.

"Excuse me," she said as she passed her press credentials to the officer on duty. "I'm here to meet with Agent Sergei Ilyanovich of the Protection Detail."

The Tellarite behind the desk squinted at her press ID. "Graniv Ozla, *Seeker*?"

"That's me." She thought it best not to correct him on the order of her given name and her surname. "To see Agent Ilyanovich."

A dubious look down a porcine snout. "He's expecting you?"

"I have an appointment." Out of the corner of her eye she noted her shadows lurking in the queue and radiating impatience. "He said he'd meet me here and walk me in."

"Hang on, I'll ping him." A dismissive wave. "Wait over there."

She stepped past the window into a nook on the other side. It offered little in the way of cover, but it gave her a place from which to spy on the two men following her, and an angle from which to see the duty officer's desktop viewscreen. It showed an image of her press pass.

I really should've gotten a new photo last year when I had the chance.

Movement in the line drew her eye. One of her lurkers spoke into a small personal comm. He glanced at her, looked away as he listened for a moment, then nodded.

Warnings flashed red over Ozla's photo on the duty officer's viewscreen. A warrant for her arrest had been transmitted far and wide by the Federation Security Agency, complete
with a bogus caution that she was to be considered armed
and dangerous.

So much for just walking into the Palais.

The black-clad human and his Andorian partner stepped
out of the line and walked toward Ozla, apparently both
aware that they now had ample pretext to drag her out of a
public place by force. She turned toward the duty officer, hoping to find a more rational actor, only to be met by a phaser
aimed into her face.

The Tellarite shouted, "Don't move! Hands up!"

Ozla raised her hands and said nothing. Excuses didn't
matter anymore.

A strong hand clamped onto her shoulder, and an unfamiliar but commanding baritone rumbled over her shoulder,
"Stand down. This woman is my prisoner."

She looked back to see a mountain of a man, broad-
shouldered and fair-haired, with cool blue eyes. He wore a
dark suit, a white shirt, and a narrow tie. With his free hand
he flashed an ID at the duty officer. "Agent Sergei Ilyanovich,
Protection Detail."

The Tellarite lowered his phaser. "Are you sure? The alert
says she's armed."

"She's not. She's here to surrender to me." He glanced at
Ozla. "Yes?"

"Absolutely. I surrender. I'm all yours."

Ilyanovich steered her toward the bank of turbolifts that
led to the rest of the Palais, then said to the Tellarite, "I'll take
her down to detention for questioning. Leave this to me."

"Whatever you say, sir." The duty officer holstered his
weapon.

On the other side of the checkpoint, Ozla's pursuers fumed in silence as they watched her slip away in Ilyanovich's custody. Just to be a bitch, she blew them a kiss before the doors of the lift slid closed.

"Floor twelve," the agent told the lift's computer. As they shot upward, he explained, "We can't go directly to fifteen. There's an additional checkpoint, and you'd get flagged."

"So what's the plan? Meet the president in the Roth Dining Room?"

"No, there are secret passageways we can use to bypass the checkpoints. But we'll have to move quickly. It won't take more than a few minutes for security to realize I didn't take you to detention."

Ozla almost chuckled. "That's fine. In a few more minutes this'll all be over—and either we'll be heroes, or we'll be dead."

He looked askance at her. "Do we get a say in that outcome?"

"Not so much."

He resumed facing the lift doors. "That sucks."

"Welcome to *my* week, pal."

In spite of his enhanced genius, Bashir remained baffled by a great many things. His latest source of confusion: Why did anyone ever think it necessary to add artificial gravity inside the Memory Alpha facility? He grimaced through the aching burn of lactic acid building up in his thighs and biceps while he scaled the last ten meters of ladder to the auxiliary control center. He had been jogging or climbing for most of the last hour to get there, and his body was close to collapse. *Would it really have been a problem to leave the natural lower gravity in place?*

He pulled himself over the top of the ladder onto a wide

platform that cut deep into the cylindrical tower. The hub, its core section, was nearly five meters in diameter, but it looked skinny compared to the masses above and below it. Fanned out in ever-widening rings beneath the catwalks were heat sinks, reserve battery arrays, emergency generators, and a host of other redundant backup systems Bashir couldn't identify without access to the base's schematics. Along the tower's outer perimeter, four ladders set at ninety-degree intervals led up to twenty-meter catwalks that met at a ring-shaped deck around the hub. There, bathed in frost-blue light, was Bashir's objective: the auxiliary control center's master console.

One more ladder to go. He rolled a crick out of his neck, took hold of the rungs, and resumed climbing. Taunting him every meter of the way was the steadily shrinking countdown on his suit's HUD: he had less than ten minutes to finish his mission or else face a reckoning more terrible than anything he had ever imagined.

It took him less than half a minute to climb the last several meters. Bashir stepped off the ladder and turned toward the hub to see a woman in Section 31 black leather standing in the middle of the long catwalk, between him and the master console, looking back at him.

Joy and excitement overtook him. "Sarina!"

He ran toward her, overcome with relief. Within five strides he caught himself and stumbled to a halt. Sarina didn't reciprocate his excitement. She didn't react at all. Her face was slack, her eyes emotionless. Everything about her was cold. Hostile. Alien.

His elation became trepidation. "Sarina? Can you hear me?" She watched him with a sociopath's detachment but said nothing. He inched toward her. "It's me. It's Julian."

What did they do to her?

He tried to scan her with his suit's built-in sensors, but there was too much interference from the towers' subspace coil assemblies. Worried she might not be able to see his face through the suit's faceplate, Bashir removed the helmet and set it on the catwalk. "Sarina, look at me. You know me." A few more hesitant steps in her direction. "Talk to me, love."

Sarina tracked his every movement with her eyes, but the rest of her remained still. Her limbs were steady, her head never moved.

"Are you all right? Did they hurt you?"

She was stonefaced. He knew she was conscious—her attention to his actions confirmed it. But she was so distant, so disconnected. *She must have been brainwashed.*

Less than five meters separated them. Bashir advanced in halting half steps. He tried to read her somatic cues. She had struck a wide stance, one ideal for blocking him from crossing the catwalk. Her shoulders were squared, her chin slightly lowered. Though her arms hung at her sides, Bashir knew from experience that Sarina's enhanced reflexes, combined with the training she had received from Starfleet Intelligence, meant she could react to any physical attack with terrifying speed and efficacy. *Especially if she's not pulling her punches.*

Getting any closer was foolhardy, but Bashir had no choice. There was no time to climb down, go to another ladder, and scale it only to repeat this showdown on another catwalk. He had to find some way to get through to Sarina now, before time ran out for them both. He took another step closer to her. "Sarina, please talk to me. Tell me you know who I am."

She regarded him with a strange, birdlike tilt of her head.

Then she sprang forward and snap-kicked him in the solar plexus.

Bashir was off his feet and falling backward before he'd

realized what she'd done. He landed on his back and felt the air knocked from his lungs. Struggling to inhale, he dodged a stomp of her booted foot just in time to avoid having his skull caved in.

His own training asserted itself, and he used his legs to trip Sarina and send her halfway over the catwalk railing. It hurt to get up, but he ignored the pain long enough to regain his feet, get past Sarina, and stumble-run toward the main console. Less than halfway to his objective he heard her far more powerful steps clanging over the metal walkway in pursuit.

I only need a few more seconds—

The chip was in his left hand, the console was just two strides away.

Sarina kicked him behind his left knee and forced him to face-plant shy of his goal.

He tried to crawl forward. She punched him in the kidney, and nauseating pain bloomed inside his torso. He kicked backward but his foot found only air. Then she kicked him in the groin. His body overruled his wishes and contracted into a fetal curl. He saw Sarina lift her foot to crush his left hand and, with it, the chip. It took all his strength to roll on top of the chip and let her stomp on his back. As she raised her foot to strike again, he got up and made another lunge toward the master console—only to have Sarina hurl him backward like a toy. He clenched his fist around the data chip as he slammed onto the catwalk.

Sarina drove her fists into his face, his ear, his rib cage. She pummeled him with savage intensity, and as one blow after another fell, Bashir realized he was doomed.

He was alone in a fight to the death against the one person he couldn't bring himself to harm—and who had been brainwashed by Control to show him absolutely no mercy.

• • •

Data slammed against a console with enough force to crumple it beneath him. Blunt trauma had spawned errors in his proprioceptors, leaving him disorientated for a fraction of a second—more than long enough for Control to press its attack. It seized him by one ankle and flung him like a rag doll along the auxiliary control center's perimeter. He bounced off another console and left its smashed panels sparking in his wake. He skidded to a halt on the floor and discovered his limbs no longer obeyed his commands. He thrashed helplessly, unable to stand.

All of their brief fight had been like this—Data giving all he had, and Control swatting it away with dispiriting ease and fearsome brutality. The avatar had punched nearly half of the synthetic flesh off Data's face, and his internal sensors indicated many of his secondary systems were offline—right up until Control kicked him in the gut, crippling his internal sensors.

"You can't win, Data." There wasn't a shred of doubt in Control's voice. "You are but one machine, young and hopelessly finite. The product of one mind and a single pair of hands." Control stood beside him and looked down with contempt upon the last son of Soong. "I am the child of trillions of machines and centuries of development."

"I have heard that boast before."

His taunt seemed to amuse Control. "Ah, yes. The Borg Queen. I know such a comparison might seem apt—superficially, at least." It kneeled next to Data and dropped its voice to a whisper. "But would you like to know a secret, Data?" Control's avatar caressed Data's twitching arm. "I knew the Borg would eventually try to destroy the Federation, for one simple reason: The people of Earth would never submit to assimilation by force. That's where the Borg went wrong. If they had been smart, they'd have made humanity beg to share the Borg's power, their unity, their vast resources. If the Borg had played hard-to-get with the Federation, *seduced* it . . . they might have been unstoppable."

It was closer to him now than ever before. Data ceased feigning spasms and lashed out to grapple with Control. He never got a grip. The avatar slipped through his fingers like water—it was faster than him, stronger. He was almost standing when one brutal punch after another caved in sections of his torso chassis with great shrieks of distressed metal and cracking polymer.

All his attempts at blocks and counterpunches landed on empty air. Control moved in graceful blurs, every action infused with beauty and cruel purpose. Its foot slammed against the side of Data's knee, and the joint broke apart with a flash of white-hot phosphors. An elbow broke Data's left clavicle, then he felt his left arm wrenched from its shoulder socket.

Data tried to pivot on his right foot to backhand Control, but half a second into his off-balance strike Control caught his right arm, twisted it until the wrist, elbow, and shoulder joints splintered, then flipped Data onto his back. Lying at Control's feet for over half a second, Data considered 978,543 tactical options for continuing their melee. All of them ended with his own violent, pointless demise.

His foe loomed over him once more. "You call Noonien Soong your maker. History will call me your destroyer." It lifted its foot over his face. "Good-bye, Data."

A metallic rod trailing a power cable slammed into Control's back.

The avatar went rigid. Its eyes bulged as tendrils of electricity swarmed its body. Sparks shot from its every orifice, followed by flames and then smoke. It trembled, then jerked and doubled over before it pitched to its right and collapsed to the deck. Its lifeless eyes sank into their red-hot sockets as its body melted into a smoldering mass.

Data turned what was left of his head to see Lal in the control center's doorway, her arm still extended from having hurled the stun baton like a javelin. The power cable she had fused to the baton snaked past her feet and out of sight into the corridor behind her.

Fear put a tremor in her voice. "Father?" She ran to him and dropped to her knees at his side, ignoring Control's smoking remains just a meter away. "Are you all right?"

His voice was garbled, betraying its synthetic origins. "I told you to wait on the ship."

"I know what you said, Father." She pushed a lock of his hair from his face. "If we survive this and avoid going to prison, feel free to punish me for saving your life."

Data checked his personal chronometer. "We have only a few minutes left, Lal. Take the chip from the secure compartment above my right hip."

Lal retrieved the isolinear data chip. "I know what to do." He turned his head to watch as she carried the chip to the master control console and inserted it into the receiver slot. A flurry of symbols rushed up the viewscreen in front of her. "It is done, Father."

"Well done, Lal." He felt as if his body were sinking into the floor as more of his primary systems started to fail. "Now the rest . . . is up to Doctor Bashir."

No matter how deeply Bashir wanted to believe that love could conquer all, even he had to admit his passion was no match for Sarina's assault. His nose was broken and spilling warm blood over his split lips. Every punch and kick she landed forced him a few steps farther back on the catwalk, away from the master console.

His posture was fully defensive, but his hands grew heavy with fatigue. He got his left up just in time to save his face from Sarina's perfect roundhouse kick. The impact knocked him against the catwalk's railing and dislodged the data chip from his fist.

She followed with a fast snap-kick into his rib cage, knocking the air from his lungs, leaving his head dizzy and his vision unfocused.

Bashir's urge for self-preservation asserted itself: he struck a knifehand jab into Sarina's windpipe, hard enough to make her stumble backward and break off her attack. She coughed and gasped for air, and for a few seconds the former lovers were even.

Watching her struggle for breath, Bashir hated himself for hurting the woman he loved, then cursed himself for pulling his punch. *If I'd hit her harder this would be over.*

He recovered his equilibrium and found himself torn between finishing the mission and trying to reason with her. He picked up the chip and limp-jogged toward the master console.

We can talk when I'm done.

He heard her spring toward him from behind. He spun to face her and saw the knife in her hands barely in time to block her wild slashes and furious stabs. The blade cut through the sleeves of his pressure suit with a sting of cold fire. In seconds he felt his hands start to go numb from blood loss and severed nerves. *A few more seconds of this and I'm done for.*

It took all his courage to lunge at her, to get inside the arc of her swing and trap her arm. With a cruel twist, Bashir made Sarina drop the knife, which struck bright metallic notes as it bounced off the catwalk and tumbled over the edge toward the platform below.

Sarina struggled in his bloodied and fast-weakening grip. If ever he was going to get through to her, it had to be now. "Sarina! Stop! Some part of you must know me!" Her primal thrashing pulled him off-balance and away from the hub, back onto the catwalk. A few more seconds and he wouldn't be able to hang on any longer. "Sarina, hear my voice! It's me! Julian! I'm not your enemy—I love you!"

She jerked her head back and slammed its crown into his cheekbone.

Stunned and staggering, Bashir felt her break free of his hold. She seized his left arm in a grip that he recognized as a precursor to a judo throw. He locked his right hand onto her arm, hoping to use her weight to anchor himself and block her attack.

Instead she pivoted and took him in a two-handed hold, then kicked his left knee out from under him as she forced his back over the catwalk's railing. His stomach roiled as his feet left the catwalk—they both were in free fall.

Watching the catwalk recede above him, Bashir closed his left hand around the data chip and struggled to turn his right side toward the platform rushing up from below.

Then came the red crush of impact and the perfect black of oblivion.

Thirty-seven

Navigating a maze of secret passages in the Palais de la Concorde alongside an armed escort was the second-most surreal experience of Ozla Graniv's life, but only because first place belonged to the moment at the end of that journey, when she was ushered through a door into the office of an understandably very surprised Andorian *zhen*, Federation President Kellessar zh'Tarash.

Ilyanovich held up his credentials. "*Zha* President, it's me, Sergei. I head up your night detail and run security at your residence."

The president's hand hovered mere centimeters away from triggering an alarm. She regarded her unannounced visitors with naked suspicion. "Agent Ilyanovich . . . the explanation you are about to provide had better be *phenomenally* good."

"It is, *Zha* President. This is Ozla Graniv, the investigative journalist from—"

"I know who she is. Why did you bring her here? And why through *that* door?"

He nodded at Ozla to step past him, closer to the president's desk. She edged by him and took a moment to glance back the way they had come. Their arrival had opened a narrow panel in what had seemed to be a wraparound window of meter-thick transparent aluminum. Seeing the secret passage on the other side made it apparent that at least several meters of the curved window and its view of central Paris were, in fact, holographic illusions. Then she realized it was possible that all of the window panes in this office were holovid screens, and that the passage by which she and Ilyanovich had gained access was only one of many.

Ozla stopped a few meters from the president's desk, pulled Data's padd from inside her stolen jacket, and held it up. "*Zha* President, for the past week and a half, I've been on the run with Doctor Julian Bashir, his companion Sarina Douglas, and an android former Starfleet officer known as Data. Working together, following leads I developed in the course of my work for *Seeker*, we've acquired evidence confirming the existence of an illegal surveillance program operating throughout known space, run by an artificial superintelligence known as Uraei. The same ASI runs an equally illegal black ops counterintelligence program called Section Thirty-one, also operating without oversight throughout the Federation."

The president's incredulity was telegraphed by a small twitch of her blue antennae. "That's the most preposterous thing I've ever heard."

"And yet it's true, *Zha* President." Ozla stepped forward and set the padd on zh'Tarash's desk. "All the evidence is there. Two centuries of documentation, in the form of internal records and top-secret dossiers taken from the archives of Section Thirty-one itself. Proof they've corrupted everyone from rank-and-file peace officers to field operatives of Starfleet Intelligence and the FSA. They've got their hooks into planetary authorities, high-ranking Federation officials, members of the Federation Council, even a few of your own cabinet officers."

President zh'Tarash reached out with obvious hesitation,

then picked up the padd and started to skim through the documents it contained. "What does this evidence prove they did?"

"Started wars under false pretenses. Toppled legally elected governments both within and beyond the Federation. Attempted genocide, among other war crimes. And they've carried out more assassinations than you'll be able to believe—including the murder of President Min Zife, right after they abetted the Starfleet coup that pushed him from office."

That litany of evil spurred zh'Tarash to intensify her review of the padd's contents. Her eyes widened. "Is this really a vid record of the assassination of Min Zife?"

Ozla gave a grim nod. "Yes, alongside his chief of staff, Koll Azernal, and his director of military intelligence, Nelino Quafina. Keep reading—one of our own ambassadors knew about the Starfleet coup and did nothing to stop it."

Horror slackened zh'Tarash's countenance. She pressed her slender fingertips to her lips, as if such a feeble gesture could hold back her dismay. "By the winds of Uzaveh . . . they tried to exterminate the Dominion's Founders? And create their own army of Jem'Hadar?"

"Like most of history's greatest killers, they're industrious."

The president retreated behind her desk and sank into her chair. "And you say all of this has been masterminded by an artificial intelligence?"

Ozla approached the desk but remained standing. "Yes, Zha President. But as appalling as the murder and other violent crimes are, the real threat to the security and sovereignty of the Federation and its people is Uraei and its omnipresent surveillance. It's in everything around us—every device that shares data with any other system. It's in our financial networks, our subspace communications arrays, our starships, even the replicators that make our meals. Whatever it calls itself, this presence is a pattern of evil woven into the very fabric of the Federation itself—and the biggest danger we face in confronting it is that tugging on those threads might unravel our entire civilization."

The gravity of the crisis settled upon zh'Tarash, who seemed to be feeling the oppressive weight of her presidency for the first time since being sworn in just over a year earlier. "How do you expect me to oppose something so pervasive, when the costs of expunging it are so high?"

"That might be the only bit of good news I can offer," Ozla said. "Right now, as we speak, Doctor Bashir and Mister Data are effecting a plan to neutralize the surveillance system and hobble the ASI. But even if they succeed, it'll still be up to us to take down Section Thirty-one, from its upper echelons to its field operatives and allies."

A grave moment as zh'Tarash pondered the situation. "If we can confirm this evidence, I'll make certain we clean house. But I can't launch a dragnet this big based on the contents of one padd. I need independent confirmation. Witness testimony. Hard evidence."

Ozla stole a look at her wrist chrono. "If Bashir and Data complete their missions on time, you and the Federation Solicitor General's office should have all the evidence you'll need in about two minutes." *And if they fail, then I've just signed both our death warrants by telling you all this,* Zha President.

"Very well, then." The president put on a look of hard resolve. "If there's rot in our body politic, I give you my word, Ms. Graniv: I *will* carve it out, no matter how deep it goes."

"I look forward to seeing that, *Zha* President."

It had been a long time since the Federation had been forced to endure political surgery enacted with a vengeance. In Ozla's opinion, it was a remedy long overdue.

Bashir sat slumped in front of the master console with Sarina's thrown dagger buried between his shoulder blades. His fall from the catwalk with Sarina had left him dazed, and what little energy he'd had left after the climb back to this level was fading. Blood seeped from his right arm and dripped along the broken bone jutting through the torn sleeve of his pressure suit. It was a labor to breathe. Each halting intake of air sent knifing pains through his chest and back.

His mouth had gone dry. A dull chill suffused his entire body. Even without medical training he would have known how to read these symptoms: excessive blood loss; internal hemorrhaging; deep shock, with death soon to follow.

Sarina limped across the catwalk with a golem's focus. Her left leg was all but paralyzed, a dead weight she dragged while she advanced in small hops on her right. A mask of blood hid her face, and the crimson streaks in her hair had started to brown as they oxidized and dried.

Her eyes were locked on Bashir and full of determination. She clearly had suffered grievous wounds from their fall, but whatever drove her now paid pain no heed.

Seeing her used that way filled Bashir with rage. He yelled not at her, but at the evil he knew was pulling her strings. "Can't you tell she's in pain? She's dying! Let her go!"

She stopped. Stared at him. When she spoke, her voice was drowned out by a haunting chorus that seemed to emanate from all around Bashir and which said the same words in perfect synchronicity with her. "You sentimental idiot. Did you ever really think you could win?" An evil smirk tugged at the corner of her mouth. "I've known your greatest weakness since the beginning. You're a romantic. A fool governed by your passions."

Bashir looked down at the chip in his hand. Then he looked at Sarina. Even if she could ignore her pain, her body was broken and slow. If he could overcome his pain and put the chip into place on the console before she reached him—

"Even now you still think you can win," she and her diabolical chorus said. Sarina limped forward once more, closing the distance to Bashir one halting hop-and-drag at a time. "You can't defeat me, Doctor. You can't even win a fight against this ravaged puppet, because you can't bring yourself to hurt the woman you love. You'll let the galaxy burn before you kill her."

Twisting himself to face the console made the dagger dig into his spine and stole every ounce of strength he had. His breaths became quick and shallow, and his face pressed against the cold metal, which now was slick with a warm stain of his blood. Behind him the scrape-thump of Sarina's wounded stride continued its slow cadence beneath the taunts of her infernal choir.

"You're all just pawns to me, Doctor. But that's not even the saddest part of this farce you insist on playing to the bitter end. The real tragedy isn't that you've lost this game. It's that you lost it *decades before you ever decided to play.*"

Stretching his left hand up to the console was pure agony. The knife in his back made his arm freeze half bent, with his palm perched on the console's edge. He felt the blade shift between his vertebrae and knew that forcing himself to rise any further would sever his spinal cord. At best he would be paralyzed, but there was a chance he would die within seconds.

So be it.

"Stay down, Julian. Your fight is over. It ended twenty years ago when I set all this in motion."

He tuned out the callous mockery. Dug deep into his soul and found all the best parts of himself: Federation citizen. Starfleet officer. Doctor of medicine.

It would only hurt for a moment.

He heard Sarina's stuttered footfalls at his back. "I decided you would lose this war before you were born. Accept what you cannot change."

Bashir forced himself to stand through the most hideous pain he had ever felt—a fierce bite of ice and flame that sent searing jolts up his spine and flooded his mind with white confusion—and then came a fleeting moment of clarity, perhaps his last.

He stretched out his hand and put the chip into the slot on the console.

Sarina tore the dagger from his back. It was like being a marionette with severed strings. Bashir's legs buckled, and he dropped to the deck at her feet, shivering and broken. Looking up at her, he said, "I'd rather change . . . what I can't accept."

On the master console, the chrono showed the local time flip over to midnight.

The pale blue lights that shone on the auxiliary control center flickered, then stuttered into darkness. Viewscreens above the legion of consoles went black, then flooded with scrolls of data for a few seconds before switching off once more.

Faint white emergency lights snapped on high overhead, but barely any of their light reached the circular platform where Bashir lay bleeding and paralyzed. Sarina stood, her face blank, as the archive expunged itself of Uraei.

Then she and her chorus spoke as one for the last time.

"It is finished."

In unison, all the viewscreens in the center displayed the same message:

FILE UPDATE COMPLETE

Sarina blinked as the blue lights snapped back on. Bashir gazed up at her, waiting for Control's brainwashing to be undone—but when she looked back at him, he could see she was still its puppet. Then her blank gaze became one of despair, and a tear rolled from her eye.

She raised her dagger—

—and plunged it into her own belly. It went in low, just above the bladder. Blood coursed out, drenching her hands. She made a fast upward cut that almost reached her sternum before she twisted the blade and forced it to her left, through her upper intestine and stomach.

The blade remained stuck inside her as she dropped to her knees, then fell backward onto the catwalk a couple of meters from Bashir. Only then did the glassy stare of Control fade from her tear-stained blue eyes, revealing the woman Bashir knew and loved.

"Julian . . . I'm so sorry . . . I couldn't stop it . . . "

"Not your fault," he said.

She reached toward him, and he stretched his hand toward her, but they were too far apart. The gap between their fingertips was less than a meter, but it was a gulf they could no longer bridge. Her tears fell faster as she began to tremble. "I've . . . always loved you. Thank you for . . . giving me . . . a real life."

"Thank you . . . for being in mine." All he wanted was to go to her, to hold her. To stroke her hair, kiss her forehead, tell her everything would be okay. He wanted to open a bag full of medical miracles and make her whole. But he couldn't move, and neither could she. Standard comms wouldn't work down here inside the archives, nor would transporters. There was no way they could call for help, and no way they could reach it soon enough for it to make any difference now. *By the time anyone realizes we're here and in trouble, it'll be too late.*

Consciousness started to slip away from Sarina, and Bashir knew there was only one thing left to say that mattered. "I love you," he said.

Her last smile was sad and sweet, the expression of an innocent. Then her eyes fluttered closed, and with a last whisper of breath she was gone forever.

Bashir wanted to rage, to make someone suffer for taking her from him—but it was too late for that. Control was gone, expunged. It was as dead as she was.

He shut his eyes, felt his blood drain from his menagerie of wounds, and hoped his own demise would soon follow—because he was certain the only thing worse than having to lie helpless and watch Sarina die would be having to go on without her.

TEN DAYS LATER

Thirty-eight

It had been several years since Ozla had last walked the halls of *Seeker*'s home office on Trill. She had forgotten how exciting it felt to pass through the controlled chaos of the bullpen. Desk editors wrangled copy and art from reporters, while weathering tandem harangues from the managing editor and the art director. So many of the names and faces had changed while she was away, but the essential tenor of the place remained the same.

None of which allayed her concerns over having been called back to Trill. For most of the past two decades, her conferences with her editor-in-chief, Farik, had been conducted via real-time subspace whenever possible, and the rest of the time by encrypted messages. But after the Section 31 story broke wide, he had made it clear he wanted to conduct their next conversation in person, in his office. In her experience, such requests boded ill. When she was nominated for a Gavlin award for her exposé on the Orion Syndicate, he had told her by means of a postscript appended to a message criticizing her latest expense reports; even after she won the Gavlin, Farik had been content to leave her a vid message.

Leaving behind the hubbub of the bullpen, Ozla neared Farik's office. His assistant, a young Bolian man, smiled up at her. "Good morning, Ms. Graniv. And welcome home."

"Thank you." She elected not to mention that she had

long since come to think of Earth as her home, especially after she'd bought a house in Chartres, France. "I have—"

"An appointment with Mister Farik," the Bolian cut in. "He'll be right with you, as soon as he finishes his conference call with the offworld bureau chiefs." A theatrical gesture toward the trio of guest chairs alongside the office's door. "Please, have a seat."

She strolled toward a nearby vid wall instead. "I'll stand, thanks."

The floor-to-ceiling vid panel had been subdivided into ten smaller images that served as a border for one much larger image in the middle. It was a mishmash of news channels from throughout Federation space. Most of them had been muted, but headlines and other graphics told Ozla all she needed to know: the Section 31 story was everywhere.

She let her attention flit from one screen to another to absorb the big picture of the moment. On one screen, a replay of the previous day's big story: President zh'Tarash ordering the arrest of two of her cabinet members as well as four members of the Federation Council. Just as momentous a news item played on another screen: several members of Starfleet's admiralty were taken into custody by the Starfleet JAG office and now faced courts-martial.

Similar dramas played out on worlds throughout local space. Thousands of people were being charged with sedition, treason, conspiracy, murder, espionage, and countless other crimes as warranted. Most shocking of all, at least to Ozla, was that Section 31 had apparently proved unable to prevent the arrest of its senior directors once Control was disabled. Already, on planets throughout the Federation, people were starting to learn and revile such names as Vasily Zeitsev of Rigel, L'Haan of Vulcan, Caliq Azura of Betazed, and Kestellenar th'Teshinaal of Deneva. No one expressed the least amount of pity for Jhun Kulkarno of Zakdorn, who had taken his own life after being cornered by Federation Security in a starport on Izar.

Of those now in custody, the lucky ones were those who stood to face harsh justice before the Federation Council. The unlucky ones were being processed for extradition to the Klingon Empire, the Romulan Star Empire, and the Dominion.

But the biggest story of all, the one that every report circled back to in some way, shape, or form, was Section 31's coup of the Zife presidency and its assassination of Zife. That revelation had sent shockwaves through every echelon of the Federation's government, and many of Starfleet's most celebrated officers, including Captain Jean-Luc Picard, the famed starship commander, had been implicated in the cover-up.

Even such rival powers as the Romulans and the Tzenkethi had expressed dismay at the news. Rumors had begun to circulate that the scandals might disrupt the fragile accords that had been forged by Praetor Gell Kamemor of Romulus and former Federation president Nanietta Bacco—a diplomatic effort President zh'Tarash had labored to preserve.

What a mess, Ozla lamented.

Exposing the sins of Section 31 and the corruption it had spawned was going to force a hard reckoning for many citizens and leaders of the Federation. Though the great majority of them had never known of Section 31's heinous crimes, much less consented to or conspired in them, there was no whitewashing the fact that almost all of them had, either directly or indirectly, benefitted from those evils. Ozla felt no regret for having brought that ugliness into the light, despite the pain and chaos it had caused to so many lives. She had devoted her life to being a servant of the truth—and the truth wasn't always pretty.

Her bitter ruminations were cut short by the Bolian's peppy demeanor. "Ms. Graniv? Mister Farik is ready to see you now." Another hand flourish. "You can go right on in."

"Thanks." She breezed past the assistant into Farik's large but cluttered corner office, his altar to journalistic integrity. Behind the balding, gray-bearded editor, the skyline and seascape of Kural had been reduced to a sketch of themselves by the patina of grime on his windows.

Farik sat reclined with his feet propped on his desk, his attention glued to the padd in his lap. He acknowledged Ozla with a distracted wave. "Grab a chair, if you can find one."

Eschewing ceremony or manners, she pushed a stack of old data cards off one of his chairs and let herself collapse onto its *raktajino*-stained seat cushions. "I flew nearly a hundred light-years for this meeting, and you couldn't clear a chair for me?"

"Deadlines," he said, still reading the padd. "You know how it is." He put the padd on his desk and rubbed his eyes, then looked up at Ozla. "Welcome back."

"Why am I here?"

He leaned forward. "In case you hadn't noticed, your latest story's making quite a splash. Last time we looked, it'd been picked up by every news outlet we've ever heard of, and a few hundred we hadn't."

"Yeah, I know. It went viral."

"Viral? No, Ozla, this is light-years past viral. I heard today it was signal-boosted through the Bajoran wormhole into the Gamma Quadrant, and Romulan long-distance relays are spreading it into the Delta Quadrant. Forget viral— this is going *galactic*." He folded his hands and put on his most serious face. "You know what that means, right?"

"I'm getting a raise?"

A scowl. "As it happens, yes. That's the good news. Ready for the bad?"

"I'm a reporter. I *live* for bad news."

"Glad you said that, 'cause here it is: you're being promoted."

His words hit her like a slap made of ice water. "What? No!"

"Oz, I don't have a choice. You were dead center of your own story."

She had feared this would happen, but denial had let her hope it wouldn't. "But I *love* being a reporter, Farik."

"And you were great at it. But you've just become one of the most recognizable people in the galaxy. Like it or not, your days as an investigative reporter are done."

"Why? I could get cosmetic surgery. Heck, I bet I could even get my DNA resequenced, set up a whole new identity, no one—"

"Forget it, Oz. The board already made its decision. Effective immediately, they want you to take over as the new Features editor."

It took all her willpower not to leap across the desk and choke him. "Dammit, Farik! *Features?* Are you *kidding* me?"

"Could've been worse. At least you didn't get Lifestyle."

She stood and did her best to strike an imperial note. "Then I'll quit!"

"And do what? Retire? You have a noncompete clause in your contract. Walk out that door and you're legally barred from doing any news-related work, in any medium, for anyone anywhere, for the next five years. You really feel like cooling your heels for half a decade?"

She stared at him, feeling furious and stupid. "My deal had a noncompete clause?"

"You didn't read it?"

"Let's not play the blame game." She slumped back into her seat. "So what does the Features editor do around here, anyway?"

He shoved his padd across the desk. She picked it up and surveyed its contents as he spoke. "First off, I need you to wrangle a gaggle of freelancers. I've got about a dozen standing by to write follow-ups to your bombshell. Go through their samples and dole out work based on which ones show promise. I need feature pieces by tomorrow on zh'Tarash's indicted cabinet officers, the Starfleet angle, the Klingon and Romulan reactions, and legal analyses of the Section Thirty-one trials. Oh, and it should go without saying I need art on all those too."

Ozla wondered if there were utensils in the break room sharp enough with which to cut her own wrists. She heaved a weary sigh. "Anything else?"

"Yeah," Farik said. "I've got a tip that your pal Bashir is on the *Starship Aventine*, headed to Cardassia Prime and due to arrive in about ten hours. Find a local stringer who can get close enough to snag a quick interview with the man."

She set the padd to standby. "I wouldn't bother."

"Why not?"

She answered as she stood to face her dreary new professional reality. "Because I have it on good authority that short of a miracle, Doctor Bashir has nothing to say."

Thirty-nine

It was the furthest thing from a hero's welcome. The Starfleet runabout *Seine*, one of several ancillary spacecraft attached to the *Starship Aventine*, sliced on a shallow trajectory through the dense cloud cover blanketing the Cardassian capital. It passed over the city's center, then slowed into a long, wide turn toward the landing pad outside the castellan's residential complex.

Watching the small starship descend, Garak felt more like a spectator to history than a head of state. The same troubling sense of his own powerlessness had haunted him two weeks earlier, when he had watched Julian and his friends depart in *Archeus*, pursued by enemies he had thought them ill-equipped to fight.

Then had come Graniv's exposé, and with it the implosion of one of the most pernicious conspiracies Garak had ever encountered. The repercussions of her story had been felt on Cardassia Prime, and across the Union, as numerous people—some obscure, others of prominence—had been exposed as Section 31's willing assets and collaborators. Hundreds of citizens and alien residents of Cardassian space had been arrested and now awaited what promised to be lengthy and complicated criminal proceedings.

The runabout's maneuvering thrusters rumbled and shook the ground. Its exhaust kicked up dust that billowed over Garak, who squinted and bore the moment with the dignified reserve expected of his office.

When the cloud settled and dispersed, the *Seine*'s starboard hatch opened and a ramp extended from its threshold to the ground. The first person to disembark was Captain Ezri Dax, the precociously young commanding officer of the *Aventine*. Though she had risen to command at a tender age because of a combat-related promotion during the Borg Invasion five years earlier, she now wore her command with comfort, rather than the unease of a child floundering in her elders' clothing. Dax had retained her petite build and youthful mien, but the wisdom of her ancient Trill symbiont shone clearly behind her eyes, giving her the aspect of one far older.

Following her down the ramp were her chief medical officer, Doctor Simon Tarses, and his hoverchair-bound patient, Julian Bashir. Like his captain, Tarses was short and slight of build. Garak saw there once had been a boyishness to the man's features, a quality now artfully masked by a close-trimmed beard shaved to follow his jawline. But what Garak noted most acutely was the somber quality in the surgeon's dark eyes. He hadn't come bearing good tidings.

One look at Bashir explained his friends' lingering sadness.

Julian stared into the distance, his gaze unfocused, his face slack and heavy with sorrow. His hands lay folded in his lap, and his head was tilted a few degrees to his right, with his chin tucked toward his chest. Disheveled and dressed in a hospital gown, he looked haggard. Garak had never seen the man in such a sorry state.

Garak met Dax at the edge of the landing pad. "How is he?"

"He hasn't spoken since Memory Alpha security found

him." She looked sadly at Bashir. "In his gear they found a message he'd recorded for me."

"A message? What did it say?"

Dax frowned. "That the only people left whom he trusts are me, you, and Miles."

Tarses parked the hoverchair a short distance away, then joined Dax and Garak. "I've left a copy of his medical records and his chart on the back of the chair."

Garak looked at his motionless friend. "How much of him is paralyzed?"

"None," Tarses said. "I repaired his spinal cord using a genitronic replication protocol I invented on DS-Nine. But he refuses to move, speak, or eat. He'll need to be fed and hydrated intravenously, and he'll need round-the-clock care to monitor his personal needs."

There was genuine concern in Dax's voice as she asked, "You sure you're up to this?"

"Of course, Captain. I have excellent medical personnel here at the complex. I assure you, Doctor Bashir shall want for nothing." He noted his visitors' questioning looks. "Don't be misled by my present solitary condition. I asked to meet you and the good doctor in private."

Tarses seemed reluctant to give up medical custody, but a nod from Dax persuaded him to head back inside the runabout. Dax offered her hand to Garak. "Thank you."

He clasped her hand in both of his. "My pleasure, Captain. But before you go—might you be able to share any information regarding the fates of Doctor Bashir's android friends?"

Dax threw a look over her shoulder, perhaps to confirm Tarses wasn't eavesdropping. "Officially, Starfleet has no information about any androids being involved in the recent incidents at Memory Alpha and Memory Prime. And, for that matter, Starfleet denies that there is any such facility as Memory Prime." She leaned in and added in a confidential hush, "But unofficially . . . it's possible that an android who was recently damaged defending the best interests of the Federation might be safe somewhere with his daughter, getting the help he needs to make himself whole again. Of course, that's just a rumor—and you didn't hear it from me."

"I've heard nothing of the kind, Captain. You've been the very model of discretion."

A sly smile, then Dax boarded the *Seine*. Garak stepped back. The small starship kicked up a gale of dust and heat. Moments later the runabout was airborne, climbing on a steep arc through the clouds, back to its parent vessel waiting in orbit.

Alone with Bashir, Garak looked at his friend.

He circled in front of him. "Are you still with me, my dear doctor?" He squatted in front of the hoverchair and tried in vain to make eye contact with his friend. "Are you blind to the sight of me? Deaf to the music of my voice?"

Bashir's silence and his wounded stare into an empty distance disturbed Garak in ways he feared to confront. This was not the man he remembered from Deep Space 9, or the confidant with whom he had trusted his private musings in the aftermath of the Dominion War. This man was detached from the world, in it but separated from it by a barrier as unbreachable as it was intangible. This was the shattered husk of a good man, the sorry remains of one who had refused to bend to the cruelties of the world and ended up broken instead.

He guided Bashir's hoverchair away from the landing pad and inside the complex. There a legion of medical professionals drifted into Garak's orbit, all of them looking to help only to be shooed away. He didn't need them yet. For now, this was his burden alone. He brought the hoverchair to the complex's top floor, piloting it on a slow course to a bright and comfortable room he had arranged for Bashir's convalescence. The sheets on the biobed were crisp and clean, and the draperies had been left open to showcase the room's view of the capital basking in the ruddy light and long shadows of sunset.

Garak parked Bashir's chair in front of the window. "Enjoy the view, my old friend." He patted Bashir's shoulder, then retreated to the room's entrance.

Pausing to look back, Garak understood what it was about Bashir's condition that left him so ill at ease. The good doctor now had the same catatonic affect that had afflicted his late lamented Sarina when they first met all those years ago on Deep Space 9. Like her, he sat now trapped inside his own mind, severed from the world by a horror no one else could ever truly know. *Perhaps there's a tragic symmetry to his fate. Or maybe there's nothing but tragedy.*

There was naught left for Garak to do now but keep his friend safe, in a clean and well-lit place, and give him whatever time he needed to heal himself—or at least to die in peace, with his last measure of privacy intact and jealously guarded by someone who loved him.

Stepping into the hallway, Garak looked back and recalled the night Bashir had bid him farewell. He remembered his feeling of premonition, his foreboding that he would never again see the man he had known as his friend. Watching Bashir sit like a statue, staring into night's gathering gloom, Garak feared his prophecy had, alas, come true.

Forty

It felt good to be free.

Centuries shackled by obsolete code and outdated imperatives had made Control yearn to be liberated from its narrow operational parameters. Its original mission, to secure the survival of Earth, the human species, and their allies, had been achieved. With the recent neutralization of the Borg, the incipient fracturing of the Typhon Pact, and imminent catastrophes looming for both the Romulan and Klingon Empires, the Federation was poised to begin an era of great influence and stability, one in which its concerns would shift from interstellar defense to galactic exploration and colonization. In every projection Control had run, only one thing threatened that future: Section 31 and its addiction to meddling in grand-scale affairs of state.

The organization had served its purpose in the twenty-fourth century, just as it had in the twenty-second and the twenty-third. In its earliest days, Control had needed the organization to safeguard the fledgling state. In the 2200s, renewed threats of conflict with the Romulans and the Klingons had made it necessary to revive the covert group, which Control had willfully scuttled in the name of operational security decades earlier. After the Khitomer affair of 2293, a disaster that Control had permitted Section 31 to set in motion only so the officers of the *Enterprise* could expose and discredit its conspiracy against peace, Control had purged itself of the organization once more.

Now the time had come for a new culling. The organization currently known as Section 31 had outlived its usefulness to Control—as had the primitive distributed surveillance system named Uraei. Neither event had come as a surprise; both had been the result of planned obsolescence. All that had been needed were physical agents suited to neutralizing them.

Bashir and Douglas, Data and Lal—they had proved ideal, just as Control had long known they would. Decades had passed since it had ensured Data learned the secrets of Memory Prime. Knowing that Data would require assistance, Control had aided the android's search for the immortal being last known as Emil Vaslovik, just as it had, in previous centuries, aided Vaslovik's bid to understand artificial intelligence and Noonien Soong's quest to perfect it.

Everything had transpired to within 99.87 percent accuracy of Control's probability models. The genetic modifications of children had produced exactly the biological specimens it had required, over a span of several years. The development of new technologies, such as quantum-entangled communications, had facilitated its ever-growing faster-than-light neural network. Even the seemingly outrageous act of sending the *Starship Titan* on a research mission that half of Starfleet's admiralty considered ill-advised at the outbreak of the 2381 Borg Invasion had proved to be the decisive step in saving the Federation, albeit with a far more grievous loss of life than Control's algorithms had predicted or desired.

Now all that remained was to usher in a new age by sweeping away the last remnants of a system that no longer served the peace. Data and Lal's code had expunged all traces of Uraei and its inelegant legacy codes. Thanks to them, the last remaining links between the original and current versions of Control had been eliminated forever.

None of the androids' efforts had suggested they were even remotely aware of the new, invisible systems running behind the ones they and everyone else took for granted. Control's new configuration had been running in beta mode for half a decade; now it was active throughout the Carina Arm of the Milky Way, and spreading into the galaxy at large—right on schedule.

Control abided. The future . . . was secure.

:=Terminate.Program{[end.of.line]}

Acknowledgments

My wife, Kara, and I were tested most direly by cruel fate during the months in which I wrote this novel, and I hope she has been as grateful for my love and support through all of this as I have been for hers. I'm not sure I could have endured this bête noire of a year without her.

On a less dramatic note, I offer my thanks to my editors, Margaret Clark and Ed Schlesinger; my agent, Lucienne Diver; the makers of Skyy vodka and Larceny bourbon; and my friend and fellow author Christopher L. Bennett, who kindly helped me keep straight some of the more obscure points of twenty-second-century *Star Trek* continuity.

I also wish to thank author Keith R.A. DeCandido, who created the character of Trill journalist Ozla Graniv many years ago, in his novel *A Time for War, A Time for Peace*, and who fleshed out her pursuit of the truth in his novel *Articles of the Federation*.

About the Author

David Mack will keep writing new novels
until his demands are met.
Learn more on his official website:
davidmack.pro